MY LIFE
UNDER WATER

Alan D. Stamp

ISBN: 1514115743
ISBN 13: 9781514115749
Library of Congress Control Number: 2015908735
CreateSpace Independent Publishing Platform
North Charleston, South Carolina

FOREWORD TO THE READER

I've been fascinated by stories all my life. Throughout this book, my stories, and the stories of others, have reminded me of the struggles and pleasures of being alive.

DEDICATIONS

This story is dedicated to my mother, Margaret Rose, whose kind heart, optimism and zealous love of life - even in dark times - has remained constant.

To Alfred James William; for what might have been.

To Robbie Lynda; a big sister in a tiny package.

To Laura Jean Overend; the most beautiful and complex creature I'd ever known. I hope you'll recognize the loving reminiscences in the pages of my story.

To Ellen Dacamara; your lasting friendship has brought me laughter and comfort in and out of the water. Your irreverence, wicked humour and theatricality can be found throughout this tale.

To Dr. Richard Taylor; for all you've done, I'll remain in your debt.

To my wonderful, incorrigible Joey. Always loved and remembered.

And lastly, to the beautiful music the water sings each day; to be surrounded by it and to be in it has brought me a lifetime of happiness.

TABLE OF CONTENTS

Chapter 1.	Watery Memories	1
Chapter 2.	Meet the Family	4
Chapter 3.	Coming Into My Own	20
Chapter 4.	Adolescent Angst	24
Chapter 5.	Chances in the Land of Oz	36
Chapter 6.	The Departure	41
Chapter 7.	Lara's Theme	48
Chapter 8.	Revelations of Jim	56
Chapter 9.	Climbing Onto the Soap Box	67
Chapter 10.	Choices	69
Chapter 11.	I Feel Love	76
Chapter 12.	Wounded Healers	84
Chapter 13.	Oil Can Harry's	90
Chapter 14.	Afterglow	104
Chapter 15.	The Decision	106
Chapter 16.	Is Confidence Sexy?	119
Chapter 17.	Queen Charlotte	126
Chapter 18.	Guess Who's Coming to Dinner?	136
Chapter 19.	Finding That Other Gear	147
Chapter 20.	An Early Morning Surprise	150
Chapter 21.	Going Into the Ditch	157
Chapter 22.	Design by Rose	173
Chapter 23.	Lara's Big Date	187
Chapter 24.	Home is Where the Pasta Is	198
Chapter 25.	Robby at the Lagoon	201
Chapter 26.	Toute la vérité et rien que la vérité ~ Nothing but the Truth	221
Chapter 27.	Happy Coincidences	229
Chapter 28.	Pop-Up Pete	231
Chapter 29.	Hearing an Old Story Anew	247

Chapter 30.   Clockwork Carrie   255
Chapter 31.   Montreal   265
Chapter 32.   Making a Big Splash   276
Chapter 33.   Words and Music   288
Chapter 34.   My Life Under Water, An Epilogue   302

1

WATERY MEMORIES

My earliest memory is my most profound one. My older sister Lynda and I were playing in Lake Superior on a brilliant summer's day. With the vast lake swelling just above my waist, I was oblivious to the large roller picking up mass and momentum behind me. Lynda noticed it approaching and couldn't resist a tantalizing opportunity. At the precise moment the rumbling wave was to crest, she gave me a forceful two-handed push against my shoulders and hollered, "Hah!" I was knocked off my feet and sucked backwards under the enormous breaker. Pulled under several feet of icy water, the force of the curling wave yanked me into treacherous Lake Superior. I'll never forget the terror of sinking deeper into the liquid darkness, the sounds of the world muffled as I shockingly looked through the waters to the brightness of the sky above. In a second of panic, I launched myself from the lake's sandy bottom, moving in a frenetic fashion that swiftly brought me from the clutches of Superior and back to the surface. I grabbed a snatch of air, then swam, kicked and thrashed until I was close to shore. It wasn't my fastest twenty-five-meter sprint, nor was it refined, but I'd made it out of danger quickly. I sputtered and wheezed my way to the safety of the beach on chubby red legs. I was coughing and had water up my nose, but was unhurt as I ran to my mother's outstretched arms. I looked back to see my unscathed seven-year-old year sister grinning with devilish delight at her wailing, white-haired little brother in his Roy Rogers bathing trunks. If I hadn't drawn a lung-full of air before my unholy baptism, I might not have come up from the depths and thus ended my life at the age of four. As I said, Superior's treacherous, but an older sister can be mean.

If my early grave was to be an aquatic one, little Lynda seemed oblivious if she unintentionally placed me in it. My sister must surely have resented her annoying baby brother. A little push was needed every so often to maintain her special sibling status. Decades later I'm certain my memory didn't happen exactly the way that I chronicled it - memories are notoriously imperfect after all (though it does make for a good yarn - much to the distress of my sister who recoils whenever I trot out the story at family dinners). In retrospect, and when I re-frame my experience, I'm indebted to my sister for showing me that I can rally against a life-threatening and fluid obstacle - that's the meaning I've taken from my recollection, as watery as that memory might be.

As far as I was concerned, any sibling rivalry between my sister and me was unnecessary. I was never a child nor an adult who wanted to grab the limelight from anyone, including my big sister. My hunch was that Lynda's desire to receive attention was well-developed before I came along. It's an eldest child trait - they're used to getting recognition and frequently expect it from others. Lynda sought attention, but also naturally garnered it. She was pretty, bright, self-assured and personable. I was shy, quiet and cautious. I liked to be by myself and loved to be in the water.

Unquestionably, throughout my life, water has held special meaning. I was born in Port Arthur, which hugs the shoreline of Canada's great inland sea. I grew up fascinatingly drawn to the mercurial lake. It could be violent - tossing twenty-foot waves onto craggy beaches, sounding off with a deafening roar - and capable of destroying many things in its path. But when calm, the rhythmic waves moving across the pebbled beach made soft, delicate shushing sounds. The constant waves polished small green and grey-blue stones into gems, scattering them across endless shores. In small coves, the lake became warm in summer and frozen icy-white in bone-chilling winters. It was an ever-changing cyclorama for a child whose knowledge of life was as small as the lake was large.

I learned to swim in nearby Boulevard Lake, where the waters were less metaphoric and decidedly safer. I'd frustrate my mother because once in the water, I never wanted to get out. I'd swim for hours, with the summer sun blistering my back and my mother keeping watch. Quickly, I became a competent swimmer. If I was a bull in a china shop (I was frequently told so), in the water I was graceful and fast. "Like a hot knife slips through butter," was how my Mum described my swimming technique.

As a young boy I intrinsically knew that I wasn't the same as others, but I couldn't articulate what those differences were. Of course, the function of a child isn't to think like an adult, is it? My awareness of being different made me wary of making or having friends, so instead I created my own unique friendship with the water. In a lake or even at the local pool, I was content. Perhaps it's surprising that I should have loved the water so much given my early recollection, but when I was under water, most everything - including secrets - that was worrisome to me dissolved. Keeping secrets was already an essential part of the life I was to live and childhood proved an excellent training ground for learning how to develop a pretend self in which to hide. In my silence I watched, far more than participated, in the life that was unfolding slowly before me.

2

MEET THE FAMILY

I've come to realize that one way of understanding others is by exploring their family history. It's intriguing to understand one's self as part of a larger context; that's where motifs can emerge. One of the themes of my multi-generational family was about being hardy, and I'd like to believe that characteristic is a part of my composition, too. Like many Canadian families, mine were European immigrants. The extended family that I was most familiar with was my mother's. Her Scottish parents were from the Isle of Arran, the largest wind-swept island in the Firth of Clyde. My Grandpa, a lanky man with striking pale blue eyes, was left by his mother when he was a toddler. His father sent him off to work at age eleven or twelve, he married at eighteen and was enlisted in the forces before the start of the First World War. Sent over to France, he fought in the hellish Battle of Somme, where over 600,000 allied troops were slaughtered by the Germans. It was in the trenches at Somme that he'd been horribly shot up in his right leg. For five days he lay in a cold, muddy trench with the dying and the dead before being rescued and returned to England. He'd been fortunate; many never made it out alive. He spent over a year recovering in a sanatorium from his injuries and a dicey bout of tuberculosis. With my Grandmother at his side, he slowly improved. Grandpa had a shortened leg and walked with a painful limp, yet never complained. To recover from lung disease, he was told to settle either in Australia or Canada where clean air was considered critical for his health. Port Arthur was certainly closer than Sydney, so in the spring of 1919 they boarded a ship in Glasgow, sailed across the Atlantic and soon began new lives as Canadians. Grandpa was very fond of the small city on the freshwater sea with views of the Sleeping Giant - what the Ojibwe called Nanabijou. Perhaps the air *was* restorative, as he regained his constitution, started a family and worked as a wholesaler for Fitzsimmons Fruits well into his 70's. In their home, he lovingly tended a backyard garden of vegetables and grew prize-winning gladiolas through the summer. Grandpa was a humorous and colourful man whose Canadian friends were varied and plentiful. He never let wartime scars prevent him from enjoying life. From his youth, he was a self-taught drawer and painter. He was well-regarded for his renderings of stormy Lake Superior, the magical Sleeping Giant, fiery red and orange autumn maples of the Cambrian Shield, the purples and yellows of his prize-winning gladiolas and the golden browns of grouses and pheasants he'd seen on his many fishing trips in the Ontario countryside.

My grandmother had a similarly challenging early life. When Nana was 15, her mother died from a botched gall bladder operation. Less than a year later, her husband died from a broken heart - that was the family story. Grandma was the eldest sister of three brothers, and after the parents died the family home became a boarding house by necessity. Nana spent her days and nights cooking meals, cleaning, doing endless loads of filthy worker's clothes in a wringer washer and hanging them on a line to dry. My Grandfather became one of her lodgers some time before he became her husband. I'd say before they even really knew each other, my grandparents were already connected through the early losses they'd both experienced. Grandpa's losses made him appreciate life - his gratitude could be seen in his drawings and paintings. Nana's losses motivated her to be a hardworking, pragmatic survivalist. She ran a tight ship and got all tasks done and done well. Grandpa was affectionate with all family, but it was a source of amazement that he was also loving towards my dour Nana. I always thought of my grandmother as narrow-minded, disagreeable, wrathful and domineering. She was unforgiving to all who may have questioned her authority - rarely were there second chances with Nana. She even looked fright-worthy: a pinched, stern face, long white hair tied in a tight bun, a razor-sharp tongue and a terrifying bust that seemed to stretch all the way down to her sensible black Oxford shoes. One look was all that was needed to understand that Nana meant business.

Both grandparents spoke with thick Scottish accents - at times indecipherable to my ear. Words such as aboot, aye, Ben Birn, bonnie, dae, crik. There was no shortage of bewildering words. And putting phrases together was as confusing: "It's a braw bright moonlit night the night." Translated, it meant "It's a brilliant moonlit night tonight." "Gonnae no' dae that!" meant, "Not going to do that." "Ah dinnae ken," was "I don't know." And my personal favourites, "Is that cat deid?" Meaning, of course, that your pants are too short and "Haud yer wheesht!" Translation? "Be quiet." We heard that a lot from Nana.

My mother Rose was born in 1933, a first generation Canadian, the youngest of four siblings. In the sepia-toned pictures of her youth she's depicted posing in her torn and ragged woollen swimming costume at the lake, playing ball with her brothers in the street, climbing birch trees with a dirt-smeared face, speeding across an outdoor rink on hockey skates or sliding down a snowy High Street in a toboggan. Always with a sunny smile, she seemed upbeat. Mum became an attractive young woman with wavy light ash-blonde hair, trim of figure and had a flawless complexion. She finished grade ten but never cared to continue. Instead, she traded her hand-me-down coveralls and school smocks for smart blouses, wool slacks and the best dresses she could afford. Mum joined the working ranks and by 1949 was employed at Eaton's department store on Arthur Street. Working in the music department, she sold the popular recordings of the day. She liked serving customers and also enjoyed dressing fashionably for her job. Being a salesgirl at Eaton's was something she enjoyed and Mum was good at her work.

Though I knew my mother's family well, my father's family was far less known to me. I gleaned information about my father's family from my mother. My father was William - called Bill - and born of working-class parents in East London. His dad was a wallpaper hanger and by all accounts quite congenial, though he liked to drink, which maddened his wife Beatrice. She was a strident Jewish woman, who, as the story goes, was harsh to deal with, frequently hostile and was disappointed by most everyone - including her boozy husband. Beatrice had a child out of wedlock, my father's older half-sister. I learned that my father's parents didn't have the means or desire to care for him during the bloody blitz of London. In Liverpool, my thirteen-year-old father was boarded onto a frigate in 1941 - one of the hundreds of child evacuees (only ten percent of them Jewish) bound for Canada. His journey began a history of distance and cut-off from his family that would encompass his life. He trekked across the North Atlantic Ocean during dangerous wartime. After six days, he arrived in Halifax and walked into the Department of Immigration wearing a pair of tattered and stained school-boy shorts and a crumpled blue blazer with a yellow crest of England stitched on his coat pocket. From Nova Scotia, he made his way to Montreal and then to the rugged expanse of Manitoba 2,300 kilometres west. Certainly, this must have been a perilous journey for a solitary boy. My father was meant to work at a farm in Portage La Prairie and attend school. However, when he met with the sponsor family, they decided against having a Jewish boy on their farm, which must have been a shattering rejection. If there were a children's aid organization, he surely didn't go to them for help. Instead, he left Portage and travelled sixty miles south to Winnipeg. Perhaps he understood that there were more chances for him in the city, but exactly how he managed remained a mystery to me. He did make several references later about how he would trade work for food, work for a bed, work for all necessities when he came to Canada. Of this period, my father never stated any gripes. There were no histrionics and no position of being a victim whatsoever. In fact, quite the opposite. From what I recall, he was prideful about being a boy in a man's world. I can't imagine what it must have been like. Any elaboration as to how he survived in Canada as a child was cursory, such as, "I just did," and didn't invite questions. My attempts at inquiry were met with either stilted responses or silence. From Winnipeg, he went to Port Arthur to work at a gas station. Still a young man, in the last two years of the Second World War he lied about his age and signed up with the Armed Forces. There are photos of him wearing his uniform proudly in far-flung places such as China and one crinkly snapshot of my father in an airfield. He's beside three men wearing bomber jackets, smiling broadly, standing close to a propeller plane. On the back of the photo he had printed (he never wrote), 'With the Airmen'. In fact, my father held a fascination with aviation and rocketry. Perhaps being bound by the gravity of his early life was a burden that he'd have liked to have escaped from.

For someone who claims such great curiosity, it's a shame that I couldn't find a route to probe my father's story. But I did understand that because of his early experiences, work became his ally, his religion, his obsession, his redemption and his foe. There's a cost to only being a worker in a world where personal relationships hold value, too. Struggling with pneumonia at home a few days before being diagnosed with terminal lung disease, my father confided that he had a wish.

"I've really thought about this - I'd like to die at work."

"Huh? That's crazy. What are you talking about, Dad?"

"I hear stories that at the end men say they regret they worked so hard. That won't be me; I'll be saying I wish I could have worked more."

"Dad," I said disapprovingly, yet I knew he was merely being truthful.

"I wish it could happen on the sales floor. Boom, done in one breath. Clean and easy, the perfect way to tee off and finish my last golf game. Wouldn't that be memorable?"

"Jeez, Dad…memorable for sure, but for who?"

Ironically, a long illness removed him from being able to work, and work was practically all of my father's identity. Regrettably for him, he never got his wish. No quick exit, he clung to life via a twenty-foot oxygen hose for nearly three years. There was nothing "clean and easy" about his teeing off, as my mother can attest. At the end he had family at his death bed, ordering us to bring him the Province newspaper for the morning that never came - not for him. Our family did a good job of caring for Dad, with my mother taking on complex roles with the utmost skill and patience. However, I'm sure Dad wouldn't have done the same for us. Nothing personal. That kind of sentimentality just wasn't my father's way.

Before that ending, there was a beginning, and like most children, I never tired of hearing the story of how my parents met.

"You met Dad skating, right, Mum?" I asked - just a boy of eight - as we walked home after a glacial Sunday skate at an outdoor ice rink in Winnipeg, my feet frozen to numb and my cheeks cherry-red.

"Not quite, sweetheart. I was at a Memorial Cup hockey game on a date with a young man —"

"You were on a date? You never told me that before. Who was it? Did you kiss him?" I asked, astounded that my mother had romantic interests before my father. My mukluks crunched the blue-white snow underfoot as I re-slung my skates over my shoulder.

"A proper young woman never tells," Mum answered smugly as she bundled a scarf around my throat.

"*Mum!*"

"Hush. When your father saw me, he was smitten and —"

"Mitten?"

"Smitten - keen for me - and found out that I worked in the music department at Eaton's and —"

"How did he know where to find you?"

"Your father wouldn't ever tell me. He skulked about the store on Friday nights in hopes I might notice him." She turned the collar of her heavy wool coat to cover her ears against the bitter cold as we walked on the hard-packed snowy sidewalk.

"Did you?" I asked, not understanding the flaw in my question.

"Well, yes, of course," Mum chuckled. "Your father came over to my cash counter with a stack of Mario Lanza 78's. But he didn't even own a record player."

How could he play —"

"Well, he couldn't, dear. He was making small talk. That's when your father asked me out for a Coke and fries at the Waverley Hotel."

"Can we have a Coke and fries when we get home?"

"No, sweetheart, I'll fix you some hot cocoa —"

"With marshmallows?" I interrupted hopefully as she laughed, her breath forming clouds of white steam against the stark blue skies.

Even with what I interpreted to be large differences in personality and family background, something drew my parents together that I found hard to fathom. According to my mother, their romantic relationship happened quickly. Mum said that they spent most all their free time together and that she would adapt to his schedule - whenever possible. That was a pattern in their relationship - my mother accommodating my father. My Grandmother's controlling and unpleasant disposition might have provided extra motivation for my mother's desire to marry - she was only twenty, after all. That being said, I imagine my father had certain charms as a young man. He'd been good-looking; small-framed, hazel eyes, wiry, dark-haired with olive skin. My mother was his opposite physically and they had significant differences in disposition. It's said that opposites attract, but similarities are what bind relationships. And Dad was ethnically Jewish, my mother was baptized as a Presbyterian. She attended church and celebrated Christmas. I don't imagine that my atheist father cared; her not being Jewish was probably a plus in his mind.

My father's considerable drive may have held the greatest appeal to my mother. After all, why hitch your wagon to a layabout? He worked a full-time day job at Gillis & Warren's automotive warehouse and pumped gas at night. Maybe that was the attraction - the stereotypical strong and silent man with an enormous work ethic. It was the early 1950s, a time where men were meant to be indefatigable. Engaged after only a few months, marriage took place in less than a year. In the pictures and films that I have seen of my parents' wedding, they looked happy to start their life together. Much later I assumed that something must have occurred between them to cause their disengagement. Perhaps it was the reality of what marriage had become - living with children. From joie de vivre to abattement. As if to highlight his displeasure, my father was aloof with his children. My mother was critical of his neglect, though he wasn't concerned about what his wife might have thought about his fathering ability. As a boy abandoned by his family, hadn't he gone beyond the scope of expectations by outfitting all necessities for his wife and children? His family had discarded him, yet he worked harder than anyone to give us the things he'd never received. In retrospect, what seemed to be the most inexpensive thing to supply - attention - was the thing that was nearly impossible for my father to furnish. He was utterly disinterested in being a parent. He was interested in work. Work was the compensatory device to reconcile all ills, real or perceived.

In his smoke-filled office, inhaling Buckingham cigarettes deeply and addictively, punishing his lungs, he found his identity and life's purpose. His sales spoke volumes, though with his family, my father did not. As a boy and a man, my own discomfort and unease prevented me from knowing more about him until a few years before his death. Musing about my father is sad. For most of my life, I had accepted that he was unimportant. Then as time and his eventual death unraveled the animosity that I had for my father, I was left with raw emotions and regret I thought had resolved many years before.

Change happens to all things, including my family and the city in which I was born. Charming Port Arthur fell into decline. As a boy, I knew nothing of my hometown's misfortune. I didn't know of the despair so many thousands would experience due to the closing of the grain elevators, or the panic over the shutting down of the paper mills. I wasn't aware of the port slowly falling into disrepair, the old wooden piers stinking of rot, shuttered-up and waiting for second or third chances. Port Arthur's final gasps of economic life were stifled when the railway pulled out. And before the last hope of the town's prosperity had passed, my father's work advancement saw the family departing the Lakehead. So off we went in my father's 1961 Plymouth Fury, driving west for Manitoba and leaving the Lakehead and the spectacular shores of Superior behind. My family's suburban trajectory was assured, bound for a new development called Westwood, where achingly similar bungalows lined the treeless streets 438 miles west of Port Arthur in Winnipeg, Manitoba. Our blue bungalow on Sansom Avenue had all the trappings of the middle class, including a dishwasher, three small bedrooms and the still-wet smell of a concrete basement.

Winnipeg isn't a bad place - unless you're there for the ten months of winter. Pardon my exaggeration; it's usually only six months. The most anticipated season of the year wasn't a cake-walk, either. Summers were searingly hot, with pesky mosquitoes and horseflies the size of budgies swooping around, even biting through seersucker to find their bloody meal. That heat was good for a few things though, like the beef steak tomatoes my mother grew in the front yard. When they were at their fragrant dark-red best she'd slice them thickly and heap them on white bread slathered with Miracle Whip for lunch. During the unrelenting heat, Mum would cook our evening meals outside, lighter fluid combusting black charcoal briquettes in our kettle barbecue. As though the smoke were a signal, hungry neighbours arrived as Mum was tossing wieners and burgers on the grill. In a huge teak bowl, Mum would prepare a summer salad from her juicy tomatoes and garden-grown white onions, cut into thin rings, adding chopped celery, torn parsley, butter lettuce, vinegar, salt, pepper, sugar and salad oil. I remember neighbours eating and laughing outside until late with 'The Twilight Zone' theme music eerily heard from opened windows - that music always unsettled me. But what really stands out about those summer evenings? The smell of fat dripping on smouldering charcoal and those beef steak tomatoes.

As July's temperatures soared, the second-hand powder-blue plastic pool with triangular rusted metal seats would be hauled from the basement and set up in the backyard. That plastic pool meant summer had truly arrived. I watched excitedly as the nozzle on the black rubber hose was cranked open and Mum filled the pool with a foot and a half of water. Within a half hour, it was also filled with neighbourhood kids and plenty of insects. My sister and I had a lot of fun in that pool - aside from the painful bee stings. Who knows what else was in that watery mix? I don't believe any of us children could have cared. It wasn't Lake Superior, but with some imagination and a few floating plastic boats, that pool would be the setting for many playtime fantasies.

Mum was very involved with Lynda and me, but I don't recall my father's presence at all when we lived in Winnipeg. Perhaps that's why my mother and I (and though my sister must have gone, my memory doesn't register her on those trips) traveled back to Port Arthur so often. Mum cherished her father and when there was an opportunity to visit, she took it. She understood that Grandpa was magical to her children - an old man who loved child's play - and I remember the excitement I felt boarding the train in Winnipeg whenever we could to see him. On the eastbound train for the Lakehead at the age of five or six, I'd press my nose to the window, looking at the shining green-black lakes, forests of silver birches with peeling bark, winding creeks and low mountains as the panorama rushed past. On one very significant trip, I sat with my mother, excited to be with her on an adventure. With candy in my denim pocket and a book at my side, I spied with great interest a man facing me a few rows ahead. He was dressed in blue and scarlet, and as my Mum would tell the story, "He was spellbound by that Mountie on the train! He could barely take his eyes off of him all the way to the Lakehead!" Mum was convinced that her son was intrigued by the uniform he wore. Well, that was partly correct, though my recollection was more fulsome and powerful. This was the first time I became consciously aware of being tugged towards a male presence. His costume was indeed striking, with his red tunic jacket and navy serge trousers with a yellow stripe, Stetson hat and brown Strathcona boots to his calves. But it was the Mountie's beauty that made me notice him; his angular face, dark brown hair peeking out from his hat and eyes that I believed watched me watching him. I felt the flush of embarrassment as he smiled at me. I wanted to cross the aisle and go to him, sit beside him, be near him. There was nothing sexual of course, because I wouldn't have known what that meant. But emotionally? Yes - there was an unmistakable draw and different from any other I had experienced. Yet I was aware that something was wrong with my desire for closeness. I'd never have acted on such an impulse. Even as a small boy, I must have clearly understood what the established norms were, noting the cues all around me. I learned to contain my urges. I knew that acting on my impulses was wrong or dangerous. There wasn't anything else I recalled about that trip except the handsome Mountie in the scarlet uniform with bright eyes and a smile that thrilled me and made me self-conscious and vigilant.

Though we lived in Winnipeg for several years, scant memories remain. One person I could never forget was the grim Mrs. Swift, my kindergarten teacher. My mother called her the Witch of Westwood. For reasons unclear, the teacher disliked me. Mrs. Swift would frequently place me in the corner and on several occasions smacked my hands with a ruler (shocking to a good boy). One morning she derided my fashion choice of Roy Rogers western leatherette boots with real chrome studs and plastic horses stitched on the sides. I was proud of my footwear (it's doubtful that the Witch would have liked my Roy Rogers swim trunks, either), but Mrs. Swift thought my boots were inappropriate and promptly sent me home to change. After all, boys must look like boys and not like Cowboy Rockettes. This produced considerable wailing from me when I arrived back home utterly humiliated. After Mum attended to my tears with kind words, she poured me a big glass of milk and relentlessly poked and tickled me in the rib cage until I was giggling hysterically. This made me laugh further until wetting my pants was a distinct possibility. Mum could always turn my unhappy tears into tears of joy. Mum would deal with the Witch of Westwood later; the teacher would rue the day she had mistreated her son.

Like me, Mum was the youngest in her family so she knew what it was like to be the perpetual baby. My father's disinterest in Lynda and me only made my desire to be around my mother more pronounced as I got older. Mum's routines were a source of considerable intrigue. I watched her complete her morning rituals in the pastel-blue bathroom in our Westwood bungalow. She'd smooth foundation across her face, drawing black lines around her eyes with a pencil, painting her lips red and smearing coloured shadow on her lids. I'd sit on the pink and blue knobby chenille bath mat riveted with attention. Mother revamped herself and finished with a light spray of Shalimar eau de cologne.

"There. The war paint's on. How do I look?"

"You're pretty and you smell like flowers," I offered.

A look of satisfaction would creep over her face as she gave her lips one more smack, tidying the corners of the smudged lipstick with her finger and rubbing the excess into her cheeks for added effect. It was comforting and fun watching Mum apply makeup and choose her clothes. Watching her dress-up up gave me permission to tie a sheet around my neck and pretend I was Superman, or wear her aviator's sunglasses in a snowstorm and imagine I was the sole survivor of a plane crash. Imagination can be a frightening thing, too. One evening Mum read *Little Red Riding Hood* to me. For months afterwards, lying in my dark room at bedtime, the Wolf appeared outside my window, complete with a top hat, tuxedo, beady, bright red eyes, blood-red tongue and salivating mouth. Each night I panicked that the Wolf would slide open the pane of glass, stealthily slip into my blackened bedroom and rip me apart in a few barbarous bites. There were more animals to come. Mum told me that for nearly a year I would tumble into her twin bed at night due to the beasts underneath mine. I would waltz in and matter-of-factly state that there were, "Far too many lions for me to sleep." I remember the security in my mother's bed. Mum must have felt better knowing that her little boy was safe from the many harmful creatures that prey on boys late at night. Perhaps she derived comfort in having her small boy close to her chest, wrapped up in her arms, a quickened heartbeat slowed by the calm reassurance of a mother's love.

As I got older there may not have been lions under the bed or a Big Bad Wolf ready to devour me, however I was very aware of needing to be alert. Looking back, it's probably quite true that an inordinate amount of time was spent maintaining that vigilance and secrecy. Exceptions were made at Halloween; a kind of Carnival for children. One frosty Winnipeg Halloween, my friend Danny Dillo and I did a gender-bender for the night. We were dressed in slippery polyester print dresses of blue and green worn over our long-johns. We had mismatched plastic handbags, imitation pearls, purple faux-amethyst brooches pinned onto our chests and adorned our mouths with bright red lipstick. Our crowning glory? Blond beehive wigs of questionable quality. On the festive night, we wobbled around the neighbourhood streets on spike heels, lurching dangerously from side to side. From a discreet distance, our mothers watched their unbalanced cross-dressing children and laughed so hard they cried, their tears nearly freezing on icy cheeks. And though we seemed to take it all in stride - and what eight-year-old boys wouldn't at the prospect of a purse full of candy - faded pictures show Danny and me looking nearly frost-bitten, our waffle-underwear failing to keep us warm, make-up smudged, faces chilled to blue. We gathered up our bejewelled selves and paraded through Westwood garnering both candy and praise at each house we tricked or treated until the night was through. This completed my one and only foray into drag. I'm not too sure about Danny; he was extremely fond of that purple brooch.

My mother became close friends with Danny's mother, Lu, a stocky woman with a shock of black hair and piercing blue eyes. Lu's husband could be hurtful - depending on his mood and alcohol intake - so she had to be judicious about what she did or else face Eddie's wrath, which on several occasions included a hard slap across her face. My Mum was only too aware of his nonsense, as she called it (today it's called abuse). The last summer we spent in Winnipeg, Eddie had been particularly objectionable. During a morning coffee klatch, my Mum decided that what Lu needed to ease her stressful situation was a new look to assert herself. If there was any ambivalence on Lu's part - and there was a lot - my mother swept it away. To Polo Park Shopping Plaza they went, picking up Lady Clairol at the pharmacy and some new clothes at Simpson Sears. Back home and bubbling with laughter, Lu was to undergo a metamorphosis - after much time with peroxide - from black hair to platinum blonde. Eyeliner applied, shadow smeared, cheeks rouged and to finish the new look my mother's normally good fashion sense faltered as she poured the plump Lu into a snug pair of black and white checkered Capri pants and a sleeveless black top. Her abundant flesh spilled out from everywhere. Lu looked like an overweight and shoddy impersonation of Marilyn Monroe. My mother told Lu that she had the right to look as she pleased, or in this case, how my mother pleased. Maybe Eddie would be excited? Eddie's reaction wasn't the type of excitement Lu had hoped for. When he arrived home from work and saw his wife's hair and new clothes he exploded, enraged at her appearance. Within seconds, poor Lu was steered into the washroom. Off came the makeup, the lipstick became unstuck, top and bottom were switched for a housedress but the hair took more work. Fade to black, literally, as she did it the next day, her transformation short-lived, her return to a raven-haired hausfrau complete. Danny told me that he heard his mother crying for hours that night while his father drank Molson's and watched Hockey Night in Canada. My mother's attempt at Suburban Style flopped badly. I got the message easily enough. Differences in Westwood families were not acceptable. Not for a woman who bleached her black hair and not for a boy who secretly sang along to his mother's collection of Broadway soundtracks, wearing Roy Rogers boots, fantasizing about a train-riding Mountie instead of watching grainy black and white hockey games on the CBC.

As far as families go, mine wasn't perfect. And I certainly can recall my sister and I grumbling, whining and grousing. But as my humourless Nana would tell us, "Whit's fur ye'll no go past ye." Meaning?

"Whatever is meant to happen will happen, so stop complaining." That was the family credo, at least in principle. It's true that my dad never complained specifically about being a father, but I knew instinctively that he'd have been happier if his children weren't a part of the equation. Children got in the way of work. My father opted out of family and all of school events. It was vaguely possible that he might have known the names of the various schools that Lynda and I attended, but he never darkened their doors. Birthday parties? School concerts? Swim practice? Um, nope, not interested. It became my mother's responsibility to atone for my father's gaps. It's a challenging role to be both mother and father but Mum did a laudable job. She volunteered at most all the schools we attended, went to school plays, attended PTA meetings, became involved in all things important to my sister and me. Still, if Bill was uninspired by fatherhood, he was very inspired to advance his career. That meant moves; lots of them. If I found moves difficult because I was shy and anxious, my sister found them to be adventurous and challenging. New school? No problem for Lynda. I viewed the moves as further reason to retreat, to bind myself closer to my mother, to grow resentful of my father's apparent lack of sensitivity. Schools were terrifying places - strange teachers, new kids and especially the bullies. Once a boy has been stuffed into a school locker in front of laughing children...well, that's a story even I don't wish to share. By the time I reached grade twelve, I had been in seven different schools in six cities from Ontario to BC. That's a lot of teachers and students. Lynda may have thrived, but I shrank from the experience. I was cautious, hawk-eyed, sensitive and fearful. At school and after school, I kept a distance from others. I was aware that I was viewed as the awkward and unfriendly one, which really was untrue. The worried one was much more accurate. I had a big secret to keep. If being hardy was my family theme, I was going to need a sizeable amount of it.

3

COMING INTO MY OWN

Throughout my growing-up years, I found solace under water. I started competitive swimming at an early age. As we moved from city to city, I was allowed to join swim clubs to help build my confidence. From the age of six or seven, I swam lap after lap all across Western Canada. By sixteen, I was tall and well developed with good-sized shoulders, slim hips, powerful legs and longer than average arms which extended my stroke. Another development - what started out as a rather unpromising thimble below the belt was gratifyingly a much larger penis by the age of sixteen. The problem with the adolescent penis - as almost every man can attest - is that it has a mind of its own. At the most unnerving moments, it would decide to extend itself beyond the boundaries of my pants or my gym shorts or ably leaping through my trousers while sitting in class. The only way to manage this beast was to slap it around a little - or a lot. That wasn't anything new. I'd started rubbing my penis when I was a small boy; putting it between my thighs and rocking side-to-side on my back. I wasn't even five when my mother wanted to know what I was doing one steamy summer night, hearing the uneven creaking of the metal bed springs. She discovered me lying flat on my back in my bed with my flannel pyjamas down around my ankles. I could tell by my mother's disapproving look that I was providing more pleasure than a boy should ever give himself. That encounter didn't go unnoticed; I made sure that I would only do the maneuver after all the lights were out and ensured the bed springs didn't creak as I massaged my thimble, already a source of great pleasure and some shame, but certainly insufficient shame to stop.

While sexual fantasies would begin after adolescence, as a boy of barely thirteen I was unaware of any. And speaking of cumming - which I guess I wasn't - that never happened in all the years of rubbing my little friend red-raw between my legs. It took a bit of research at the local library to find out exactly what a randy teen with surging hormones should be doing. I found the book *Boys & Sex* supposedly featured by the librarian, the fearsome Mrs. Faulkner. She embodied the stereotype admirably, wearing brown tweed-pleated skirts and a never-ending supply of starched buttoned-to-the-double-chin white blouses, sensible shoes and bifocals which she pushed down her crooked nose to glare suspiciously at students signing out books. Each month, her Fun Features - books about African Safaris, Geology for Teens and How-to manuals about making paper airplanes and ice candles from used milk cartons - were displayed on the rotating book carousel. She personally selected the most appropriate books for children as Mrs. Faulkner was a staunch supporter of wholesome reading. However, something tells me that *Boys & Sex* might have been left on the carousel in error. I don't think it would have been one of Mrs. Faulkner's Fun Features, but perhaps she was more progressive than she appeared. Regardless, there it was in plain sight, the title emblazoned in yellow on the blue dust cover. Finding courage that only a hormonal boy can, I picked up the book and took it to the steely, four-eyed librarian. Giving both the book and me the once over, Mrs. Faulkner smirked and rolled her eyes through thick myopic lenses as I flamed crimson and checked it out. Hurrying to my locker and making sure that no one was about, I scanned through *Boys & Sex*. To my delight, there were pictures of genitalia; male genitalia. At this point, many of the boys I'd seen were hairless and undeveloped. In my Fun

21

Features book there were drawings and pictures of the penis - and let's call it what it is - cock - big cocks with hair and large low-hanging balls. I was flushed with excitement but petrified that someone would catch me reading it. Quickly, I rushed into the boys' washroom with my prized book held tightly against my chest, bounded into the stall and jammed it under my armpit so that I could push down my dungarees. I sat on the toilet and took the book from under my moist pit. Finally, now I could read all that it had to say about being a thirteen-year-old sexual boy. When I got to the part about masturbation it was nothing less than a revelation.

"Wow," I murmured under my breath. "So I'm supposed to hold it in my hand like *that?*" As implausible as it sounds, I was only aware of putting my penis between my legs and rubbing it against my thighs. Now I could use my hand! Made perfect sense. How stupid I felt. Reading further, the book stated that masturbation would cause an orgasm. That sounded like a fabric my mother once said her dress was made from. According to the book, I would ejaculate sperm at the time of orgasm. *This can't be possible,* I said to myself, suddenly not so charged with excitement but more worried that I was going to be leaking seminal fluid like a faulty bottle of LePage's Glue. Tucking *Boys & Sex* discreetly into a bunch of homework binders, I pulled my pants up, bolted from the boy's room and sped home with one thing on my mind.

You might be thinking at this point, didn't your father tell you about sex, birds, bees, stamen and semen? I'll tell you this: sex talk was not on the agenda at our house. If my father, with whom I'd shared precious little with since birth, had waltzed into my room and started talking about penises and erections I would have - well, I don't know what I would have done as it was so beyond possibility. Instead, tucking *Boys & Sex* under my tee-shirt, I stealthily crept down the hallway, locked the bathroom door, dropped my pants, opened up the book and read about the way to masturbate as though it was an instruction from God. I'm not a religious person, but the only way to describe this moment was reverential. I read the words, *Grasp your penis and gently move your hand back and forth* as though they were written on a stone tablet. And being an obedient student, I did just that. My hand tugged at my erection and I rode the wave of sensation for several minutes, building up slowly and the sensation quickly turning into a familiar pleasure. And then I was moving towards something I hadn't experienced before and couldn't stop. In moments it culminated with a rush of heat in my groin and a veritable geyser of semen. When I stopped gasping I looked at the frightful mess I'd created. There was sperm on my hands, stomach, chest and splattered all across *Boys & Sex*. I unrolled some toilet paper and started wiping it up, but my ejaculate fixed the pages together. I tried in vain to get the pages unstuck, unintentionally tearing out a section on fetishes. "Jeez," I exclaimed, immediately flushed with embarrassment when I envisioned myopic Mrs. Faulkner assessing the damages to the boy's sex manual I'd checked out. *She's going to give me a colossal book fine.*

If there were life-changing nodal events where I'd come into my own - literally - this was one of them. At that pivotal moment in my bathroom with the blue-knitted Poodle toilet-roll cover, sitting on the john and covered in semen, I became less of a boy and even more of a secretive dreamer, indulging in fantasies and eagerly anticipating the time when I would become a real man.

4

ADOLESCENT ANGST

I'd describe my adolescence as a cruel joke - testosterone levels skyrocketing like missiles, an unsteady voice cracking like thin ice, a penis with its own idiosyncratic whims, joint pain that defied my youth and a face which routinely erupted in blotches of acne, controlled only by giant doses of tetracycline and fuelled by a diet of potato chips and corner-store candy. If all that wasn't sufficient, painful shyness affected the most minor of social interactions and turned me into a red-faced, sweaty, stammering mess. I wasn't alone - many boys experience adolescent angst and girls may have it worse. At least boys never had to cope with a menstruation cycle.

Adding to the tumult, school was an anxious tribulation. There were even a few moments of abject terror, like when the physical education teacher grabbed my throat and pushed me up against the cinderblock wall of the gymnasium. My crime? I wasn't paying sufficient attention when spotting a classmate on the trampoline. A momentary dereliction of duty, but not a reason to nearly break a boy's larynx. Hack was the same brute who requested all boys wear jock-straps and inspected us as we slipped into them - just to make sure it was worn correctly. A jockstrap is a bizarre invention. Many thirteen-year-olds had little to protect, not to mention the weirdness of wearing something that highlighted the ass end. (However, there were a couple of boys

I recall being well-developed for their age.) The professional that he was, Mr. Hack would marshal all the boys into the change room at the end of class. If a boy had not tried his best, or failed to wear his jock, he faced the humiliation of having to bend over the change-bench in the buff and be the recipient of Mr. Hack's substantial paddle. This happened in front of the other boys to intensify the degradation. We called it 'Hack's Whacks', and according to Brian Finster, who was Hack-whacked several times, the experience was not helpful in stemming a lacklustre gym class performance nor did it incite any new-found love of the elasticized jock-strap. Mr. Hack's predilection for striking the bottoms of young boys paled in comparison to his shower antics. He would ensure that all boys had showered after gym, standing naked before them for some unknown reason, except for a clipboard and a Bic pen, eyeing us as we lathered and rinsed until his requirements for hygiene had been satisfied. *Or something had been satisfied.* It was difficult to think that such a routine was appropriate, though we boys never questioned it nor dared talk about it with adults. Half-way through the school year, I heard a story from Brian that Mr. Hack had finally crossed the boundary with his hygiene drill.

"Did you hear about Robby Berd?" he asked in a hushed tone at the library workstation. We were paired off to work on an assignment about the building of Canada's national railway for Social Studies.

"Robby? The guy who runs cross-country?" I asked. I knew of Robby Berd; a high school athlete and very good-looking older teenager.

"Yeah, that's him," Brian whispered, barely suppressing his excitement.

"No, what's happened?"

"It's just nuts; listen to this. Hack was watchin' him do laps at the track after class. Robby finished an' headed for the change room to shower-up an' Hack followed him."

"So what? Hack follows us to the showers all the time."

"Yeah, to the showers, but this time Hack stripped off an' stepped *into* the showers." Brian's voice cracked and broke. The librarian shot us a narrow-eyed look.

"Shhh," I tried to get Brian to lower his voice. "Jeez. What did Hack wanna check this time?"

"Whaddya think? And there's more."

"Tell me," I whispered hoarsely.

"Hack wanted to —" Brian covered his mouth with his hand in an effort to appear discreet, *"give him a rubdown in the shower."*

"Holy crap." I felt a sense of dread about what might come next.

"That's what I thought. I heard Hack wouldn't stop feelin' him up. Robby tried to get away but Hack grabbed him by the shoulders, 'an Robby swung out an' hit Hack's jaw with his fist."

"He whacked Hack?"

"Yeah, but after Hack got slugged, he shoved Robby backwards an' he slipped an' hit his head on the tile floor. His head cracked open like a walnut with blood everywhere. *Everywhere.*" Brian's eyes were wide as saucers as he made his report.

"Gawd, is he okay?" Hearing there was bleeding made me feel sick to my stomach.

"I dunno. I heard that he ran down the hall buck naked to get the nurse. She got him to hospital so they could stitch him up. Hasn't been at school since."

"Unreal. What about Hack?"

"This is the good part. He's gone, gone for good. A couple of days ago he quit," Brian said brightly, clearly delighted with the news.

"Not soon enough."

"Yeah. Apparently the reason they said he left was 'cause he's having family difficulties." Brian snickered, then the two of us laughed loudly with relief. The librarian scowled at us from the sign-out desk.

"Shush! You two boys, quiet in the library!"

"You know what this means, don't you?" Brian murmured. "No more bending over in a jock-strap to get a Hack-whack," he said in a steady voice. "I just hope the new Phys Ed teacher isn't worse."

"No way he could be worse than Hack," I said.

"We'll find out next week."

We went back to the assignment about the CNR and the Golden Spike, but my mind was preoccupied on the frightening experience in the boy's shower. Did being young mean that a boy was easy prey? I didn't need any incentive, but Brian's story gave me extra reasons to be cautious.

2

My father's striving meant new opportunities for him, constant pressure to adapt to change for my mother and ongoing anxiety for me. When we lived in Burnaby my mother seemed happiest. My father was a general manager of a large automotive warehouse. Mum had a beautiful family home in a pleasant neighbourhood. Lynda and I were in excellent schools and Mum was satisfyingly employed at the Hudson's Bay at Georgia & Granville. The accoutrements were complete and all seemed content. All except my father, of course, whose desire to buy his own business superseded our family's emotional stability. Even as I write that statement I can hear my father's voice groaning, "You've gotta be kidding."

The second-last family move came when we moved from Burnaby to far-away Abbotsford. (Tulip Crescent was a sunny name for such a muddy and ugly street.) My father had bought his own auto-parts store - a dream for him and a nightmare for the rest of us. We were on the move to a bucolic (which really meant foul-smelling - *not* pastoral) town in the Fraser Valley. Eventually, it proved to be a wise choice for my father, whose instincts for building revenue through ridiculously hard work were realized most clearly with this last move. My father pumped all his money from the sale of our Burnaby home into his venture, leaving us nearly penniless. My urbane mother left her sales position at the Hudson's Bay, work she'd adored, chatting with customers and even hawking clothing to Nancy Greene on several occasions. (There's pride in helping clothe a woman who skied down a mountain to win a couple of World Cup and Olympic gold medals.) My Dad was excited about his next undertaking, but for Mum to leave her work? Well, the move was difficult for that reason alone. Abbotsford would prove to be an oppressive place, complete with churches and temples on every corner, representing every possible version of faith - with the exception of Judaism. And yet, for all their pretence of good spirit, this community seemed anything but helpful to those who didn't share the same views on religion. Apart from a sweet elderly couple whom my mother had taken a shine to next door, the residents of Tulip Crescent were unfriendly at best.

One Sunday winter's afternoon, I was Windexing the inside of the front windows and noticed something puzzling. After finishing my chore, I put down the spray can and went to the kitchen to tell my mother. She was dicing onions and making a batch of pea soup for supper.

"Mum, those people across the street keep pulling back their curtains to stare over here."

"They're staring at our house? That's odd." Mum stopped chopping and went with me to the living room and gazed out to see neighbours from several homes peering through their front windows.

"How long has this been going on?" she asked, her curiosity growing.

"I dunno, maybe fifteen minutes or so. It's weird, isn't it?"

"Something's wrong. I don't think it's our house they're looking at. Get your jacket and runners on."

My mother slipped into her rubber boots and donned a windbreaker. We went outside in the rain to the front of the house and began a quick survey.

"Oh, dear God." Next door she saw Mr. Pottinger collapsed beside the car he was working on just outside their carport. We scuttled over immediately and stood over his horrifying body. Instead of coming to his aid, our neighbours stayed indoors, moving their German lace curtains aside, idly and inexplicably observing Mrs. Pottinger's husband of forty-seven years in his death repose, his eyes wide-open to the cold rainfall. His hands were formed into fists and his face and body contorted as if his last living moments were subject to great pain.

"Mum, is he...?"

"Yes. Stay here with him and don't stare - it's only going to upset you," Mum advised, taking a breath to settle her nerves as she rang her neighbour's doorbell. I stayed inside the carport, terrified at what I was seeing, a body sprawled on the asphalt, the rain pelting the corpse. Mum was right, I shouldn't have gawked but I couldn't look away. I'd never seen a dead body before and seeing him I felt instantly nauseous. Mrs. Pottinger answered the door and immediately grasped the tragic dilemma, rushing to her deceased husband. Those same good christians (they don't deserve a capital letter) crowded their windows, curious at the old woman's horrid loss. My mother wrapped her arms around the sobbing Mrs. Pottinger and gently coaxed her inside to call the police. Before she entered her door, Mum glared across the street.

"Goddamn you!" she cursed bitterly, shaking her fist at the un-neighbourly christian onlookers of Tulip Crescent who continued to dispassionately observe the unfolding drama of the death of their neighbour.

♒

Abbotsford wasn't Burnaby, Calgary, Winnipeg, Waterloo, Hamilton or Port Arthur. There was nothing special about the place, just miles of stinking farms, dusty feed stores, dingy homes, a dilapidated general store and an unpaved gravel main drag. It was a shock to my city-loving mother to find herself removed from her stylish Burnaby house and living in a shabby rental with worn-out purple shag carpets, peeling moss-green kitchen linoleum, a musty dark basement (where I slept, Lynda got the small upstairs bedroom with pink candy-floss carpeting) and a swampy, grassless backyard. For nearly a year I recall Mum looking forlorn in a place that seemed to be the antithesis of family life. I worried about her sadness. Mum was someone whose laughter was frequent and infectious. It was the first time I ever saw her look glum for a prolonged time and there was nothing that a boy could do but try to make attempts to cheer her. It's a challenge when a child worries about their parent. There's so much that's worrisome about just being a youth. I told myself that her unhappiness, as well as my own, was the fault of my father. I couldn't see the move as being in the family's best interests, as he had explained. I started further down the path of declaring my father as being insensitive to my mother's needs and in doing so, continued to construct the barriers that became a prominent part of my relationship with him for most of my life.

A change for the better was the last family move across town to a house on Birch Street a year later. Though a lovely home, the best feature was a giant maple tree in the front yard. The maple was extremely old; over a hundred years. I loved that tree. The house needed some work on the inside and my mother was ready for a creative project. Mum spent years decorating it. Painting, wallpapering, Oriental rugs, parquet floors, French silk curtains, new furniture; all was fair game. If she had to live in Abbotsford, she could distill images of elegance from the pages of Architectural Digest and create her own tasteful home. It made living in a Ditch more bearable.

I was in a nicer home, but life didn't necessarily get nicer for me. If there was one experience that cemented my disparaging view of Abbotsford, it happened when I was in Grade 11, the night before Halloween. After school, I went to the community library to work on a paper. By the time I was heading home it was dark. I had a two-mile trek home up Hazel Road, blackened by the lack of street lights, devoid of vehicles. The only person on the street was me. One long section of the steep hill had a fifteen-foot concrete retaining wall on the right, the road was on my left and a sheer drop-off past the left shoulder. As I continued my way home I thought little of the lights from a vehicle approaching me from behind. A short while later a flatbed truck slowly pulled up alongside me and I had an immediate sense of dread.

"Hey, faggot!"

Okay, I thought, my heart racing, adrenaline being pumped to my brain, *just stare straight ahead and keep walking.*

"I said, *faggot!*" one screamed at me.

That same person yelled out my last name. They knew who I was. I was in trouble. I dared to look at the now-stopped truck. There were three young men in the front of the truck's cab and two other young men in the flatbed of the truck. *This didn't look good.*

"Fucking faggot-boy! Fuckin' dirty cocksucker!"

As I instantly turned away, something was thrown at me. The object crashed hard against the sidewalk; a baseball-sized stone. My heart thudded in my chest. The others picked up rocks from the bed of the truck and began tossing them at me as they snarled a series of hateful slurs. The driver followed, moving the truck at my quickened pace, my fear and panic surging. All at once the stones began to fly; thrown at my legs, chucked at my back, tossed at my head, one hitting me square in the ear, breaking the skin as blood coursed down my jaw. My rucksack full of books protected the space between my shoulder blades, but otherwise, I was a vulnerable target. I ran as they laughed and followed me. I tried to dodge the stones by keeping my arms around my head but they found their target, one jagged rock smacked my forehead, snapping my head back, stunning me with excruciating pain and causing me to drop to my knees. Two or three young men hopped out, arms laden with rocks, ready to - what? Stone me to death? With the concrete wall on one side, the truck on the other, and a steep hill ahead, I was trapped as they pelted me. I immediately got to my feet and sprinted, dazed and fright-filled as I ran for my life up the steep grade. A spray of rocks hit me as I bounded around the first corner after the retainer wall, charging down a path, into the bush, deeper and deeper and into a thatch of cedar trees. Panting, sweating, I crawled through the blackness on my hands and knees and I cowered under the trees. I was scratched deeply by sharp branches, wounded and bleeding. I stifled my rapid breathing and listened helplessly to their spews of hatred. Their voices sounded near. I waited for them to find me. I heard them scuffle around the area, muttering, laughing, kicking at the ground, teasing me with their taunts, screaming out.

"That dirty faggot's gonna die when we find him. Come outta there, Stamp, you fucker."

I held my breath, shaking with fear. After a few moments, the voices seemed more distant - and then silence. *Did they go, or am I being baited to come out from hiding?* I didn't know for certain but I couldn't leave. I was planted to the ground as solidly as the trees I was hiding under. Paralyzed with fright, I waited in the cold and dark. My forehead was wet with beads of ice-cold sweat, I had bleeding injuries on my head and chest, my ear was swollen and bloodied and my heart pounded in my chest so loudly I thought the noise would give me away. After a while - I can't say how long - I decided to venture out. I was fearful of moving and making a noise but my legs were cramped and sore. I quietly stood and stepped tentatively from cover, vigilant of every sound I made and every noise I heard. I walked from the woods and closer to the road. I saw no truck, no others in the street. I smoothed myself over, wiped the dirt from my matted hair and rotted leaves from my pants and slowly, timidly started to walk the rest of the way home. Every approaching car sent me running into the darkness, waiting for any vehicle to pass, adrenaline surging. Twenty minutes later I scampered into my parent's home; breathless, blood on my neck and shirt, forehead bruised and bloody, my face scratched from the branches and bramble, jacket and shirt torn, the sweat caked filthy grime on my face. My mother saw me stagger in through the kitchen door and gasped as I stumbled in and dropped my rucksack.

"My God! You're bleeding! What's happened?" she cried as she rushed to me, looking as stunned as I felt. She put her cool hand over the bloodied goose egg on my forehead then grabbed a dish-cloth and wet it from the faucet and held it on my wound. She looked over at my startled father who stood at the counter, watching but not knowing what to do.

"I'm okay," I managed to lie shakily. "I took a shortcut home from school…through the ravine and had a bad fall."

"Through the ravine at this hour? In the dark?" Mum asked. Dad remained silent. By the appraising look on Mum's face, she could tell that I hadn't slipped in a ravine.

"I don't believe you. You're white as a ghost. Who did this to you?" she demanded.

"I fell, Mum, that's all. I wasn't watching my step. You know how klutzy I am. I'm gonna take a shower and clean myself up."

I left the bloody cloth in the sink and walked away swiftly; there were no further inquiries from my mother, or perhaps my leave made it clear that the question period was over. I went to the bathroom, looked at my shocking image in the mirror, ran a shower, shed my ruined clothes, allowed the hot water to wash away the stinking sweat of terror and a body encrusted with blood. The water stung, forced my wounds open and caused more bleeding. I stayed under the wa-ter, disbelieving what had happened to me. Me…strong me, a swim-mer, an athlete, a young man, indestructible, beaten, bloody, bruised and shaken. Shower over, I gently dried myself. It hurt to touch the towel to my body. Humiliated, I went to my bedroom, closed the door and bundled myself with blankets. I lay on my bed, shaking, freezing cold after a scalding shower. I stared at the ceiling and mused about whether I should've told my parents. *But how could I tell them their boy had been gay-bashed with stones in the righteous town of Abbotsford?* It was better for my parents to not know what happened and better for my father, whose store was coming along. I didn't want it known that I was stoned. What would people say? Upon reflection, it could have changed my life if I'd been honest with them. It could have started me on a different path, perhaps a more truthful one. It didn't make sense that I was as afraid of telling my parents as I was of being terrorized that night, but it would have been the truth.

Being called a faggot was paralyzing for me; what might come next? There would be other hateful incidents that rattled my composure, but none like the evening I was the target of homophobes bent on my ruin. What happened that night took planning - they had to know my movements - so from that night onward I was extra-cautious about being myself. If being me meant that I was an object worthy of hatred and violence, then I had to be someone else. I walked stiffly, spoke less, pitched my voice lower when I did speak, avoided eye-contact with most everyone (lest they see me for who I really was), swam harder, faster and farther than any other young man on the team. I pledged to never, ever be the faggot walking up Hazel Road and bombarded with rocks. Never.

Swimming was a way that I distracted myself from thoughts of my sexuality and living in the despicable valley. Up at 5 AM; in the water by 5:30 AM. By the time most people were waking up, the team and I had done four kilometres of swimming plus kick board drills. Freestyle and butterfly were the strokes that I had success swimming, with backstroke fast enough, but always hard work for me. My breaststroke was slower than most, mainly due to a whip-kick that aptly demonstrated my less-flexible hips and feet and thus weaker propulsion. Even with my lacklustre breaststroke I swam the IM - Individual Medley - butterfly, back, breast and free in the 200 metre distance and was easing into swimming the 400 metre IM. By the time I'd reached sixteen, I was shaving tenths of seconds off every at every swim meet. I had set some good short-course times but I had an innate belief that I could go faster. I immersed myself in training. I was committed to being a hard-working swimmer whose efforts would pay off.

At seventeen years of age, I had completed secondary school in the un-prestigious Abbotsford High School. I wished that I was anywhere else, and if I had to be in Abbotsford, the best place for me was under the fluorescent yellow lights in the cloudy waters of the dingy MacMillan Pool, swimming lap after lap, getting quicker and stronger. Every morning before practice I stood on the pool deck and swore: *If I go fast enough, I'll swim right outta here.* There may be no place like home, but I hadn't found mine yet.

5

CHANCES IN THE LAND OF OZ

I had applied to UBC and was ecstatic when I received a letter of acceptance to begin a Bachelor of Arts program. I'd saved money from part-time lifeguarding, but it paled to the costs of tuition and other expenses related to attending university. My parents weren't in a position to support me but I'd had a long-term plan. UBC swim trials were taking place in late-April of 1975 at the new Vancouver Aquatic Centre. For two years it had been my intent to try out for the team in the hopes of securing an athletic scholarship. I'd dedicated my energies for that opportunity. I was no Mark Spitz, but I was well-trained, had a good slip through the water, and most importantly, I was determined to leave Abbotsford. I wanted my chance.

Ever been to a swim meet or a swim trial? It's an exciting event for swimmers; perhaps even more so for spectators who don't have to contend with the inherent anxiety of athletic performance. By swimming decent times through the season I'd given myself a chance for the UBC trials. The day of the meet, I woke up early, showered and dressed in a blue nylon tracksuit. I had some muesli and fruit at the kitchen counter, packed a lunch and left my Mum a note telling her that I'd be back later in the evening. Grabbing my wallet and my swim bag, I left the house and walked down to the bus station in a steady rain, my damp tracksuit clinging to my legs. By 5:45 AM, I'd paid for my ticket outside the small terminal and waited as the bus slowly ambled into the bay. I breathed in the heavy diesel fumes as I climbed aboard the Greyhound. After a few minutes, the bus pulled out of the station and was on the highway, the rain stopping and the sun beginning to illuminate the landscape of the town I desperately wanted to leave. I thought of the day ahead, started planning my swim strategy - my starts, my turns, my closings. I went over it many times in my head, visualizing it, telling myself what was going to happen. After half an hour, the sounds and movements of the bus had lulled me to sleep. An hour later I woke, mouth dry, eyes adjusting to the light. The bus was travelling west down Hastings Street. I could see the tall buildings in the approaching downtown, the city spreading out through my window, the bluish mountains of the North Shore and the snow still dusting the top of the Lion's. It made me think of Dorothy viewing the Emerald City for the first time and my excitement grew.

The Aquatic Centre was a bee-hive by the time I had registered. Officials were setting up the timing system, parents paced nervously and anxious swimmers focused on the day of competition ahead. Soon all athletes would be called and the wait to swim a series of heats, semis and finals would begin. It was an all-day affair with swimmers across the province competing for twenty-five or thirty spots. I knew some of them, but my primary competition was Matt Lowe - he out-swam me at every competition. Standing at 6'2", he was tall, lean, well-muscled and seriously fast. He and I shared events: 100 free, 100 butterfly, 200 IM and 400 free. Quickly locking up my clothes in the change-room, I donned my blue-and–white striped Speedo suit and walked down the tile deck and shook my arms loose. I slipped a latex cap over my long hair and placed my goggles into position. I jumped into the dive tank to keep <u>limber</u>, taking some easy, long strokes along with other swimmers who didn't look nearly as worried as me. Swim meets usually last a couple of days. However, my heats were in the late morning. I was grateful to have advanced to my finals and was ready to compete later in the afternoon. My first final was the 100 metre freestyle. I had a bad start off the block and finished fifth with a near-pedestrian 59:88. A disappointment; I'd gone out with too much adrenaline and been passed by Lowe after the turn and he'd taken the win easily. The 100 butterfly was better; I took fourth place and 1:05. Lowe took first again. The 400 metre free was my next final. I liked the longer distances. I could get more of a rhythm in the race because after many years in the water I'd developed a high level of stamina. For the 400, I churned out a decent time - 4:32. Enough for a third place finish with a swimmer I'd not heard of winning and Lowe finishing in second place. I had a break and ate the food I'd packed before swimming my last event. At 4:30 PM I was waiting with the other swimmers for the 200-metre Individual Medley, a prestige final. It was essential that I medaled if I was to be considered as a swimming hopeful at UBC. Matt Lowe was determined to win. He had posted the best time in the heat: 2:09. Like most swimmers, Lowe went faster at finals. He was assigned to lane 4 and I would be right beside him in lane 3. The official announced the race. We stepped up onto the starting blocks. I faced forward, not looking at the other swimmers. Instead I breathed deeply, assumed the start position with my hands grasping my feet and waited for the gun to sound. It felt like a long wait. There was dead quiet in the building as I focused my attention on the lane ahead. Muscles <u>twitching</u>, head <u>reeling</u>, a combination of excitement and nausea. My heart was <u>thudding</u> with anxiety and *pow!* The starter's gun sounded and I was up and off the block, a good start, powering up and then slipping easily into the still water, legs and hips beginning the <u>undulating</u> dolphin kick to push me back to the surface...*1, 2, 3, 4,*

5, 6, 7 kicks - and up! My shoulders rotated out and I began the butterfly stroke, catching the water, holding it, pushing it backwards as I kicked; *pull, kick, kick, fly!* I could see no one beside me; Lowe was not in my range of sight. Propelling myself down the course with all the speed and power I could muster, I was breathing every third stroke, then every second, then every first. My arms stretched out, hands pulling, shoulders burning, rising up and out of the water and falling back in, stroke after stroke, hips aching with pain. *Five metres to go. Hold on, close to the wall now, touch! Good turn for backstroke, push off hard. There's no one near me, kick hard, breathe out underwater, my lungs hurt, spectators yelling, shit, water in my nose, don't cough, don't choke, look up, churn the water, push, pull. I'm getting closer to the end, push! Flags above me; six more strokes, push hard, touch and turn fast now! Breaststroke, go! One underwater pull...big kick...up again to breathe, grab a gulp of oxygen, shit, I'm slow! Pull hard, don't puke...no, don't, goddamn it - vomit in my mouth, spit it out next breath, don't choke, okay, swimmers on my right and left; damn! Did Lowe pass me? Fuck.... just pull, pull, pull!* I heard screaming from the bleachers. *Almost finished the breast, 5 meters left, pull! Grab gutter...open turn, push hard off the wall! Glide a second, underwater now, up, up. Okay, at surface, pull hard, power the freestyle...kick from the hips, ride the water. Power through. Stroke, stroke! Can't see, goggles fogged, muscle strength's going... kick, pull, breathe! Close to finish... almost there, hang on, pushing...pulling, don't fade... don't fail! Ten metres to go, 8, 5, 4, 2...kick to the wall, stretch and touch!*

I stood up, pushed off my goggles, gasped and held on to the lane ropes for support. All around me was a watery melee of noise and confusion. I saw Lowe and the other swimmers; we were looking at each other; the last swimmers still had not completed. I stared at the board in disbelief. I'd come in at 2:09:45, a third-place finish, but a PB, with Lowe in first with 2:05:74. His name was announced as the winner, and while the cheers and applause were for Lowe, I had a sense of overwhelming relief. Tears came to my eyes, masked by the water running off my swim cap. Even with my lousy breaststroke complete with a mouthful of vomit, with two losses and two third-place finishes, I'd done enough to make the university team. Screw that despicable Ditch. I'd get my own chance in the Land of Oz.

6

THE DEPARTURE

Leaving home was a long-awaited fantasy for me. The departure happened a few days before Labour Day of 1975. Being a university student was mind-blowing and I was very proud of having an opportunity to attend UBC. I had few belongings to take with me; two pairs of weathered jeans, a stack of white tee-shirts my mother laundered for me, some books, a worn quilt, my swimming and running gear. I was able to get all my life into two bags; one a swim bag and the other a large leather rucksack. All I had left to do was say goodbye to my parents. I worried that my mother would have difficulty with my leaving. My sister was living with her boyfriend and Mum would be alone with my father and I wondered how she'd manage with the change. After all, I'd been a confidante to whom she spilled the beans about my father's frequent inattentiveness and miserable behaviour. I'd listened to her frustrations, heard her gripes about living in a town that she only now was beginning to accept. I'd been dutiful, driving her to get groceries, taking her to medical appointments, going with her to the mall, commenting on her fashion choices and tried to be a conscientious - if at times irksome - son.

I sat down with her in the family room. Mum was drinking a large glass of white wine with ice cubes in it, the crystal goblet wet with condensation. *A little early for wine.* She looked pensive, sitting there, waiting for me to speak. She knew once I left I didn't want to come back to Abbotsford. I shut off the constantly playing television. She turned towards me, smoothed her dark-blue corduroy pants and noticed my rucksack.

"Looks as though you're packed up."

"Yup. Thanks for washing my tee-shirts. How'd you get 'em so white?"

"Javex. You'll have to do things like your own wash now."

"Mum, don't you think I know that? There's a laundry just off campus."

"There's no need for me to worry?"

"About having clean clothes?"

"Don't be a smart-ass. About being away at school and looking after yourself."

"No need, you know I'll be fine."

"It's a big change."

"I know, but Mum, it's a good change. You have no idea how much I've hated this place."

"I'm not an idiot. It's all you've talked about since we moved here."

"I wasn't the only one," I zinged hurtfully. My mother sighed, piqued by my comment. "Weren't you glad when you left Port Arthur for Winnipeg?"

"No, of course not. It was very trying for me when we moved."

"Because your hometown was special to you. This place is gross, except for you, Mum."

"Well that's something," she said, then drew a long sip of wine. Though I'd had many different schools to attend, our frequent cross-Canada moves meant that my mother had to say goodbye time and time again to people and places she'd cared for. It couldn't have been easy for her, either.

"Wasn't it an adventure? And you got away from Nana, too."

"It's not that simple. Besides, Nana had expectations wherever we moved." She smiled sadly. "And speaking of adventures, I'll tell you a secret, dear." Mum put her wine glass on a coaster and leaned in slightly, lowering her voice.

"I'm all ears, Mum."

"Well…you're heading off to university —"

"That's not a secret," I interrupted.

"And you're not listening," Mum said, slightly scolding me.

"Sorry." I took a breath and tried to be patient.

"I wanted to go to school, too. Not university, but I'd planned to take interior decorating at a technical school in the Lakehead. After your father and I were married."

"Really? I never knew that. Why didn't you? You had the panache, for sure." Mum had an eye for colour, fashion, scale and an interest in many aspects of design. She had an undeniable aesthetic.

"Because your sister came along in a year, and then you a few years later. We moved and I gave up on the idea. It was a big job, having children, keeping the house and then starting a new job at the Hudson's Bay. Your father and I had a mortgage and money was short. I gave up the notion of being a decorator and sold clothes instead."

It was a good secret; I hadn't heard this before. My mother had dreams I knew nothing about.

"But weren't you angry? Giving up on something that important?"

"Angry? No, not at all. I indulged my whims by sprucing up our houses. Who knows? Perhaps I'd have been a terrible decorator."

"I can't believe that. Look at what you've done here."

She looked lost in thought for a moment and perused her family room - chocolate brown walls, white wainscoting, a red oriental wool area rug, navy blue sofa with blue and brown plaid toss cushions and my Grandfather's art hanging in ornate frames that she'd antiqued with gold paint and a wire brush.

"Years tumble by so fast. You'll see. All at once you and your sister went from diapers to diplomas." Mum took another long draft of her wine.

Yeah, a useless high school diploma from this terrible place.

"You know how important this opportunity is for you?"

43

"Mum, we've already talked about this. I swam hard to earn my scholarship. I'm not going to screw it up."

"Yes, but you're still so young. Other students are older when they go to university. Some have worked for a couple of years."

"I doubt I'd make a scholarship a few years from now. I have to capitalize on how I'm swimming right now. I'm super-lucky to have this chance."

"It's a mother's prerogative to worry." She sipped her wine. "Is there anything else that you need?" she asked.

"No," I said, patting my rucksack, "I've got it all. Mum, are you going to be okay without me here?"

"Sweetheart," Mum said, furrowing her brow. "You're being theatrical again." She moved hair from my eyes with her hand. "Your hair is too long. It should have been cut before you went to university."

"Mum...stop. Besides, long hair is in now."

"Well, at least it's clean, isn't it? *Isn't it?*"

"*Mum.*"

"Did you know I still have your baby locks from your first haircut? They're white-blond and curly. I've kept the clippings in an envelope in my dresser drawer if you ever want to see them."

"I've seen them a hundred times," I groaned.

"Yes, I suppose you have." She smiled at me and put down her near-empty wine glass. "Promise me you'll work hard at all your courses?"

"I'll work hard at all my courses," I parroted.

"I hear young people are getting into trouble at those disco cabarets on Granville. You'd do well to stay clear of them," she advised.

"I barely go out at night, let alone go disco dancing. I'm always in the pool. I won't get into trouble, Mum." *Good boys like me never get into trouble.*

"Let's hope so. I'll fret, regardless. Now, call me collect when you get to your room and let me know you're safe and sound."

"Mum, I told you, there's no phone. I'll call you when I can, okay? After I'm sorted out."

"Yes, after you're sorted. Give your mother a hug. I'll miss you," she whispered. I felt her arms enclose me, smelled the Shalimar perfume she loved, the softness of her flesh against my own. I immediately felt a lump forming in my throat. Holding her close for a moment and then letting go, I said, "I should head out now. I gotta get to the bus station by four this afternoon."

"Do you want your Dad to take you to the depot?"

"Could he? It's kind of hard to haul this stuff down by myself. Could you ask?" *Because apparently I'm completely unable to ask my father for anything.*

"Of course. Bill, your son needs a ride to the station! Bill!" she hollered upstairs. "Here," she said, reaching into her corduroy pocket, "I've saved up a little money for you but don't tell your father." Mum handed me five crisp fifty dollar bills.

"Wow, thanks. This'll really help." I stood up and tucked the money in my wallet.

"Don't forget, this is always your home." Mum noticed her depleted wine and walked to the kitchen for a refill, her cords swishing. I gathered up my belongings and went outside to stand beside the giant maple tree. A few leaves were burnished with early autumn's gold. It seemed that the maple was readying for change, too. The trunk was over five feet in diameter; it was a marvel and I'd miss seeing it. *I'll miss that tree more than anything else here - except for my mother, of course.* My father unhurriedly came down to the car. He took a brief sideways glance at me, then unlocked the trunk and I tossed my bags in it. As we pulled out, I saw the shadowy form of my mother in the window, waving.

The drive to the bus station with my father was eventful in its silence. It reminded me of the times he deigned to drive me to school - part way only, of course. On the way to the station, there was nothing said that hinted at the importance of a son leaving home, of going off to university, of becoming a man. As the big black Ford pulled into the station my father cut the engine, got out, went to the trunk to collect my bags and passed them to me.

"Son?" My father looked at me with something - expectation?

"Yes, Dad?"

"Be good, Junior," he stated plainly.

"Uh-huh. Sure thing. Bye, Dad." I grabbed my belongings and held them tight against my chest. My father nodded his head, then turned away, slipped into his car, started the motor and drove off. I waited alone for the bus, musing about the nature of boys and men, of sons and fathers. I wondered if any family had seen my father off before he trekked across the ocean at age thirteen? Did they regret their decision? Or did they trust their boy could make his own way? I was lost in thought as the coach pulled up and I climbed aboard. It was a two-hour ride to the city via the Fraser highway. As the nearly-empty bus travelled the milk-run there was plenty of time to ruminate. It was liberating for me to be free of family and to start university life, but I worried about my mother. Would she manage without all our laughter and banter? Or was I being theatrical as she stated? After nearly two hours and various stops in Aldergrove, Langley and New Westminster, the coach finally arrived in Vancouver, inching its way into the depot on Dunsmuir. I collected up my gear and walked a few blocks up Richards Street to the next bus stop. I waited in a deserted bus shelter and in twenty minutes caught a city bus over the Granville Bridge, then west to Broadway where I had to transfer buses again to get to Kitsilano. I was quickly tiring of the efforts it took to get to my destination. I climbed onto the last grimy bus and breathed the stench of stale sweat. *There's a lot of humanity on this bus. A little too much.* After getting as far as I could on the MacDonald bus, I hiked the rest of the way to Tolmie and 10th, my gear making my back ache. The trip from downtown took a long time and though the room I rented was close to campus, I was far from the city. *I'll hunt for a car sometime in the next year from the money I made from guarding. Yes, a car would really help out, make things easier.* I'd found a cheap and decidedly un-cheerful place to stay in an old bungalow close to UBC on Tolmie

Street. I'd be living in a small room in an otherwise unfinished basement with no shower but at least it had a sink to brush my teeth - cold
water only. I arrived in the early evening, spoke to the Slav landlord
who mostly understood English, got my key and my instructions. I
was to enter only from the back through a low door I had to duck
under. I put my swim gear and rucksack in my tiny space and started
another part of my life. Though I'd be living in a small cell, I was
eager to discover what it was like to be a free young man. Perhaps my
father felt the same way when he was young?

I settled into university quickly. UBC was a big campus; there
were more students at university than the entire population of the
Ditch. I learned where I was meant to be for classes - at the Buchanan
Building and other lecture halls - and began my liberal arts education. I worked hard at my studies, as I'd promised. Psychology was
my major. I would be training at the Empire Games Pool, an outside
fifty-yard pool and the new indoor fifty-metre UBC Aquatic Centre
a few steps away. In a week I started working part-time as a lifeguard
- I'd been certified in Abbotsford a year earlier- and was grateful for
the hours. My coach was Jack Lerner, who lived up to his reputation
for being tough on his swimmers, certainly tougher that any coach
I'd ever had. In his late 40's, Lerner was considered one of the top
university swim coaches. He and his staff expected a huge effort in
the pool. From the start, I showed them how grateful I was having an
athletic scholarship and did exactly as directed. I wasn't interested in
futzing about or making friends on the team. In fact, I was distant to
all and cautious about where I was looking in the showers after practice - vigilant at all times. Failing to do so could be disastrous. I barely
admitted this to myself, but I felt lonely on a campus of thousands,
though clearly there was danger in being known. If I found a friend,
it would have to be someone special.

7

LARA'S THEME

My first significant adult friendship was with a winsome, strong-willed, freckled, red-haired young woman named Lara. She was three years older than me. We met in French class during our first year at university. Her skill at French was already advanced, so for her the course was a lark. We partnered for practice sessions with the more experienced helping with the less. She took sympathy on me as my French - though I put in much effort - was not up to snuff. She tried to help me increase my basic language skills - compétences de base en français, au mieux. Within a short time, we got along famously. I found out that Lara also loved to sing. She had studied voice from a young age and sang whenever possible for extra money. At the Student Union Building - the SUB - she sang occasionally during Pub Nights accompanying herself with her guitar and also played the piano beautifully. Lara sang at weddings and funerals around the city which helped her improve her bank account. Lara had studied bel canto and had a plummy, rich soprano voice suited for classical composers, but with her deeper chest voice she sang everything from Joni Mitchell to George Gershwin. Lara breathed music; even when she spoke her voice had a kind of lyrical sing-song quality.

In the brief time I'd known Lara, and from what she'd told me, I'd say she'd experienced a challenge in becoming an adult. Like me, Lara was the youngest child but had three older brothers. Her parents had high expectations for all their children and singing was not on Lara's parents' list of future achievements. Her mother called it *Lara's hobby*, which she thought was dismissive at best. Her parents had charted out what she would study, where she would attend university, what she would eat and even what sports she was to participate in. Her mother wanted her children to be successful, though her daughter may have been an ill choice upon which to heap such objectives. Lara wanted to be successful on her own terms and for her own abilities. Her mother was determined that her daughter follow her guidance towards a proper and solid career. One afternoon following class Lara and I were talking about her mother as we walked to the SUB for something to eat.

"Did you know that my mother nursed at Vancouver General?"

"Did she?"

"Uh huh. For years. Her mother taught Home Economics - so there's an understanding about what women do for work."

"You mean —"

"It's either wiping asses or making baking powder biscuits and macramé owls." Lara made a sour face.

"Today women can do whatever they want, right?"

"That's what Cosmo says, but it never seems like I've had much of a choice. Anyway, she worked very hard - both my parents did. And I'm to have a professional career; very important," Lara stated flatly as we climbed the stairs and walked into the crowded SUB.

"So that's where the push to teach comes from?"

"I don't think my mother would say she is pushing me to become a French teacher. Her phrase is *encouraging me*. And she's right - I'm decent in French. My mother claimed I had an aptitude for it and thought it was logical to parlay that into teaching, which makes sense. I mean, what else do you do with a French degree? Mother is very logical."

Lara and I entered the cafeteria, got in line with about twenty-five other students and surveyed the displays of food behind scratched plexiglass.

"But how do you know you'd be content?" I asked as we moved quickly past the trays of wieners and canned beans, grey creamed cabbage, greasy pizza and to the stainless steel vat of pale-red tomato soup, which was what we decided to have.

"I dunno. Guess I'd have to try and see. I mean she's right, it's logical."

"Do you know how many times you've used the word logical?" I asked as we took two heavy white ceramic bowls and put them on purple plastic trays and filled the bowls with some dubious looking soup.

"Let me put it this way, Sunshine," Lara answered as she picked up a pile of crackers as we lined for the cashier. "According to my parents, singing is not logical, even though I adore it. Teaching's not horrible I guess, and I love French. I'd be an okay teacher, I suppose. If it weren't for the children, of course." Lara's face turned into a scowl.

"They sorta try your patience, huh?"

"Are you kidding? They're horrible little creatures. You've heard about teachers that lock-up misbehaving students in the science lab with the unlit Bunsen burners gassing full blast as they run for the border?"

"Uh, well, not —"

"I'm afraid that's the kind of teacher I'd be. Maybe I could learn to tolerate the snotty-nosed monsters, but what if teaching's just plain drudgery? Day in and day out of conjugating French verbs until my hair falls out."

"Ugh," I said reflexively.

"Exactly. After a few months I'd have to be fitted for a wig. And a woman is nothing without beautiful hair." She satirically flicked her red bangs from her face à la Farah Fawcett. "Anyway, here I am in the French Education Department."

"A fait accompli?"

"Looks that way," she sighed. "You wouldn't believe the scraps I've had with my mother about this. But I guess you know all about family fights."

"Our family doesn't fight. Instead, we wait until the offending person is in the shower and then we flush the toilet."

"You always scald the one you love," Lara laughed as we moved along. "When I question her judgment my mother gets *ruthless* with me and I just lose it. I scream that everything she's ever believed about me is wrong."

"You *are* opinionated," I said seriously.

"Don't I have a right to be?"

"Of course, I just —"

"But then the guilt-trip starts - *'Don't you know what I've sacrificed for you to go to university?'* and my personal favourite, *'How did I ever raise such an ungrateful child?'* which sends me skulking off, apparently the worst daughter in the universe. After all, I'm not supposed to upset my mother, am I?"

"Funny, I thought that was exactly what we were meant to do," I snickered, having tried to never upset mine willingly. Lara and I fished out some change and paid for our soup. We moved to a table with a stack of leftover crackers.

"They're paying for university and taking care of the cost of my accommodation so I feel obliged to follow-through and not disappoint."

"Even if it isn't right for you?" I asked, crumbling the packets of saltines into my bowl of soup, as did Lara. I stirred mine up and took a taste.

"Well, that's the confusing thing. I'll never tell them this, but I don't know that it's *not* right for me. It's remotely possible that I might like teaching children. My parents could know what's best. And really, when it's all said and done, I don't want to fail them. I want them to be proud of me."

"It's perplexing, huh? I mean, if singing's what you really love —"

"Well, yes, but even if I have a talent where would it take me?"

I couldn't answer her question and Lara didn't continue on the topic. She brought a spoonful of the pink chunky soup to her mouth, rolled it about and frowned. "God, Sunshine…how could they screw up tomato soup?" She put a spurt of ketchup in it, stirred it about, grimaced and passed the bottle over to me. Lara tasted it again and made a face. "This is very suspect." Lara licked her lips. "Since when is tomato soup gritty? I'm done." Lara put down her spoon.

"Starving students don't get to be food critics," I said, eating the rest without complaint. Lara passed me her bowl and snacked on crackers, not saying anything more about her mother's presumptions or her path at university. But I was ready to listen; an inexperienced young man with a voix doux and understanding ear. At any time, Lara had my full attention. As I grew to know her, I began to understand the notion of the kindred spirit. I either called Lara daily from the pool's house phone or ran into her on campus. And no week was complete without a meal or two shared together, though sometimes that meal took the form of Sara Lee cheesecakes - usually one blueberry and one strawberry. We scarfed down many of those, still frozen and eaten from the aluminum containers in the parking lot of a Mac's convenience store. Along with the laughter, Lara would confess worriedly (and sometimes tearfully) that she didn't know where or if she fit in the world. To me, it was astonishing that such a talented person questioned if she would achieve anything in life. I didn't have the courage to share my own musings. My own worries about being truly known motivated me to maintain a discrete emotional distance while I listened to her concerns and tried to help as much as an inexperienced young man could.

Unlike Edith Piaf's great song, I've had regrets. One was not being able to love Lara the way that I knew she wanted me to. Our relationship could never be more than platonic, though if things were different I've little doubt that I would have found a way to stay with her as long as there was air to breathe. While I admired Lara's beautiful voice, her sharp mind and her lithe, athletic body, I didn't have sexual thoughts for her. That's all; nothing more and nothing less than my sexual disinterest for Lara - for women. If I didn't have the ability to be sexual with her, I shamefully didn't mind if our relationship offered an illusion to those around me.

Though my mother would have disapproved, Lara and I often went out to dance, or as it was known at the time, to boogie. It was the era of Donna Summer, Elton John, ABBA, Fleetwood Mac, Stevie Wonder and KC and the Sunshine Band. Everyone was shaking one's booty. Thankfully for callow me, dancing required minimal skill and a minor bit of coordination. One notable Friday night we went to the Commodore Ballroom on Theatre Row to dance for several hours. A disco group was the headliner and we danced for hours, hardly leaving the bouncy wooden floor for a sip of water. Twirling, jiving, dizzy with our youth, our deep friendship and the pounding beat of disco music ringing in our ears, we danced as though we were the only ones there. At the end of the evening, both sweaty and reeking of stale cigarette smoke, we pushed through the crowd and onto the street. We chatted and walked until we found my car - a used red VW Fastback. For the next short while we circled around the city centre. Peering out of a constantly fogged-up windshield, we drove through the wet and shiny downtown streets. I wiped the steamy glass with the palm of my hand so we could see the neon signs on Granville glowing with fantastical colours. Through the mist, we drove down Robsonstrasse en route to the Blue Horizon Hotel. We had a late-night supper at the restaurant on the thirty-first floor. Three-hundred-and-twenty feet above the rain-soaked streets, we looked out on the towers of the West End. Beyond the darkness of English Bay, far away freighter ships' lights burned late into the night. The view was spectacular. Lara thought it sweet and touching that I was taking her to dinner when my finances were so meagre. I was delighted to spend what I could on her. We must have appeared to be a happy couple that night as one of the staff wanted to take our picture with her Polaroid camera.

There I was, a nineteen-year-old having my picture taken with a twenty-two-year-old woman who surely everyone thought was my gorgeous girlfriend. *Perhaps this is how grown straight men feel - prideful.* We leaned close together at the table as the hotel staff took our photograph, the flash of brilliant blue-white light forever freezing us in time. We ate our grilled steak and butter-drenched lobster, munched crispy Caesar salads and contemplated having dessert. We chose Mississippi Mud Pie, savouring the chocolate ganache that topped the cake and sipped cups of strong black coffee. Lara smoked occasionally, perhaps surprisingly for someone who sang, and lit a Virginia Slims after our meal. Never at a loss to ask questions and to create conversation, Lara was beguiling. I noticed men looking at her with more than passing interest - and why not? With her sinewy bare legs, deep-brown eyes, burnished hair and captivating smile, Lara was a compelling creature. Any man would have been fortunate to have had the opportunity to be with her on this or any evening. I admit to being jealous of those men who gazed at her. They could give her something I never could.

After our dinner, the showers ceased and the skies cleared. We walked along Robson Street, back to the car and took a slow drive on Stanley Park Drive, stopping at several points to look at the views. With the windows flung open, we breathed in the rain-freshened smell of the cedars. After climbing up the steep grade to Prospect Point, we got out to look across the magnificent Lion's Gate Bridge, ablaze with hundreds of lights, cars slowly making their way to and from the North Shore. As we walked on top of the gusty bluff, we shared some fantasies - us running a marathon, me living in a stylish apartment by the sea and Lara singing all over the world in the most famous of halls but coming home occasionally to live in her modest country log house. Time vanished; we spoke for hours that seemed like moments. Getting into the Fastback, we continued driving past Third Beach, beyond the Teahouse. A couple of minutes later we parked and got out of the car to walk. With conscious and careful thought I boldly took Lara's hand. Silently we strolled along the newly-completed seawall section at Second Beach, clamshells cracking under Lara's wooden platform shoes, the darkness beginning to fade as the Eastern sky gave way to a crimson purple daybreak, the tide softly pushing against the rocks with a steady and gentle constancy. I recall my contentment, my appreciation of being alive, of this perfect moment of happiness coupled with my belief that such a moment was to inform me of what bliss might feel like, to give me an understanding of what I could experience.

Though many years have passed, I've never forgotten that evening. I kept that aging Polaroid photograph of Lara and me safe in a scrapbook. Every so often I gaze upon it wistfully. Two ruddy-faced youths, the flash of hope and promise incandescently reflected in our eyes, dining in the sky on the thirty-first floor of the Blue Horizon.

8

REVELATIONS OF JIM

L anguage is evocative, isn't it? *He's gay.* Those two words have carried a history of condemnation and judgment. Deranged, bent, queer, odd, queen, unclean, sissy, faggot - and there are many more adjectives, of course. They're derogatory, meant to offend, to shame and to oppress. It's no wonder that gay boys (and girls) of every generation have had to develop skins as thick as an alligator to make it to adulthood. The majority of the world condemns us as if we had a choice to be anything else but who we are. There's no point in debating that being gay is merely a variation of sexuality, and yet I imagine the argument will continue indefinitely.

As a young man of nineteen, I may not have had rocks thrown at me anymore, but I was nonetheless bound by my own fear that others may uncover the verities about myself and that I would pay a significant price for it. Even in university, homophobia was rampant, and not just in the locker room, but in the hallways, in the classrooms and in the SUB. Gay Liberation may have been launched at the Stonewall Inn after Judy Garland died in June of 1969, but that world of body politic was just beginning in the Vancouver of 1977. Hyper-vigilant, I tried my best to appear straight. Having Lara near me may have helped the charade, but it wasn't the reason why she was so important. We had created a deep friendship and spent much time together - studying, writing papers, practicing French (she tolerated my ineptness), making cheap meals from low-cost grocery stores (Kraft Dinner was too expensive; we cooked bulk macaroni and stirred in Cheese Whiz and Keene's dry mustard), going to movies, dancing at the weekend, running on Spanish Banks and drinking copious amounts of tea sweetened with stolen packs of sugar from the cafeteria. We lived fairly close to each other, though our residences were a study in contrasts. Lara's bright and airy studio apartment was in Kitsilano and had views of the water and mountains. My dark basement room had a tiny fixed window, room just enough for a twin bed and more than enough mold to make sinuses close and my clothes pong from mildew. My washroom was in a tiny alcove with the iciest tap water this side of Pluto. The toilet facilities were raised on a block and therefore made it impossible to stand and urinate as the ceiling was lower than my height by nearly a foot. I had to squeeze and fold myself into the tiny space and sit down when nature called. Not the best accommodation, though at fifty bucks a month it was several times less expensive than Lara's digs. I wasn't complaining, but I loved to get outside whenever I had the chance.

If my room was less than stately, the campus and its surroundings were. Sprawling UBC was perched on the edge of Point Grey and surrounded by a forest of dense old-growth trees. At the bottom of the Endowment Land's cliffs were several long and sandy beaches. One beach was unique: a nude beach. I'd heard about it but for the last two years I hadn't found the gumption to journey to Wreck Beach. Late on an early-May afternoon, with classes finished, I stuffed a towel in my rucksack and directed myself across campus. In twenty minutes I found myself on North West Marine Drive beside the cliffs that towered over the beach. I was anxious as I made my way to the trail. What if I was seen? Me, going down the steps to a nude beach? *Idiot, barely anyone knows you and surely no one cares what you do.* There were students, older people and alternative-types hanging around the entrance to the trail. The people I saw looked assured and carefree, unlike me, flushed with worry as I scuttled down the dirt path and stepped on the first of four-hundred and sixty-five wood steps that went to the beach below. I noticed a thick canopy of new green growth all around me, nearly obliterating the sunlight. Step by step I descended, carefully watching my way as to not falter down the steep path. Bubbling with laughter, young people ran past me wearing coloured shorts, tie-dyed shirts, with rolled-up blankets stuffed under their arms, singing, holding hands, speeding into the darkening forest. Minutes passed as I continued my small trek until I was just thirty steps from the bottom. I heard the sound of water rushing across a beach that opened expansively before me. I stepped into another world of water, sunlight, of men and women moving naked against a backdrop of near-white sands and a slate-blue ocean. It took a while for me to accept what I was seeing, but this mélange of unclothed bodies was real. If the women were a curiosity the men were a revelation - suntanned guys with large penises flopping and swinging as they strode the beach. And there were regular and small penises as well. But the large cocks? They got my attention. But more than that, it amazed me - how unashamed people seemed. *How many people are here? Hundreds at least.* Strolling the beach, standing alone, in pairs or in groups - it was an incredible spectacle. Viewing nudists intensified my own conspicuousness - dressed in yellow cotton shorts and a red tee-shirt. There were so many people about that I decided to find an area where I could be more circumspect. Going to my left was instinctual. That meant walking south on an established trail, clambering over some large rocks and around fallen cedars to continue in that direction. It was warm, so I removed my shirt, stuffed it into my rucksack and walked for another ten minutes until I came across a large, open sandy patch with scores of wave-worn logs bleached by the sun.

The area was dune-like and went all the way back to the start of the incline of the forest, about forty or fifty metres and perhaps two hundred metres across. Tufts of grass grew up from the sand and I found a spot to spread out my big red towel. I was perspiring at my forehead and chest from the increasing heat of the afternoon sun. Tugging at my laced runners until they came off, I removed my socks and immediately felt the coolness of the breeze on my overheated feet. My damp shirt was next, then my cotton shorts. Underneath I had a purple-striped Speedo swimsuit on, which was already becoming moist. I sat like that for a time, the warmth of the sun penetrating my skin triggered sweat on my torso. I relaxed and succumbed to the heat. I felt as though my body was melting into the sand beneath me. The sounds of the birds, the slight breeze smelling faintly of smoke and salt contributed to a near-hypnotic state as I stretched out and fell asleep.

"Ya look real hot," a disembodied voice said. *To me? Distant, a dream?* I roused myself.

"Uh, s'cuse me?" I uttered, squinting at a figure against the backdrop of the searing afternoon sun, aware of being disoriented.

"Looks like ya fell asleep in the sun. Ya look hot."

Alert, I sat up, my chest and nose felt scorched. I put my hand to my face, rubbing my eyes. "Oh, yeah, thanks. Guess I nodded off."

I could now see that the man who was speaking to me was nice-looking, perhaps thirty, with a tan body, long brown hair parted in the middle, and of course, completely nude. His cock was large and right in front of me. I hadn't engaged in conversations with naked men before. It wasn't comfortable, yet I knew I'd try my best to talk with him.

"Ya been here before?" he asked slowly with a slight American drawl, looking me over very well.

"Well, uh, no, actually, this...this is the first time I've ever come down here." I felt his eyes on me and was aware of my swimsuit becoming constricted. Sweat was beading on my forehead.

"Ya should really cool off. Wanna come with me to the main beach for a swim?" He wiped the sweat off his brow with the back of his hand. Apparently he was also affected by this early May heat. "Leave yer stuff here; it'll be safe," he said with confidence.

"Uh, well, I guess I could go for a swim."

"Course ya could. It's good that I go with ya; someone might wanna scoop ya up," he said with a <u>devious</u> grin.

"Why would anyone do that?" I asked defensively, my fear apparent.

"Cuz yer cute. What are ya, sixteen?"

"No, I'm nineteen." I was <u>cognizant</u> that I was moving into completely new territory.

"Old enough," he uttered plainly. "Let's go. I'm sweatin' like a pregnant nun at Sunday mass."

We started off towards the main beach together. My heart was pounding. This wasn't conventional - walking with a naked male stranger across a nude beach. As we spoke along the way I stole glimpses of his body, which was undeniably attractive. *There's no harm in a walk to the water for a dip, right? Just relax, go with the flow of the afternoon. Don't over-think this.*

When we got to the beach it was more crowded than when I'd first arrived. There were a few people wearing clothing, but in the water, nudity was de rigueur. There was some serious <u>frolicking</u> happening at Wreck Beach.

"Leave yer swimsuit here; no one'll run off with it."

I thought about it. Though I had been swimming for years, the only time I was nude was when I took a shower. Swimming naked in the sea with a man I didn't know was an <u>enticing idea</u>. A bit too enticing; I was hard in my Speedo, the sight of which was not lost on the man I was with.

"Hey, no problem." He pointed at my suit. "Pitchin' a tent don't matter here."

"I'd rather wait a bit; sorry, it's not always under my control." I was more than a bit embarrassed.

"Sure, yer nineteen. Ya know, we can take 'er easy till the little guy has settled down some. C'mon. Let's make tracks."

And we continued to walk towards the water, I watched the tide flooding the shoreline, pushing the water insistently to the beach and turning to briny white foam as the waves slid across the glittering sand.

"Okay," I said a few minutes later. "I'm ready to go in."

And with that, I pushed my Speedos down, tossed them onto the beach and took my first naked steps into the ocean. The sea was cool in places and in other areas warm. I inched my way to my midsection, grinning with how good it felt. The man was watching me, smiling, egging me on to take the plunge. He waded in, watching me from a short distance. I dove under the water, swimming out a hundred metres and then back, pulling against the tide, riding the swell of the waves to the beach. It was an exhilarating feeling being naked in the ocean with the sun high above. How did a young man never have the experience of swimming like this? I swam some butterfly against the waves, then played around with my piddling breaststroke. After twenty minutes, I swam back to where the man was standing and walked towards him.

"Whoa, buddy! Ain't you somethin' in the water!"

"I never swam like this before!" I shouted, laughing and splashing the waters around myself with my hands.

"So, whaddya think, kid?"

"Incredible." I absorbed what I was seeing and experiencing: the sounds of the ocean as it boomed to the shoreline, the heady scent of coconut oil, salt, sweat, pot and the adults playing like children in the sea. The North Shore mountains framed the scene, a deep cobalt sky to the east, contrasting the green firs and cedars of the forested cliffs. It really was another world and merely a few minutes from campus.

"I really should get back." I picked up my suit and rinsed the sand off of it in a shallow pool.

"I'll walk ya there," he said. "I'm Jim, by the way." He extended his hand for me to shake.

"Nice to meet you," I said, putting my Speedo back on.

During the walk back from the main beach, Jim disclosed that he'd been coming to Wreck Beach for years - since arriving in Vancouver from North Carolina. He liked everything about it, he told me. I didn't inquire further, as I understood that it either meant he enjoyed being nude or enjoyed the activity that I took place whilst nude. I assumed that activity was with men but I didn't have confirmation of that, though it was difficult to fathom that an older man was striking up a conversation with me out of a desire for friendship. We arrived back at my spot south of the main beach in a few minutes.

"Ya know, when I was here - one of the first times, I guess - a hot man came on ta me. Dunno what his name was." Jim scanned the beach and scrub area. "Actually, it was pretty much right where we are now."

Here we go.

"Huh. And what did you say to him?"

"I told him I liked women, but I was sorta interested in what it felt like ta, ya know, touch a guy an' play around a bit." Jim paused, carefully sitting his tan buttocks down on a large piece of driftwood opposite me as I sat back down on my blanket, cross-legged. "Ya know, sorta like an experimental thing. I mean, guys turn me on, too."

Of course they do. That's why you're trying to pick me up. He winked at me or it might have been a nervous twitch.

"An' so, this guy, he goes right up ta me, close-like, and in my ear he whispers, *Come with me - right now.*" He paused for a moment. "An' I went with him, see, just like he said. Don't think I'll forget how nervous I was, but excited, too. Didn't really know what I was doin'... well that's not completely true - I knew a couple things. So, we were already naked, 'course, an' it was obvious that he wanted me ta suck his dick, an' it was a nice one, real thick. He puts his hands on my head an' pushes it to his cock. Ya can't get clearer than that." Jim watched to see that I was paying close attention before he continued. "Well, I sucked him for a few minutes, an' liked it. Then the guy, he just turns me 'round so that my rear end was exposed, held my hips in his hands an' then somethin' cold an' slick was at my ass, pushin', an' in another second he was fuckin' me….it hurt, hurt like hell at first an' I yelped. But he didn't stop. He told me he wouldn't stop and fer me ta shuddup till he was done. So, I shuddup an' it got better. I waited for it ta be over; didn't take too long, 'bout five minutes. He pulled outta me 'an didn't say nothin' else. He just walked off. Left me naked in the bushes right there." Jim pointed behind us where the woods formed at the bottom of the trail. "An' I just stood there… stunned. I was bleedin' a little bit, so he sorta tore me up some, too."

"Gawd, that's horrible. Were you okay?" I'd never known anyone who told me such a story - a rape - what else could it be called?

"I collected myself an' licked my wounds a bit…but I decided right I wouldn't ever hurt anyone the way he had. Sex is suppose ta be a pleasure, ya know, not supposed ta hurt, right?"

"Yeah, of course. I'm no expert though," I said weakly. "And have you done it that way again since that time?"

"Sure, many times," Jim said. "An' I got to likin' it after I figured out a few things. Got to likin' it lots." Jim laughed.

"And it isn't painful?"

"Well, no. But I'm more into throwin' than catchin', if ya know what I mean."

I did. Though this whole concept of anal sex was truly something I didn't much think about, and when I did I was a little fearful of the obvious; what if there was, umm, soiling in the process? And what to do then? I didn't find my own rectum to be a place of scintillating delights, either. I thought of it as something to clean with tissue after having a bowel movement and then to shower immediately after. I had never sexualized my ass - no disrespect to Freud and his Anal Stage. It wasn't an erotic area. It was a means to an end or perhaps the other way around.

"And," Jim continued, "I make sure my bottom's havin' a hot time."

"*Your* bottom?"

"No, my bottom's bottom."

"Oh, I see," and clearly didn't. I looked skeptical and Jim picked up on it.

"Listen, buddy, when a bottom's ready to be fucked it's super-sexy," stated Jim emphatically. Perhaps a bit too emphatically. He appeared puzzled with my lack of understanding.

"So, I take it ya never had a cock in yer butt?"

I shook my head.

"Pity, cuz you've gotta great ass. But every guy goes at his own pace."

"Umm, sure, that sounds right," I said, nodding.

"What about gettin' sucked?" Jim asked.

"What about it?"

"Well, do ya like it?"

"Yes, of course I do," I lied, having never having been sucked nor done anything else remotely sexual with anyone but myself.

"Okay, well, let's go. I can tell yer excited. I can start." He quickly moved down from the driftwood; a naked, bronzed man with long searching fingers undid the ties of my Speedo. I didn't resist; should I have? No. I was on a nude beach, with a man whose hand was quickly pulling my swimsuit to my ankles and exposing my aching penis. Just the slightest touch of his hand on my cock was electric. But when Jim moved his brown tousled hair closer and slowly put my cock into his warm mouth I thought I was going to explode. Too much sensory overload. I controlled myself, didn't allow myself to cum, thought of school, of swim practice, tried to recall the Fathers of Confederation. *John A. MacDonald, Mowat, Carter, uh, Tilley.* It worked. Jim continued to suck me with expertise, or so it seemed to a nineteen-year-old virgin. He spent time lapping at the head of my penis, then stroking it at the base, never losing contact with it. He caressed my scrotum gently, touching my thighs, murmuring how much he liked my body and what was between my legs. After a few minutes of bliss, he stopped and kissed me deeply, his tongue touching mine, exploring, tender. I held his head in my hands and every nerve was alive, tingling with sensation. Never had I felt so profoundly aroused as I had in those brief moments.

"Now it's yer turn." He stood up and without pause, I knelt before Jim's large hard cock. In the late afternoon sun, I moistened my lips and for the first time moved my mouth towards a man's penis. I took him into my mouth, tasting his sweat, gliding my tongue all over, amazed at the soft velvet of the head, the firmness of the shaft, feeling the prominent veins, the length of it, the way it felt in my throat. I was galvanized with excitement, my own cock throbbing beneath me as I continued to learn how to pleasure a stranger on the beach. Jim cooed encouragement to me, telling me what he liked and what I should do. He told me to keep my throat open as though I was about to yawn, then he'd thrust his cock deeply. The more I learned what he liked, the more excited I became. He told me to suck harder, faster, to tug his balls. In a few moments Jim said that he was going to cum, then shouted that he *was* cumming and I was told not to stop, to keep on sucking. I heard him yell out and then I felt him explode in my mouth and down my throat. It tasted nothing like what I'd thought. Jim was spent, nearly falling down against the driftwood.

"Great job, bud. That definitely feels better; much better. Ya give good head. Gonna be around this summer?"

"Uh-huh, yeah, I think I will be," I said, my penis pulsating, my head whirling with what I'd just done. "I'm a student here so I'm close. And school's mostly over now, so…I'll try to come down a few more times."

"Ya remember what we talked about, 'kay? We can try somethin' else if yer into it. Fer next time."

"Next time," I said. "Yes, sure, if you'd like." *Very unlikely.*

"Oh, I'd like, buster. Yer gonna remember me, right? Name's Jim, jus' in case ya forgot." (I never did forget.) He smiled, "Next time fer sure." Jim slapped my ass gently, laughing.

"Right, can't wait," I said, not knowing at all what I was saying.

Jim pressed his slippery body to mine. "Adiós," he said and ambled off. I watched his long hair whipping backwards, his sun-bronzed butt fading into the distance as he padded barefoot across the sand, leaving me naked with a painful erection. I sat there, stretched my legs and became aware that other men were in the secluded areas and glancing my way. Perhaps they'd seen my actions? It seemed that all the people in this area were men. *I'm a little dense.* This part of the beach was apparently for gay men. My instinct to come this way was correct, though. I thought for a moment. *My Gawd...I've had sex for the first time with a man on a nude beach.* I chewed on that and considered the importance of this event. I laughed and shook my head. The Revelation of Jim. I had got through nearly twenty years without having any intimate physical contact. Inside of a couple of hours, it seemed as though my life had changed. Watching the sun lower on the horizon and colour the sky with shots of deep oranges and blushing pinks my thoughts meandered... *I'm not as cautious as I believed. I took a chance today. I didn't fall apart and I don't feel ashamed. Quite the opposite. Still, I won't be shouting it from the rooftop - not yet.* I sat on the beach and watched the sun dip behind Vancouver Island, igniting the skies above the Strait of Georgia with a spectacular blaze of purples, pinks and blood-reds. I gathered my towel, brushed the sand from my yellow shorts and dressed for my trip back up the trail. I walked slowly, almost jubilant, joining the other happy people about to scamper up and back to a different reality. As I prepared to climb the bluff, I cast my gaze on that inspired sunset and tried to think of an appropriate analogy about how the sun rises and sets on our lives, but I'm not the best with metaphors.

9

CLIMBING ONTO THE SOAP BOX

For me, having sex with another man was nothing less than a soothing balm to heal a scarred psyche. For gay men and women, the act of sex can be an acknowledgment of acceptance in a world that may otherwise have been hostile towards them. Having a sexual experience - however <u>fleeting</u> - was critical to advance my identity as a gay man. Years of feeling burdened by the shame of my nature were lightened. Of course, being gay isn't merely about having sex; that's far too simplistic. When it comes to sexual orientation we just are who we are. And yet how much time is spent describing, analyzing, defending, medicalizing, debating and advocating for the permission to be gay or lesbian? I can't choose to form an intimate physical, sexual and emotional relationship with a woman and be satisfied and true to myself let alone the other person. Anyone who thinks otherwise is simply refusing to understand human nature. People ask, what is being gay about? I sometimes find the question offensive. Perhaps we should be asking, what is being straight about? And while we're at it, please tell me - what's it like living where you are provided so much acceptance? In an ideal world, we'd be attuned enough to know such inquiries are unnecessary. For me, living a life of secrets and being fearful and cautious affected me in ways that were adverse. I don't believe that a straight person, with all the built-in acceptance that heterosexuality affords, can appreciate or understand the experience of being gay in a homophobic world. And, let's face it - they aren't asked to. So, if I were to answer my earlier question, I'd say that being gay is being brave. Brave if you come out and brave if you stay in the closet. After all, it takes a lot of resolve, pluck and determination to live a lifetime of oppression.

Okay, enough of my bleating. I'll climb down from the soap box. Back to my story.

10

CHOICES

My first two years of UBC went according to plan. I'd found my courses rewarding - when I wasn't falling asleep in the lecture hall. Swimming took a lot out of me and I did crash every now and then in the midst of psychology class. During the summer of '77, I continued working as a lifeguard at the UBC Aquatic Centre. Due to my schedule, I saw Lara infrequently. She'd become involved with her French Literature teacher. Sure, he was older, intelligent and worldly-wise - but her French teacher? I had an opinion about it but decided to garder le silence. I had my own secrets, after all. I'm guessing Lara had a few of her own, though I was told about Professor Jean-Paul Daguile.

My forays into gaydom were proving to be a slow-going endeavour. University was my focus - not my sexuality - and had been flying by. Swimming remained a constant through the summer. It seemed I was under water more than I was ever on dry land. Water supported my mental health as much as any therapy could have. It was calming - during practice, not meets - and gave me an instant sense of peace when I was in it, just like when I was a child. During a swim practice of two or more hours, lap after lap, and even with all the flailing swimmers around me, I would remain in my own liquid Nirvana.

I had proceeded to develop under the coaching of Jack Lerner. His influence on my athletic performance and was significant, and I was indebted to him. Lara thought he controlled me, and I guess that was true, though Coach Lerner was slowly transforming me into an elite swimmer. And I wasn't yet at my developmental peak. I had several more years of high performance possible, including trying out for the National Swim Team when Lerner thought the time was right. It was often in my thoughts; my many years as a swimmer wouldn't be complete without accomplishing something extraordinary.

Lara would sometimes show up at my practice sessions, watching from the spectator section. Late in my workout on Thursday night I could see Lara in the stands as I did a set of flutter and dolphin kicks. I waved at her from the end of the lane. She looked a little worried. After my set, I jumped out of the pool to the deck to make it appear to locate another kick board - a ruse to say hello to Lara.

"Hey!" I called out to her half-way up in the stands. "You okay?"

"I'm fine," she shouted back. "What are you doing after practice? I'd like to talk."

"Sure. I'm done at six thirty. Do you wanna meet at the SUB?" I asked.

"No, let's meet off campus. What about going to Naam's? You'll be famished after your practice."

Naam's was a Vietnamese place on Fourth Avenue that was cheap and vegetarian. Lots of students could be found there on any given night, chowing down with the alternative crowd of older hippies from the 1960's.

"Naam's it is. Listen, Lara, I gotta get back in here. The Coach is giving me the stink eye." Lerner was about to yell at me, so I made it seem as though I was stretching my shoulders out - they did get sore from keeping my head and neck hyperextended during kick sets.

"Hey! In the water...move it...now!" he hollered, making it unquestionably clear that I was not where I should be. My wile was transparent.

"Oh God, this man really thinks he owns you." Lara looked disgusted.

"Um, he sorta —"

"Don't say it. Meet you there at 7:30 - and don't be early," Lara said, exiting the Aquatic Centre. I leapt back into the water and finished the practice and worriedly wondered what Lara wanted to discuss. Swim finished, I took a short, hot shower, tossed on my Levi's, a clean white tee-shirt, a battered pair of black penny loafers and jogged down to Marine Drive to collect my beloved Fastback, with its slow-leaking tire, tired battery, lousy heater and a clutch that was unnecessary to change gears. I fired the ignition and the air-cooled motor loyally whirred to life. I headed across campus and headed east on Fourth Avenue for my meeting with Lara. Parking the VW on a hill (just in case), I walked through the Naam's door and down the centre of the dimly-lit restaurant to find Lara already there, sitting by the window, watching me come towards her.

"I'm not early," I said, tapping my Timex: 7:40.

Patting her hand on the bench, Lara declared, "Sit down and let's order. My stomach feels like my throat's been cut."

I pulled myself around the bench and took a seat. We decided on steamed brown rice, vegetables, bean curd satay with peanut sauce. It came fast and we tucked in. Lara was slender, perhaps 120 pounds on her 5' 7" frame. And though her appetite was large, she remained willowy.

"What's on your mind?" I asked, chewing slowly on some rice. I was never famished right after a swim, though I didn't tell Lara that. I usually got hungry a couple of hours later.

"I've made a decision about something, and I need to tell you about it."

"What is it?"

"Okay." Lara laid her fork on the side of her plate. "I'm just going to blurt this out. I've decided that I'm not coming back to school in September."

"Whoa, hold on a sec. You can't - why are you dropping out?" I was thunderstruck, nearly choking on my sticky brown rice. This news didn't fit with our plan of getting our degrees together. We'd talked about it for years.

"My heart isn't at school. No matter how I've tried to motivate myself, no matter how many talks we've had, I just can't continue."

"Lara —"

"I hope you'll understand that I've been just…terribly lost and unhappy at university. And I've never been surer of *not* wanting to be a teacher."

"Yes, but what about —"

"But I *do* want to find out if I have something special to offer."

"Lara —"

"And I can't find that out by studying French." Lara stopped talking, sighed deeply and picked up her water glass to take a big drink.

"I can talk now?" I asked.

"Of course. Say what you want, Sunshine, but you won't be changing my mind no matter what you say," she said firmly.

"I understand. But how could you think you aren't special now? The way you sing? There's music coming outta your ass."

"You're comparing my voice to flatulence?" Lara asked sharply.

"No, of course not, that came out wrong, pun unintentional. Everyone loves to hear you sing. That alone makes you special."

"Thanks," she said quietly.

"Tell me, are you absolutely sure that leaving school is the right thing? Have you considered the Music Faculty? Maybe there's another —"

"It's the right thing. I've thought it out completely - a thousand times. And I don't want to be in *any* faculty, music or otherwise. I don't want to be at university. I know you think this sounds flaky, but I know my future's not there."

"It's a huge decision you've made," I said, my intonation not able to hide my disappointment. Lara picked it up immediately.

"Yes, Sunshine. This is a real bummer for you, isn't it?"

"A bummer? It's the worst." I looked at Lara's brown eyes. "I'm sorry for being selfish," I sighed. "Does anyone else know?"

"Apart from Student Services, you're the first," Lara explained.

"And Jean-Paul? He'll be the next to know, I suppose?"

"No, he won't know. I decided not to see him anymore," she stated ruefully.

"Why's that?"

"Jean-Paul told me last week that he's been married for eleven years."

"*Married?*" I couldn't hide my shock.

"Well, he never told me and I didn't bother to ask. Guess that makes me his dirty little affair. I wondered why he never gave me his number." She smirked, shaking her head. "God, I can add mistress to my resume."

"I'm...uh, I'm sorry to hear... a married man, huh?" I decided to try to suspend the judgement I felt. She looked frustrated or perhaps disappointed with herself but didn't seem to pick up on my bias.

"Oh, I'm quickly getting over him. The embarrassment might take longer. The bastard was lousy in bed anyway."

"Is that possible? He's French."

"Please, I should refer to him as the *Five-Minute Frenchman*. And that was on a good night. Forget about what you read about French lovers. Once you get past the accent, they're really nothing special."

"Jeez." I took a breath and asked, "And what about your parents?"

"They're also nothing special."

"You know what I mean, Lara."

"My parents? Fuck my parents."

"Well, okay. So, what are you going to do? What's the plan?" I asked, believing that a scheme was essential. After all, I did park the VW on a hill.

"For now, the plan is to see what happens," she said calmly.

"That's a bit risky, isn't it? I mean, there's rent, food, expenses and, well, everything else." I couldn't disguise the worry in my voice.

"I'll keep waitressing. It's more than paying the bills. And I'll look for singing work. There's always the funeral homes; they seem to like me, and the cash is good. Of course, it's all a bit ghoulish."

"Ghoulish?"

"Well, yes. Especially the open casket services."

"Oh…" I didn't wish to hear more, but Lara continued.

"Picture me perched on a riser in a long black dress singing a dirge, like 'Shall We Gather at the River' or 'The Old Rugged Cross'. It's always something heavy and sorrowful."

"Am I missing something? It's a funeral, Lara," I stated incredulously.

"Yes, of course. Anyway, I'm howling away, verse after verse and I can't help but look down at the poor stiff all done up in their best outfit and with make-up just *troweled* on."

"Uh…" My stomach started to churn.

"Rouged cheeks and that horrible fixed smile - do they really glue the lips together?"

"Jeez, really, I don't —"

"They try to make it look as though the departed's going to sit up and join the get-together for a drink and a few canapés. The way the dead are dressed and posed is so macabre, don't you think?"

"Um, yes, it's really disturbing." I gulped, feeling more squeamish and recalling Mr. Pottinger's horrifying rain-soaked corpse from many years ago.

"Isn't it? Still, I'm told my singing's a comfort and there's usually great food afterwards. Last time there was crab quiche; I snuck a few pieces in my music folder - discretely, of course. Oh, and the money's good," she said brightly.

"Yeah, you mentioned that." Involuntary shudder. I'd heard enough.

"I'll take my guitar around to more restaurants and coffee places. Where else do singers get work?" Lara asked herself softly.

"I wouldn't have the faintest —"

"No, of course you wouldn't. I'll find out. And I'll stay at my apartment for now. I'll tell my parents at the end of summer. They'll probably drop dead - but not before they wrack me with additional guilt until I develop an eating disorder, if I don't already have one. I can just hear my mother's voice telling me what a moronic decision I've made - a singing waitress with a guitar - and what a disappointment I am to our family of professionals. But I don't want you to be concerned."

"I'll try, Lara. It's just, that...well...of course, I understand."

"That's all I'm asking. I'm just so relieved, so be pleased for me, okay? Let's have some Blueberry Tea and celebrate my freedom from the trappings of UBC."

There wasn't anything for me to say. Lara was committed to her choice. *Wish her well, hope for the best outcome to a decision you think is full of risk.* Lara waved over a handsome young server to order a boozy concoction. The waiter had a head of dark curly hair, liquid brown eyes and a complexion that was reddened - perhaps by exposure to the late spring heat and sun. I realized that I recognized him from Wreck Beach. He'd been walking along the trails when I'd been there, but with decidedly less attire. *Does he recognize me, too? That's an odd coincidence*, I pondered, as I allowed myself to be distracted by the strangeness of the moment. After a couple of minutes, he returned with two glasses of hot blue tea that smelled as unappetizing as it looked.

"Well, then," Lara exclaimed brightly. "University ends and another part of the story begins!" She raised her glass for a toast. I lifted my Blueberry Tea to hers and we gently clinked the cheap glasses.

"Here's to the next chapter," I said with an unconvincing fête. Smiling brightly, she agreed. I sipped at the wretched concoction and coughed. I stole a glance at the young man with the curly brown hair, wondering when new beginnings might happen for me.

11

I FEEL LOVE

By 1978 Vancouver's gay community had fully surfaced with a large number of bars, many bathhouses and clubs catering to a wide range of tastes. The West End was a gay residential ghetto with most gay businesses concentrated on Richards and Seymour Streets between Robson and the Granville Bridge. After many decades, Vancouver had become gaymopolitan. Even with the abundance of places where men could connect, it had taken me until adulthood to have a few fleeting sexual experiences. I *did* understand the importance of having a community where acceptance, rather than intolerance and hatred, was the norm, but it was a challenge for me to access it. Since my experience with Jim at Wreck Beach the summer before, I was motivated to practice my rudimentary skills further. Practice, practice - it's the only way to get to Carnegie Hall, as the old joke goes. I did want to practice, and returning to Wreck Beach provided me with some additional opportunities to grasp the mechanics of sex. I was interested in being with men for the purpose of experimentation, most surely, but going to a nude beach was only one of several routes of exploration. I was curious to try other ways such as clubs. I wasn't someone who liked to drink, so I had never been interested in going to a bar. I hadn't even purchased alcohol at a liquor store. My father had a problem with booze; I was aware of it in my youth and his drinking only intensified as he grew older, drinking Scotch every night until he was slurring his words. I watched him pour the liquor and top it with a drop of soda water. After a few drinks, he became more irritable and surly than he would ever be sober. Mum would have a few glasses of wine but didn't allow herself to become intoxicated. To her, being drunk was déclassé. His drinking, not to mention his incessant smoking, had control over him. No one dared to confront my father on his alcohol use. Therefore, it wasn't a problem if no one discussed it. My family held onto that belief as firmly as the cork was held in the bottle of his Glen Fiddich. So as a boy and now as a young man, alcohol had negative associations. Still, if I was to explore the gay scene, I would need to become familiar with clubs and bars.

After Saturday's swim practice, I donned a new powder-blue polo shirt and a pair of tan chinos with the only other pair of dressier shoes I owned - dark brown loafers with tassels. On a warm evening, I drove to a corner store on Robson at Denman Street where I'd been a few times before. Walking through the door, bypassing the produce area and the shelves full of used books, I headed for the maze-like Adult Section, where there were hundreds of sex magazines, though that wasn't what I was interested in. I was looking for flyers about what was going on in Vancouver's gay scene. There were several men there, most of whom appeared quite uncomfortable, skulking with downcast faces. I came across what I was hoping to find: a mimeographed pink-coloured paper brochure listing the gay bars and clubs in the downtown area.

"Gotcha," I said, a little too loudly, causing two of the men to look up from their periodicals nervously. "Oh, sorry," I apologized. "I didn't mean you. I just found what I was looking for." I waved the pink paper at the uncomfortable older men. I folded up the handout, placed it in my pants pocket and burrowed my way out of the Adult Section of the local produce store. From my paper treasure, I had selected a bar to frequent that night. The place was called Faces, located on Seymour Street. The name sounded friendly enough and so with much conviction and less courage, I headed out. Within ten minutes I'd arrived and waited in my car until opening time, steeling myself for what I was about to do. There was an important lesson I learned that evening: never be the first man at a gay bar. It leaves an impression of desperation. I walked to Faces and tried to open a door that was still locked at eight o'clock. I stood outside, expectant and as uncomfortable as the men had looked in the produce store. When the club opened a few minutes later, I went to the bar to order an orange juice. The craggy, bearded bartender gave me the thrice over and said, "Never seen you here before, son."

"Yeah, I've never been in this bar before." I'd actually never been in any gay bar.

"Are you old enough to be in here? I'm gonna need to see some ID, kid."

I did look young, younger than my age. I pulled out my wallet and my driver's license, fumbling a bit, embarrassed that I was being asked. *Shit, don't blush and look even younger.*

"It's pretty slow tonight, huh?" I asked with as much authority as I could muster. It was a tough sell considering I was red-faced and sweating. Seeing my ID, the man nodded, then poured the juice into a tall glass.

"Well, you're the first one here, but don't worry. It's always busy Saturday night."

"Great. I'm just gonna hang out," I said, paying my two bucks. First hurdle done. *Now...bring on the men.* I walked over to a far table and tried to make an orange juice last for an hour. The place seemed pleasant enough, though I didn't really know I was expecting. I'd been to people-packed glitzy discotheques with Lara, but that was my extent of clubs. All I could say about Faces was that it was dark and smelled of beer. Faces certainly wasn't like the Anvil bar that I'd read about in Blueboy. I sat in the shadows, mirrored balls twirled above me, throwing multicoloured bursts of light on the dance-floor. A few men meandered into the bar and within an hour there were many men. Some walked by me, casting what appeared to be approving looks. Or it might have been sympathy. I looked out of place. I was the only person sitting in no man's land, so I sashayed up to the bar, plopping myself and my orange juice down and waited to be picked up. That was the start of my facial freeze. I couldn't seem to get the half-smile off my face. I wasn't particularly happy. I most surely looked ludicrous - my face locked in some type of delusional grin, which, far from inviting hordes of attractive men to bed me down in wild orgiastic pleasures, instead sent them fleeing in droves. I was clearly uncomfortable, sweat staining the underarms of my formerly fresh polo shirt, anxious and worried that no man would speak to me and perhaps more worried if one did. The crowd seemed to be a nice mix, too. Younger and older men, some with beards, others clean-shaven. Jeans, khaki shorts, dress shirts and tee-shirts. Tall, suave, short, stocky and geeky; all types were represented.

The bartender leaned over the sticky counter to catch my eye and close enough for me to smell his Old Spice. "You look like you gotta zucchini stuck up your ass."

"Huh?"

"You know what I mean. And really, you're not a bad-looking guy, 'specially if you stopped sweating."

"Um, thanks," I said, tightly pinning my armpits to my torso.

"Lemme give you some advice, okay? You're scared, right? It's a bad look, son," he advised, wiping down the counter.

"I'm not scared," I lied defensively. "It's all a bit new for me," I admitted.

"Right. Here's the thing. Not every guy's comfortable in a gay bar. But you gotta look as though you are."

"Right," I nodded, agreeing with his psychological assessment.

"Do you wanna meet a guy tonight, son?"

"Um, kind of, yeah. I think so." I stumbled in my response - no one had ever asked me that question before, but of course I wanted to meet someone.

"If you wanna hook up, you gotta look more approachable."

I took a breath. I didn't know what he meant. How could I not look approachable? I nodded and smiled some more.

"And lose that smile, it's creeping everybody out, me included."

"Oh, Jeez," I groaned. *That's my best feature.* "Any suggestions?"

"Do something to relax. Why don't you ask someone to dance?"

"To dance? No, I couldn't —"

"Then have a *real* drink, and try to loosen up. You're uptight and guys, well, they really can sense it," he said.

I knew that he was right, but I felt even worse about myself.

"Gawd, I know, I just can't seem to...thanks, I've gotta go." I walked out of Faces, head down, chagrined, displeased at my complete ineptness. *So much for getting picked up in a gay bar,* I mused, hitting the street. As I walked, I looked at my reflection in the shop windows. I was tall, strong and healthy, but I might as well have been Quasimodo. I'd swum dozens of races, won some, been stoned by gay-bashers, persevered, managed to get to my third year at UBC, had sex on a nude beach and yet I couldn't even figure out how to have a drink and be sociable in a gay bar? What a bunch of crap. I solidified my resolve and pulled out the pink brochure. There was another bar close-by on Robson Street called the 616 Club. I made my way there. In a few minutes, I walked boldly into an already crowded club, strode across to the bar, saw what every man was having and ordered a Budweiser. Still perspiring, but frozen smile completely thawed, I downed half the beer, disliking the taste. I finished the second half, wiped my mouth and ordered another. Instead of taking my beer to a far-away table I stood my ground during the next hour waiting for something to happen. It didn't. A few courteous smiles came my way, though my smile back didn't result in any romances, but rather a kind of passing disinterest. I waited longer, the smoke thick all around me, making my throat hurt and my eyes water, the blare of the music causing my ears to ring. Obviously, other people were having fun; there was music, dancing, drinking and camaraderie. I looked around, thought about dancing by myself and two hours later, I left. Deflated, I walked to Seymour to collect the VW, feeling like an outsider. Whatever it took to connect with others in a crowd-ed, smoke-filled and rowdy club I apparently did not have. And yet I understood the heat of the bar, the excitement of men looking to hook up with someone. It was novel to me; men being quite unabash-edly around other men. I gave myself a reality check and said that I wasn't going to give up. Unlocking the Fastback, I slid into the seat, buckled up, started the motor and headed for the Burrard Street Bridge, leaving the bars and the men behind. It might have been Oz for a lot of guys that night, but I was clearly an undesired Munchkin. I cranked down the window to blow the smoky stench off me. Driving up Robson and turning onto Burrard, I felt the pulse of the city; traf-fic, people, noise, excitement. There were attractive men lining the streets, going to clubs to have an evening out. I looked out at many of them and wondered why I couldn't join the ranks. Turning on the radio, I heard Donna Summer singing *I Feel Love* for the first time. A Eurotech synthesized song with a sexy beat - very different. Over the next six minutes, the singer's steady, insistent, repeated admissions highlighted by her sensual, sultry voice - even on my tinny Blaupunkt radio - had reaffirmed my conviction that I wanted to feel some love this summer, too.

Many years after I was more comfortable in my own skin, I reflect-ed on that summer. I didn't have any idea about approaching men. I made a few efforts and became instantly flustered and awkward in my clumsy attempts to construct small or any type of talk. I think that all the stimulation - the men, the lights, the noise, the music - also con-tributed to my unease. I didn't know how to communicate in a bar; it was noticeably unpleasant for me.

Coming to grips with being gay was only one aspect of a larger picture. The next part was being comfortable living as a gay young man. I had thought that the former was the easy part, but for me, this was an ongoing challenge. If I needed to understand how intimate human relations operated in the construct of same-sex relationships, then I would have needed some practice earlier on. This is where straight men have an advantage. Think of it - a boy grows up in a world geared towards heterosexuality. Every message he receives - in family, school, media, print - validates and fosters the experience of being straight. Therefore, when it comes to girls, he is primed and ready to explore without anyone or anything telling him it's wrong. By the time he's a twenty-year-old man he may have had seven or more years of dating, of sexual relations, of intimacy, of knowing the ropes (and I don't mean bondage, but if that's the knot that binds you, far be it from me...) in how opposite-sex relations operate. And if he were unfamiliar with girls, there were parents or siblings who might be quite eager to talk about it. Even if his family wasn't willing to discuss his potential relationship woes, there would be a bevy of friends at school who he could either commiserate with or brag to about his real or imagined conquests. If a boy never spoke about it with others, the world around him is still geared towards heterosexuality in all institutions. That's heavy stuff when you think about it. There's a huge heterosexual advantage to growing up that cannot be measured. Our family is the place where we begin to learn about ourselves in relation to others. What happens to a gay boy or girl when their family - perhaps unconsciously - encourages them to be oriented towards those of the opposite sex? Children like to please. Gay children understand they must be duplicitous in order to both secure parental approval and avoid danger with human contact - sometimes even within their own families. Certainly for me, I expended much energy being an undercover gay in a family that was either unaware or unwilling to see who I was. Thriving with being gay was also a large but infinitely rewarding developmental task. Like going to a gay nude beach, starting new conversations, hearing stories, listening to other people's experiences, creating a family of choice, going to a bar (while not successful for me, there was nonetheless a sense of freedom and liberation merely by being there) or living as an adult in a community where I could begin to be accepted for who I was without question: this is the second coming out. The process never stops, though it could be made easier, starting early in family life. I had many fantasies about my family sitting down with me to have *that* talk - I mean different from the one I eventually had. Here's how I'd pictured it: my parents would sit me down in my mother's beautifully decorated living room. With the utmost taste and decorum, they'd gently inquire about their gay son. Asking respectful questions about what it was like to feel and be different, they would help me articulate the struggles I'd experienced. Telling me I wasn't alone, my parents would guide me through the risks of being dissimilar in a world that insists upon sameness. After saying a few simple words I'd never forget, my mother and father would hold onto me tightly and then release me so that I could discover my own special home.

12

WOUNDED HEALERS

My long-term plan after university was to continue my education at an Institute that taught family systems therapy. Of all the theories I'd studied, systems theory resonated with me. It postulated the therapist's practice was influenced by experiences and unresolved issues in their family of origin. It was the work of the therapist to understand how to mitigate the emotional triggers originating in family when working with clients. As part of the coursework there were small learning groups, theory and practice classes and a family clinic. Overseeing the learning were practicing clinicians. The supposition that therapists and other professional helpers - therapists, social workers, advocates, nurses, teachers, pastors, rabbis, physicians - were wounded healers wasn't anything new. Many had experienced difficulties in early life that predisposed them to support the health of others psychologically, spiritually and physically. Frankly, it's not a ringing endorsement for all of us in the helping profession. Let's just say that there are potent implications for those who are motivated to care for others who are frequently more than a little scarred themselves.

Through doing my undergrad, I more clearly understood my role as an observer in social relations. Participating was fraught with potential risks. I listened well because I thought I was good at it and less good at speaking. I asked questions because I had an inquisitive nature, knowing that questions were something I could hide behind if necessary. But being at university was changing me. Expressing myself was getting easier. Being away from my family helped me to assert myself in situations where I was expected to form and express opinions. Some courses in my last year concentrated on theory and there was a practice component in a mental health clinic that I was anticipating with pleasure - sort of a trial to see just how suitable I was to offer psychological services. I shared much of what I was learning with Lara and it was the basis of many discussions about family. Both Lara and I had a long way to go in gaining compassion in parent-and-child relationships. Lara wanted her mother and I wanted my father to be different in order for us to be happier. It just doesn't work that way; not for us, not for anyone.

As a young man, I recall being furious with my father for being, well, himself. I couldn't accept that he'd been disinterested in me, disengaged, exclusively work oriented and for moving us from place to place without consideration for a sensitive boy with adjustment problems. Adjustment problems? Hmm, maybe it was my adjustment that needed correcting. After a certain point it's tiresome to blame others on my state of unhappiness or discontent. My father might have said - though he never did - that he sacrificed many things to provide our family with everything we needed. I don't know, perhaps that's true. I do know that a boy needs a father to guide him to manhood. I felt his absence in my life even when he was there; that's angering and disturbing to a growing child. When I went off to UBC I told myself over and over again that I would be nothing like him. Of course, I am like my father in ways I dislike and in ways that I value. And if nothing else, my father taught me by his significant level of un-involvement that I was responsible for meeting my own needs and for finding ways to look after myself. That's an important lesson, though it seemed too sophisticated for a young man like me to have grasped.

I would re-connect with my father a few years before his death. Dad proved to be a complex person, which shouldn't have been a surprise to me. It takes energy and effort to be distant and inexpressive, to cover up one's emotions as well as he did. I knew all about that; at least my father and I had that in common. There was no doubt that he was wounded but my father didn't seem able to behave in the healing part of the equation.

As per my plan, I was completing a four-year internship at a training institute and was conducting individual interviews with my parents. I was getting a surprising amount of new information about their background, their families and significant life events. By the end of the interviews, they had shared so much with me that I had decided it was time to tell my family that I was gay. At this point of my life, I was thirty-four and had been involved in a relationship for several years. Most people would assume that two men living together in a one-bedroom apartment in the city's West End weren't roommates. I came out to my Mum and her first response? "But what about my grandchildren?" she tearfully asked. *Hmm.* There's just no reason in this world. Later that evening, my father came home from work (semi-retired, he worked at a golf shop, perhaps the happiest scenario possible for him), entered the family room and knew something was up.

"What's been going on?" he asked.

I was nervous, nauseous, sweating, but I faced my father, eye to eye.

"Well, Dad, I was speaking with Mum and…I told her that I'm gay." I watched my father who slowly turned away from me and faced the window. I thought to myself, *Okay, get ready, he's going to call me a faggot. He's going to say that I'm not a real man but a disappointment; that I made everyone upset and to leave immediately and never return.* "Dad, are you alright?" I felt as though time had stopped, my breath was catching in my throat.

My father turned to face me and spoke haltingly, "I'm afraid… that you've lost respect for me."

"I don't think I understand," I said honestly.

"I've known that you were...for a long time," my father said, struggling to find his words. "But I never had the guts to ask you about it."

My father had caught me off-guard; a completely unanticipated response.

"Oh." I didn't know what else to say.

"I'm sorry," he said softly, marking the first and last time I ever heard my father utter those words to me.

"Dad, It's okay. I've made everything work. I've got someone. And we're happy."

"Yes, I can see that. And he's one of the family."

"Uh, pardon, Dad?"

"If he's with you, then he's a part of our family, all right?"

I felt the blood pounding at my right temple.

"Thanks, Dad. I'll tell him when I get home. He'll like to hear that."

My father went to the cupboard to take a large glass and poured himself a double Scotch. "You don't have to talk about this again. Not with me and not with your mother."

And we didn't. Even though my family's familiarity with my more intimate details was limited (though my sister did want to know who the female was in the relationship, demonstrating ignorance isn't bliss, it's just stupid) by a complete lack of curiosity, they did their best to make my boyfriend welcome in their home. Expecting more was implausible given the guarded willingness to accept me, let alone the man who was schtooking their son. What I found so fascinating about telling my father I was gay was the immediate transformation of my relationship with him. It was as if the thirty-four years of withholding who I was vanished in an instant. I wouldn't exactly describe the conversation as healing, but even with my father's stolid reaction, my mother's dashed hopes for a grandchild and my sister's limited view of sex roles, I have no complaints. Well, except one - the wait to be honest with my family wasted far too many years.

As a consulting therapist, I'd get asked to do presentations for specific groups. One memorable request was for an Art Therapy workshop for gay and lesbian youth at Britannia Community Centre in the mid-90's. I was expecting a handful but was stunned when over fifty youth showed up. After taking a risk and telling their families about being gay, most youth were cast from their homes to fend for themselves. The majority of them were between fourteen and twenty-four years old and were living hand-to-mouth. This was an exceptionally dangerous time in the gay community let alone for gay youth. By being honest about who they were, they lost the benefit and safety of their families who should have protected them. Could living a secret have kept them safer until they made the transition into adulthood? Many youths told me that they created their own families with friends from the street, a few had survival jobs, some resorted to stealing to get by, others worked in the sex trade to pay for food or shelter. There were great risks being honest in an intolerant world. I tried to send a message to them about marshalling their tenacity and toughness and staying connected to their "family of choice" without sounding patronizing. I knew nothing of being tossed from my family as those youths and my father had been. Even with my abundant and long-standing criticisms of my father, after that presentation I clearly understood that I wouldn't have managed to survive without him.

Several years later, I was asked to discuss depression on a live Vancouver morning talk show. It was a struggle to keep up with cogent responses to the battery of live callers and their questions. I'd been an inept guest expert. After the show, I went to work and came home that night dog-tired and very disappointed with myself. On my answering machine there was one call. It was my father, suffering from COPD. His once-strong voice was hoarse and faltering.

"Hi, Junior. Mum and I listened to you today. You did a great job and sounded so knowledgeable...and...so professional." During the last few words, my father's voice was quaking with emotion. "I called to tell you...I've never been more proud of you, my Number One Son," and with that, he ended the phone message. I was stunned. This was the first time my father had ever told me that he was proud of me. I was forty-one years old. It had been a long wait. I sank to the floor. I didn't know what to make of it. I couldn't figure out if I was touched that he left the message or pissed that he had never said those things before. But he'd made the effort to tune in to the program, told me I'd been a pro when I'd been bungling at best. His pride in me made an indescribable difference in how I thought about myself. As I sat cross-legged on the cold tile floor, I wondered what to do. I wiped my eyes, cleared my throat and called him back to thank him. I couldn't deny it. Seemed like my dad could be a wounded healer, after all.

13

OIL CAN HARRY'S

Donna Summer had scored a huge and direct hit with *I Feel Love*, but so far my summer of love was an utter misfire. I'd gone to the bars a few times and tried my best, but found I was comfortable as a swimmer with a nosebleed in a pool full of sharks. And clutching a rapidly warming orange juice in the darkest corner of a bar only contributed to my appearance of a misfit. I admit that I was no Al Cavoto, but I must have been worthy of at least a conversation. However, in a bar, my social inadequacy meant zero confidence and zero sexuality. Additionally, in an era of hypermasculinity, dark moustaches, forests of chest-hair and gaudy gold chains, I was mildly counter-culture; blond, clean-cut, polo-shirted, chino-clad, wearing loafers and most always freshly shaved. I had wrapped myself in a pleasant enough package, but beneath the decoration I projected unease and insecurity. Other men could smell me out like cheap cologne and stayed away en masse. After all, there were no shortages of men who radiated what I lacked. So, healthy clean-cut looks were seemingly less important than confidence. While I was supremely confident at jumping off the starting block, I was supremely non-confidant projecting any kind of winning style. I practiced eleven or twelve more times at several gay bars without any positive result. I went to the Castle Pub - known for being a friendly place; not for me. I tried the Playpen Central on Seymour; there was no play for this guy. As if to rub it in a bit further, there was a club called Playpen South on Richards and Seymour; I was invisible. Also on Seymour was the Luv-A-Fair, a hot disco with a promising name. Promising, most assuredly for some, however I found no affair was forthcoming. I went with the express purpose of being an object of some man's desire, but I might have been the only young man in Vancouver who was never picked up in a gay bar. And I'm embarrassed to say, not even spoken to let alone propositioned. That summer I saw guys getting picked up left, right and centre, and believe me, some of those chaps were a little sketchy. Rejection is tough, but being completely ignored time after time felt much worse. So I stopped going to gay bars. The summer was heating up, but my love life was as cold as ice.

In late April I had written all my exams. Reports and projects were banged out late at night on my second-hand Olivetti typewriter - much to the annoyance of my landlord. I experienced the great surge of relief when classes were over for the summer coupled with the anxiety that I hadn't worked hard enough. Unlike school, swim practice wasn't finished. Lerner continued coaching those of us who were hopefuls right through the season. In swimming, speed and stamina can be lost within a week or two if not training at a high level. So I committed to a practice and competition schedule, preferring the training to competing. A few times I had persuaded Lara to come to the pool and work out with me if she wasn't doing a shift at the restaurant. One evening after a swim we climbed into the Fastback, both red-faced and smelling slightly of chlorine and headed out. Lara was hungry and needed to eat. On the way down West Broadway we decided to nosh at a popular place on Granville where the food was plentiful and inexpensive. The Aristocratic, or as patrons called it, the Ritsy, was an iconic Vancouver diner. Parking just off Granville I could smell the fried food a block away. We walked into a crush of diners chatting, eating and smoking. A tired-looking older server wearing a polyester robin's-egg blue miniskirt and a stained white blouse took us to a booth with red vinyl seats, still damp from being wiped down. She dropped a couple dog-eared plastic-covered menus in front of us. After we ordered and the food arrived, Lara became talkative.

"Let's go out tonight," she said as she dug into her meal - a tuna melt.

"We are out," I said, munching my Whole Earth Salad. It was the least deep-fried item on Ritsy's menu with seeds, nuts, sprouts, and, of course, deep-fried onion rings on top of slightly rusted iceberg lettuce.

"No, I mean l wanna go somewhere else tonight. I'm not working and you're free. We haven't had a night on the town for absolutely ages."

"Lara, I dunno, I have work tomorrow." I was guarding at 10 AM.

"Come on," Lara pleaded. "We can celebrate your birthday a bit early."

"Lara, my birthday's not until —"

"I know when your birthday is. Okay, a lot early. It'll be a blast. There's a jazz place I'd like to go to."

I slowly chewed on a Whole Earth walnut. "I guess we could. So, what place are you talking about?"

"Oil Can Harry's on Thurlow Street. You know it?"

"Heard of it," I said. It was a club that had been around for several decades, having a reputation for attracting hot jazz and blues singers and musical groups. Of late the club had fallen on hard times due to changes in musical tastes. Word was that Oil Can Harry's was going the way of the dinosaurs within the year.

"C'mon, I promise you'll have a ball," Lara enthused.

"When did you start going to jazz clubs?" I asked.

"Sunshine, I'm not some disco-dummy. I do like other music, you know. I love jazz, I *sing* jazz. I'm not an uncultured plebe," she said, not masking her displeasure.

"Jeez, it was just a question."

"Never mind. Listen, last week a customer gave me a couple of free tickets for tonight's show." Lara took big bites of her tuna melt. An enormous side of French fries was nestled alongside. "He's involved in promoting the singer." Lara promptly finished her sandwich with a slight licking of her lips before continuing. "He told me she's outta sight. I can't recall her name, but he said that I'd enjoy her. I told him that I also had a friend who was crazy about music and that he'd just be *dying* to go." Lara got to work on her fries, then stopped eating just long enough to reach into her purse. She retrieved two tickets and passed them to me.

"Dying to go, eh?" I looked at the tickets and Lara noticed a server passing our table with a tall piece of pie. It got Lara's attention immediately.

"Oh, look at that! I just adore that Mile High Lemon Pie. How many calories do you figure? Or what about Peach Cobbler with Double Vanilla Toffee Ice Cream?" Lara looked excited as she continued working on her plate of fries.

"What do you care?" I said, smiling. "You went swimming tonight; there's built-in calorie immunity. Besides, it looks as though you could use some double-toffee-lemon-whatever on that skinny ass of yours."

"Sweet-talker. How can I resist?" Lara asked glowingly and decided on the lemon pie. "So, we're going to Oil Can Harry's?"

"Oil Can Harry's it is," I muttered. I was tired and dreaming of sleep, but Lara could be persuasive.

After dessert, we headed downtown. I parked on Alberni, tossed our swim gear in the front trunk and walked a few blocks to the club. After presenting our tickets we hiked up several flights of stairs and went to the bar to get some drinks - white wine for Lara and a tall orange juice for me. Oil Can Harry's had a surprisingly large crowd of patrons, drinking, smoking and schmoozing. The establishment was showing its age. The floors were uneven, the upholstery was <u>tattered</u> and stained, the tables were chipped and the walls needed some fresh paint. Oil Can Harry's was being hard-hit by the disco dance clubs that were snapping up customers all over the city. Though its days were numbered, their owners managed to get some excellent performers such as Almeta Speaks, the singer we were to hear. By the time we got to our table with drinks in tow, Speaks had been introduced. She acknowledged the appreciative audience and sat down at her piano on the small stage and sang gospel, some blues and some jazz-tinged material. Over the next hour, Lara and I listened to Speaks sing in a deep voice never overshadowed by her own sensitive piano-playing. She closed her set with 'My Eyes Are on the Sparrow' and the audience demonstrated its approval with warm applause.

"Wow," I said after Speaks left the stage. "She's really good."

"Isn't she? I admit I'm jealous. She's doing —" Lara was interrupted by a tall, strikingly handsome man who put his hand on her shoulder.

"Evening!" he said, bending over our table with a wide smile and spoke loudly over the <u>ruckus</u>. "I was hoping that you could come to hear Almeta. Are you enjoying the show?"

"Yes, very much, thanks." Lara beamed. "Oh, Sunshine, let me introduce you. This is my handsome customer Steven, from the restaurant. Or Steve, I can't recall what you prefer," Lara stated.

"I prefer Pete, actually," he said, grinning with impossibly white teeth.

"Are you sure?" Lara laughed, then exclaimed, "How terrible of me! Well, I forgot your name but I didn't forget how good-looking you are."

Nice one, Lara, I thought as she completely recovered from a potentially embarrassing situation. Never an awkward moment. Poise under pressure.

"And your name is Sunshine?" Pete asked me, slightly amazed.

"No, you see, when Lara and I met in French class the first thing she said to me was, Votre sourire est comme le soleil, or —"

"Your smile is like sunshine. I see Lara's point," he said, smiling incandescently himself. *So Pete knew French...very nice.*

I stood up and introduced myself to Pete - my real name.

"That's an unusual first name," Pete said. "Don't think I've heard that before."

"Oh, yes," I started to elaborate a bit further. "My father, he...well, it's a bit of a story. I don't like my name much so I'm really fond of the one Lara gave me."

"Suits you," he nodded.

"Oh, um, thanks." My face burned. "And thanks for the tickets. I don't get out to things like this."

"It's my pleasure. Glad that you're both here this evening," he said warmly.

"Let me get you a drink," I insisted, hoping that he would stay longer.

Pete had glossy jet-black medium-length hair, dark eyes and long lashes that most women would give up their firstborn for. Long nose, trim physique. He spoke with a clear, deep, distinctive voice and was dressed in a dark-blue suit and white shirt with one button undone. *No pectoral-showing polyester shirts for this guy.* His face was lined a bit, especially around the eyes. *Very attractive.*

"Really, that's not necessary."

"It's the least I can do for giving us tickets."

"Then I'll have an OJ, please. I like to be sharp," Pete said, winking at me with his long dark eye-lashes.

"Comin' right up," I said, getting up quickly and thinking that he was perfect for me - he liked orange juice as well. I turned to Lara.

"More white wine?" I asked. She nodded graciously and I left Pete with Lara, who seemed quite pleased to be sitting at the table with him, smiling and inviting conversation. I couldn't wait to get back. *You're a fool.* I quickly walked over to the bar and waited for the drinks I'd ordered. *Lara is smitten with a man who wanted her to come to this jazz club so that he could speak with her, perhaps ask her out. Be cool, don't be an idiot, don't think about how you are attracted to him, don't...*

"That'll be $5.25," the barman said.

I took out three two-dollar bills and left it on the counter. "Keep it," I said and hustled back to the table.

Through the blue haze of a few hundred smokers, I could see that Lara and Pete were getting along well, with Pete listening attentively. I came in part-way through their conversation.

"Thanks," Pete said, smiling warmly and gently taking the glass of juice from my hand, inadvertently brushing his fingers along mine.

"Yes," she said, raising her glass. "To new friends. De nouveaux amis," she said, clinking her glass to Pete's.

"Wait, and your glass, too," he said, looking at me as I sat to his right. I picked up my warm drink and clinked my glass to theirs as the music started. For the next twenty-five minutes, the quartet performed, but I wasn't paying attention. I was in the midst of having a crush on Pete - with Lara front and centre. I was hyper-aware of my movements, my statements, my interactions and my eyes, which wandered over to him at any discrete opportunity. I noticed his rich voice as he spoke, his fluid movements at the table, the touch of his hand on my thigh. Perhaps an accidental brush as he went to reach for his wallet? I couldn't tell, but his brief touch felt like an electric shock. I was flushed; my discomfort and excitement were a troubling mix.

The quartet finished; Speaks was to sing her last set after a thirty-minute break. Pete wanted to get some drinks for Lara and me. I was fine, but Lara was eager for another glass. I could tell by her florid skin that she was feeling the effects, but that could have been explained by the strikingly handsome company sitting with us. Pete excused himself and went to line up at the bar.

"He's such a nice guy." Lara's speech was slightly slurred. "Isn't he?"

"Seems to be. Exactly what does he do? He didn't talk about it."

"He didn't? That's *all* he's been talking about."

"Oh, I guess I wasn't paying —"

"Talent representation. I'm not exactly sure how it all works, but I'll find out. I was telling him about my sinning…oh, I meant my singing." Lara giggled at her Freudian faux pas. "It could be very helpful knowing someone like Zeke."

"Zeke? It's Pete, Lara. *Pete.*"

"What? Jesus, of course it is. Oh, and he's so good-looking. A real dreamboat. Don't you think?"

Lara glanced at the bottom of her empty wine glass and then at me. I didn't answer her question. I hoped that she wasn't fishing for my assessment.

"You sure you want more wine? I think you might be a bit drunk," I said.

"I might be a bit," Lara said stubbornly. "But it's your birthday, after all."

"Right, I forgot about that, so shouldn't it be me who gets plastered?" I asked, laughing.

"Drivers don't get to be plastered, Sunshine. Maybe that's why I never learned how." Pete had made his appearance back at the table."
It's his birthday," Lara blurted out, pointing an unsteady finger my way.

"No! Really?" Pete asked.

"No," I stated. "Lara says that whenever she wants an excuse to get drunk."

"So, do you have a lot of birthdays?" Pete inquired sincerely.

Lara and I looked at each other and started to laugh.

"Not nearly enough," she said.

I was having fun, certainly the most fun I'd ever had at a club in my life.

"Okay, I gotta use the boy's room, if anyone knows where it might —"

As I stood up to find the loo, Pete said, "It's on the lower floor and the basement stairs are way over there, where you see the exit sign." Pete pointed across the distant hall of the nightclub. "It's a bit of a hike."

"Thanks," I said, and went in search of the toilet across a crowded floor. The smoke was acrid, burning my eyes as I walked through it, trying to see where the stairs were for the basement. It was further away than I thought; then down three flights of worn wooden steps to the bottom floor. Now far away from all activity, the sound of music was faint, just a diminished echo. I wondered if I should even be where I was - it didn't seem right. But there, at the end of a hall was the toilet. The door creaked open as I walked into the dimly lit men's room. There was a water leak somewhere; droplets were steadily falling onto the floor. I went over to the turquoise tiled urinal wall. *Wow, this is a relic of the past. Crazy things, these urinal walls. Gawd, there's probably piss splashed everywhere; it reeks. Who'd have thought up this nutty idea of a twenty-foot tiled trough to use as a pissing pit? It's impossible to pee standing up without drenching my pants or feet with urine.* I was contemplating just how I was going to do that, with my zipper unzipped and my best friend hanging out when I heard the door creak. Clearly, it's never a good thing to surprise my best friend, because it makes the job much, much harder to do. My peripheral vision was able to pick up that someone was coming alongside me to the trough. I didn't dare look as I was stick-handling my penis and feeling very bladder-shy. I fixed my stare downward on the goods at hand as the stranger was pulling out his dick. I decided that the urination part of the visit to the urinal wall wasn't going to happen (I really had to pee; however, I wasn't going to embarrass myself further by going into a presumably filthy stall). I stuffed it back in and zipped up.

"Don't leave on my account."

Pete. He sidled up beside me.

"Sorry," he said. "I have the same problem. I have to wait a minute for it to get the message."

I looked over at him. He was grinning, holding his cock in his large right hand, which it filled up completely. I was silent and continued to glance at his beautiful dick, unable to look away.

"My mother told me when I was a boy that if I held my penis in one hand and tickled my balls with my other hand it would make me pee," Pete said.

"Really? My mother told me if I touched my penis I'd go blind."

"Why don't you try it?"

"You want me to go blind?"

Pete said, "Here, watch," and deftly reached under his cock to stroke his large, round balls; once, twice and then took his fingers away and quickly a stream of urine poured out steady and strong, hitting the wall of the trough. I confess I was a little turned on watching this handsome guy take a leak. He shook the remaining drops from his penis, left it out and said, "Your turn."

"I dunno, what if the only way I can pee from now on is by standing in front of a turquoise urinal wall tickling my balls?"

"Funny guy," Pete said, moving closer. Much closer. Close enough that I could smell a heady combination of his fragrance and slight perspiration.

"Here," he said. "Why don't you let me show you how it's done?"

With that, Pete unzipped my pants and placed his warm, meaty hand on the underside of my scrotum. I jumped reflexively. He caressed my balls softly, gently touching me. Instead of letting the pee out, I got hard - fast. Surprisingly, I wasn't embarrassed whatsoever.

"You sure that you came all the way down here to pee?" he asked me, as he slowly unfastened the top part of my chinos. I had no answer for him. "You're a handsome guy. Do you know how sexy you are?"

Before I could tell him about being ignored at every gay bar in the city, Pete looked at my red face and said, "No, you don't, do you? Well, then. I'm going to have to tell you a few more times."

Me, sexy? I'd wanted to hear that. Even if it's in a decrepit urinal stinking of piss, I'll take it.

Pete continued to hold my cock in his hand. There is no way I can describe what that was like, so I won't try. •

"Oh, Gawd…is it okay to do this here? I mean is it safe? What if someone comes in?"

Pete answered by grabbing onto my cock and leading me to the back stall, holding it tightly. I couldn't do anything but follow him into the darkened, graffitied enclosure. He unbuttoned my shirt, pressed his lips to mine and kissed me deeply. He then brushed his tongue against my nipples, then touched them with his fingertips. Pete took off his blue jacket, hung it on the metal hook on the stall door, took his shirt off quickly to reveal a dark-haired chest. He shoved my pants to the floor then pushed me to the toilet seat and dropped to his knees, put his beautiful warm mouth on my cock - gently at first - then devoured it. He reached up to stroke my nipples lightly. I put my head back and moaned quietly. Part of me was thinking that this was insanity, the other part wanted more craziness. Pete continued to suck my cock, making me nearly hyperventilate with uncontrolled deep breaths. He put my balls into his mouth and gently sucked them. He licked the underside of my scrotum, and then further, underneath to my anus. *My anus!* Jesus Christ, he was moving his tongue around my rectum, driving it deeper. I was shocked and then it felt so incredibly exciting that I suspended my judgment and allowed him to continue. He stayed there for a bit longer, making me hunger for more. I felt his finger at my spit-lubricated anus.

"Stand up," he ordered.

I did as I was asked, excited and apprehensive.

"Turn around and let me see that beautiful ass."

No hesitation. I complied willingly.

"Gorgeous…unbelievable…so smooth."

Pete bit my buttocks lightly, then used his tongue to probe the area, making it alive with unanticipated excitement. He stood up and gently pushed me forward at the waist so that my buttock was fully exposed. I felt his large, thick penis rubbing against me. He held onto his cock and massaged me with it, teasing my butt gently then pressing with more force. I could feel myself open slightly, tense against his cock and wanting it inside of me at the same time. In my mind my thoughts flashed. *I shouldn't be doing this with a man I don't know in a men's room. This is all wrong.* Yet, I wanted him in me. I wanted to know what it felt like. I was thinking and wanting and suddenly Pete pushed his large penis into me - all at once. I took a deep breath. I waited for it to hurt, to be split apart. It didn't happen. What I felt was fullness, and then as he began to carefully stroke his cock inside of me, newfound pleasure. Pete expertly controlled his movements - steady and assertive. I was overwhelmed with excitement; my cock was hard in my hand as Pete began to fuck me aggressively. I twisted my head back so that I could kiss his mouth. Pete didn't let up as he continued to pull out of me and then thrust back in with long, forceful movements. I was completely engulfed in the physical and emotional gratification I felt from him inside of me and was unable to keep myself from cumming.

"Oh, man, I can't hold back," I strained softly under my breath. My climax came in pulses, each stroke of his cock in me resulted in a heightened ejaculation onto the toilet seat. Pete didn't stop. He was more excited now that I'd cum. He continued fucking me for another two or three minutes, my spent half-hard cock flopping back and forth. Then he uttered, "Urgh!" and climaxed inside me. Pete held me, his sweaty chest to my back, spent. Wordlessly, I wiped the semen off myself as best I could in a tiny cubicle. I turned around to see Pete smiling in the near-dark, his polished teeth bright, his formerly sharp-pressed pants wrinkled and lying on the dirty floor. I did up my shirt, pulled up my trousers, stepped out of the stall with Pete and then it hit me. I looked straight into his dark eyes.

"Lara," I said.

Intoxication can cause a loss in the perception of time. While Pete and I were composing, rearranging and de-crumpling ourselves in the men's room, Lara was working on finishing her fourth glass of wine. We cunningly got to the table at slightly different times. I heard her asking Pete where I was. I hoped she wouldn't be able to put the two of us together fucking in a washroom stall. Pete shrugged uncertainly.

"Dunno where he is. Might have gotten lost on the way to the washroom. That basement's kinda confusing."

The explanation seemed sufficient for Lara, who probably needed to visit the ladies' room herself.

"Sorry," I said, appearing a bit disheveled as I walked to the table seconds later, making it appear that I was coming from afar. "A guy ran into me downstairs," I uttered, which was a version of the truth. I caught Pete smiling. "You know, I think we should get going, Lara. It's getting late for me. Whaddya say?" I noticed Pete was looking around the room, likely planning his departure.

"Ah, there's Frankie; he's a client of mine." He tried to get his attention. "I wanna talk to him before Almeta does her last set. Listen, it was good to see you, Lara."

"You too, Pete. When you come by the restaurant can we finish our conversation?"

"Of course. Be there next week, okay?" He gave her shoulders a squeeze. Pete was anxious to make his exit, stage left.

"Bye," Lara said, smiling weakly, a few sheets to the wind, turning away and sipping on ice water. Pete winked at me, eyelashes fluttering and briskly walked off. I felt lightheaded.

"He's really so nice," she said absently, putting down her glass of water and looking for a napkin to wipe her mouth.

"Yeah, you said that before. What conversation?" I asked.

"Huh? Oh, he said we'd talk about my singing." Lara looked a little green.

"That's terrific. Hey, are you alright? Are you feeling sick?" I asked, fearing the worst, which could involve projectile vomit all over the Fastback on the ride home. I did have vinyl seats, but still...

"No, I'm just getting sleepy, Sunshine. It's late. I'm drunk. You're right. I wanna go home now. Please." Lara scrunched up her napkin and held it against her mouth for a moment.

"Okay, let's go," I said, knocking back my OJ and thinking of the twenty-minute drive and the state of my still-full bladder. I never emptied it in the washroom and I couldn't go back downstairs. Getting up from the table Lara smoothed her skirt and steadied herself as we headed for the exit. As we moved through the nightclub, I noticed the men's room along the hall. I didn't have to go downstairs. Pete surely knew that; pretty crafty of him.

"Hold on for a sec, Lara. I gotta go to the boy's room again. Must be all the beer."

"You were drinking orange juice, Slick."

"Yeah, go figure. I'll be right back," I said and I excused myself so that I could alleviate the pressure. I barely made it to the urinal and unzipped before the dam burst. I didn't rinse my hands but went straight back out to find Lara leaning up against the wall. I took her by the elbow to steady her and we went out the nightclub's front door and into the breezy night air on a busy Thurlow Street. At the crosswalk, waiting for the green signal, Lara looked at me and asked pointedly, "So, how'd you enjoy it?"

"Huh?" I was startled to hear Lara's question.

"Oil Can Harry's. I promised you'd have a ball, so did you?" Lara inquired.

"Oh, yes," I said with relief. "I had an absolute ball."

14

AFTERGLOW

After a thankfully vomit-free ride back to Kits, I walked Lara to her apartment, chatted awhile, made sure that she was okay, gave her a big hug and said goodnight. Even though it was late, I wasn't eager to drive back to my mouldy room. I fired up the Fastback and went up Alma Street; the downtown peninsula glittered in the distance. I headed north and turned west onto Fourth Avenue. The street was deserted. It was shortly after 1:30 AM and I should have been exhausted but I felt exhilarated, thinking about what had transpired. I dropped the engine into fourth gear and continued along the avenue, the engine clattering reliably as I drove further west, the windows down, my hair lifted by the breeze, my head trying hard to retain each scintillating detail of my bathroom encounter. Turning onto Tolmie, I drove to the end of the street and found a parking spot adjacent to Locarno Beach. I cut the motor, climbed out and walked down to the deserted beach. I sat on a huge piece of driftwood. *What had I done or said to Pete that indicated I was gay?* I thought I hid myself very well. *Perhaps I'm more transparent than I thought.*

The wind had really come up. *Unusual for it to be blowing this hard at night.* The tide was surging in, the waves reaching far up onto the beach, the foam reflecting the moonlight. Looking east, the city was laid out beautifully before me, glowing against the black skies. The wind stirred the fragrance of English Bay as I sat for a few minutes, taking in the visuals, the sounds and the scents of the evening. I was happier than I could ever recall. I smiled to myself, lost in the ability to experience things I'd only fantasized about. The breeze continued to pick up, pitching the water, creating whitecaps just barely seen in the starlight. I breathed deeply then stood up, removed my shoes and placed them where they would remain dry. I unbuttoned my cotton shirt and placed it on my loafers, then unzipped my wrinkled chinos, dropped them to my ankles and stepped out of them. My white boxer shorts were still damp from perspiration. I could smell the sex I'd had, leaving its odour on my flesh and on my undergarment. I pushed them down from my hips and placed them on the pile of clothes. The wind felt warm against my skin. I walked to the water's edge. For a few minutes I stood naked in the building winds, recalling the caresses, the feeling of being kissed, of a man being inside of me. My head reeled at the recollection. The sand was grainy and cool, the water cooler still against my bare feet. As I moved further in, my calf muscles tightened with the anticipated cold. I moved deeper into the waters, past my waist, then deeper still. The waves grew larger, tossing the sea nearly up to my chest. The cold, salty water took my breath away in one quick gasp. Defenceless, I stood there, swelling black water to my throat, the sand beneath me slipping away. I cast my eyes at the few visible stars, whose light flickered, seemingly by the currents of air. I let the water push me, cleanse the sweat and the scent of sex from me, a memory only as the waves overtook me and I was under water.

15

THE DECISION

I'd gone through my first three years of university with the anticipated trials and tribulations realized; the full course-load, swimming four to five hours a day, varsity swim meets through the year, travel, work and assignments. My fourth year of university would test me further with an increase in academics, athletics and work. My swim times reduced through the autumn and winter and I'd had some excellent results at key meets. With school coursework and a practicum at a mental health clinic, the demands were heavy. The clinic placement confirmed my wish to work in the counselling field, consolidating my belief that attending graduate school and further training was the right direction for me.

I saw Lara less frequently as she'd been dating a short, self-absorbed and incredibly hirsute German named Arnie. I'd met him a couple of times over at her apartment and failed to warm up to him. Arnie was the classic narcissist that I was reading about - the dangers of a psychology major, I suspect. He never stopped talking about himself, his hiking efforts in the local mountains, endlessly showing his outdoorsy photos ad nauseam. He never said a word about Lara's struggles with singing, so I questioned how supportive he was of her. But who was I to criticize? My so-called relationships amounted to no more than a few fleeting hours of sex. Because of school and Arnie, Lara and I saw less of each other and I missed her. Reaching for the phone at the SUB after practice, I dumped in a dime and gave her a call at home. I knew it was her day off. The phone rang five times before she picked up.

"Hello?"

"Lara, it's me, how're you?" I asked. "Something's wrong," I added. Right away I thought Lara sounded off-kilter.

"Oh, Sunshine…you're right. It's Arnie."

"What's happened?"

"He broke up with me just before February the fourteenth," she sighed.

I had to think about the date she referred to - it hadn't a meaning to me, but to Lara, Valentine's Day was special.

"Wow. Bad timing. I'm sorry to hear it," I lied convincingly.

"I'm pretty bummed out. I don't think Arnie liked dating a waitress. Probably a few classes beneath him."

"Arnie sells double-knit suits at Fred Asher's," I said. "I wouldn't say he's a few classes above anyone. Besides, doesn't he know you sing like Callas?"

"Apparently Blondie is more his style."

"There you go, point taken. Any chance of getting back together, or is it —"

"It's definitely Dump City," she stated seriously.

"Um, okay. Well…let's see. Maybe he's left you with a couple nice memories?" I tried a positive reframe.

"What he's left me are long black hairs in my Porthault sheets," Lara groaned.

"Jeez, Lara."

"Like sleeping with a Neanderthal."

"Well, he was from Germany."

"True. You know, it wasn't just his chest and back. It was a Black Forest below the belt, as well."

"Yech. I didn't know that."

"It wasn't pretty."

"I can only imagine. What did he say the reason for the break-up was?"

"Which reason would you like to hear?"

"There's more than one?"

"Oh, yes, there's quite a few. Like he wasn't ready to make a commitment."

"That's unoriginal."

"Isn't it? Such a tired cliché. Christ, I had no desire to be a hausfrau and make him Rindergulasch. I just liked his...company."

Rindergulasch? Don't ask. "Huh...so you *enjoyed* spending time with Arnie? I guess I find that a bit surprising."

"Well, I could understand that. I'm not telling the whole story."

"Okay. So?"

"I liked the sex," Lara admitted.

"The sex with Arnie was okay?"

"It was surprisingly more than okay. Arnie droned on and on about himself and had body hair that could be parted with a comb, but he had another attribute that made up for any deficits."

"Oh," I said. "I think I know what you're saying." I figured my best friend just told me she was a Size Queen.

"At least I was happy with the sex. And until very recently he gave me the impression that he was, too," she lamented.

I was sympathetic. "I dunno, Lara. Arnie's let go of a very special person. But I gotta tell you, he wasn't the classiest character."

"What do you mean?"

"On that thatch of black chest hair he wore a giant St. Christopher's medallion, and it hung off a fifteen-pound gold chain. I sorta noticed."

"Tell me about it," Lara said, a snicker in her voice. "By the way, that chain was gold-plate. I've got the green stains on my boobs to prove it."

"You see? You can do better. Next time choose a quieter guy with a better chain."

"I have to tell you, Sunshine. I'm thinking of having a man-break."

"My mother says that a break is as good as a holiday," I added. We were well-versed with clichés in our family.

"You're the psychologist."

"I'm a part-time lifeguard who can barely keep his eyes open most of the time," I countered. "Hey, why don't we go see a movie this evening? Get your mind off that hairy beast. How about Star Wars?" *Sure, take your best friend to a sci-fi picture; that's sure to help mend her broken heart.* "It's playing at the Stanley. Everyone's talking about it."

"I don't think I could bear rocket phallic symbols and testosterone right now." Lara paused for a few beats. "What about an art film? La Menace by Alain Corneau is on, and it's a Canadian movie. Or that Woody Allen picture, Annie Hall? It's at the Starlight at nine."

"Tell you what; it's Annie Hall tonight, and Star Wars another time, okay?" I compromised quickly. I could see the sci-fi flick anytime and I didn't want to spend two hours reading subtitles to a plodding foreign film.

"Deal, Annie Hall and neurotic Woody Allen. I could take a bit of someone else's neurosis right about now," Lara stated. "Oh, by the way, I'm hungry."

"You sure got over Arnie fast," I said.

"Don't be clever. You know how stress gives me an appetite."

That's very true. Stress, happiness, sex, movies, phone call break-ups.

"How 'bout we talk over a greasy ham and pineapple with extra cheese pizza at White Tower?" I asked.

"A No. 3? Sounds terrific."

"And Lara, to be frank, I didn't care much for Arnie."

"You didn't? You never said."

"You seemed happy with him. I didn't wanna be unsupportive and tell you I thought he was a narcissist."

"Being a narcissist wasn't the worst of it," she said softly.

"There's more?" I asked, grimly thinking of what he might have said.

"Yes. What really hurt was that Arnie thought I was all hot air."

"What did he —"

"He said I was a big dreamer who'd never get my shit together. He said he couldn't go out with someone like me, a waitress who didn't have a scheme, who was just waiting for a bunch of fantasies to magically materialize. He told me I had enough hot air to fill the Zeppelin, and you know what happened to *that* balloon. Arnie was blunt but maybe he was right."

"Lara, that's not being <u>blunt,</u> that's being mean. Obviously, he didn't understand what singing means to you."

"I don't know that I explained it very well to him. We didn't spend much time talking."

"I see."

"It's not Arnie…it's just that another guy's dumped me. It's…so humiliating." There was a pause over the phone. She might have been holding back some tears. *Get her something to eat.*

"Listen, we'll talk it out, okay? I'm coming by right now to pick you up," I said and hung up the phone. Fifteen minutes later Lara was outside her building waiting for me. She was wearing a printed prairie skirt in blues and greys with a denim jacket and had wrapped a long orange scarf around her neck. Her throat was always wrapped in cool or damp weather. Though dressed in colourful layers for the nippy evening, she looked wispy-thin. She smiled warmly at me and climbed into the foggy Fastback. After driving to the West End we parked the car, walked into the White Tower and soon Lara was devouring a large No. 3 with extra cheese. She was either extraordinarily hungry or very upset. We didn't talk much; she wasn't in the mood and I didn't press it. After the pizza, we quietly walked up Denman to Barclay Street and lined up outside the Starlight Cinema. It was a cloudless evening, un-characteristic for February in Vancouver, and very chilly. There was a large crowd of people queuing up to get inside so we had time to talk. As we shuffled along slowly I asked Lara, "How long did you go out with Arnie, anyway?"

"Oh, I dunno. Guess we dated for five months or so," she replied, counting it out on her fingers. "You know, guys are gung-ho with me at the start, then a change happens; I guess the novelty of dating me wears off."

"Lara, you're many things, but I'd never describe you as a novelty."

"Thanks, but I can tell when there's a loss of interest. Perhaps I lose my charms?"

"I wouldn't think so," I said, blowing warm air into my cupped hands.

"Maybe I'm lousy in bed?" Lara inched towards the cashier's wicket.

"C'mon, I doubt that."

"Yeah, I've never really thought so. But I didn't tell you...Arnie broke up with me on the phone a few hours after we had sex. Who does that? Said it 'just wasn't happening'. Well, it seemed like it was happening just fine when he was porking the bejesus outta me for three hours." Though Lara's voice was restrained, it easily carried. Ahead of us in our line-up, I noticed an older lady with a younger woman - perhaps mother and daughter - who turned their heads and looked shocked at Lara's comment. They glanced at each other and continued indiscreetly eavesdropping on our conversation. Blithely, Lara continued on. "He said the last four or five times we slept together he just wasn't feeling turned on any longer and that we weren't compatible. Apparently, the last romp was the final ride on the pony."

"I don't understand. Why would he even *want* to have sex if he planned on breaking up?" I asked under my breath.

"Oh, Sunshine. He's a man, that's why. One last fuck for the road," she hissed angrily. The older eavesdropper rolled her eyes to the back of her head as though she was going to pass out. The younger woman looked eager to hear more.

"That's cruel."

"Isn't it? I must be a glutton for punishment because I foolishly asked him if there was anything else he wanted to tell me."

"Why? Is that when he —"

"Yup, the Zeppelin. Hot air, das Gewäsch."

"Wow...unbelievable. What'd you say to that?"

"I told him he was a Heinie pig and never to call me again. He reassured me he had no plans to. I was going to slam the phone down for extra emphasis but he'd beat me to it."

"Jeez, what an asshole," I said.

"And that's insulting an asshole," she sneered and then exhaled a huge sigh. "Of course, Arnie was right. We weren't compatible, though I tried. Really, I did try to be compatible."

"I don't see how compatibility can be conjured up. Not with Arnie or Jean-Paul or - who was that guy you went out with last year on day parole?"

"Oh, you mean Michel," Lara answered sheepishly. "Good-looking, but dating a convict wasn't my best choice."

"Not really," I agreed.

"Though on the plus side, it almost killed my mother."

"I remember. Also, Michel did have some very interesting tattoos, I mean, from what I could see."

"Oh, you have no idea. Did I tell you that he's back inside? I got a call from his lawyer - Michel was using me as a fake alibi. Anyway, it's only grand larceny this time." The two listening ladies glanced back and forth, jaws nearly dropping to the ground.

"Only?"

"Never mind." Lara looked skyward and shook her head in exasperation. "Tell me, Sunshine, why do men always leave me feeling as important as last week's tuna casserole?"

"Because you settle," I let slip.

"I settle?"

"Lara, you step into the girlfriend role pretty fast. You're very accommodating with men - from what I see."

"I think you're right." Lara nodded her head affirmatively.

"What, no argument?" I asked. I was anticipating a scrap.

"None. I agree. I do settle. When a man pays me attention I go right into relationship mode and completely lose myself in the process. When it ends - it always does, and badly - I'm shattered. But then

I repeat it all over again," Lara said, shaking her head. "It's stupid and moronic and ridiculous."

"Something to think about?"

"No, it's something to change." Lara paused and then said, "Sunshine, I'm a reasonably bright person. I'm not horrible to look at and I'm hardly inexperienced when it comes to sex. I shouldn't have to settle, should I?"

The eavesdroppers exchanged a darting look, waiting for my answer. Lara took out her wallet from her purse and pulled out some cash.

"You don't have to settle," I said confidently with no experience or legitimacy whatsoever to back it up. We got to the box office.

"Two, please," she told the cashier. "I'm getting this," she told me. "I wanted to see Annie Hall, so the least I can do is cough up." Lara was insistent. "What about some popcorn and drinks? Here," Lara pressed ten dollars in my hand as she finished paying for our tickets and we moved into the crowded lobby. The food counter was busy and Lara wanted to stay back from the crowd so I went for the goodies.

"It's hard to believe you're hungry after scarfing down that big pizza."

Lara observed that both women continued to snoop, so she made her final declaration.

"Well, it's been said I'm insatiable. A lotta men've told me they're amazed at what I can cram into my mouth," she called out briskly. The older woman gasped slightly. The younger one snickered as the other took her by the elbow and marshalled her into the theatre. I grimaced and went to order from a pimply-faced girl, her mousey-brown hair slick with oil. She was wearing dull metal braces on her yellowed teeth. When she half-smiled I noticed a piece of food had stuck in her dental hardware. I swallowed and felt a twinge of nausea. Adolescence was not being kind to her. I tilted my head a little to read her lopsided name-tag: Brunhilda. *Gawd, another strike. My name's not so bad.*

"Hi, a large popcorn and two Fresca's. Hey, Lara," I called out, "I don't suppose you wanna hot —"

"Oh, I'd love a hot dog! Onions, mustard, pile it all on," she boomed brightly. I paid for the treats, thanked Brunhilda and resisted the urge to tell her that she'd be okay in a few more years. With food in tow, we found a couple seats and hunkered down in the cinema with a couple of hundred others to watch the musings of Woody Allen playing Alvy Singer and the delightfully imperfect Diane Keaton, appealing in most every way, her performance dazzling. Keaton's characterization of Annie Hall struck a familiar chord with the singer on my right. Lara could appreciate that Annie Hall was a young woman of similar age who was a struggling performer and whose self-doubts inhibited her from moving ahead. Lara's vocal talents were Mt. Everest-like compared to Annie Hall's little mound of a voice. Annie Hall was a wonderful flick, and as we were leaving the Starlight I was lost in thought. I was contemplating how much I learned about heterosexual relationships from watching movies. Flicks featuring gay relationships were few and the characters were so tortured or ashamed by their sexuality that death was their frequent outcome. There weren't a lot of happy endings for gay men or women in film.

"What's going on?" Lara asked as we briskly walked down Denman looking for a gelato place.

"Huh? Whaddya mean? I was just thinking —"

"About the movie?" she asked quickly.

"Yeah, sort of." I buttoned my pea jacket against the night's cold and stuffed my hands in my pockets.

"Me, too."

There was a long pause as we walked past shops and green grocers. Lara gushed, "You know, that Broadway-babe Elaine Stritch sings like she's puffed a couple packs of Camel's and downed a bottle of Jack Daniel's."

"Huh? Was she in the movie?"

"No, of course not. She's got such ferocious drive it doesn't matter how horrible her voice sounds. She's been a phenomenal success for decades."

"Okay…" I ventured, more than a little perplexed.

"And there are girls with voices like angels who can't get work and resort to blowing old men in alleys just to pay their rent," Lara gasped.

"Lara, what the hell are you talking about?"

"Jesus, Sunshine. Don't you see? I've gotta have the balls of Elaine Stritch and a voice like Leontyne Price," Lara declared with excitement. "And I'm going to sing."

"Ah, Lara, right here and now, on Denman Street?" I took my hands from my coat and vigorously rubbed them together.

"No, stupid, I mean, I'm going to try to sing," she proclaimed.

"You do sing, and very well." I was obviously missing the point. Lara stopped walking and grabbed my cold hands with a formidable grip.

"Listen to me. I don't wanna haul plates of burgers an' fries in some dump. I'm not gonna spend my life dodging a bunch of middle-aged men grabbing at my ass just so I get a couple quarters for tips."

"It's a nice restaurant," I said. It really *was* a nice restaurant. I also thought she was guilty of dramatic license with the 'ass-grabbing' comment.

"It's a dead end, and you know it." Lara let go of my hands and fixed a defiant glare.

"What are you saying? Are you telling me that from now on you're going to be singing for your supper?" Lara stared at me, and though I felt her annoyance growing, I continued. "Isn't that a bit risky? You have a big appetite. Look at the meals you had for dinner tonight." Dense as I could be, I finally realized my playful banter was not where she was at. Her mood had shifted a while ago and I wasn't in sync with her distress whatsoever.

"Sit down." Her voice began to shake with emotion.

"We're on the street and it's freezing. I'm not plopping my *tuchas* on the curb."

Lara took me by the arm and steered me to the bus stop bench a few feet away. The traffic and street noise surrounding us made it difficult to hear but I could tell by Lara's voice that she was near tears.

"Look at me. I'm a…a…colossal failure," she stammered softly. I tried to refute her statement, but she shook her head. "No, let me finish. I'm twenty-four. I should know what I want. My parents think they know what I should do but they're wrong. *Dead wrong*. I don't know how I'll do this, but I'm committing my energies to music, to performing, not just singing at a funeral once a month and hoping some crummy café hires me for two hours. No more half-measures. And if I futz this up, well, it'll be just another one of my calamities, like studying French for fifteen years," she sobbed. "Or having these strings of useless relationships! Jesus Christ, I've even screwed my French teacher."

"Your *married* French teacher," I added quietly.

"Yes, yes, my married French teacher. If that wasn't bad enough, I slept with a Neanderthal and a prison inmate, for God's sake."

"Well, not at the same time, and technically Michel *was* on parole," I commented softly.

"And what about the others? Just like you said, I settle. They're pointless time-wasters. They never cared for me and truthfully, how much did I like them? I'm just as bad." Lara's face was flush with despair, tears falling from her eyes, smearing her mascara. "But forget about them - it's me that's failed," she wept. "I wanna make something of myself. I'm tired of being someone's girlfriend or someone's obliging daughter. I wanna be a someone in my own right." Lara's voice was cracking, straining so that she could be heard above the street noise. Her nose had become a watery mess. "I probably look like hell, don't I? *Don't I?*" she demanded.

I was afraid to answer, but she was right - her eyes were badly smudged with black mascara, her face was red and blotchy. I absently handed her the napkin from my movie hot dog, previously stuffed into my pocket, not noticing the thick remnants of mustard.

"Here," I offered. "You're gonna need this."

"Thanks." Lara took the napkin and wiped her nose and dabbed her eyes. Bright yellow mustard smeared across her cheeks and under her left eye already scarily smudged with mascara. Now was not the time to tell her.

"I'm so pissed at my parents," she uttered loudly. "I've tried to tell 'em a thousand times I'm not who they think I should be. I'm not a teacher. I'm not Annie Hall, either. I'm not anyone," she cried. Lara's exasperation was growing by the second and I didn't know what to do. "Sunshine, I'm so unhappy with myself. I've got nothing to offer," she whimpered softly. "Even Arnie knew it; that's why he dumped me, why they all dump me. I've become that stinking, horrible, disgusting tuna casserole."

"Lara —" I tried to interrupt her, but she continued her self-critique.

"I've wasted all this time and energy and for what? No, I've gotta get on track. I've got to make…myself…proud. I'm more than a singing waitress, I know I am…or can be," Lara stammered, tears choking her voice. "Will you…can you…please…help me?" Lara howled like a hurt child, lurching full tilt into heaving sobs. Onlookers seemed either curious or concerned as they waited for the Robson bus. I put my arms around her shoulders as my best friend continued to cry. *Was this the existential angst I'd read about?*

"Of course I will," I said, doing my best to comfort her and not knowing what helping her meant in the professional or musical sense.

"What can I do?" I asked as the bus pulled up. People passed us by and clambered onto the electric trolley, casting lingering glances at Lara, deeply upset and bawling. *Maybe they think I'm some kind of cad?* They stepped onto the bus, scrutinizing the odd pair holding onto each other on the bench. I repeated my question, "Lara, please, what can I do?"

"I dunno. Just...make me...stop blubbering, for starters," she sobbed as the trolley lumbered off, "or I'm going to pass out."

"Think of the war in the Middle East?" I <u>lamely</u> offered.

"Idiot," she wailed. "That's not helping."

In all honesty, I didn't know what to do. *Cross off a career in crisis counselling.* I sat there for the next few minutes, waiting for something to change. Lara snatched a couple of breaths quickly, settling herself in four or five minutes on her own. The world continued to whirl around us; passersby, buses and traffic for a brief while longer. Then Lara's sobs ceased completely, her breathing restored to normal. "Okay," Lara said, wiping away the tears with the mustard-stained napkin, leaving yellow smears under her blackened raccoon-eyes. The unintentional frightening look was something she'd have to remedy later. She inhaled deeply and blew out a massive breath before standing up. "Better. Much better. I've made the decision. For Christ's sake," she said, grabbing my arm to get me moving. "Get up off this filthy bench and let's find a bucket of gelato. I'm famished."

16

IS CONFIDENCE SEXY?

My four years of university were coming to a close. Though I still had some papers to complete and exams to write, I'd graduate at the end of May. University had been a positive experience for me, though I felt a massive loss when Lara dropped out. I wasn't particularly social with others on campus - my interactions comprised of vague and general comments from time to time. As always, my teammates were kept at a distance. I was getting more attention for my athletic performance in the pool, so I became even more cautious about the kind of image I projected.

My graduation ceremony was meaningful to me, and my parents were invited to attend convocation. My father said that he couldn't get away from the store, however my mother came. She sat in the Fredric Wood Theatre with other mothers and fathers and watched me receive my degree. Though my mother's presence at the ceremony was gratifying, it was my father's absence that reminded me of what I'd lacked since I was a boy. Simply a father's interest in his son.

When I reflect on pseudo-father-figures a prof here and there comes to mind, but there was another man who inspired me. I taught adult swimming lessons for extra income and one of my students was a thirty-eight-year-old man named Nick. He was the husband of a running buddy of Lara's. Nick was an <u>affable</u> guy who became a competent swimmer. We got to know each other quickly - that often happened with my swimming students. Nick shared that since he was a child he knew exactly what he'd wanted to do: become a veterinarian. He explained that his desire to care for animals was established by the time he was five years of age. All activities were directed towards that goal. He said there "was no hesitation, no ambivalence" in his pursuits. His deliberation about his path amazed me. Nick described how he set objectives and worked towards them. That same attitude was evident as he learned how to swim - prepared, hard-working, disciplined, committed. Nick taught me about setting targets and helped me to crystallize the direction I was moving in regarding my education and career. He listened and was curious about my plans in a way that I'd dreamed a dad might have been. Nick's personal life was as unambiguous as his professional life. He married young; he and his wife Colleen had been together for over sixteen years. According to Lara, Nick and Colleen had a highly active sex life - most every day and sometimes twice a day. *How could people in their thirties manage this?* I met Colleen at a barbecue that she and Nick had invited Lara and me to. I studied them both and could see why Nick was so attracted to her; she was beautiful and intelligent. It was readily apparent that Nick and Colleen were well-suited for each other. Never critical, they laughed together, held hands, treated each other like best friends and according to Lara's reports, fucked like bunnies after a carrot binge. Nick wasn't a GQ model, yet clearly Colleen found him decidedly attractive. A quiet confidence radiated from Nick and I wondered if that was the appeal for Coleen. I asked Lara about it indirectly at the Aristocratic when we were stuffing our faces with mushroom burgers with fries and coleslaw. Luscious peach cobblers were perhaps to come for dessert.

"Is confidence sexy? Well, a confident man can be an aphrodisiac and an overly-confident man can be an asshole." She pushed aside the slaw to get to the crispy French fried potatoes. "Why do you ask?" Lara popped a few potatoes into her mouth, shook salt onto the remaining ones on her plate and reset her gaze on me.

"Oh, I'm reading on personal development and it came up."

"It's an interesting question," Lara stated, continuing to munch.

"That's what I thought."

"Sunshine, are you asking if I think you're confident?"

"Well..."

"No one's more confident in the water. But equating confidence with sexual attraction? Surely people who aren't confident have sex. After all, Marilyn Monroe had zero confidence and yet she's still the world's greatest sexual icon." Lara popped the last of her mushroom burger in her mouth.

"Maybe she was only sexually confident?" I pondered.

"Or maybe she created an illusion. She *was* an accomplished actress." Lara had an eye on my uneaten French fries. "Aren't you going to eat those?"

"Go ahead." I dumped them on her plate.

"Thanks. I can't explain it, but I'm just ravenous tonight. The only thing I could think about today was food. Maybe it's because of winter. Don't we eat more in winter?"

"I don't know, Lara, maybe."

"I've been doing these crazy exercises for my diaphragm," she said, forking a few fries in a stainless steel cup of mayonnaise and lifting them to her eager mouth. "Putting telephone books on it and panting on my back like a madwoman. I'll show you later. Maybe that's making me hungry."

"Or hungrier?" I asked, marvelling at her appetite. She was savouring her mayo-laden fries.

"So, were you wondering about anything else?" Lara asked in between bites.

"Okay...so if confidence *is* sexy and attracts people or if the confidence is fake, I wonder what sustains the attraction over time? 'Cause you said that the sex will pass."

"Yes, I'd say that's true for most, though Nick and Colleen wouldn't agree."

"Perhaps they're the exception to the rule?"

"Possibly, though there's much more to relationships than having sex, as fun as that might be." Lara abandoned her fork and used her fingers for the few remaining fries. "Oh, speaking of Colleen, did I tell you I met her mother last week after she and I did a run? She prepared a huge plate of cucumber sandwiches on this incredible pumpernickel with bowls of fresh fruit - sliced peaches, raspberries, blackberries - and a pitcher of ice tea with lemon. It was all set out on Colleen's porch when we came back. How thoughtful was that?"

"It's all about the food, isn't it, Lara? What's her mother like?"

"Oh, my gosh, she's so charming. Asked me questions about music and singing; really showed an interest. Completely the opposite of my mother. We chatted for an hour. I could see right away where Colleen's good nature comes from. They're really quite similar."

I pushed my coleslaw to the other side of the plate with my fork.

"I've been reading about that - how we inherit personality traits from our parents."

"Yes, can you imagine?" Lara shook her head.

"Listen, if that's true and I'm really like my father I'm going to buy a polyester golf shirt, take up chain-smoking and go on a twenty-year drinking binge," I dead-panned.

"Aren't you being a tad melodramatic? Besides, you're more like your mother. And really, if we were only the sum of our parents' traits, I'd be a cold, logical, sexless and talentless person."

"You aren't most of those things."

"I hope you're saying I'm logical."

"No question about it," I said, grinning.

"I decided the person I am is my choice," Lara said firmly. "After all, it was good enough for Aristotle," she added.

"Aristotle?" I asked incredulously.

"I paid attention in Philosophy 100," she said smugly.

"Who am I to argue with Aristotle? But I think there are some things you can't choose, Lara."

"Yes, perhaps, but I can choose what's right for myself. You said we always have a choice. Even Arnie; his was to say so lange für jetzt."

"Huh?" I asked, raising my eyebrows.

"You know, auf wiedersehen, goodbye, adieu, so long for now."

"You're sounding suspiciously like the Von Trapp children."

Ignoring me, Lara asked, "Anyway, isn't it all just a big jumble? Eventually, it seems that people find their way in or out of relationships. Confident people might have more stable ones, but who knows? Let's be honest, I'm hardly a reliable source for understanding romance. My record's scratchy. What's that verse? Oh, right, I've been through the mill," she sang.

"Ah, Judy. The Man That Got Away," I enthused, then regretted doing so.

"Huh...I'm always impressed with the number of Garland songs you know," Lara commented curiously.

"Guess I've heard you sing a few of 'em," I lied, then changed tracks. "So even with all the family stuff that shapes my personality - ultimately you're saying that we have a choice in how we turn out. We're not locked in just because of our family's patterns or behaviours."

"Free will states that we're more than that. Just wait until you're with someone. Relationships sort of - I dunno - highlight your behaviour in new ways." Lara finished her fries and sighed contentedly.

"At this point it's all conjecture," I said.

"Maybe now, Sunshine, but things change, all kinds of people get together," Lara said warmly. I denied there was any subtext to her statement.

"Tell me about it. I see 'em paired off everywhere, at school, at the pool, hand-in-hand on the seawall —"

"God, I see them on the seawall, too. Makes me insane! Just yesterday I passed a couple jogging in matching burgundy velour tracksuits. It was all I could do to stop myself from tripping them," Lara sneered.

"Um, yeah...and I guess I wonder if that might be possible for me."

"Oh, sure, just stick your foot out; they'll shoot right into the water."

"Lara, you know what I mean. Having someone - or maybe it's a series of people - to go through life with. Who said it has to be just one?" I shrugged.

"Clearly not me," Lara answered dryly.

"Why am I even worrying about it? I'm only just starting out, aren't I?"

"You're just a puppy," Lara said lovingly.

I smiled, exhaled and nodded in agreement, started to eat the last part of my mushroom burger instead of playing with it, happy to conclude this conversation.

"Going back to what you originally brought up, about confidence and sex," Lara paraphrased.

"Uh-huh," I said cautiously.

"Well, I've never asked you this before," Lara started, looking a little uneasy. "But, ah, have you been with anyone? Sexually, I mean?"

Hmm. Here's your chance, smartass. Be honest.

"Umm, sexually? I, uh...well, yes. I have. A few times." My mouth was half full of food, and I instantly became more than a little uncomfortable.

"Oh, I'm surprised...and you never told me? Who is the...no, I shouldn't ask. And are you seeing someone now?" Lara looked anxious to hear my response.

"Oh, Gawd, no," I exclaimed, horrified. "I meant that I've sort of, you know, had...sex. Just sex. Nothing more than that." I looked down at the table, cleared my throat, swallowed, took a breath, had a large drink of water and reached for the spoon so I could play with it.

"That's...great. I mean that's *really* great. I had no idea." Lara paused for a moment, looking stupefied and uncomfortable. "Will you see *them* again?"

"No, I don't think so. It's been...one-time things, if you know what I mean."

"Really? Wow. Huh. Don't take this the wrong way, but it's so hard for me to picture you with someone sexually. I guess 'cause we've been friends for so long. That must be it." She looked away, lost in thought, her brow furrowed.

"Uh, Lara, do you need to picture it?" *Am I that sexless that she can't even imagine me with someone? Someone like Wreck Beach Jim, or perhaps Pete?*

"No, of course not; how stupid of me. I'd just love to know who it was, though." I shot her a sharp glance. "Oh, you *really* don't want to tell me, do you?"

"Not now," I said. "I don't wanna get into it. Let's finish up and get some cobbler, okay? With ice cream." I stopped playing with the spoon and took a deep breath.

"Oh, Sunshine," Lara smiled at me and looked relieved. "C'mon, let's just pay the bill and go," she said. "Je ne veux pas le dessert plus. I'm not hungry for dessert anymore."

Frankly, I was a little dismayed that she couldn't conceptualize me as a scintillatingly sexual young man. Did my lack of confidence leave me without any sexual swagger? I was on the verge of telling Lara that in my rare free time I did some ribald things but didn't, of course. Instead, I opted for secrecy. I noticed that she referred to the other with whom I had sex with as not having a gender. *Kind of her. That's because she knows you're gay, you clod. Or maybe not. Do you know anything?*

17

QUEEN CHARLOTTE

Before graduating in the spring of 1979, I was constantly thinking of moving from the Mildew Manor and into my own apartment. I attributed my ongoing sinus congestion to the visible mildew in the peeling wallpaper and walls. The closet stank of mold and I began to think that I must have smelled the same. I'd been there long enough. Having saved nearly four-thousand dollars from guarding, I could afford a better living situation. I liked the West End for some pretty transparent reasons - there's safety in numbers - but also because it was so close to both Stanley Park where I liked to run and the beaches where I could meditate in the summer or bundle up and storm watch in the winter. The West End was the centre of Vancouver's gay community and within this small region, there was a growing social awareness and acceptance of gays and lesbians. When the time was right, it made coming out more than just feasible.

Beginning in March and whenever I had some extra time, I searched for rentals. I looked at several great places I couldn't afford and some that were near-derelict. A boy has to have some standards, even if I had spent nearly four years living in a moldy pit. Scouring the Westender newspaper, I saw a unit for rent on Nicola Street at the Queen Charlotte Apartments. Available April 1st, I dialled up the resident manager to view it. The pleasant-sounding lady stated I could see it at three o'clock. I fired up the Fastback and located the five-storey character building. I noticed the apartment had a Spanish Colonial design that I recognized from watching Hitchcock's great film Vertigo. That's where the spectacular Kim Novak fell to her death from the Mission San Juan Bautista - twice. Surrounded by walnut and tulip poplar trees, the apartment building's exterior was impressive. I could see the Spanish touches on the red-tiled rooftop, the twisted metal on the balconies and in the overall design. I'd never seen it before, probably because it was tucked away and surrounded by many trees. As I made my way to the front of the apartment at 2:58 PM, an older woman was waiting for me.

"Pleased to meet you. I'm Hannah McBride," she said, simultaneously extending her hand. Well-dressed in a pair of dark-brown tweed pants and a cream blouse, grey-haired Mrs. McBride was rather slight-looking, but seemed fit. Despite her last name, she had no Scottish accent. After just a few minutes of chatting amiably with her outside the building, I thought that Mrs. McBride, like the Queen Charlotte, had much character. She gave me a tour of the outside of the apartment, commenting on the history that she became aware of during her many years as the building manager. Mrs. McBride pointed out that the Queen Charlotte had originally been built as a new type of luxury hotel in 1928, but in time had been converted to twenty-five apartments. We went through to the lobby.

"All of the rooms were beautifully detailed with the best workmanship of the day." Mrs. McBride looked up to a badly patched piece of ceiling. "But now the old girl is showing her age." She guided me further into the tall and open entrance that had been designed to impress, albeit many years ago.

"It's beautiful still," I said, casting my eyes around what was once an elegant residence. Somehow its faded glory made the Queen Charlotte more charming. Compared to my eight-by-nine-foot unheated room the building was Versailles. And there was a special feel to the place. In addition to a beautiful wooden carved ban- nister and attractive stairway with threadbare red Axminster car- peting, there were original architectural details throughout. In the once-grand lobby with light streaming through the large windows, I had a sense of its past opulence.

"I think you'll like this, dear. Step smartly this way." Mrs. McBride took me to a handsome ornate brass birdcage elevator at the rear of the lobby.

"I've only seen this in movies," I said, stepping into the lift and waiting as Mrs. McBride closed the cross-hatched door.

"It's a Turnbull, dear," she said proudly. Inside the elevator were more polished metal fittings and a small, dark-red cushioned seat that flipped up against the wall to create extra space. She took me to the third floor, passing the levels slowly, its gears creaking with mechanical effort. The lift door clanked as she opened it and we stepped out into the wide hallway. Unlocking apartment 302, Mrs. McBride ushered me into a spacious, freshly painted unit with var- nished uneven hardwood floors. In the corners of the ceilings were intricately sculpted plaster mouldings. The large foyer led into the living room. French doors opened onto a narrow balcony. Facing south and west, afternoon sunlight flooded the apartment, with the sides of the tall trees brushing several of the windows. A white-paint- ed Adam fireplace centred the large room. Mrs. McBride showed me the bedroom; it was a good size, even considering I had no bed. The windows had lead in the design - and were spotless. They had been opened to air out the paint fumes; a cool spring breeze flowed through. The next stop was the galley kitchen; smallish, but there was a pantry closet that was substantial. The stove was gas and a white fridge stood on the opposite wall. I hadn't had a refrigerator since I'd lived with my family. This meant I could have cold milk, juice, vegetables and could keep food for more than overnight. Mrs. McBride led me through a second set of French doors into a modest separate dining room with a built-in shelf for dishes. I did have some hand-me-down multicoloured Melmac plates that may have been as indestructible as they were ugly. I continued to tour the apartment and was shown the bathroom where I wouldn't have to sit down to pee because of a low ceiling. The bathtub had iron feet and an old round metal shower-head. Being able to shower whenever I wanted and not just after swim practice was luxurious. The apartment was just affordable at $185.00 per month. Complicating things, I only had a few bowls, a radio-record player from the thrift shop, the odd utensil that my Mum had given me, my worn-out electric kettle and cardboard boxes full of textbooks.

"So, dear. What do you think? How does the apartment look to you?" she asked.

"Where do I sign, Mrs. McBride?"

"My, that is happy news. I must tell you that you're not the first to look at the apartment, but you are certainly the first I've liked. Have you someone to help move all your belongings, dear?" she asked.

After telling her that I didn't have much to move into the apartment, she kindly offered to give me a few things that old tenants had left behind. After I signed a tenancy agreement and gave her a signed cheque and a deposit, she took me downstairs to see if there was anything I could use. Though the lift went to the basement, Mrs. McBride wanted to show me the staircase to the same place at the rear of the building. Accessed by a long hallway, the staircase was made of iron that had a distinct green patina. As Mrs. McBride trod on the steps, her footfalls made a sharp metallic clinking sound that echoed through the room. We descended into the cool, dark area and when we reached the concrete floor she turned on the electric light switch. Bare lightbulbs on electrical cords inexplicably swung like pendulums, illuminating the space and created shifting shadows. There must have been a strong draft somewhere, though I couldn't feel it, for how else could the bulbs have moved? Past the laundry facilities were areas that were cordoned off with heavy drapes. The space was unsettling to me, but then I was not fond of dark cellars. I was glad she was with me and then I had a flash that Mrs. McBride - that sweet good-natured elderly lady - was going to butcher me and keep my dismembered body parts in a deep freezer. I was a little freaked out and my imagination was once more getting the better of me. The Queen Charlotte's bottom floor reminded me of my Grandmother's basement on Egan Street in Port Arthur. Nana's cellar was dank, dark and smelled from the vegetables kept in the root cellar. After my Grandfather passed away, my mother and I went back for a visit during the summer and I was sent to bed in the cellar. Nana's dressmaker forms eerily stood watch and my Grandpa's half-finished oil paintings were propped on paint-splattered easels, his grey rags in metal buckets still smelling of turpentine, as though he had never passed away. Nana refused to take the easels down. Those were fitful nights, turning over in my little cot, fearing opening my eyes, just in case I'd see something that I didn't want to. I imagined it was haunted by all manners of ghosts, one being my Grandfather. In the bowels of the Queen Charlotte, I allowed my fanciful imagination to conjure all manner of possibilities. Snapping back, I saw there were tables pushed against the walls, dusty chairs, sofas covered with sheets, old utensils, boxes and things I couldn't identify in the dim light.

"See anything?" Mrs. McBride asked, her friendly voice not succeeding in overcoming the discomfort that I had in a strange and gloomy place.

"Well," I started, looking around some more, poking at the crates, slowing moving around the huge room. "There's quite a lot of stuff. How did it all find its way down here?"

"You'd be stupefied at what people leave behind, dear." She added, "Over the years, things just accumulated. And of course, people pass away."

By your murderous hands, Mrs. McBride?

"We've had many long-time tenants at the Queen Charlotte." Hannah McBride blew the dust off a dark-red painted dresser. "We could have discarded the items, but I think there are many pieces that new tenants could find useful. I like that objects can belong to someone else once more."

"I see." *There, nothing wrong with that. She's being very helpful. What's wrong with you? How can you be so suspicious?* "Oh, that's a beautiful dresser," I said, spying a burled-walnut cabinet. It had brass handles and when pulled open showed six separate compartments for clothes with two bottom drawers. It appeared in excellent condition. "That's really a handsome piece."

"Isn't it lovely?" she said, admiringly.

Being bold, I asked, "Would this be something that you would consider loaning me?"

"Oh, dear, consider it yours. It's a relic, but it is a rather pretty relic. I'd be delighted if it found a new home in your apartment. It's quite heavy, though. You'll ask someone to help you?" she asked pointedly. Lara was going to have to help me with this piece of furniture. I'd have to make her a big dinner.

"Yes, my friend can help me," I said.

"Good." Mrs. McBride smiled. "Now, there must be something else here that you can use."

"I couldn't ask for anything else. You've been more than generous."

"Oh, stuff and nonsense. It's all collecting dust. A university graduate needs a leg up and I'm only too happy to help out." Mrs. McBride found a beautiful small round dining table with four chairs which I gratefully accepted. "Now, there's a chesterfield around here somewhere and it's quite upmarket." Mrs. McBride moved through the towers of crates. "Ah! Yes, here it is." She was moving towards a sofa covered with a white drop-cloth. Hannah grabbed the cloth and pulled it off with a flourish. A shaft of light illuminated the sofa, which had four large overstuffed cushions forming the backrest; sumptuous and stylish.

"Wow," I exclaimed. "That sofa's so plush."

The fabric was velvet; a rich, dark brown with a subtle pattern of teal and dark blue peacock feathers. Much later that it reminded me of the pheasants my Grandfather had painted and that I admired as a boy. The sofa was clearly well-taken care of, from a different age and none the worse for wear. In fact, it looked new. I sat down on it. It was firm but yielded comfortably to my weight.

"It's perfect! I really love it. You're sure I can have it?"

"Dear, of course. I'm glad you like it. It belonged to a lovely friend who lived at the Queen Charlotte many years ago. He's gone now, the sweet man."

"Moved away?" I asked, ever hopeful.

"Yes, in a manner of speaking," she said pensively.

I knew what that meant; I quickly stole a glance about to look for a freezer. *Don't even think about it.*

"I'm very grateful, Mrs. McBride." I stood up from the sofa and smiled at my rapidly growing possessions.

"Hannah, please. And you're welcome. I hope that you're very happy with us here." She looked left and right. "I know there's a bed here, too," she mused. "Yes, over here. No, that's not it. Help me, now. You're a strong young man." She moved to the other end of the basement. "Come over here," she commanded. "Move this away," she directed. I did what she asked, pushing some wooden window frames past to reveal a dull brass bed frame and a double mattress leaning against the wall.

"Mrs. Mc...Hannah, I can't possibly take a bed, too," I said, hoping that she'd contradict me. The bed frame was very attractive, if unpolished.

"Take it, you must," Hannah affirmed. "You can't sleep on the floor, my boy. Now you'll be sleeping in style. Some fresh sheets and a duvet are all you'll need. Is there a girlfriend that will be sharing your bed, dear?"

Her unexpected question caught me off guard.

"Oh no, Hannah. No girlfriend. I mean, I have a girl friend - Lara - but we aren't girlfriend and boyfriend."

"I understand. Perhaps a boyfriend, then?" she asked, not missing a beat, raising her eyebrows for effect. Hannah McBride was a wily one.

"No, no boyfriend, either. It's just me, ma'am," I stammered, turning crimson and thankful for the low light.

"Well, you're a young man." She smiled assuredly. "There'll be romance when the time's right."

Well, we'll see about that. So far I wasn't winning too many popularity contests.

Changing the subject, Hannah told me that I could collect the goods anytime and move into my apartment in April. Things were looking bright, however, down in the dark cellar of the Queen Charlotte, being around the items of those likely deceased tenants was grim. I noticed that Mrs. McBride was rubbing her arms as though she were chilled. It was cool and the lights didn't bring much illumination to the space. I found it oppressive. Suddenly there was a deep groaning sound - a pipe, perhaps. It unnerved me and she noticed.

"Now, unless you want to shop some more, let's go upstairs and I'll make us some hot tea. I'm chilled to the bone and I find it a touch sinister down here this afternoon. Don't you agree?"

The next week, I unceremoniously said farewell to the Mildew Manor and hello to Queen Charlotte. Lara agreed to help me load the antique cabinet and the brass bed-frame into the birdcage elevator and move it into my apartment. It proved to be quite an effort. The velvet peacock couch, dining table and the mattress were too cumbersome for her and me to move, so Hannah sweetly asked one of the neighbours in 206 - a surprisingly burly window dresser named Tommy - to help. I gave him ten dollars and together we hefted the remaining furniture up from the basement. The sofa looked terrific against the far wall, making space for the things I'd yet to purchase. To celebrate my new digs and to thank her for her help, I invited Lara for supper Saturday night. At a thrift shop I'd picked up a few kitchen items like pots and a frying pan so that I could make a meal. At the Super Valu on Davie Street, I bought a whole fresh spring salmon - a splurge - brown rice, green beans (which I hated but Lara adored - how can you eat anything with fuzz on it?

Perhaps I should rephrase…), breadcrumbs, salad greens, fresh herbs, red onions, peppers, feta cheese, tomatoes and butter-fried croutons. From the Paris Bakery on Denman Street I purchased a mustard-seed loaf of crunchy bread and Lara's favourite strawberry cheesecake with a lemon-cookie crust. I lugged the groceries back to the apartment, careful not to ruin the dessert. Thankfully, my mother had taught me how to cook. Mum believed boys should be able to prepare their own meals. She encouraged me to cook and to make as many mistakes as I needed to gain confidence. The importance of experimenting with new tasks can yield to greater confidence in many areas, even cooking. Mum must have been on to something - perhaps it's really all about practice.

Hurrying to my apartment, I unloaded the food and got to work. I combined grated lemons, dill, eggs, breadcrumbs, green onions and cracked pepper, stuffed the salmon generously and put it on a large baking dish. A few minutes later, I had the brown rice simmering in vegetable stock with dried cherries. The rice would be re-heated after the fish was done. The beans would be sautéed and dressed with toasted almonds at the last minute. The greens were washed, dried and placed in a pretty blue and yellow crockery bowl from my mother (her kitchen colour scheme from several years ago). I carefully placed the dessert in the fridge to keep cool. Like my mother (who wasn't Jewish but cooked as though she were), I had enough food for twenty-eight people. Lara did have a big appetite, but nevertheless I was relieved when she called me on my new phone an hour before dinner asking if she could bring someone over. As I spoke to her I discovered the length of my extension cord as I set the mismatched Melmac on the dining room table. Hannah found a few more pieces of the plastic stuff in the basement for me, adding to the questionable collection. The dishware looked oddly attractive on the table, I admired as I chatted with Lara.

"Of course," was my answer to her question about whether she could invite a guest. "The food's reproducing like alien pods in a bad science fiction movie. Who're bringing?"

"Well," she started to answer my question. "Funnily enough, it's someone that —" before Lara could complete her sentence I had a problem. The rice was boiling over and onto the gas flame, creating a giant cloud of steam.

"Oh, Gawd, I'm sorry, Lara, something's gonna explode - I gotta go. It's great that you're bringing a guest. Don't be late. Ring 302. Bye!" I hung up and raced towards the stove to avert a cooking disaster.

18

GUESS WHO'S COMING TO DINNER?

I was looking forward to my dinner date with Lara. She'd told me that her singing income had increased significantly, but didn't elaborate - that talk was for our dinner. Mostly she sang with just her guitar so she was limited to the type of place that would hire her, usually cafes and bistros. Occasionally there would be a pianist playing her arrangements which allowed her more freedom to perform. Regardless, Lara was always positive about her music dates. From her singing work plus waitressing, her rent was paid and other expenses were covered. *Pretty good.* No asks from her parents. Howie and Maggie withdrew their financial support when she quit university. *Understandable. This is her pursuit and her risk.* Lara explained to her parents that she could be a steadily-working singer in a couple of years. Her parents were horrified, unable to accept Lara's choice and told her so in a hurtful letter she'd shakily shared with me. As troubled as her parents were about her quest, Lara's commitment remained steadfast.

The buzzer blasted at 8:10 PM. I was unshaven but showered, wearing a pair of khaki pants with a salmon coloured (to go with the meal?) polo shirt and my usual bare feet. I opened the door to see Lara before me. Beguiling, smelling of flowers, her red hair was brushed back off her luminous face, her brown eyes warm and sensual. Her blouse was an amethyst silk, loosely covering her freckled chest and she'd cinched a purple and blue polka-dot men's tie around her small waist. Her slacks were royal blue and she wore high-heeled brown shoes, elevating her considerably. She thrust a bottle of white wine at me. I gave her a hug, kissed her cheek and brought her into my apartment. I took another appreciative look.

"Lara Jean, you look beautiful," I commented. She beamed.

"Oh, Sunshine, and you're so handsome in your pink shirt."

"It's *salmon*, Lara. Where's your friend, by the way?" I asked.

"Well, this is sort of funny..."

"Your friend couldn't make it?" I asked, worried about the amount of food I'd prepared.

"No, he's here. Guess who's coming to dinner?"

"Sidney Poitier? I hate guessing. Where is he?"

"Just when we came into the lobby an older woman asked if he could help carry an order of groceries up to her apartment —"

"Was she smallish and grey-haired?"

"Oh, of course, that's Mrs. McPickle, right?" Lara asked, futzing up the name knowingly and swiftly moving into my apartment. "I remember seeing her when I gave you a hand."

"I'm surprised she needs a hand with anything."

Lara plumped one of the big cushions and sank into the velvet couch.

"It's very chic!" she cried, taking a good look around at my spartan home.

"Very minimalist, I think they call it," I said dryly.

"Really, you've had a great help, haven't you?" Lara ran her hand across the sofa. "What is it about velvet?" she murmured to herself.

"Thanks to Mrs. McBride. You know, she furnished this entire place - the sofa, the dining table, the dresser; these chairs, even my bed."

"Of course I know. I schlepped all of it up here and almost broke my back for you."

*

"Yeah, from a basement right outta Edgar Allen Poe. I'm convinced that Mrs. McBride has a body hidden down there - maybe more than one. And listen, I've heard a groaning ghost in the cellar. She heard it too, I swear, but she didn't want to admit it."

"A ghost? Oh, Sunshine! You never told me about a ghost!" Lara laughed warmly.

"Well," I sniffed dramatically, "I didn't want to alarm you."

"It was creepy, but I don't think Banquo is lurking about."

"I don't think it's Banquo, Lara," I said seriously.

"Where do you get such ideas? By the way, dinner smells just...oh, here he is." Lara rose and went to the open door as her guest entered.

"You remember Pete, don't you, Sunshine?" Lara smiled and stood by him. "From Oil Can Harry's?"

Immediately I turned a deeper shade of the spring salmon being served for supper. Closing the door, Pete grinned and quickly strode over to shake my hand.

"Pete..." I managed to stammer his name.

"Great to see you! Still swimming? All finished school, I suspect?"

"Uh..."

"So nice of you to have me to dinner; unexpectedly like this. I hope it's no trouble." Pete pumped my hand vigorously. Aware of breaking out into an immediate sweat, I swallowed hard.

"No trouble whatsoever. It's great for you to have me, I mean for me to have you...here, of course," I stumbled, laughed uncomfortably and went to the kitchen. "What can I get you to drink? Lara brought wine. I have chocolate milk, lemon juice and for some reason, Hawaiian Punch," I said from the kitchen.

"What year is the Punch?" Lara asked facetiously.

I picked up the can. "Umm, let's see, it says best before 1987. Does that help?"

"Very much. I'll have wine, please...Pete?"

"I gotta go with the Punch," he called out. "With some ice, if you have it, Sport."

Uh, did he just call me Sport? He could call me anything he wanted. Pete looked good. Very good. His attire highlighted his slender body; form-fitting dark jeans, a blue and gold striped rugby shirt with a stitched emblem and a pair of expensive-looking moccasins on his feet. His watch looked pricey - in comparison to my $21.00 Timex. Raising my voice to be heard, I said, "You're in luck. I bought ice today, straight from the Arctic. Why don't you all get comfy? I'll be there in just a sec."

If Pete was uncomfortable he wasn't showing it. Probably because he wasn't. I dropped the bag of ice on the floor and spilled sticky Hawaiian Punch across the counter a moment later.

"You okay? Need a hand?" Lara asked.

"I'm fine, be there in a sec." I tried composing myself as I mopped the mess up. I opened up the Chardonnay that Lara brought, poured it into a tumbler, filled Pete's glass with ice and punch and brought the drinks to them as they sat on the couch chatting.

"So," I said. "So..." I repeated and then hesitated, not knowing what else to say as they looked at me expectantly.

"What do you think of the neighbourhood?" Pete asked, helping me get my needle unstuck.

"Oh, I really like it. I'm close to the beach and in a couple of minutes I can be running in Stanley Park. I'm over the moon to leave Mildew Manor."

They looked at me, towering above them with their drinks. I wondered if I sounded a bit too excited. *Over the moon? Who says that? Take a moment and calm yourself.* "Your wine and a big purple Hawaiian Punch for you, with ice." I took a deep breath. *I'm doing okay; relax.* "And the building is very interesting. It has a lot of character."

"Yes, there's no lack of charm here," Pete said, looking directly at me.

"Although I think the landlady might be a murderess," I blurted.

Pete raised his eyebrows, baffled at my comment. Lara made an attempt to explain my paranoia.

"He thinks that the landlady has killed her husband and some of the tenants, chopped them into pieces and stuffed them in the basement freezer," Lara explained to a rather startled looking Pete, who immediately seized on a golden opportunity.

"All *kinds* of things can get stuffed in a basement, can't they?"

I smiled at Pete, remembering our bathroom tryst. He winked at me. The panic was fading and I started feeling calmer.

"Well, truthfully, Mrs. McBride is outta sight. She's been great," I said.

"Yes," Lara agreed, "but I think she's got a crush on you, Sunshine."

"Huh? Whaddya mean? Mrs. McBride?"

"Please," Lara smiled, looking at Pete. "I've seen how she looks at you. And she's always calling you dear. Don't you notice?"

"She calls everyone dear, Lara. It's how she ends her sentences. Starts 'em that way sometimes, too. It's old-fashioned and… endearing."

"See? Now you're doing it! You'd better be careful or you're going to wind up just like her," Lara giggled.

"Mrs. McBride is a real sweetheart," I said in Pete's direction.

Pete smiled, toothy and impossibly white. "For a serial-killer, you mean," he stated dryly.

"Have you heard something?" I asked without guile.

Lara was watching me closely, ready to rush in if I needed assistance; so far, so good. Changing the subject, I asked, "So, um, what have you and Lara been up to?" I moved towards the galley. "And tell me while I toss the salad."

"Well," Lara started, "Pete's been helping me." Lara walked over to the kitchen counter where I was putting the greens into the salad bowl. Lara picked up a box of Tosca croutons. She opened the box and scattered some butter-fried croutons in the salad, helping herself to a couple and crunching them appreciably, and knowing Lara, hungrily.

"Helping you?" I asked.

"Remember that Pete specializes in talent development? He's been coaching me, sending me to clubs and events, introducing me to people. I've been working with a voice teacher a couple times a week. It's paying off. Pete's been talking to his contacts in the biz and selling me - musically speaking."

"Whoa, I didn't know that," I said with surprise. Lara was usually an open book. "Is that why you're getting more work?"

Before Lara could respond, Pete made his way to the kitchen and said, "Yes, without a doubt. First and foremost, she's got a great voice, but my job is to pull everything together, to help with the package."

I'd like to help you with your package. "Wow, that's super. You haven't told me what's been going on, Lara."

"It's been a work in progress. I've been keeping things under wraps until I was more secure. I didn't want you to think that I was all hot air. You know, like Arnie? No plan?"

"I wouldn't think that, Lara. It's great that you have a plan. How did you and Pete come together? I mean come to work together?" I instantly reddened at my unintentional double entendre. He shot me a knowing look.

"Pete has a phenomenal reputation and I knew I needed his help. So I went to his studio with my guitar and sang for him - 'Lost in the Stars', the song you like - and he agreed to take me on. These past seven months I've been writing my own arrangements for piano and for the last few weeks practicing with a trio. Can you believe it?" Lara stood up, eating bits of salad from the bowl. She looked at Pete warmly. I wondered - mentor worship or romance? Who wouldn't have a crush on Pete? I tossed the beans and almonds in butter to sauté on the gas flame as she continued to talk, watching Lara pacing anxiously. "Pete sees me as a cabaret artist - like Jane Olivor." Lara grabbed a bean from the pan and popped it in her mouth. "Mmm, delicious. So, we're bringing all these songs together in a two-set act. Right, Pete?" He nodded encouragingly.

"Yes. And in the meantime I'm working on getting her an important date, one where I can invite people to hear her sing. I'm sure she's going to surprise them. She's got a voice that is different from the rest."

"I've been listening to Lara sing for years. She's great," I agreed, dumping the beans into a bowl, "but how do you get people to really notice her?"

"Her talent has to be professionally showcased to the right people. I know how to ready her and present her so that she's in demand." Pete looked at Lara, who'd stopped pacing and was listening intently. "And, I'll tell you, it's easy to see that she's special. In addition to being able to sing nearly anything, she has something extra, in the voice."

"What is it?" I ventured. Lara was keenly paying attention to his response.

"Well," Pete pondered before continuing. "Her voice can be loud as a trumpet or whisper a high note like a cello. And beyond the technique, her singing hits us here," Pete said, pointing to his stomach. "That's what I can't describe. People have to experience Lara." Pete smiled at her. "Then they'll get it. And these next steps are happening very fast."

Lara looked contemplative as she listened to Pete's explanation. She swirled her wine in her glass and looked at me.

"Putting it another way, Sunshine, these next steps are a giant leap of faith."

Sensing a good segue I said, "Well, so are my cooking skills. Let's eat." I opened the French doors to the small dining room with the beautiful walnut table topped with a variety of Melmac dishes. I'd lit five or six small candles of differing sizes and placed them haphazardly around the table. The effect was soft and warm. Pete looked handsome in the flickering light.

"Oh, this is beautiful," Lara sighed with Pete nodding in agreement.

"I couldn't carry off my mother's panache when it came to a sophisticated dining experience, so I settled for the starving-student-swimmer-with-plastic-dishes look."

"It works quite well." Pete flashed a smile. Even by candlelight, his teeth beamed bright white and I felt a rush when he looked at me. Pete chose the chair to my left, across from Lara. I brought out the brown rice, the horrible hairy green beans with almonds, the mustard-seed bread and salad, setting them on the table. There was a pot of herb-infused butter for the bread and a generous amount of wine for Lara. I put a big tin of Hawaiian Punch on the table in front of Pete. "Nice touch, very tasteful," he said.

"Thanks. I hope you like salmon," I said as I collected the huge tray of stuffed fish from the kitchen and plunked it onto the table. "I cooked forty-six pounds of it."

"Wasn't it meant to be just you and Lara tonight?" Pete asked, sizing up the salmon and raising his eyebrows.

"Yes," I said. "My apologies. I'd usually have much more." Lara scowled at me then plopped some salad onto her plate. "Bon appetite, everybody. That's nearly the extent of my French." I passed around the fish, the vegetables and bread. Lara's plate was fully loaded in a few moments and she was looking eager to dig in.

"De bons amis et une bonne vie," Lara toasted, raising her wine glass.

"Ah, to good friends and a good life. Good one, Lara." I said.

"Oooh, it all looks delicious! And I can't wait to tuck into that dessert. I spied it in the kitchen." Lara looked giddy with anticipation. Pete and I laughed at her comment. For the next couple of hours, we also tucked into interesting conversations about the latest news stories such as David Berkowitz, a discussion about Conservative leader Joe Clark, who Pete thought looked like a depressed beaver, the death of John Wayne and the troubling state of Iran. Pete was informed and worldly-wise, much more aware of politics than Lara or me. When there was a break, I brought out the cheesecake.

"Sunshine, no Sara-Lee tonight. But it must have cost a small fortune," she said, glowing at the sight of the impressively tall dessert covered with strawberries, dripping with a sweet crimson glaze and sitting in a crisp lemon-cookie crust. I cut large wedges of cheesecake for Lara and me; Pete requested a tiny piece. The cheesecake was lusciously rich. Lara managed to eat the filling first so that she could savour the sweet crust at the end. Watching her enjoy her meal brought me nearly as much happiness as she had eating it.

"Lara must be a very good friend for you to make this special meal," Pete said, putting down his fork without finishing his dessert.

"Oh, yes, I'm nothing without her."

Over the dessert that Lara and I continued to eat, Pete told stories of some of the people he represented; he was a bit of a raconteur and had some terrific tales. After Pete finished theatre school in Montreal, he worked as a stage actor for about six or seven years. He came out to play Shakespeare's Macbeth in Vancouver at the Playhouse Theatre. There was a lot of hoopla about the production and his performance, but after the run was finished he went back to auditioning for parts he never got. He decided he'd stay in Vancouver for a few years. "But it was tough-going," he said, "and I needed to go in a different direction." For him, that meant promoting actors and singers - people with talent but without the support necessary to succeed. Times were just getting a bit better for actors on Vancouver's stages, which there were more of, including the new Art's Club Theatre on Granville Island. Pete used his background as a stage actor to full advantage. Working with his singers, he taught them to break down a song into acting components. Pete worked with Lara on her numbers to coax out any meaning that she was not accessing. Lara's confidence being what it was, she needed his guidance and mentorship. She seemed confident in Pete's abilities to move her along professionally. I realized that he was the first man Lara was involved with that I liked - really liked. The irony was not lost on me.

Lara and I stuffed ourselves with more cheesecake. Lara and Pete continued to chat across the table about people she was to meet when he moved his leg over to touch my bare foot. It was a gentle, barely discernible pressure against my instep. Whatever they were talking about, I couldn't say. I was only aware of the sensation of being touched, a man's foot on mine, slightly stroking it, a caress. I drifted back into the other reality, aware that Lara was talking and that I wasn't listening.

"...and so the song had to be completely re-scored in a lower key. I sounded like Cleo Laine with a head cold trying to sing that high note!" she laughed. "Oh, Sunshine, you must be bored to tears, listening to me."

I might look as though I'm in another world, but I'm not bored in the least.

Pete commented, "She always calls you that, doesn't she? Why doesn't she use your given name?" he asked.

"I dunno. What about it, Lara?" I started laughing along with her.

"Only when he's done something spectacular and I'm still waiting. *If it takes forever, I will wait for you,*" she sang out melodramatically, a little drunk and a lot off-key.

"Let's say you save what's left of your voice. Come on, let's go out for coffee. I've heard there's a place on Davie that's open late," I said, getting up to go.

"No, I wanna help you clean up this mess." Lara began picking up the Melmac and carrying it to the kitchen.

"I'll help, too," Pete offered.

"Please leave it." They ignored me and started carting away glasses, dishes, emptying food scraps, putting the leftover salmon in the fridge. In twenty minutes the clean-up was mostly done. I thanked them and told them I'd walk them out to the street. Lara first needed to make a stop in the washroom to empty her bladder of a considerable amount of wine. Pete and I had a few moments alone. Without saying a word, he stepped toward me, running his hand across my scruffy face, feeling the roughness, touching his fingers to my lips, moving closer still to kiss me, his mouth tasting of strawberries and cream. He ran his hands all the way down my back to my buttocks, then slid them into my front pockets and skillfully moved them towards my groin. I was completely immobilized; kissed on a muggy spring night by Pete. My head was swimming. He leaned into me further until I thought I might tumble over backwards. I felt his cock harden as it pushed against me. He took one hand from my pocket and put it behind my neck, pressing his mouth against mine - then I heard the toilet flushing. I released myself from Pete, stepped backwards, straightened my hair and wiped my lips. Lara made her way to the kitchen for a few moments then entered the living room where Pete and I were standing. I was flustered; I hoped she couldn't see how much. She looked happy and bright-eyed.

"God, that feels better! I'm ready to go. Loved dinner, thanks! Oh, I took a piece of cheesecake on the way out, hope you don't mind." Lara held up a giant wedge wrapped in tin foil and slipped it in her purse. "Sunshine, what a great night!" Lara embraced me then lightly kissed my cheek. "You need a shave; your beard's making your face beet-red." Lara grabbed his arm. "Pete, don't you think it's time you took me home?"

As they turned to go, Pete looked back and winked at me. I felt a twinge of confusion as I watched Lara departing on the arm of a man who'd locked my lips a few moments before. I quickly collected myself, picked my keys up from the small bowl on the floor by the door and walked Lara and Pete to the street. I said my goodbyes, came back to the apartment and straightened up. I started to undress, remembering to take my keys from my pants and to put them back into the bowl. I dipped my hand into the front pocket and as I retrieved my keys I also removed a neatly-folded fifty-dollar bill. It wasn't mine. Pete had put it in my pants with a magician-like sleight of hand when he'd kissed me. I shook my head and stood in the middle of the living room in my white boxers. Flicking off the lights, I took the rest of the cheesecake into my bedroom, plopped onto my brass bed and with a big spoon ate my way to caloric paradise. I stuffed the last of the cheesecake and strawberries down my throat, dropped my boxers to the floor and went to the toilet, sat down to pee and contemplated my next move.

19

FINDING THAT OTHER GEAR

After having an enjoyable night with Lara and Pete I should have dropped right off to sleep. But instead, I tossed and turned, preoccupied with how to come out. I was flat on my back fretting over all the options and then dropped off to sleep and woke, anxious that I might have overslept. I squinted at my watch; it was five in the morning. Stumbling into the kitchen, I guzzled some juice from the carton and fixed a high-carb breakfast. After brushing my teeth, I buzzed my face with the Braun, dressed in shorts and a sweatshirt, gathered my swim gear and headed to the pool. I had to drive further to UBC now that I was living in the West End, but in the early morning there was little traffic. At the pool, I stretched for a few minutes, glanced at the workout board, checked in with the coach, made some perfunctory greetings to some of my teammates and hopped into the water. Expertly avoiding others in the frothy, blenderized waters whipped up by a couple dozen swimmers, I warmed up and went into think mode. This morning's meditation continued the theme of the previous fitful night - coming out. I couldn't wrap my head around how to do the task or even if I could. After just one kilometre in the water I'd lost focus on my swim. I tried to get into my zone for the next portion of the practice; repeating sprint sets of 100 metres with diminishing breaks. Coach Lerner noticed my lethargy as I started the speed set.

"Hey, put some effort into it, kid! What's the matter with you? Pull hard, hard! C'mon! Find another gear!" Lerner blared, pacing up and down the deck beside the lane gutter. Lerner was right, I was sluggish and I certainly wasn't sprinting. I did a fast flip turn off the wall and renewed my goal - sprinting each 100 metres in 56 seconds with a 10 second rest. I was off the pace by 6 giant seconds; completely unacceptable. I got my head into the swim. Slipping through the water; nine 100's to go. The huge pace clock keeping time, barely seen through my foggy goggles. Breathing deep into my body, catching the water, pulling it backwards, legs and arms in sync and perfectly coordinated. Chest forward, balanced on the centre of my axis, seeing my body in my mind, picking the pace up with each extended stroke, kicking harder, whipping the water off my feet, propelling me faster. *Better.* I swam the next 100 in 58; next one at 57; next 100 on track at 56 seconds. *My arms feel powerful. It's like I'm still and the water's moving past me. Like I'm swimming downhill.* Something clicked, a switch going off in my head - finding another gear. More 100's. I dropped the rests. *I'm moving fast.* My confidence grew with each 100 completed; 55:50, 55:00, 54:40. Each pull a strain. *Quads burning with lactic acid; how many seconds? Can't see the clock.* The water was churning; my hips high, my body slipping through the water, arms pushing columns of water behind me. *No rest. One last 100.* I catapulted through the flip turn. I was aware of nothing but my breath, a deep breath from my toes, flooding my lungs, my muscles, driving my hands to catch the water, riding on the surface, the blurry black line beneath me. Coming close to the wall for the last turn - *flip now* - pushing off underwater and kicking deeply, thrusting myself through the water, my chest bursting for oxygen, no sense of time, just of pain, of driving forward, end not yet in sight, seeking the pleasure in the finish, in the completion. *How many more seconds? Can't see, where's the wall? There! Take one last breath, head down, stroke, reach for the last pull. Don't look up, reach, reach! Drive forward, pump hips, kick, do it! Reach, stretch, reach! Wall close, swim faster, faster! Just another second! Pull, pull! Touch!* I grabbed at the gutter, my chest heaving with exertion. I looked up to see Lerner standing in front of me, his face a scowl. *Shit, now what have I done wrong? I swam as hard as I could, for Chrisakes.*

"Hey, Stamp - way to go! You knocked off two 53:10's. I've been waitin' for this!" Coach Lerner pumped his fists with excitement, but his tone became serious and he barked, "Breathe for one minute thirty. We're gonna do it again. Let's see how fast you can really go!"

I'd never managed to push past 55:30 before. Suddenly - in addition to the quandary of coming out - I had a new problem. I'd swum the fastest 100 metres of my life. *How did I do that and how do I repeat it? The Nationals are in four months. After years of competing, I've got a chance at something bigger.* I took a deep breath, pushed off the wall and for the first time in my life repeated another set of 53-second 100 metres.

20

AN EARLY MORNING SURPRISE

W hen I swam faster, the expectation was that this was the new standard. Anything slower was a failure of me, my training or my coaching. Because I was edging closer to great times in several events - and not merely great Provincial or Varsity times - the coaching staff arranged for me to have an increase in my conditioning, including more time in the weight room, which I secretly disliked. The extra work *was* yielding results, and though my breaststroke had moderately improved, other strokes had become quicker and more explosive. I was steadily moving towards my goal: the 1979 Nationals at the end of the summer. The step before Nationals was qualifying through time trials in June at the Western swim meet in Edmonton. In the interim, I struggled with the pressures of having to train harder and swim faster. My coach's belief in me was important as my faith in myself was inconstant. I pushed myself and my coach pushed me and the rest of the team. For the next while practices were taxing - two daily trainings as before, with an emphasis in swimming the bigger distances; 5 km in the morning, up to 7 km at the evening's workout. I was often sore; shoulders, chest, back, quads - all were tender. I couldn't eat enough to increase my weight let alone maintain it. I started losing weight that I wasn't replacing with muscle. I was down to one hundred and sixty-four pounds on my six-foot frame. To compensate, I worked my upper body in the weight room and did extra work with the kick board; up to 2.5 km of my workout involved sets of kicking. I had large quadriceps and soleus muscles, so I exploited them as much as possible. A strong kick was used by me and every swimmer as a big weapon at the end of the final length of a race. Those swimmers who had put emphasis on a training kick often were the ones who climbed onto the podium. There's more power in our legs than our arms, but a super-powerful kick is short-lived and quickly burns out. Timing the kick is an important part of the overall strategy for winning races.

I had a reinvigorated passion for swimming, but I had let other things lapse. My Mum hadn't seen me for the entire school year. I phoned Lara Saturday afternoon, cancelling our planned Sunday afternoon movie, explaining I was valley-bound in the early morning. She knew how important my Mum was to me and how infrequent I'd visited. Waking up Sunday morning, still reeking of chlorine from the last practice, I had a long, steamy shower. Towelling off, I donned some Levi's from the dirty laundry hamper, slipped into a nice Oxford-cloth blue shirt, dusted off my brown loafers, brushed my teeth and headed out the door with bagels from Siegel's. Only mid-May, summer solstice was more than six weeks away and it was still dim outside. I forgot where I left the car the night before and continued looking for the VW, eagle-eyeing my way up Nicola. Walking past rows of apartments and what seemed to be thousands of cars, I spied my red Fastback squeezed between a panel truck and an illegally parked expensive-looking black sports car.

"Christ," I said, nearly five minutes after starting the search. I jogged towards the VW, unlocked the car and tossed the bagels in. Before I could sit down, I heard a man's voice shout, "Morning!"

Few people are up before sunrise on a Sunday in the West End. I mean, no one is rushing to church. Mostly people are in a deep state of unconsciousness, some helped to that state with a liberal helping of booze the night before. I turned my head towards the voice. *Pete?* Pete. Looking somehow chic and put-together before dawn.

"Hi," I called back. I closed the door and stood by the Fastback as Pete crossed the street in jaunty steps. He was dressed in dark blue cargo pants and a white polo shirt. I was pleased to see him, if very surprised. "What are you doing outta bed this early on a Sunday morning?"

His dark hair was lustrous and framed his angular face beautifully.

"What makes you think I've even *been* to bed?" Pete chuckled. "I haven't, not yet. Maybe you wanna join me?" He leered with all the sexual innuendo he could muster. He could muster quite a lot. *Gulp.*

"Good one," I smiled. "Only I'm on my way to the Bible Belt where they stone people within an inch of their lives just for asking that question. Perhaps you wanna join me?" I asked, only half-joking.

"Umm, think I'll pass," Pete said shaking his head. "But that other offer still stands." Pete the irresistible. Pete the charming. Pete, the man with face to launch a thousand ships and a dick large enough to impress the captain.

"I didn't know you lived here, in the West End, I mean. Or do you? I guess I never asked. So do you? That is…if…if…you wanna tell me." *Great. Stuttering to a certain death by embarrassment.*

"Vaseline Towers."

"I'm sorry?" I asked, bewildered at his answer.

"You know. I'm at Vaseline Towers on Beach Avenue. Thirty-five stories? Opposite the Aquatic Centre. Don't know it?" he asked, rather surprised.

"Nope." I stood beside the VW. Pete moved closer beside me.

"I assumed that every gay man has heard about Vaseline Towers."

"I gather from the name that residents aren't infants with diaper rashes?"

"Definitely not." Pete faced me, his breath smelling faintly of coffee.

"I see." I was clearly out of my league. "You hungry? I've got some Siegel's bagels in the car."

"Uh-uh," Pete declined. "I've got a big appetite for you, though."

"Never at a loss for words - amazing."

"Former actors don't like to drop their lines. So where exactly is this Bible Belt you speak of?"

"In the valley - Abbotsford. I not so fondly call it the Ditch."

"The Ditch? Doesn't sound like a place for a downtown boy like you."

"No, you're quite right, it's hideous. But she's expecting me." I glanced quickly at my Timex. "And I'll have to get going soon."

"And is she as pretty as you are handsome and sexy?"

Did I say Pete was charming?

"She's very, very pretty," I said drolly. "Sounds like Lara's doing okay," I said, quickly changing the topic. She'd told me that she and Pete had been meeting with several club owners with her first demo tape in hand.

"Oh, much more than okay. She's become exquisite."

Yes, that's a very good word to describe Lara.

"Really?"

"Oh, yes. No one I've represented has worked as hard. I've been stunned at her development and she's continuing to surprise me," Pete added.

I nodded. Lara was beautiful, talented and had a fantastic voice. Stunning was an accurate appraisal and she'd surprised me a few times herself.

"Even you might be astounded. I've got a hotel interested in having us do a show on Wednesday or Thursday night; I'm hoping for both. I was working on the contract last night. It's going to be at a place nearby. Lara's pretty fired-up about it." Pete saw my puzzled expression. Lara hadn't told me about any potential gig. "But of course Lara didn't want to jinx it by telling you about it," he added smoothly.

Hmm, Lara hasn't been sharing much about her work for months. Maybe we've all got reasons to keep secrets?

"Well, no I wouldn't her to jinx anything."

"Hey, sorry 'bout the other night," Pete offered sympathetically.

"Sorry? Don't think I understand."

"Well, I could tell you were startled to find me at your door. And we didn't have any time to really talk at dinner."

"Oh, no, completely understandable. And thanks for the generous donation, by the way," I said, referring to the money Pete had slipped into my pants. "You didn't need to do that," I said, thinking that I needed to get going. The longer I was standing with Pete, the more I wanted to ditch the Ditch.

"It was the least I could do. It was a great evening."

"Thanks. Did you want to talk to me about something before I head out?"

"Yeah, of course. It's the reason I'm beside you..." Pete moved closer, nearly touching me. He was fluid and sexy and charming and confident; everything I wasn't. "I wanted to let you know I was thinking 'bout you." Pete watched me for a moment. "You know, you're a quirky guy. You're unsure about me, aren't you?"

"Pete..." Of course he was right.

"But you're into me." Pete fixed his dark eyes on me like a laser. "I can tell at a glance."

'What a swell night this is for romance'...Gawd, a ridiculous time to suddenly remember a Cole Porter song. Get it out of your..."You can, huh? That's quite a talent," I said, trying to sound sophisticated and savvy. It didn't come off. Pete put his hand in my hair, ruffling it. I immediately flushed.

"I've got other talents, too, but you know that." Pete moved his fingers through my long hair from the crown to the nape of my neck. "You've got soft hair. Beautiful eyes, too. So blue...the first thing I noticed about you."

All right, he's complimentary, he's attractive, he's obviously found a way to locate me at 5:30 in the not-quite-bright morning - isn't that a bit creepy? Should I be worried? Maybe he's disturbed? Like 'Looking for Mr. Goodbar'? Am I destined to be found naked in my bed with a chef's knife in my chest and

Vaseline in my butt? Wait a second…I don't even own a chef's knife and all I've got is Nivea.

"You know, it was kinda awkward at dinner, sitting there with you and Lara not knowing about, well, you know. She doesn't know, does she? I'd be mortified if she knew that you and I…got together." What would Lara think about me going behind her back and doing it Greek-style with her agent?

"No, not at all. It's copacetic," Pete reassured. "There's nothing about our tryst that Lara knows about. Makes it even more titillating, doesn't it?"

"It makes me wanna vomit blood."

"That's a bit theatrical."

"Funny, I've been told that before," I said. "Look, it's just that I'm not out, if you know what —"

"Of course I know what you mean. I don't make it a habit of telling people either. Lara hasn't asked about me or for that matter, you."

"Good. I wanna tell Lara myself, in my own way, when I'm ready."

"Certainly. It's not my place. Mum's the word."

I relaxed a little. "Okay." *I'm not so freaked out now.* "And speaking of Mum, I really should be off," I sighed. I opened the car door a second time. It squeaked a bit. Climbing in and firing up the motor, I rolled down the window and asked, "Can I give you a lift somewhere?"

"No need, I'm right behind you." Pete rested his hands on my car door.

"Pardon?"

"Lara told me last night that you were going out to see your mother at some insane hour this morning. I was up anyway and thought I'd come by to catch you before you left. I grabbed a coffee and parked behind your VW and waited for you across the street. I figured I'd give you an early morning surprise. So how was it?" Pete grinned.

"Illegal," I quipped, not answering his question.

"Excuse me?"

"Your car," I said, pointing to his well-waxed black Porsche Carrera as I put my dusty VW in first gear and slowly angled my way out between his car and the truck in front of me. "It's in a No-Park Zone," I hollered above the engine's air-cooled rattle and headed out in a blue-grey cloud of smoke. I looked in the rear-view mirror. Pete was looking back at me, leaning against his sleek car as I hurtled down the street. *That was an odd exchange. What was the deal with Pete lurking about like that? How did he know the Fastback was mine? Did Lara tell him what my car looked like? Well, it's not like I can ask her.*

The car bounced over the uneven pavement on Davie Street. My leaky left tire fully inflated, gas tank filled to the brim, oil topped up, I turned left on an empty Burrard Street, turning right past the elegant Hotel Vancouver and speedily made my way east on Georgia towards the viaduct. Traffic was negligible and I clipped along, hitting green lights at nearly every intersection. Around me were the towers that had welcomed me several years before. Many new skyscrapers were changing the city's skyline at an outrageous pace. I went over the viaduct to Main and onto First Avenue, heading east for fifteen minutes before connecting to the freeway entrance just past Renfrew. The sun was low and bright; I put the visor down.

Perhaps I should have stayed with Pete instead of going out to the Ditch. We could have gone back to my apartment and talked or I could have made scrambled eggs and toast with some of that peach conserve my mother made. Get a grip, Betty Crocker. No...we'd probably wind up on my velvet couch, or better yet, my brass bed. Imagine...spending the morning naked with Pete.

I wasn't paying attention to my driving and drifted onto the freeway shoulder, then quickly brought the VW back to the centre of the lane. I dropped the Fastback into fourth gear, floored the gas until it accelerated to 100 kph - the new metric speed limit - and watched the speedometer climb up to 110 kph and cruised the Trans-Canada highway, bound for my parents' house.

21

GOING INTO THE DITCH

The drive out of the city heading east left me discomforted. In Vancouver, I was visible when I wanted and invisible when necessary. Motoring to the valley, I had a sense of unease and vulnerability, of my own conspicuousness. If that weren't enough, I blamed the town for the unhappiness and humiliation I experienced when I'd lived there. I thought about that and reasoned my logic was flawed. One group of people doesn't constitute an entire community. I should have directed my outrage toward the few citizens who had been violent and hateful towards me. Mine was an emotional reaction lacking in rational thought. *Still, after all this time it's hard to think differently.*

As my car clicked off the kilometres, I soon missed my Vancouver home. The Port Mann Bridge - a long graceless expanse of orange-painted metal and concrete - was the last vestige of the city before heading east for the seemingly endless drive to the valley. The Fraser River far beneath the bridge was murky and brown, winding around the communities of Coquitlam and New Westminster behind me. I carefully drove onto the bridge, watching my speed, looking forward, not caring to find myself hurtling down to the river a hundred metres below.

A visit to my parents' home was overdue. Even over Christmas break, I'd decided to stay in Vancouver and get as much work and training in as possible, much to my mother's chagrin.

The grey-green fields and the objectionable stench of farms was all that was noticeable during the tedious drive. Vancouver radio stations became static-filled and impossible to listen to the further east I went. Turning off the radio, I sang a few songs very loudly, trying to keep myself entertained for the duration of the trip. An hour-and-a-half after bidding handsome urbanite Pete good-bye in the sunny West End, the Fastback had transported me to the darkest, farthest reaches of the universe - Abbotsford. I took the exit off the freeway onto McCallum Road and was going into the Ditch. I know it's harsh that I call it that, and I should be more charitable, but I didn't like the way it smelled, appeared or felt. The feeling? Oppression. Not one of the better emotions. Boys like me knew all about that one. Still, my parents and my sister lived and made their lives there. *I'll put aside my reactivity for a short visit.* I motored through a tired-looking Essendene Avenue, made a couple of turns and down-shifted the Fastback to climb the steep hill on Hazel Road. As it slowed on the rise, I passed the spot where I'd been gay-bashed. A jolt of anxiety ripped through me like an electric current, recalling the night I was pelted with rocks. It was a brief sensation, and though it passed in a moment, I nevertheless noted the adrenaline that blasted my body and brain. Many years after the incident, my response took me by surprise. Perhaps it was a warning to always be vigilant?

A couple of minutes later, I turned onto Birch Street. Near the end of the road was their Cape Cod-style home. The well-nourished lawn was mowed in meticulous dead even rows - my father's work. There were flowers in hanging baskets along the side and the front of the two-storey home. Purple and white fuchsias, already in bloom, were trailing down from the moss-lined baskets and formed a striking contrast against the sunny yellow-painted house with white shutters. That was my mother's effort - colour and form. I was pleased to see the giant maple tree that shaded the house. A newly formed bright green, the maple leaves turned a spectacular fireball of oranges and reds in late October. It loomed large beside the driveway and its branches covered the top of the carport. I recalled the beautiful Pileated woodpeckers that spent many days and weeks thunking their beaks against the hard maple wood to create their homes. The morning breeze rustled the leaves as though in a welcome to me as I parked the car and walked to the entrance. *With all the rubes in this place, at least the tree was genteel.* Before I could chime the bell, the heavy panelled front door swung open and my mother was standing before me wearing a radiant smile and a long dark-blue terrycloth robe. Her blonde hair was in pink and blue velcro rollers.

"Oh, I heard the car! You're here! Come in right away! Wait! What do you think of the baskets?"

"Hi Mum, well, they're really —"

"Gorgeous, aren't they? And how was the freeway?" she asked, grabbing my forearm and bringing me into the foyer.

"The traffic was —" I stumbled over the door jam.

"Watch your step, dear. Light, according to CKNW. I hope you didn't have breakfast, did you?" Mum shut the door.

"It was pretty early when I —"

"Oh, then I'll make us something nice," Mum said, giving me a warm embrace and quickly ushering me into the foyer. She took an appraising glance. "You're not eating enough, are you?"

"Of course, Mum, but I'm swimming such dis —"

"I have a package for you! Canned salmon, toilet paper and jeans, two pairs. The kind you like, Levi's button-fly, size 32. They were on sale. Let's hope they aren't too big on you. Of course, I can tuck them in a bit, if need be."

"Mum, you didn't have to —"

"I wanted to! Is that the shirt I sent you at Christmas?"

"Uh, I guess it —"

"Yes, it's the Oxford cloth, of course; very nice with jeans. You could use a brown belt, though. Do you need one? I'll pick one up at Woodward's next time I'm there. Blue is such a good colour on you." Mum took her hand and ran it through my locks and said with disapproval, "You don't have hairstylists in the city?"

"Yes, of course, Mum, but time's been —"

"There's always time to get your hair cut, dear. It's nearly to your shoulders! You look like a pirate. All you need is a parrot on your shoulder and you're ready for the high seas. Oh, listen to me!" Mum spun her head upwards to the staircase. "Bill, your son is home!" My mother turned back to me.

"Come to the kitchen. I'll make whatever you'd like."

"Really? I'd love one of those big veggie omelettes with hash browns."

"I'll fix pancakes."

"Oh...okay, pancakes would be —"

"Have you seen the changes in the kitchen?"

"No, Mum, I —"

"Of course not. You haven't been home in a hundred years. Come see and let's get you something to eat, okay? What did you say you wanted?"

"Huh? Oh, pancakes are fine, Mum. I'll help." I was a little dizzy and it wasn't low blood sugar. It was a bit overwhelming to have one year's worth of my mother's love in a few moments of utter manic attention. But she certainly wasn't depressed.

"I don't know *what* your father is doing up there. He knows you're coming to visit. *Bill!*" she cried upstairs in a voice loud enough to wake the dead.

Mum and I walked down the long hall and into the recently redone red and white kitchen. The floor was tiled in white ceramic squares, the countertops were tomato red. The cabinets had been painted in a glossy white with red pulls. The red and white vertically striped curtains were offset by the horizontal red Venetian blinds. Another person might have made it look like an enormous candy cane, but my Mum had managed to make it all work in a striking and unusual way. It must have cost my father a pretty penny. I pulled out a large red bowl to mix up the batter and she hauled out the cast-iron griddle. There was fresh coffee in the Bodum, but I put on the kettle for some tea. The light flooded the kitchen from the east and illuminated my Mum's face. In her forties, she remained beautiful, her blue-green eyes bright and her fair complexion unlined; pale without makeup. Mum caught me looking at her and smiled.

"I like the changes, Mum. It's really different."

"Oh, it's a little bold, isn't it? But quite smashing." Mum looked approvingly at the stark colour scheme. "I went for something entirely different this time. It's very today, don't you think?"

"Yes, very today," I said, not knowing exactly what my mother meant. "It's great to see you - it's been a long time, hasn't it?"

She nodded. "Far too long. I've been looking forward to you coming out. Tea? Water's boiled." Mum beamed. I smiled back weakly, plopped an Earl Grey tea bag in the red and white mug and poured the water over top. Contrary to my mother's statement, I certainly hadn't come out - not in the sense that preoccupied my mind. I had a hard time convincing myself to trek out to the valley, but whatever the gulf of physical space, Mum and I always managed to be close.

I found the pancake mix as my father entered the kitchen. I was holding a red bowl and a box of Aunt Jemima and I put them on the counter. There was a slight half-smile from him, but that was pretty much it. Dad had on his golf pants - shiny orange polyester - and a white, lime and orange flowered synthetic polo shirt. I blinked a couple times. There was my father, brighter than the sun in golf apparel that could outshine Liberace in Vegas, and his man-loving son, wearing a blue button-down Oxford cloth shirt, jeans and loafers. We stared at each other. It was an interesting study in contrasts.

"Number One Son," he deadpanned. I never asked him why he insisted on calling me that. But we didn't ask each other many questions.

"That's quite an outfit."

"Got it at the Pro Shop. It's the latest. Wrinkle-free. Not a crease to be found."

"I can see that. So...how's the store?" This question was one I asked every time I spoke to him. I went to shake my father's hand.

"Hah," he grunted, running his free hand through his wiry thick silver hair and pumping my hand a few times with the other. "Sales could be better. It's hard, this working for a living," he responded. It was another one of his sayings (there weren't many) that he came up with routinely. I didn't pursue it further.

"Yeah...so you've got a game this morning?" I asked him without scoffing. Why else would he be in such a gaudy outfit? For as long as I could recall, my father had worked six days a week and golfed the seventh. Always on Sunday - he rarely missed, even if he hit balls off a driving range into the snow.

"I have a tee time at 10 AM. Precisely."

Of course you do. And you'll be there in your wrinkle-free Carmen Miranda outfit, on that tee, ready to play at 10 AM. Precisely.

"Good weather for it, quite warm," I ventured, once more collecting the bowl, dumping in the pancake mix and some tap-water and passing it to Mum. "For May. Apparently, there's never been a spring like it." No response. *Well, this is painful,* I said to myself, swallowing. I watched as my father pulled out a Buckingham's from the ever-present package kept in his shirt pocket. He lit it with his ancient stainless steel lighter, the kind with a cotton wick and filled with butane. He went through his ritual of dragging the smoke deep into his lungs and blowing strikingly symmetrical smoke-rings. He coughed a bit and took the coffee that Mum handed him - two sugars and a healthy dose of cream - in the same faded black and white checkerboard cup from years ago, spoon in the cup. He liked to stir it himself at the counter; twenty times around the cup. Not twenty-one and not nineteen. I'd counted a hundred times. Clink, clink, clink. I thought of grabbing the spoon from the cup and flinging it out the window in an act of post-adolescence defiance, but the window was closed and I was too afraid of his response. Instead, I coughed from his foul smoke and if he noticed, he made no acknowledgment.

"Mmm, now that's coffee," he murmured, sipping cautiously. He grabbed the paper and sat down. A twelve-inch colour television was at the end of the kitchen table. *Great place for the TV. That ensures no one has to talk during a meal. We should put it on a chair and give it a placemat.* I started getting agitated. *Well, I lasted a few minutes, anyway. No, try again.*

"So…you've been okay?" I persisted, willing myself to settle.

"Not bad for a man of a hundred."

"I guess it feels like that sometimes, eh?" *If all else fails, try sympathy.*

"You have no idea."

I had some idea. Okay, I haven't seen you in a year. I'm willing to ask you questions. Granted, they're tedious, but you have a part in this, too. Try asking me a couple of things. I'll talk. No questions were forthcoming. His smoke was an impenetrable wall. Mum was watching her son and husband from the counter, stirring the batter and waiting for the griddle to heat up. She knew the difficulty that my father and I had to exchange more than a few words. Seizing any opportunity for a getaway, I exclaimed, "I was going to help. Do we have any blueberries, Mum? That would be nice in the pancakes."

"Yes, they're in the fridge."

"Oh, not the freezer?"

"No, the fridge. They're fresh. Your sister bought them for me from a farm out in Mission. They were selling flats of blueberries from Chile. *Chile!* Can you imagine? I have a container of them in the crisper and I froze the rest of the flat."

Mum was deliriously delighted about the berries. *So my sister bought some fruit. What's the big deal? It's not like she gave her a sack of gold nuggets.* Lynda saw my parents frequently and lived close by. She had her own family now, a little girl just a year or so old. Our efforts to stay in touch with each other were minimal.

"It was so thoughtful of your sister, especially with all the terrible things going on."

"Huh? What terrible things?"

"Oh, I'll tell you after we eat. The berries were a special treat."

"Yes, really good of her," I conceded, curious about what was happening with my sister. Mum took a container of blueberries from the fridge and put them in a glass bowl.

"They're quite sweet." She placed the bowl of berries onto the red countertop. "Of course, I don't care for them much," she added.

"You don't like blueberries?" I popped some in my mouth.

"It's because my sisters and I used to pick them - wild blueberries - each summer. The brothers always found a way to weasel out of it. Your Grandpa would take us down to Wild Goose Lake and we'd spend all day picking little blueberries at the water's edge. We'd put them into metal pails until they were full - berry by berry; so tedious! They were tiny purple reminders of the Depression. After we'd bring them back home, Mother would spend the day putting them up in jars so we could have berries all winter for dessert, sometimes with ice-cream, but only when we could afford it."

"She put them in jars? Why didn't she just freeze them like you do?"

"Your knowledge of Canadian history is a bit lacking, son. What did they teach you at school? Most of us only had an ice-box. Fridges weren't affordable until after the war." Mum tested a teaspoon of water on the hot pan; it danced on the surface. "Looks ready," she said. "I'll add 'em to the batter now." She dumped the berries into the mixture and gently folded them in. "You liked blueberry pancakes since you were a boy. Of course, you weren't persnickety about food like your sister was. You ate anything I put in front of you." My mother opened the cupboard to get the syrup.

"Except *that* awful stuff. Maple syrup tastes like tree sap."

"That's not very Canadian of you," Mum admonished me. "And, my university educated son, it *is* tree sap."

"Yech. That explains it, then. Oh, Mum, I forgot. I brought you some bagels from Siegel's. They're in the car. I'll get 'em and you can have them later. I know you like them, right?" My mother looked pleased.

"Yes, sesame bagels? I just adore the sesame bagels toasted."
"Mum…"

"You always remember how much I love the sesame."

"They're plain, Mum."

"Oh," she hesitated. "I love the plain ones even more," she laughed.

"Mum!" I started laughing along with her. I noticed the pan was starting to smoke. "That griddle's red-hot. You don't wanna set your new kitchen ablaze." I handed my mother the pancake mixture. Mum turned down the heat and began pouring batter onto the griddle. It bubbled up immediately and started smoking.

"Oh, Aunt Jemima!" She grabbed a metal spatula and began flipping pancakes - charred instantly on one side and liquid on the other. "Christ!" she cried out, howling. The kitchen filled with billowing smoke, blueberry batter was splattered across the counter as the scorched flapjacks were flipped on a dangerously hot griddle. I turned the exhaust fan on, went to open the window and looked over at my father. He was resolutely stone-faced; would not join the fun happening five yards away. He kept reading the paper with the television loudly broadcasting the morning news. I looked at Mum, gestured at my stoic father and shook my head in disapproval.

In ten minutes, the three of us were seated in my Mum's red and white kitchen at the smoked-black glass table with bamboo and chrome chairs. In the middle of the table was a tall stack of blueberry pancakes. We put several on our plates, good side up.

Mum drenched her stack with butter and maple syrup. Dad did the same and we dug in.

"Dear, you're looking very thin," my mother commented.

"It's not intentional. I'm swimming five hours a day and my weight keeps falling." I tried scraping off the blackened part of a pancake.

"Maybe you're sick," my father stated curtly, looking up from his breakfast as his piercing hazel eyes met mine.

"Sick? No, of course I'm not sick, Dad." I chomped down on the burnt pancake. *What a stupid thing to say.* "I'm feeling just great. I have a lot on my plate, with swimming and work and hopefully grad school in the fall." *How about a bit of understanding? Stupid asshole.*

"That's good, Number One. I thought perhaps you'd come down with something serious." He drank his coffee and pecked at the burnt offerings. He looked unimpressed with his breakfast, then opted instead for another Buckingham's, continuing to fill the red ashtray. *Keep on smoking like this and you'll be the one coming down with something serious.* I stood up and opened the kitchen window wider in an attempt to rid the stench of cigarette smoke from my breakfast.

"Anyway, you haven't seen my apartment yet. I've got some furniture from the landlady. She's really been great to me; helped me out *so* much." *Unlike you, Dad,* I thought, with a touch of passive-aggressiveness. "Maybe you'd like to come by this summer and see? Spend the night, if you'd like. I've got a couch I can bunk on. It'd be fun. I could show you around the West End or we could take in a movie." I sat back down and watched my father's toxic smoke thankfully drifting out of the opened window.

"Yes," Mum said. "We'd love that, wouldn't we, Bill. Bill?" Mum pushed her plate aside and looked at her husband inquiringly. Father looked lukewarm about my offer. *You're going to say no, aren't you?*

"Well, summer's a busy time at the store. Maybe later in the year."

"Dad, it's not a trip to New Brunswick. It's less than ninety minutes on the freeway."

"I'm aware how long it takes. I've managed to drive downtown before. Another time," he said icily, picking up the paper and forming a smoke-free but nevertheless formidable barrier. There might not have been smoke rings in the air, but there was tension hanging between us.

"I'll come in," Mum exclaimed. "I'd love to spend some time with you in your new apartment." She stood up, gathered the plates from the table and started putting them in the dishwasher.

"That'd be great, Mum," I said as I stood to help her clean up. Dad stayed put as usual.

"And why not today?" she asked pointedly.

"Huh?"

"Why don't I go back with you this morning? Your father's golfing and I was going to be by myself. Yes, now's a good time." My mother looked contemplative for a moment and said, "I can take the Greyhound back home after visiting for a couple of days. I've got cash upstairs; always have some extra tucked away just in case, and, well... nothing's on this coming week. That's alright with you?"

Mum's enthusiasm was nice to see, but I was surprised at her assertiveness.

"Of course, Mum. It'll be great to spend time with you. Maybe we can go out one night. In fact, there's a chance that Lara will be performing at a hotel this Wednesday or Thursday night. Would you like to go and hear her sing?"

"Lara's got a gig?" Mum stopped cold.

I shook my head in disbelief. "Mum, you know what a gig is?"

"Young people aren't the only ones who know about music and nightclubs." She smiled widely. "What marvelous news. I'll toss a few things together after I tidy up." My mother turned to her husband and exclaimed, "Oh, Bill, there's all kinds of food in the fridge. While I'm away you can fix something, can't you?" Before my father could respond, she answered her own question. "Yes, of course you can." I helped as Mum wiped off the griddle, rinsed out the bowls and looked at her mostly cleaned up red-and-white kitchen. My father could boil an egg, but that was the degree of his culinary skills. Even though he had survived the last two years of

WW II, Mum often believed that he was incapable of making himself a sandwich and coping with a few days of her absence. Over the years, I'd tried my best to disabuse her of that notion. My father could easily exist on bread, butter, cheddar, coffee, cigarettes and Scotch and be eminently satisfied. He'd never starve willingly.

"Go get ready, Rose," he said flatly, barely looking up from the television. My father was the antithesis of excited. The more charged-up Mum would get the more impassive he would be.

"What a treat," Mum declared. "I'd better get these rollers out of my hair and make myself presentable," she exclaimed as she dashed upstairs to pack a thousand outfits into one overnight case. I cleaned up the rest of the kitchen and looked at my father. "Dad, I hope that you might come and visit, too. I can show you some great spots, maybe we can tour around." I swallowed dryly and managed to croak, "We could play Pitch and Putt in Stanley Park."

"You know that the store comes first, Number One. I've got the staff to look after plus the daily reports have to be tallied. There'll be another time."

As clever as I imagined myself to be at twenty-one years of age, I didn't have a clue about my father's dedication to his store. He was of a certain age when adventures with his son would have taken him away from his top priority and therefore would be perceived as an indulgence. I get it now, but then? Nope.

"Okay," I said. "I'll see if Mum needs help with anything."

I raced upstairs to my Mum's Cambridge blue and terra cotta bedroom. I found her blonde hair de-rollered and combed out, the scent of Aqua Net lingering unpleasantly in the room. Dressed in ivory pants and a navy-blue cotton blouse, she was examining several outfits laid out across the bed. *That was a lightning-fast change. I wonder if she'd planned this out ahead of time?*

"What do you think of this one?" she said, pointing at a black and gold flower-print dress. "I have a gold belt somewhere to wear with it."

"It's very elegant."

"Yes, or else I have this outfit. I want to look smart when we go to see Lara." My mother gestured at a black crêpe pantsuit and looked at me with raised eyebrows. "Your opinion?"

"Hmm, both are nice, but I'd bring the dress. Mum, you're just going for a couple of nights, right?" I looked at the spread of clothing. Ignoring me, Mum put the pantsuit and the dress on top of her luggage and said, "Oh, and the tan slacks - that's my foundation. Pass them, will you?"

This will be fun for her. Let her take whatever she wants. Stop being so controlling. "Here, Mum." I handed the slacks to her as she carefully placed them on the bed with several blouses and a half-dozen cotton tee-shirts of various colours and patterns. "Mum, is Dad alright with you going away? He's so grumpy."

Mum was putting some accessories together; scarves of blue, green, dark orange, some belts, pearls, earrings and several pairs of shoes.

"Grumpy? When isn't he grumpy these days?"

"Are there any problems with the business? He didn't talk about it much."

"It's fine. He's obsessed with the store. He doesn't trust that the staff can do the work if he's not there - not true, of course. It's the store first and golf on Sunday second. But that's nothing new." Mum was opening drawers, taking out belts, stockings, jewelry; putting them out on the bed, reviewing them and then returning some to the dresser.

"He's smoking a lot more than I recall," I said.

"First thing in the morning and last thing before bed. He says he's going to quit and makes feeble attempts but in a few days he's so irritable I shove a smoke in his mouth and pass the lighter. He's too miserable without cigarettes. Don't forget, your father's been smoking since he was thirteen."

"Jeez. Unbelievable. What about the —"

"Don't ask me about the Scotch," she stage-whispered, reading my mind.

"That's horrible, Mum. He'll get ill. Maybe that's why he's so snarly. Has he told you he's not feeling well?"

"Your father complains all the time; endless aches and pains. He eats aspirin like it's candy and drinks Bromo Seltzer like soda-pop." She held up a pair of gold shoes for my opinion.

"Classic." I nodded my approval.

She smiled and put the shoes in a side compartment of her luggage with a bewildering supply of make-up. I continued to think she was suspiciously well-prepared for a spur of the moment trip.

"Well, he doesn't seem to wanna say much to me," I said.

"No, it's not you. Your father never had the gift of gab, you know."

"That's an understatement."

"And as he's gotten older he shares even less."

"Even with you?"

"Oh, especially with me. He mostly chats with his golf buddies," she sighed. "And with me, he's quiet as death. Your father's so maddening at times. I think it'll be good for me to be away for a bit. Frankly, I think he's delighted to have some time alone."

"He is? How can you tell? Delighted or depressed he's the same."

My mother held two sweaters against her face.

"The chartreuse merino or the blue raw-silk knit?"

"The blue knit. Chartreuse makes you look like you've got hepatitis."

"I'll take the knit," she said, folding the sweater neatly.

Mum was putting the finishing touches on packing her items and wasn't interested in speaking further about my father; she was excited about her time in town.

"We're going to have a great visit. We'll do whatever you like. We can visit Stanley Park if the weather's nice. It's nearly in my backyard."

"I'd love to go to Eaton's. There's a big sale on, you know."

Doesn't anyone want to go to Stanley Park?

"Eaton's, wherever you'd like to go. I know my place isn't exactly Shangri-La, but I'm sure we'll have fun, okay? I can even take you to a singles bar on Richards Street I've heard about. You know, a meat market," I blurted.

"A meat market?" My mother looked curious.

"Well, now that you are Dad aren't getting along maybe you'll have a fling."

My Mum rolled her eyes. "A fling? Don't be daft. Men out for a fling want girls that look like Farrah Fawcett or Catherine Deneuve."

And some men want a fling with boys that look like Al Pacino or Harrison Ford.

"Mum, it's not like you're dead. Pack extra war paint! You're still a looker. Bring something low-cut, maybe that red dress, something to show off your boobs! You'll get picked up in a flash!" I gushed. Mum looked at me as though I'd lost my mind and shook her head in disbelief.

"Sometimes I wonder what I gave birth to."

"Honestly, sometimes I wonder the same thing." From the bed, Mum lunged at me and tickled my armpits and hysteria ensued, relieving the disquiet of being in my parents' home. After a few moments of frenzied fun, she gathered up her camel coloured bag and zipped it closed. Satisfied with her choices, she asked me to take her bag downstairs. If the upstairs hilarity was heard by my father in the kitchen, he never commented as we reappeared red-faced and slightly exhausted. He was sitting, chain-smoking his Buckingham's and watching television.

"Well, we're off, dear," Mum said with half-contrition, picking up the cardboard box with food, toilet paper and jeans meant to go back with me to Vancouver. Smirking at her suitcase, make-up bag, an overstuffed purse and with more than a trace of sarcasm my father asked, "Sure you have everything?" He didn't say how lovely his wife looked: hair done, fresh make-up, dressed stylishly for her city sojourn. Mum didn't respond, instead raising her eyebrows and slightly pursed her lips in displeasure.

"We didn't have much of a chance to visit," my father said, looking back at the television. Mum observed quietly.

"No, but we can still have a talk now if you like." *Please, say no.*

"Well, I'm off soon myself. Got a game with Chip."

Why do all your golf buddies have names like Chip and Butch and Ciggy and Porky? "Oh, right, at 10 AM. Well, have a great game." I started to walk towards the kitchen door with Mum beside me.

"Take good care of your mother."

I stopped and dutifully turned back and waited for the routine to start.

"I will, Dad."

"How's that Kraut-can running?"

"Um, my *car?* It's fine, Dad."

"Tires?"

"Inflated, tread's good."

"And the radiator?" My father's trick question.

"*Dad.*"

"When have you last changed the oil?"

Ah, the oil question. I took a deep controlled breath.

"Just last week, Dad," I lied. "Every five thousand miles, just like you told me."

"How's your cash situation?"

My mother spoke before I did.

"He's fine, Bill. He's working at the pool, remember?"

Dad ignored her. "Well? How is it?" he persevered.

"I'm flush."

I should have said, 'Thanks for asking', but couldn't manage it; the words refused to be uttered and froze in my throat. My guard was up, always up. Why was it so difficult?

Mum came over and kissed my father quickly on the lips. "See you in a few days. I'll call you before I come home so you know when to pick me up at the bus station," she said and briskly walked out the door with me labouring to carry her impossibly heavy suitcase. I smiled at Dad. "Three days and thirty-six outfits," I said off-handedly.

"Typical woman," he stated dryly.

Yeah, nice one Dad. Lara would just love to hear you say that.

"Bye Dad," I grunted as I heaved my mother's luggage out the door.

"Number One."

22

DESIGN BY ROSE

I've had many good conversations with my mother in the car. After all, we were strapped into a hulk of metal hurtling down the freeway at a high speed. Anything could happen, so why not be forthright? About most things. On the way back to Oz, Mum gave me the news about Lynda. Her relationship with her husband Stewart was in rough shape. The birth of their daughter didn't improve the situation. Mum told me Lynda's husband was having an affair for the past several months. I was taken aback.

"You're kidding. Do you think it's true?" I asked.

"One hundred percent. Several people have seen him and the other woman pawing each other in the mall Food Court."

"Gawd, the Food Court?"

"At the Orange Julius. Apparently, there's —"

"No accounting for taste? And does Dad —"

"I've told your father; he wasn't surprised in the slightest."

"Who's the woman?"

"We don't know yet."

"I assume that Lynda's aware of —"

"I'm not sure what she knows. I haven't uttered a word about this to your sister."

"You haven't? When will you, Mum?" *What are you waiting for?*

"Actually, I'm not sure it's my place," Mum said plainly.

Hmm, that's either respecting your daughter's privacy or merely being ill-equipped to have a conversation that would be deemed as difficult.

"Well, who's place is it?" I asked sharply.

"You're the psychologist, perhaps you should speak with her?" Mum asked as we sped along the freeway in light traffic on an increasingly warm spring morning. I rolled down the window and the Fastback became a wind-tunnel.

"Mum, I'm not a psychologist," I said raising my voice to compensate for the roar of air rushing into the cabin. "I think you're the one who should speak with her. She wouldn't listen to a word her little brother had to say, especially about an affair. And Dad's certainly not going to do it."

"Your father? When pigs fly," she snorted. "I suppose that I could broach the subject. And you really think that's best?"

"Well, let's say that Dad was sleeping with another woman. Wouldn't you want to be told?" I asked.

"Yes, certainly. And I wouldn't rest until I found out where she lived."

"That'd be important?"

"Of course. How else would I know where to send the fruit basket?"

I gasped slightly and my mother added smugly, "And then I'd be on the next flight to Paris. First class, champagne included."

"Mum," I mildly protested, chuckling under my breath. "Paris? But then what would you do?"

It was farcical. My father would never step out on my mother. Who would have my father? The non-stop working, complaining, drinking, smoking and golfing? That's the kind of catch a woman wants to throw back immediately.

"All right, how should I approach this?"

"Mum, I'd tell Lynda what you've heard - that Stewart's romantically involved with another woman. Even if it hurts her, even if she didn't want to know, even if she does know. She'd at least be informed by her mother rather than hearing it from - I don't know, a friend of a friend who saw them making out at an A & W."

"It was an Orange Julius," my mother corrected me.

"Whatever. It's so degrading. I assume she'll leave him? It would be rough now that she's got a child. She'd have to go back to working full-time."

"Oh, I could do the child-minding, if it came to that," Mum casually offered.

I swerved from the centre of the lane. "Watch the road," my mother said with alarm.

"You can't be serious. That would be a huge commitment, Mum," I said. *And yet another huge mistake.* I thought of when Lynda got married. Dad told her moments before he was to walk her down the aisle, "We can stop this wedding right now. You don't have to go through with it." Lynda burst into tears, and certainly not tears of happiness. She was enraged that her father disapproved of her partner choice - right up to the last moment. Wicked of Dad? Possibly, but his instinct that Stewart was a poor match for Lynda was prophetic. Mum's statement brought me back.

"Yes, but we'd figure it out somehow. That's what families do."

An hour later I exited the freeway via First Avenue and headed west, leaving the VW chattering in top gear. By the time we'd zipped our way through Pacific Boulevard and into the West End, I could tell how worried she was about my sister's predicament. I started feeling bad for Lynda's situation. I wanted to help but knew my limitations. Motoring along Beach Avenue and crossing Thurlow Street, beautiful English Bay became visible, spreading west and north, the blue bay dotted by early-morning sail boats and distant red freighters waiting to get into port. People were already out, enjoying a walk or run. I drew a deep, calm breath, relieved to be home. Several minutes later I parked a half-block away from my apartment. I gathered up Mum's luggage and left the other box of items for later. As both April and May had been much warmer than normal, most trees were fully leafed in dark green. There were masses of flowers in pots, window boxes, baskets and beds, lighting up the street. I loved watching spring unfold for the promise of what summer might bring.

"This is it," I said and gestured to my apartment building bathed in dappled light. I gazed around quickly, half-wondering if Pete was hiding in wait behind the foliage, ready to pounce. How would I explain that?

"Oh, it's so charming! Let's see your new apartment!" Mum's excitement was like my own when I first saw the Queen Charlotte. We walked up the tiled steps to the heavy teak and brass double-door with me toting her luggage. We stepped through the entrance and into the lobby. Mum right away noticed the high ceilings, the ornate crown mouldings and the brass finishes.

"So lovely," Mum said, gazing at the lobby.

"Wait, Mum, whaddya think of this?" I asked as I led her down the hall to the birdcage elevator.

"I haven't seen one of these in years. Not since we left Port Arthur. Is it safe?"

"Yes, of course it's safe. Fully operational," I said as I hauled the luggage and ourselves into the small space. I shut the cage door and pressed the button for my floor. The lift jerked and we slowly descended. "That's odd," I said, hitting the third-floor button. "We should be going up."

"Is it always so dark in here?" Mum asked as the remaining light faded with the wobbly descent.

"No, the bulb's burned out." The lift made a clanking sound.

"Good grief." Mum was unnerved as the elevator lurched shakily to the basement. We peered through the birdcage's frame and into the blackness. Outside had been so bright, and my eyes were not quickly adjusting to the darkness of the elevator nor the cellar.

"I don't wanna scare you, but I've heard a ghost moaning down here," I whispered in my mother's ear half-jokingly, pressing the third-floor button several times. Suddenly, the brass door swung open and I was astonished when a horrifyingly white face appeared from the blackness and quickly came towards us. Mum loudly gasped in terror and placed her hand over her mouth.

"Gawd!" I hollered.

"Oh, so sorry, dear! How terrible! I was just coming back upstairs. Heavens, I can see I've caused a fright." She glanced at the lift's ceiling. "Is that light out again? I'll have to fix that." Mrs. McBride looked at my stunned mother. "And who's this with you, dear?"

My heart thudded in my chest as I answered, "This is my mum, Rose, Mrs. McBride."

"How nice to meet you. And it's Hannah, of course," Mrs. McBride said brightly. She stepped into the elevator, extended her hand to my mother who shook it and smiled wanly.

"Your son has said such pleasant things about you." Mrs. McBride took a quick look at my mother's luggage. "How long shall you be staying at the Queen Charlotte?" she inquired. Before my mother could answer she said, "Oh, silly me, let's move this old thing along, shall we?"

I couldn't have agreed more. I closed the brass door, she pushed the third-floor button and we ascended, the mechanical workings shuddering with effort as we slowly passed each level. The lift took us to our floor and we stepped out.

"This way," I said to my mother, fishing my keys from my pants and juggling my mother's suitcase. "Here we are. We'll see you later, Mrs...Hannah."

"Yes, yes. So nice to meet you, Rose. You must have tea with me while you're here at the Queen Charlotte."

"Well...I'm afraid it's just a short visit this time." Mum had other plans.

"Oh, then I must tell you here and now what a treat your son is. Helps me whenever I ask and even when I don't. And a talented swimmer! I see him coming back from his practice looking so full of vitality. Exercise is important for young people. Puts them right, don't you think? Runs in the family?"

"Uh, do you mean —" Mum started.

"Were you also an athlete like your son, Rose?"

"Me? Oh, no, Mrs. McBride." Mum explained, "Unless marathon shopping in high heels counts," my mother said seriously.

"My, how clever! Do enjoy your stay with us. Bye, bye dear!" Mrs. McBride sharply turned and walked away, chuckling down the hallway to her apartment in 308.

"Does she think we're all living in a hotel?" Mum whispered with an arched brow.

"No, I think she's just proud of the place. She's managed it for years."

"And what on earth was she doing alone in that dark basement?" Mum asked quietly as we went down the corridor.

"She's always taking things down there and likes to root around. It's a treasure trove. Wait till you see the stuff she's given me." I dropped my mother's heavy satchel and unlocked the door. "Here we are," I said, swinging open the door and bringing the luggage and my mother through to the cool apartment. I'd opened the windows before leaving. After my stint at the Mildew Manor, I couldn't get enough fresh air.

"It's sunny and bright, isn't it? And surprisingly spacious." Mum moved towards the tiny terrace. "And you have a balcony, too. Wonderful to sit - oh, it's quite narrow. Perhaps you could stand out in the morning for your coffee."

"I don't really drink —"

"A Juliet balcony. It's meant to give a certain appearance from the outside," she said, taking stock of the apartment, "but it also makes for much more light." She spotted the dining room table. "This table is gorgeous. It's an expensive piece. The landlord gave it to you?" she asked as she ran her hand across the smooth finish.

"No, the landlady, Mum. Mrs. McBride."

"And Mr. McBride?"

"There is no Mr. McBride, unless she's got him stashed in the basement freezer."

My mother frowned. "What a horrible thing to say."

"Murder's a horrible thing, Mum."

She disregarded my statement and asked, "The couch is unusual, isn't it?" She glanced quickly around. "And with so many windows, sheers would soften the light."

"Sheers are for geriatrics," I said flatly.

"Like me I suppose? You'll need a bookcase," she stated, seeing my texts stacked on the floor. "A coffee table and a couple side tables, too. And some art on the walls. There's no life without art, is there?" Mum walked into the kitchen. Peering into the fridge, she was aghast at the lack of food. "No wonder you're so thin. There's nothing to eat in here."

"Mum, please. I'm not thin and I haven't gone to Super Valu yet."

Opening the cupboards, Mum commented on the lack of cutlery, pots and pans. Spying my dishes, she winced. "Melmac? For a picnic, maybe." Wandering to the bathroom, she noticed that I had two mismatched towels taken from last year's swim meets. "I think we can do better," she said optimistically. In the bedroom she was impressed with the cabinet and gleaming brass bed but was distressed at the cover and the sheets; though laundered, both had seen much better days. After pulling out a pen and paper from her purse, Mum did a ten-minute tour solo, coming back to find me sitting on the kitchen counter.

"I've taken an inventory and a shopping trip is in order. Today." She took another appraising look around the apartment and noticed the slightly grimy tile kitchen floor. "What are you washing your floors with?"

"Uh…"

"And Javex as well," she said gravely.

"Mum," I protested slightly, "a lot of purchases aren't in my budget this month, or next month. You're going to have to just rough it for a couple of days. We don't need anything for us to have a good visit."

"No, we're going shopping. I want to pick up some things for you."

"Mum, I —"

"Call it a housewarming. Woodward's has an amazing bargain floor. Marked-down goods of every description. I insist, and there's to be no question about it." My mother was heading towards the door.

"Okay," I relented, following her. "But let's not go overboard. I don't want you to spend all your money on me."

"Don't be ridiculous," she said, taking my elbow as we headed out the door. "It's your father's money, and spend it we will."

Before our shopping trip, we decided that a full stomach would be necessary for the anticipated exertion, so we had lunch at Hamburger Mary's on Davie Street. A funky new 50's inspired diner, it had a near-ly-exclusive gay clientele. I think Mum was too interested in visiting with me to notice the handsome men all around us. Our server was an older bald man with a giant black moustache. He wore a pair of leather suspenders and faded, very snug jeans; so snug I could con-firm he was circumcised. My mother was talkative with him, though I was afraid the conversation might tip towards discussing who lived in the gaybourhood. After our lunch of baked macaroni and cheese, we left for Woodward's on Hastings Street.

With an enthusiastic step, Mum pushed through the revolving doors and entered her place of devotion - the department store. On the bargain floor we jostled with the crowds and within a couple of hours had picked up a thick green comforter (Mum said it would look beautiful against the brass of the bed-frame), quality white sheets, pillows, plates in eggshell to set off the table, a set of stylish cutlery, a cast-iron frying pan, cotton napkins, ceramic mixing bowls, food storage containers and stainless steel pots and pans. I hauled all the goods back to the Fastback and went back for round two. She found a beautiful yellow and blue cloisonné vase, heavily discounted and as my mother emphatically stated, perfect for the bedroom cabinet. We shopped around in the discontinued furniture area and found a handsome oval glass coffee table, a pair of glass and chrome lamps and side tables; those items to be delivered on Monday. My mother took out her Woodward's charge card and I worried at the cost. After all that effort we went to the bustling Woodward's Food Floor. It was an amazing cornucopia of everything edible and inedible, including bleach. In a frenzy, Mum whipped round the aisles, filling the cart to the brim with peanut butter, sugar, cereal, canned beans, tuna, butter, bread, vegetables, rice, pasta, oats, dairy, ready-made items from the deli, fresh fish and enough poultry to start a fried chicken franchise.

"Mum, enough already. If I eat all this stuff I'm gonna look like Shelly Winters in the Poseidon Adventure."

"Really," she sounded slightly imperious as she struggled to push the overloaded cart to the check-out. "A boy has to eat."

On Sunday, I didn't have swim practice nor did I work. It was clear and warm - a perfect day for going for a run or taking it easy, but I'd done nothing of the sort with my Mum visiting me. With much effort we brought back all the merchandise to my apartment. She ousted the old bedding and replaced it with new. The kitchen was filled with food, an array of bowls, dishes and gadgets. After getting the purchases put away and organized, we made a dinner of broiled chicken, roasted potatoes and fresh spring asparagus, my favourite veggie, though Mum was allergic to it. She had white wine with our meal; I stuck with water. Mum made my best-loved dessert; apple crisp with cinnamon and allspice. Sated from the meal I stretched out on the couch. It was getting late; I started getting ready for bed. In the living room, I shook out the new cocoa-brown woven cotton blanket that Mum bought me. I'd be sleeping under it and on the sofa for the next few nights.

"Thanks, Mum." I expressed my gratitude with a hug. "You whirled around like a Kansas tornado today."

She sat down on the sofa and sighed. "I'll tell you something, sweetheart. When Lynda was married, your father and I helped them with a down payment, bought them a washer-dryer and paid for half of the wedding. But we haven't done much for you. I've been wanting to help you with some things, but your father thought that we should wait until you finished school. He said it was good for you to know what it's like to struggle, you know, like he had. You've been working and swimming so hard to get through university. Now you've got your own home. Why wait further? That's why I'd hoped to come back with you this morning. I wanted to set things up for you, give you a start, at least in a small way."

"In a big way. You're a great Mum, the best."

"Well, I don't know about the best, but I'm not half-bad." She smiled and looking pleased with my compliment.

Yawning, I said, "Sorry but I'm pooped, and five o'clock comes pretty quickly."

"I remember," said my mother, who never saw 5 AM in her life, not fully awake anyway. "I don't want to kick you out of your bed. I'm fine sleeping on the couch," she said. "Really, I'm sure that I'd find it quite comfy." The only time my mother slept on a sofa was for her daily naps.

I shook my head. "The couch is paradise, honestly. G'night, Mum." My mother gave me a small embrace and stood up to get ready for bed. "Mum, wait a sec. Did Dad know you were going to buy all this stuff for me?"

"He will, dear, when the Woodward's statement arrives," she cooed as she headed towards the bathroom. *Brilliant*, I thought, grimacing. With that I plopped myself down on the velvet sofa, snuggled in and drifted off to sleep, exhausted by our shopping spree.

During my Mum's visit, I maintained my regular work-swim schedule and Mum planned out her activities. After staying home Monday morning to accept delivery on the tables and lamps she went to the Hudson's Bay to see her old colleagues for lunch and shopped at Eaton's. After her hair was cut and coloured at a salon on Howe Street, she continued marathon shopping for me (I now had a slew of toss cushions, a wall mirror and a bearskin rug for the floor - how she got all the goods home on the bus was an amazement). Mum disinfected my apartment, made casseroles and packed them into my new storage containers for the freezer. In the last two days, my mother had been a superhuman; sorting, bleaching, sweeping, buying, arranging and cooking. On Tuesday night I arrived back home after swim practice. At the door was a shoe-rack, a brass umbrella stand, a small table for my keys and a Berber floor mat. In the living room, Mum had placed the bearskin rug at the perfect angle under the glass oval coffee table and strategically arranged a few art books and a small jade plant in an oriental ginger jar. Against the wall was a small rattan bookcase, filled with my textbooks. The velvet couch's cushions were seriously plumped and there was a teal throw casually draped at one end. Two large framed A.Y. Jackson prints of Georgian Bay were above the sofa, softly lit by table lamps. In the corner beside the fireplace was what Lara would call the *cerise sur le gateau*: a beautiful dark brown leather chair. I gasped. Mum was standing beside the kitchen, keenly watching my expression.

"Mum, this is too much! Way too much!"

"You like the chair?"

"I love the chair! But no, it has to go back. You've spent a fortune." I moved towards the chair and ran my hand across it. "It's beautiful. Should I sit in it?"

My mother's pleased look crossed her face as I gazed unbelievingly at the chair.

"Yes, of course you should. It's Italian. Tell me what you think," she said, moving into the living room. I sat my tired butt down. The chair was sumptuous, soft, over-stuffed and had a heady smell. It was masculine, opulent and extremely comfortable.

"How much?" I asked, grasping the armrests tightly and cocking my head.

"It was on sale. I got a great deal." She smiled, pleased with the purchase.

"Mum! Price, please. I'm serious."

"So?" she asked. "You love it?"

I looked at my apartment, decked out with things I could never have afforded on my own. And now a gorgeous chair, to boot. I reconsidered.

"I love it. I love all of it. Graduation gift?" I looked at my Mum imploringly.

"Yes, of course. Graduation gift, and well deserved, too."

"Dad's going to freak out. He's going to go out of his mind."

"Do you know how much your father spends on golf each month?"

"I have no —"

"It's a lot more than your chair. The price doesn't matter. You always wanted a leather sofa; a chair is a good place to start."

"How did you have a chair and everything else delivered to my apartment in one day?" I asked, marvelling at the accomplishment.

"Like you said, dear, I'm not dead. I know all about salesmen and I still have a few charms left," she said, winking.

"Who are you, Blanche Dubois?"

Mum sparkled with pride. In a couple of days my apartment had been thoroughly kitted out. Design by Rose. It was a transformation I was incapable of achieving.

"Lara called me at work this afternoon. Her agent confirmed that she'll be singing at the Sylvia Hotel both Wednesday and Thursday nights. We'll go and cheer her on tomorrow night, okay?" I dug my fingers into the chair. Just thinking about Lara made me worried.

"Yes, love to. I'll call your father and let him know I won't be back until Thursday afternoon. Is Lara anxious?" Mum asked as I rose, went to the fridge and retrieved a bottle of white something-or-other from the previous night and poured her a large glass in one of my new wine goblets. Mum sat on the sofa then reclined, stretching out her tired legs.

"We didn't have much time to talk. She was racing off somewhere." *She'll be a train-wreck. I have to call her tonight, see if there's anything that I can do.*

"And what about her parents? Will they be there, too?"

"I dunno. I expect they will be for one of the nights." I brought over her drink and she had a sip. "Lara asked them to come. Remember you met them at a barbecue once - Howie and Maggie?"

"Oh, extremely dry."

"Lara's parents?" I asked, moving to the other side of the room.

"No dear, the wine is extremely dry." She pursed her lips slightly.

"Oh, you could be describing her parents. They're incredibly upset with her decision to pursue music. Lara thinks they're punishing her. I can understand they were disappointed when she dropped out of school, but —"

"Let me tell you something," Mum interjected. "Parents want their children to look after themselves when they're no longer around. And to be realistic, how many people actually make their living by performing in nightclubs?"

"But Mum, that doesn't —"

"Lara's a good singer and she's so lovely...but I'm sure that her parents - they're conservative people, aren't they?"

"I'd say that's an understatement," I said, sinking once more into my leather chair.

"I'm sure they think singing is a foolhardy career choice for anyone, let alone their daughter. Too dreamy and unrealistic - even if she's talented. Better if she does it on the side, like a pastime. It's how they'd see it; pragmatic."

"It *is* how they see it, and on the outside I know that makes sense, but Pete told Lara that she's more than a singer, that she's something special."

"He's an agent, sweetheart. It's what they're meant to say."

"No, Mum, I believe him. She *is* special. I don't think she's ever heard that from her parents. They've really hurt her; they've been unfair - her whole family."

"Perhaps seeing her perform will change their minds."

"Yeah, for Lara's sake, I hope so." I knew what it meant to Lara to have recognition from her parents. Already thinking ahead, Mum asked, "And what time should we be at the hotel?"

"Dunno. She said tomorrow night."

"You'd better find out. There are many hours in a night," she said, running her forefinger across the condensation on the wine glass.

"Yeah, I know how many hours are in a night, Mum," I said sharply. "I'll give her a call, later, okay?" *Don't get flippant, she's bought you a room full of furniture and done all that she could to be helpful. Don't be a jerk and become a sarcastic asshole like your father.*

"Alright," she said, calmly, taking another long appreciative sip of her wine, "I can't wait."

23

LARA'S BIG DATE

O n Tuesday night I rang Lara at home several times before I
gave up the ghost. I decided to call her Wednesday morning
after swim practice and before my guarding shift began at
10 AM. I got through on the first ring.

"Hello?"

"Lara, it's me. I've been calling you since last night. Everything
okay?"

"I was rehearsing all last night. Honestly, I'm a little freaked out."
Her voice was hoarse and tremulous.

"Oh. Because of your big date tonight?"

"No, Sunshine, because I missed the Queen's Silver Jubilee. Of
course because of my big date tonight!"

"I'm an idiot. Sorry."

"I'm a bit tense, just ignore me," Lara sounded unusually cranky.
"It's such a huge deal. I want it to go well, I don't wanna fall on my
ass."

"No, of course not."

"Do you know the place?"

"It's that old hotel right beside English Bay Beach, right? With the
vines?"

"Yes, I'll be singing in The Tilting Room lounge. It sounds ominous, doesn't it? One bad note and they're going to tilt me off the stage right into English Bay."

"Well, you're a pretty good swimmer," I joked.

"Let's hope I don't have to find out *how* good," Lara sighed. "I'll be singing for about a hundred and fifty."

"That's a big crowd." I couldn't imagine singing in front of *one* person.

"It's 'cause of Pete - he's invited people to see me perform tonight. All part of the plan. But I look like such a beast," Lara groaned.

"What are you talking about? You're a babe," I said.

"Yeah, well this babe's uterus is falling out," Lara said, her euphemism for having her period.

"Oh, that's not good timing."

"I can't time when Aunt Flo comes. You do know that, don't you?" Lara sounded sharp and more than ready for a scrap.

"Yes, of course." *Clearly, I know nothing about the female reproduction system.*

"Sorry. I'm snappy. I've got lousy cramps, I'm forming a huge crater on my face and blood's flowing outta me like a river."

"Oh." *Please, no more about blood.*

"Wait till you see my dress. I'm wearing a hideous sea-foam and it's so low-cut that I'm afraid my boobs are going to leap out all on their own. They're gigantic right now and jostling around like over-inflated beach balls. I'm not even going to tell you what's happening with my freckles. Pete says I look fetching. He's just buttering me up. I've never looked fetching; not in sea-foam and especially not during my period."

"I'm sure you'll look fantastic. Pete knows what he's doing."

Why is she wearing sea-foam? What the heck is sea-foam? "Lara, forget the dress, stuff yourself with a huge pad and take a few Midol. Everyone loves your freckles. And make-up will take care of Mt. Etna. Stupefy them with your voice and they won't notice your runaway knockers." I heard her titter. *Good, maybe I can help her relax a little. If all else fails, make jokes about her breasts. Very sophisticated.* "What time should my Mum and I be there?"

"Before 9 PM. Don't be late. Really, I mean it. I'll be doing two sets, if they don't toss me out into the street."

"Lara, if you bomb they'll toss you into the bay, remember?"

"Right," she sighed again. "I'm looking forward to tonight like these bloody cramps," she said, then countered herself. "No, I shouldn't hex myself."

"Of course. Lara, you'll —"

"I've been working on the songs, but like you've said before, I can't control what people - including Pete's guests - will think of me."

"Listen you," I said. "You're gonna take a deep breath and sing your skinny butt off. I'm going to be cheering you on like a crazy person and if they don't like you, well, their taste is in their assholes."

"Oh, Sunshine," she started convulsing with laughter. "That's too funny!"

We both started to chuckle at the absurdity of the jitters we both could get - her before singing and me literally throwing up before and even during swim meets. Afterwards, we would reflect and think, *'Why was I such a mess?'* Anticipation was much more anxiety-producing than any actual event.

"Try to enjoy each moment tonight, Lara. It's the start of something big for you, I'm certain of it." I could feel the intensity of her concentration - even on the phone. I waited a few beats in silence before continuing. "I'll be there - we'll both be there - to hear you. Lara…you'll knock their philistine socks off."

She snorted, "I'd settle for a few drunks who don't have perfect pitch." Lara drew a deep breath and blew it out in a long controlled exhalation. "I'll be okay."

"Okay? *You'll be swell, you'll be great* —" I sang out before Lara cut me off.

"You're a lousy singer," she interrupted, "but a good friend, Sunshine." Lara's voice was calm and centred, the hoarseness gone.

"I'm not a good friend, I'm your best friend. I'll be seeing you. Now there's a song you should sing sometime," I suggested, said goodbye and hung up the phone. After my pep talk, I finished the last of my swim practices before heading home, anxious for the evening to come. Mum called my father to say that she'd be back Thursday for a three o'clock pickup at the bus station. It sounded like Mum was telling him about Lara's upcoming performance, but it seemed - I was subtly eavesdropping - that he was disinterested. Was my father one of those plebeians? I left the room and she spoke for a few minutes longer. Mum hung up the phone and firmly said, "That's all settled." I guessed she meant about being picked up, but it could have been about the expenses that she had incurred on my behalf. She *did* seem a little tense. I was glad that life would be returning to a semblance of normality in the next day; tomorrow night I'd be tucked into my brass bed with my new comforter. I loved having my mother with me and I was extremely grateful for all that she'd done to make my apartment a home. But I was a sociable loner and I craved space and time that was mine alone.

We had a light dinner bought from the Woodward's deli a couple of days earlier - some rotisserie chicken, bread from the Paris bakery, some olives, cheddar cheese and a huge green salad. We sat down at the table.

"Hey, Mum, was Dad angry with you? On the phone, I mean."

"Angry? No, of course not. Why would you ask such a thing?" she asked, stabbing salad onto her fork.

"I dunno, just a hunch. You only spoke for five minutes." I stuffed some bread and olives in my mouth and was eyeing a large wedge of cheese. Mum passed on the chicken and was content with her salad and bread slathered with lashings of butter.

"It was much less, actually. There's nothing wrong. He's just not that interested in hearing about what I'm up to in the city."

"Huh." *Nothing wrong? There's nothing right about that comment.*

"There," she said, pushing herself from the table. "No more for me. I'm going to get myself ready," she said heading for the washroom. I cleared the table. I'd already showered at the pool. To celebrate both Lara's evening and my last night with my mother, I'd ironed a pair of dark grey dress pants to a razor's edge, picked out a striped burgundy shirt and slicked my hair with pomade. After twenty minutes, Mum reappeared, looking spectacular. When she'd gone to the hairdresser she'd gotten a feathered cut with streaks of lightest blonde framing her lovely face. For tonight she donned a new dress. The top half was adorned with gold bugle beads that glittered in the light. The bottom half of the dress was jet-black satin. On her feet she wore black pumps. Her eyelids were highlighted with dark blue shadow and her lips were neutral in colour, but glossy. White Linen perfume completed the presentation. She stood in the living room, asking for my opinion.

"Do I pass the grade?"

"Mum...wow." Her dress fit beautifully, highlighting a well-proportioned body though she'd never worked out a day in her life. *Really, she could still get any man she wanted - if she wanted to.* She looked happy and confident. *A few days away from my father must be therapeutic for her.* She'd had a good time in the city; talkative, assertive and more engaged. My mother struck a provocative pose with her hands on her slender hips.

"So, tell me. Am I one of those Foxy Ladies that I hear about?"

Though she looked terrific, I didn't want to think of my mother as foxy, but...

"Mum, you're the foxiest." I gave her a peck on the cheek. "It looks like the best-looking date in the city is mine tonight," I said with admiration.

"Thank you. Now, as you young people say, I've got my Bogey shoes on and I wanna Bogey with you. It's that Kacy Summer, you know."

Mum was a little mixed up on her Disco Lingo.

"Umm, no, that's Boogie, Mum. Boogie shoes and boogie with you. And it's KC and the Sunshine Band, not Kacy Summer."

"Are you sure?" she asked as I locked the apartment door on our way out. I didn't want to point out who Donna Summer was. That would be unkind.

❧

It had been warm - even hot during most of May - until Lara's opening. It was cool and windy with rain threatening the skies. We took an umbrella for Mum and walked to the Sylvia, just a ten-minute stroll. It was busy on the street and I noticed many men who were clearly Friends of Dorothy. We made our way down to Beach Avenue, the wind picking up on English Bay. Rain started falling as we neared the hotel. The soft drizzle glazed the green ivy that covered the entire Guilford Avenue side of the Sylvia, making it glisten in the remaining light. As we walked up the marble steps and into the lobby, I felt a twinge of nausea. Patrons were getting their drinks and making their way into the lounge area before the set started. Mum had ordered a glass of white wine but I was too nervous to even have a glass of water. I looked at my watch; it was just ten minutes before the hour. I gave my name to the front-of-house lady with the sky-high auburn hair. She gave us our complimentary tickets that Pete had arranged for my mother and me and we walked into the commotion of the Tilting Room. This scene was nothing like the bistros she'd sung in before. *Pete must have done a very good job in getting people to hear Lara sing tonight.* It was packed. I spotted a few locals personalities; Eric Peterson, an actor and playwright, CKNW news broadcaster Jack Webster and Pia Shandal, who worked on *Vancouver,* an evening talk show on CKVU with the handsome Wayne Cox. My mother and I milled about for several minutes. Mum was getting approving looks as the light danced off the beads of her dress. I'm sure it gave her a sense of enjoyment knowing that she could still turn a few heads.

I hadn't been to the hotel before, however my mother knew about the Sylvia. As we waited, she told me it was built in 1912 by a Jewish man for his daughter Sylvia. Mum commented that movie star Errol Flynn died in one of the rooms in 1959. There was a rumour that a woman had been murdered in the defunct basement swimming pool in the 1920's. I was surprised at the colourful tales - loving stories the way I did - and wanted to hear more. Before I could, there was an announcement the set was to begin. I grabbed by Mum by the forearm and selected seats in line with the microphone eight rows back. Lara could look at us, if need be. *Always be prepared.* On the platform stage was a black baby grand piano, an upright bass and a drum set. The musicians took their places, the house lights dimmed and people settled into their seats. I then recognized Pete, sharply dressed in a black suit. He briskly came onto the stage and flicked the microphone with his forefinger.

"Good evening everyone. Tonight we're very pleased to present an exciting young singer. When you hear her incredible voice, I think you'll agree with me that she's absolutely thrilling. Here she is, Lara Jean!" Pete flashed his smile then stepped back from the light and disappeared into the shadows. We started to applaud. And suddenly there was Lara, her glossy red hair upswept, stylishly dressed in a 1950's-inspired chiffon dress. Now I knew what sea-foam was - pale green. The dress was cinched at the waist and as she said, it was very low cut. She eased her way into the darkened room, unsmiling and looking uncomfortable. The applause built steadily as she quickly stepped onto the low platform. As Lara took her first hurried strides downstage, the toe of her left shoe became caught up in her microphone's heavy electrical cord. Her shoe stuck but her body continued moving forward. In the blink of an eye Lara lost her balance, shrieked and catapulted herself onto two tables in the front row, her shoe onstage but Lara definitely offstage. Her impact upset not just the table but the drinks on them. There were gasps in the audience (including my mother's and mine) as she landed with a thud on the floor, spilling the patrons' drinks on herself, soaking her beautiful red hair and green dress with wine and beer. The effect? She was turned into a booze-drenched, sea-foam monster; like a creature from Lost Lagoon. Hair soaked on one side with spilled alcohol, her dress askew and stained. Lara was stunned, immediately pushed herself up and stared blankly at me - frozen in embarrassment. I didn't know what to do. Mum looked at me in shock. This is something Lara couldn't have prepared for. *Should I hurl myself over the crowd and make it right?* Lara continued to stare out at the silent and stupefied audience for several painfully long seconds. From the darkness, I could see Pete beginning to jog over. Lara saw him and waved him off with a subtle movement of her hand. The audience murmured, not knowing what might happen next. She picked up a couple of the glasses and several bottles of beer from the floor, apologizing to the astonished guests, righted a small table and gingerly came back onstage, one leg a few inches shorter than the other, limping gamely. She mouthed something to the trio, straightened up, repositioned her breasts which had precariously edged its way nearly right out of its cup, smoothed the creases from her damp dress and faced a now-silent throng. She bent over, picked up her shoe, wiped the beer from her face with a tissue the drummer supplied, stepped up to the microphone and held up her shoe to the expectant spectators.

"Oh, I'm so sorry," Lara uttered breathlessly. She paused further, chewing her bottom lip. "My agent told me just before I came on to break a leg, but really..." The audience warmly laughed as she slipped her shoe back on. She smiled and I gave her the thumbs up sign. She acknowledged me by way of a tiny nod. Lara smiled at the pianist and mouthed, "Okay." The expectant crowd settled; the trio began Jimmy Van Heusen's sultry 'Here's That Rainy Day' and Lara started to sing. Her phrasing was delicate, holding back slightly against the beat, the piano soft, the drum cymbal being softly brushed and the steady beat of the bass unobtrusive.

> '*Maybe I should have saved,*
> *Those leftover dreams,*
> *Funny but here's that rainy day...*

With a voice that was clear, subtly nuanced, rich and soaring, people started to forget what had happened a few minutes earlier and began to notice that she was singing beautifully - and against the backdrop of a downpour. But the rain and wind only helped to provide the perfect setting for her superb vocals. The trio played the bridge and then Lara, who had been standing with her head slightly down as the trio took their musical solos, raised her head and looked out into the crowd as the trio modulated the line into a higher, brighter key and she continued with the last verse,

> *'Funny, how love becomes,*
> *A cold rainy day,*
> *Funny, that rainy day is heeeeerrrre!'*

Lara sustained the last loud note with a throbbing vibrato that nearly shook the room. Lara's effort was met with an enthusiastic response. In front of us, she changed from awkward gamine to sophisticated debutante. Lara began a set of standards that reflected her newly-developed vocal prowess. Songs by Cole Porter, George Gershwin, Harold Arlen. Her voice made distinctive versions of the classics. She grew in confidence with each number. I was amazed at the yearning in her vocals. She'd found a way to connect to the lyric that was deeply personal. Lara finished the set with an Arlen song, 'Stormy Weather' which only seemed appropriate given the blustery conditions outside. She sang the first verse softly, then with each subsequent chorus all of her power was unleashed. She stepped away from the microphone completely, her large voice filling the room.

> *'Can't go on,*
> *Every hope I had is gone,*
> *Stormy weather,*
> *Since my man and I ain't together,*
> *Keeps raining all the time!'*

Hands outstretched for the soaring last phrases, the thunderous applause made it clear; the crowd loved her. Lara bowed once, twice, smiled then rushed off.

"Jeez, I've never heard her sing like this. It's an entirely different voice." Clearly, her collaboration with Pete had given rise to something spectacular. It wasn't just about her voice, but with how she acted out the songs; each a play in four minutes. We had a twenty-minute break to catch our breath and then she was to come back for her last set of songs.

Lara strode out for her second set with confidence. She sang some Canadian content; songs by Joni Mitchell and Gordon Lightfoot. A few obscure and beautiful Gallic songs followed. 'La Vie En Rose' was exquisitely rendered, Lara's eyes glistening with tears at a dramatic moment. I kept it under control but noticed an ache in my throat. Lara sang a collection of pieces in the form of a medley and ended with another Arlen number, 'Any Place I Hang My Hat'. Each verse had an upward key change and at the end she hit a long-held high note to rapturous applause. She thanked the trio, acknowledged the audience, beamed like a searchlight and hurried off, skipping through the room. Pete was waiting for her and whisked her out of the lounge. I watched my best friend perform with an uncanny presence I'd never witnessed before. I admit being star-struck. Mum and I gave up on seeing Lara as there was a crush of people trying to speak with her in the reception lobby. *I'll talk with her tomorrow.* As we made our exit the rain was dripping still, but the wind had calmed considerably. Mum opened up her umbrella.

"Wow," was her first comment. "Wasn't she just fabulous?"

"She must have worked her ass off," I said. "She was incredible."

"Who was the man that introduced her and followed her offstage?"

"Oh, that's Pete, Mum, her agent. The one I talked about."

"Do you know him?"

"Um, yes, a bit. He's been a huge help to Lara."

And a huge help at pounding me senseless in a men's room, I admitted to myself shamefully. But not too shamefully; seeing Pete filled me with craving.

"Yes, that seems obvious. He's very good-looking, isn't he?"

"Um, is he? I guess so," I answered cautiously.

"Is he married?"

"Married? No, he's not. Why do you ask?" *Gawd...what do you want to know?*

"Well, are he and Lara seeing each other?" Mum asked as we dodged people on the streets trying to get out of the rain. I thought about that for a second. *Is it possible that he's also showing Lara the full range of his expertise? Anything's possible.*

"No, Mum, I think it's all above-board and professional."

"Hmm, I think that's best. Mixing business with pleasure doesn't tend to work out very well, does it?"

"Dunno, Mum. I haven't a clue," I confessed. I slowed my walking and touched my mother on her arm.

"Hey, Mum, you know what day it is?"

"Yes, of course. It's Wednesday."

"No, I meant the date. It's May the thirteenth."

"Oh, Christ. Your father's birthday." Mum stopped in her tracks. "That's a first."

"That you forgot it?"

"No, that I didn't care that I forgot it," she said crisply, ducking further under her umbrella, striding the rain-soaked and shiny streets to return to the Queen Charlotte apartments.

24

HOME IS WHERE THE PASTA IS

I said goodbye to Mum the evening Lara sang at the Sylvia, thanking her for turning my apartment into a home. I had swim practice Thursday - only a few hours away - and Mum would be fast asleep when I was heading out.

The next morning, I rose and went about my routines quietly, even though it wasn't necessary - my mother could sleep through a cataclysm. On the side table I left a note asking her to push the extra keys under the door when she left. I collected my swim gear and took a quick look at my attractively transformed apartment. Hurrying outside, I thought of how my mother always looked after me, no questions asked. Peering up, the sky was dusky pink as I hunted for the Fastback. After Lara's show on Wednesday Mum seemed tired, so I didn't want to talk about her cavalier attitude about missing my father's birthday. I was trying not to triangulate so much. I wondered if Dad was disappointed that his birthday had slipped my mother's mind? *Doubtful.* Perhaps he was relieved that he had additional time to himself. *Distance is the provider of equilibrium for relationships. That's what my textbooks say. Certainly there's lots of distance between my mother and father.* I often thought about all those things - relationships, the man I wanted to be but wasn't - when I was in the pool. Swimming lap after lap, there's a lot of time to ponder my life under water.

After hunting down my car, within half an hour I arrived on the pool deck, got my instructions from Coach Lerner and read the training routine. I nodded my head to a couple other swimmers and I took my lane. I warmed up in the froth of the other swimmers - a practiced chaos. I was doing an extensive workout with speed drills, long kicksets, distance training, resistance work and time in the weight room. I was now spending up to seven hours per day swimming, divided between morning and late-afternoon practices. It meant that I was often tired and frequently had muscle tenderness. Ice-baths often followed my practices; I despised them. My coach said that my muscle pain would pass as I entered another phase of fitness, but I was still impatiently waiting.

At work I phoned Lara but there wasn't any answer. *Is this girl ever at home? I'll try ringing her later tonight.* I put down the phone in the guardroom and finished my break with a couple of tuna sandwiches from the SUB, three Mars bars and an apple. I climbed onto the guard chair and tried my drowsy best not to nod off, pinching my thighs until they were bruised. It would be a disaster if I fell asleep on shift; I'd be fired immediately.

Arriving back home that night after my second swim practice, I noticed an appetizing smell coming from the outside hallway. Entering my apartment, I excitedly followed the scent to my kitchen. Mum had made a large pot of meatballs and tomato sauce, leaving it on the unlit gas stove. The spaghetti had been cooked and was in the fridge in a plastic bag with a note attached - instructions on how to combine the two. *Thanks, Mum, but I can figure out how to put sauce and pasta together. I'll have to call and let her know how much I appreciated the meal.* I soon sat down to a giant plate of pasta flavoured with Mum's love and a heavy dose of oregano. With the help of a large spoon, I twisted the pasta onto a fork. The contentment of carbohydrates. It seemed that most of my post-pubescence was spent lifting pasta and bread into my mouth. *Not a bad way to get through life.* It was eerily quiet in my apartment. Solitude. I had another plate of pasta and felt stuffed and slightly uncomfortable. I removed my pants and lazed about in my boxer shorts. My days - wake, eat, swim, eat, guard, eat, swim, eat and sleep - were organized and predictable. I stood on the balcony and looked at the tranquil street. I made a mug of sweet tea, sat down on the sofa and called Lara. No answer. After a few sips of tea, I was having difficulty keeping my eyes open. I shook my head, tried to stay alert and called Lara again. No answer. My eyelids were weighty and it was taking an effort to keep them open. *Why not let them rest?* I put down my tea and stretched out on the couch, my tired body supported and soothed; a state of complete relaxation fuelled by pasta. More like a spaghetti stupor. The dying light danced around the room as it turned from bright to dusk. Lying motionless in the growing dimness, I felt my hair falling around my face and in my eyes. As I melted into the cushion, I heard my mother's voice saying I needed a haircut. For a moment I wondered if she was still in my apartment. The room turned to dark and I drifted into a dreamless sleep.

25

ROBBY AT THE LAGOON

I hadn't heard from Lara for several days. I presumed that she and Pete were busy planning the next steps after her appearance at the Sylvia Hotel. Sunday was the day I did chores: laundry, cleaning, scrubbing the bathroom, food shopping and getting ready for the week ahead. For me, most activities were on a schedule and that included a Sunday phone call to Lara. I'd wanted to tell her how impressed I was with her singing Wednesday night. After eating breakfast, I washed the dishes and contemplated going back under the sheets, but thought better of it. I stripped my bed, picked up any stray clothing from the bedroom, put it all in a large wicker basket and hauled it down to the ghostly cellar where the laundry was located. After my washing was finished and put away, out came my bucket and the enormous bottle of bleach that my mother bought me. I was scrubbing the toilet when I heard the phone ring. Drying my hands on my cotton shorts, I ran to the living room and picked up the receiver.

"Hello?"

"Sunshine, it's me!" Lara exclaimed.

"Lara, I was gettin' worried —"

"I'm sorry but I haven't been home much. I've been working with Pete on getting more dates."

"Music dates?"

"Are there any other kind? He's been talking with some of the music people who came out to the Sylvia, and I've been doing some schmaltzing. I think that's what Pete calls it."

"I think you mean schmoozing, Lara."

"Yes! That's what I meant."

"Has something come of it?"

Lara excitedly said, "Yes, we've gotten work. Summer dates in Vancouver, Victoria, Seattle, Portland and - listen to this - a special appearance at Festijazz in Montreal on the Labour Day weekend! It's a huge break and there's incredible exposure to the performance scene. Can you believe it?"

"Gawd, Lara, that's unreal!"

"Isn't it? Pete flew out the Festijazz organizer - Doudou Boicel - from Montreal to see us at the Sylvia."

"Pete flew Boicel out? Wow, that's gutsy."

"It worked. Boicel's giving us a shot at the jazz fest!"

I was amazed. "Lara, I know Pete's helping you, but you were stupendous the other night. We were all blown away by your singing."

"Thanks. I was so glad that you and your mother came."

There was a pause at the other end. One of Lara's deep breaths was heard. I continued into potentially sensitive territory and asked, "What did your parents think? I didn't see Howie and Maggie the night that Mum and I were there."

"No, you wouldn't have because they weren't there…"

"Ah, you mean they came the next night?" *Oh, Gawd…*

"Uh-uh. No shows. My own parents were no-shows. My brothers too; my mother probably told them to stay away as if I had the plague."

"Jeez."

"It was mean of them. They knew what it meant to me…"

"Do you know for sure that they weren't there? I asked, dumbfounded.

"Sunshine," Lara said quietly. "It's a small room. If they were there, I'd have seen them."

"Well, that's, I dunno…have you spoken to them since?"

"No, I didn't actually. I just got on with things. Fuck 'em."

"I shouldn't say this, but that's shameful of them."

"Isn't it? Anyway, I refuse to let this get to me."

I didn't know what else to say - it was cruel. Even though they disapproved, there was no reason for her parents to neglect their daughter's important evening. Counter to what she said, it must have hurt her deeply. Changing subjects, Lara asked, "When exactly are you in Montreal this summer?"

"The last week of August."

"I'm at the jazz festival for the Labour Day weekend, so we'd be there at the same time. It's more than a weird fluke, Sunshine, it has to be."

"Lara, you know I don't believe in stuff like destiny and Jupiter aligning with Mars."

"And yet you're convinced there's a ghost in your cellar?"

"Well," I said, thinking of how to defend myself.

"Never mind. I'm just thinking how we can support each other in Montreal."

"First I have to make the time-trials in Edmonton, Lara. It's not a slam-dunk."

"The way you're swimming? You'll do it," Lara said assuredly.

I thought for a moment. "When will you perform? I asked, thinking ahead.

"Looks like we're the last act on Saturday night, September the first."

"If all goes according to plan, I'd be done Friday night. Regardless, win or lose, if I'm there I promise to hear you sing."

"And I'll be in the stands for you on Friday night - the 400 IM, right?"

"Yes. And that'd be extra incentive." I took a deep breath. "Jeez, Montreal….I've always wanted to go. My French is atrocious. I hafta practice. So, I guess Pete's going?"

"Uh-huh. All the people I'm dealing with in Quebec are his associates."

"Associates?" I asked. "Sounds a little Godfather, doesn't it?"

"I don't think so, Sunshine. How'd you get so suspicious?"

"Yeah, I dunno. Mum really took notice of Pete, you know. She thought he was a super-hunk."

"A super-hunk? That doesn't sound like anything your mother would say."

Gulp, watch yourself, Einstein. "No, funny, huh? She wanted to know if you and Pete were, umm, dating, but she probably wanted to know if you were sleeping together."

"And what did you tell her?"

"I said that you were all business with each other."

"Well," Lara said, "Your mother's right about one thing. He is a super-hunk, but I'm not his type," Lara stated emphatically.

"Oh, I see." I didn't pursue this any further. I didn't want Lara to tell me the reason why she wasn't his type.

"You know, I think Pete's a real player," Lara continued.

"A player? How so?" I asked tentatively.

"Well, he's just too good to be true. Always perfectly turned out - his clothes, his hair, that expensive black Porsche he drives. He's surrounded by pretty women hanging on his every word. If he wanted to, I'm sure he could be screwing every empty-headed bimbo in sight. Maybe he is."

Ouch, that hurt, I thought. But Lara was probably correct, she just had the wrong gender.

"I dunno 'bout that, Lara."

"I'm not naive. He goes after and gets whatever he wants. Pete's unstoppable, which helps me with my career, but he's not good boyfriend material. Those kinda guys are just fuck machines, excusez mon Français. They can't be faithful. Besides, I don't want a dual relationship with my agent. With my history? Can you imagine what would happen?"

"Uh, well..."

"Frankly, I haven't been thinking about men for months. Music's been getting all my attention. When's the last time you even heard me talk about men?"

"You haven't been telling me stories of bad dates and break-ups for a long time. So, tell me - what's next?"

Lara spoke about some local upcoming gigs and how she and Pete were doing a marketing campaign; part of a plan that Pete was executing. I shared some of my news about swim practice and how I was turning in some excellent times. It was comforting to be talking with Lara, like earlier days when so much of our time was spent in conversation. I loved her optimism. She was creating her own future in the present. *That's very mentally fit.* I finished up the call by saying, "Okay, I gotta go back to scrubbing my toilet. I'm hoping I won't collapse from the bleach fumes."

"I think your mother visited too long," she laughed. "Make everything sparkle, you never know who might drop over. Bye, Sunshine."

Who might drop over? Nah, no one's gonna be dropping over.

I swam twice daily six days per week and worked when I wasn't swimming. What happened on Sunday? I donned a pair of pink rubber gloves, collected a big pail, got out the Javex and scrubbed stains off the toilet, swept and washed floors, did laundry, plumped pillows, made meals for the freezer (as per my mother's instructions) and generally busted my butt until four o'clock. I appreciated that I lived in an infinitely better residence than the Mildew Manor, and I loved a clean apartment just like the next person, but there was certainly more to my one day off than drudgery, however necessary. Where was the fun? I showered in my sterile tub, put on a pair of blue running shorts, a freshly-laundered black tee-shirt, my Nike runners and headed out the door. It felt fantastic getting outside in the warm air. I walked the first block on Nicola before running lightly, turning left on Nelson Street by the old brick No. 6 Fire Hall. I headed down Nelson across Denman and towards the tennis courts in Stanley Park. I broke into a moderate run, heading down the small hill to the dirt trail that circled Lost Lagoon. It was a favourite haunt that I enjoyed running around before heading into Stanley Park. Having had a hot shower a few minutes before made my sweat come even faster. I jogged along the dirt path, avoiding both geese and people. Soon I was half-way round, past the huge water fountain and coming up to the north side of the course. The shallow waters of the lagoon were heavily dotted with birds, including a dozen beautiful trumpeter swans. There were seven or eight large turtles basking on the rocks close to the lagoon's edge. The lemony-green weeping willows were magnificent, the branches bowing in the breeze to gently bob into the water. New wild roses perfumed the humid air. I was happily running, drenched in sweat, taking everything in. As I came up to the stone bridge where the creek entered the lagoon, I noticed a young man casually standing at the rise of the bridge, about twenty feet from me. I slowed to a stop. This was an area that was cruisy, meaning that men met men there. The young man had long, well-muscled legs, a handsome face, short blonde hair, a faded jade singlet that revealed an ultra-sinewy upper-body and a pair of snug-fitting white running shorts slightly dampened at the waist with perspiration. There was something about him that caused me to stare. He caught me looking his way and returned the glance with a friendly grin.

"How's the run going?" he asked. I moved a few steps towards him, putting my hands on my hips.

"Good, thanks. Pretty humid, isn't it?" If nothing else, my family had taught me the banality of talking about the weather. "I was sopping wet after fifty metres." *Okay, not the best way to engage a hot guy in conversation by talking about how much you sweat.* He nodded his head.

"How far were you going today?" he asked.

How far would you like to go? There was something familiar about him, but I couldn't place him. I was having a serious bout of deja vu. Before I considered how to answer his question, I asked him, "Have we ever, um...I mean, I think I know you. From a long time ago? Maybe in school?"

"Uh," he said, looking at me more carefully. "Don't think so," he responded, appraising me. "I went to high school at Burnaby Central. Sound familiar?"

"Yes. Did you run track, per chance?" I had a jolt of recognition.

"I did." He moved closer to chat.

"You really grew up." I smiled at the reminiscence. "You're Rob, aren't you?"

"Robby Berd, yeah. Wow, you've got a great memory!"

We shook hands. Robby's grip was firm as it held mine. I told him my name and said, "I remember you because of that asshole gym teacher, Jack."

"Hack," he corrected me.

"Right. Hack's-whacks. How could I forget?" I rolled my eyes, re-membering the stress of gym class. "That guy was seriously disturbed."

"Did you know the real story about Hack?" he asked.

"Well, we heard many stories; there was speculation about what actually happened." I hoped he might pick up on my curiosity.

"Would you like to know?" I quickly nodded and Robby proceed-ed to relate in detail how Hack assaulted him in the shower which led to the gym teacher's dismissal. Robby talked about it for several minutes and though the incident had occurred many years earlier, he spoke with a fresh and an indignant anger. Robby declared, "I was just a kid taking a shower and he tried to fuck me. Splitting my head open was my lucky break. See?" Robby pushed his short hair up to show the scar where his wound had been. The scar tissue was white and spread four or five inches past his hairline. After nearly ten years, it still looked ragged.

"Your lucky break? How's that?" I asked, thinking that having an experience and a scar like that was anything but lucky.

"As soon as the blood pouring outta me I knew he was done. The thing is, it could've been much worse for me."

I swallowed, thinking of how disturbing and frightening it must have been. I visualized Robby's blood swirling down the shower drain and felt nauseous.

"What happened after the assault? What did your parents do?"

"They didn't take it too well. My mother wanted to press charges, but my father was dead-set against it."

"Why? It was a sexual assault of a minor."

Rob explained ruefully, "My father said that charges *'would bring undue attention to the nature of the incident'*. I never forgot his words. He was afraid people would think I was involved in something with Hack."

"You don't mean...a sexual thing?"

"Hah, can you believe it? My father's response hurt a hundred times more than Hack ever did. So, nothing was done and my father was spared any embarrassment." Robby absently rubbed his scar. I could imagine my father also being more concerned about what others might think of his son and potentially embarrassing him. "Hack was given the option of resigning - I didn't get a choice about anything. I was told that he wouldn't be able to teach again, but I doubt that. The ironic thing is that I'm gay. Hack could probably smell me out, the fucker." He paused for a moment. "You too, right?" Robby looked at me questioningly.

"Huh?"

"You too? Gay?" Robby asked as I took a few seconds to respond.

"Oh, um, yeah I am," I said, feeling vulnerable all at once. "But I'm not really out, if you know what I mean."

"Sure, I know what you mean," Robby said with a frown. "But this is a different time. It's not high school. I dunno about you, but I don't make excuses for being who I am. Especially in the West End. It's nearly a gay institution here. And as you can probably tell, I'm no shrinking violet."

"I can see that. Did you want to walk a bit?" I asked. I liked Robby's attitude.

"Sure," he answered, smiling. "Why not?"

We slowly wandered by the creek that flowed into Lost Lagoon, then towards Second Beach and past the huge salt water pool full of children playing in the water. Further along was a small cove which looked out to Vancouver Island. We sat on a log, looking out at the sea as we chatted, slowly getting to know each other's story. Robby was scarcely an inch away, his leg brushing against mine occasionally as we talked. He told me about his family - things were not good between them after he came out at eighteen. He was now twenty-five. *They still have a hard time accepting it - make a mental note, make sure that the timing is right when you come out to your family.* I spoke for the very first time about my disturbing incident on Hazel Road in Abbotsford and how it haunted me years later. I felt shaky as I shared my gay-bashing experience for the first time.

"Scars?" he gently asked me.

"Well, no, not like your scar."

Robby was sympathetic; he listened to my story with interest and explained that he wasn't surprised that I was fearful about coming out.

"I'll tell you something. There's much more hate in the world than love for people like us," he said. "But there's no excuse to hide or be a pretender. Not anymore."

Robby explained he was also attending UBC in the Theatre Department completing a Master's degree in Fine Arts, with next year being his last. Ultimately, he wanted to work as a stage director. He was candid, assured and unapologetic. I took notice and liked what I was hearing.

"Are you in student housing?" I asked.

"No, I've got an apartment on Harwood that I share with two others from school. It's not perfect, but I won't be there forever."

"And when you finish your MFA, what'll you do?"

"Work, if it were only that easy. It's gonna be a challenge. Not many directors get work in Canada, let alone Vancouver. I'll probably work as an AD - that's Assistant Director - for a few years. I'll need to get some legitimacy by getting paid work in the theatre. Maybe film. I'm looking into all possibilities. I have this year to make some decisions. Eventually, I'm going to have to go where the work is, maybe the States. And really, I'm not bound to any particular place," he said.

I was thinking that there were now several people - Lara, Pete and now Robby - whose challenge was a career in the arts. Though Pete was doing well, he had to give up acting. Consistent work, let alone career success didn't sound easy to achieve.

"You're a good listener," he smiled, holding his gaze on mine for a few seconds. "Do you go to Rawling's Trail often to pick up guys?" he asked abruptly.

"I'm sorry?"

"Don't be. You know, Rawling's Trail where we met. I figured that you were hoping to hook-up with someone this afternoon. Right?" he asked.

"I just wanted to get outside," I admitted and shrugged. "Honestly."

"You sure 'bout that? Nothing else?" Robby's smile revealed a small calcium deposit on his front tooth; very sexy.

"Maybe I did want to meet someone," I hesitated for a moment, took a chance. "I really liked talking with you."

"Well, we can keep on talking or we could find a more private space and fool around," he said boldly. "No one's accused me of beating around the bush. Hope you don't mind."

"I don't mind..."

"Great. Whaddya say?" Robby put his hand on my neck, rubbing it gently, sending a shiver all the way down my back.

MY LIFE UNDER WATER

"I can't believe I'm going to say this. I hate clichés, but do you wanna go back to my place?"

Robby grinned. "Lead the way."

"We *could* do a run first." I had to get my roadwork in as per schedule. And to do it alongside a handsome young man would be a bonus.

"Sure...uh, just a warning - I'm not a jogger," he said seriously.

"Yeah, I figured. I'll try to keep up." I stood and gently twisted my torso from side to side.

"Okay. Let's see. We can run on the seawall, past Siwash Rock and head up through the trails. I hadn't finished my run today, either."

"Did you get distracted?" I asked, hoping he might agree.

"I'll say," Robby said, winking.

I re-tied my Nikes and stretched my lower back.

"You're real fit, aren't you?" Robby hiked up my damp tee-shirt. "Whoa, some abs. I'm jealous," he said, approving of my flat stomach. Robby turned and started running across the sand towards the seawall. "C'mon, let's go!" Robby called out, moving quickly. I followed, stumbling in the sand for a few steps and then was close behind. We ran on the seawall, the waves of English Bay sloshing beside us as we fell into a syncopated rhythm. Robby was strong and fast but adjusted his running so that I could keep up with him.

"You...obviously...have kept up...with your...training," I panted.

"Yeah, I still try to run fifty or so kilometres a week. I feel fantastic afterwards. Like the world makes sense again."

Robby was speaking as easily as he had when we were sitting on the beach and not even perspiring. And then there was me, the National swimming hopeful, already a sweaty, heaving mess, my shirt and shorts drenched after just a few minutes. In my defence, Robby's pace was fast. He was holding back and I was having to really dig deep to keep up. We ran on the seawall past Ferguson Point, then along Third Beach. Robby rocketed past Siwash Rock and back-tracked into the park and up onto Merrilees Trail. The steep trail wound its way up to Prospect Point under a canopy of cedar and pine trees that nearly obliterated the sunlight. It was an effort to for me to run up the incline. At the top of the rise, there was an incredible view across the Strait of Georgia to Vancouver Island, the blue-green sea shimmering in the late-afternoon sun. We didn't have much time to see it as Robby took me hurtling down North Creek Trail, around Beaver Lake and through the middle of Stanley Park on Bridle Path, keeping up a pace that was exhausting for me and likely leisurely for him.

"How ya doin'?" he called out, hearing me gasping for life itself.

"Great," I lied, wiping sweat from my forehead, my chest burning and my legs aching with the strain. Robby was flying along the trail back to the lagoon after a fast-paced thirty-five minutes. I was impressed with his legs - sun-tanned with pale skin peeking through the bottom of his white shorts, his calves ropey with muscle. I stumbled along, but Robby was nimble with each perfectly measured stride; he was an artful runner to observe. We were running side by side, with the velocity decreased to a more manageable speed for me.

"Okay, you set the pace," he called to me, "back to your place."

"Right." I dropped the clip further and was no longer panting which allowed for a comfortable talk on the way, running west of Denman, then up the last hill on Nelson Street past the No. 6 Fire Hall and arriving at the Queen Charlotte. I was profusely sweating but immensely happy with an endorphin rush.

"Wow, that's not how I usually run." I mopped at my face with my wet tee-shirt which pushed perspiration into my already stinging eyes. My hair was plastered to my head. I bent over, grabbing at my knees; even they were wet. Sweat ran down my legs in rivulets to my socks. Robby had some perspiration on his brow; his faded singlet was darkened slightly with perspiration at his lower back; we were a study in contrasts.

"You're a pretty good runner - for a swimmer."

"Thanks," I said, "And you're a good runner for a runner. But I'd like to get you into the pool, Bill Rodgers."

"A bit of revenge, eh? I'd drop like a stone; there's no doubt about it."

"Let's get some water or something, okay?" I opened the unlocked front door and we walked into the lobby. Mrs. McBride was holding a galvanized watering can and was about to douse the two large ficus plants in massive green-and-black Asian clay pots. She stopped when she saw Robby and me enter.

"Oh, my," she exclaimed, assessing my sweaty and exhausted-looking body. "Did you overdo it, dear?"

I smiled, wiped sweat from my forehead and said, "Yes, I think I did, Mrs. McBride."

She did a quick study of Robby. "And is this your brother? You look so much alike!"

We didn't. Though we were both of a similar height, Robby was much leaner by at least twenty pounds. Our hair was both blond, though mine was shoulder length and wavy and his was nearly a crew-cut and much lighter. Our eyes were different coloured; his were hazel. Robby was beautifully proportioned with fine features, every part of his frame in balance and was refined-looking and I was more thickly constructed.

"Ah, my brother?" I asked with raised eyebrows.

"No relation," Robby quickly stated, hesitating slightly before adding, "I'm a friend." Robby quickly picked up on my discomfort.

"Oh, how nice. I've not seen you before. You must be a new friend, then?" *Oh Gawd, please, no more questions...*

"Yes, sort of," Robby said straight away. "I was taking a break from my run at the lagoon when he saw me - thought that he knew me - and asked."

"I see. Lost Lagoon?" she inquired.

"Uh-huh." Robby looked at me, surreptitiously winked and turned back to Mrs. McBride.

"How lovely. I've heard the lagoon's quite a popular place for young men to make friends."

"Yes, that's so true," Robby proclaimed with an angelic twinkle brightening his eyes. "I've made several friends there myself."

I swallowed hard, felt a little dizzy and continued to sweat.

"Have you? How lovely! Oh, I didn't get your name, dear."

"It's Robby."

"Well, Robby, I'm certain you two boys want to clean up. Perhaps I'll see you again at the Queen Charlotte." Mrs. McBride smiled broadly at both of us, then picked up her large watering can and started pouring water gently on her tall ficus plants.

"The Queen...? Oh, yes, perhaps."

We made a fast retreat from the lobby and made our way to the staircase.

"There's an elevator but it's faster to use the stairs."

"In a hurry?" he asked, racing behind me to the third floor.

"I'm disgusting," I huffed, fishing out my keys from my damp pocket. "She's right, I need to wash up."

"I've always thought that sweat is sexy," he said, as I unlocked the door and we stepped into the apartment.

"On you it's sexy, on me it's just messy."

"Whoa." Robby inhaled deeply and asked, "I know that you spend a lotta time in the water, but why does your place smell like chlorine bleach?"

"It's my mother," I sighed.

"Your mother smells like Javex?"

"No," I laughed. "I mean she'd been here for a visit. My mother likes everything bleached: the floors, the bathtub, the toilet, clothes, sinks, the phone, food, children, pets. When I clean I do it the same way. It's a family tradition."

Robby looked around. "It's an antiseptic aesthetic," he said. "Great place."

"Thanks."

"Hmm. Glass table, velvet couch, bearskin rug, leather chair." Robby cast his eyes around quickly. "It's like one of those pictures from a decorating magazine - so neat and structured. It's well thought out."

"You notice a lot." The sweat was running off my legs and arms, forming puddles on the hardwood floor.

"When we're creating a set onstage, we try to reflect the characters by their living environment. You know, to give the audience a sense of what they're like."

"Huh," I stated, needing a shower desperately but was nonetheless interested in what Robby was talking about.

"All tremendously scientific," he laughed.

"So, does my set tell you anything about me?"

"For sure. You're orderly, imaginative, on a budget and like spending time by yourself," he ventured.

"That's pretty good. How'd you get that?"

"Well, everything's arranged precisely. There's many different colours and textures, some things new and some vintage. And a guy who makes his place look good must enjoy being there, including time by himself."

"It's really my Mum. She's into decorating and put things together for me." I looked at my apartment. I was pleased that it was tidy, clean and polished.

"Then she knows what you like," Robby said.

I thought about that. Did my mother really know what I liked? Or perhaps my place reflected my mother's likes more than mine? Would she like Robby?

"By tomorrow morning everything will be in tatters, guaranteed." I kicked off my running shoes. "Let me get you something to drink," I said, walking to the kitchen and opening the fridge door. "I've got water or juice, or...something purple and very old," I said, spying a large can of Hawaiian Punch in the fridge. *I really should get rid of this stuff, but it's strangely reassuring seeing it there.*

"Water's fine, thanks. Why don't you grab your shower? You're drenched. I'm good here. I'll stretch for a bit and rinse off after you're done."

"Okay." I poured a big glass of water for Robby and left it on the counter for him. "I'll be back," I said, making my way to an overdue shower. I turned on the water, slid off my Timex, stepped out of my shorts, took off my socks and peeled off the soaked black tee-shirt and got into a hot shower. I was under the spray for a couple of minutes and was a trifle alarmed when the curtain was pulled back. In front of me was Robby. Naked, he stepped over the tub and came up beside me.

"I'm rinsing off now. Okay?"

"Uh, very okay," I stammered.

Under the water, his lean muscles were even more defined. Robby's butt was perfection, round, smooth, firm, bright white. His penis was thick; the pubic hair was fairest red-blond. I'd been around a lot of attractive male bodies; Robby's was peerless. He picked up the soap, moved closer to me, began to lather my chest and the back of my neck. His touch was sensual, running his hands across my chest, applying pressure to my shoulders, then to the small of my back, my flesh softening under his firm hands. I returned the favour, exploring his body under my fingertips. My engorged cock sprang up in front of him. Robby took another step towards me, pulling himself into me, holding me in his arms for a moment. The steamy hot water fell on us as he let go and moved back a few inches. Wordlessly Robby squatted in the shower and placed his mouth on my cock, sucking me slowly and deeply.

"Jeez," I sighed. "That's —"

"Good?" Robby stopped long enough so that he could finish my sentence.

"Uh-huh."

"Your cock's so big; dunno if I can take it all," he laughed, taking it to the base quite easily.

"Hey, no sarcasm allowed."

Robby stood up and kissed me, his tongue lightly pressed against mine, tentative, then assertive, urgent. We stayed in the shower for a short while longer, kissing, touching each other. I turned off the scalding water.

"Let's dry off and head down the hall," I said. After a few swipes of the towel, I took his hand and we went to the bedroom. Though it was still light outside, I lit a candle and put it on the cabinet. I pulled back the green comforter and we tumbled into bed. For hours, we lay in each other's arms and mostly kissed. It sounds improbable, fantastical, but that's how long we locked lips for. Robby was the master of the kiss; long, tender, probing, passionate. At one point I felt as though I might have an orgasm just by kissing him. His mouth on mine seemed to heighten all other senses to a feverish pitch. I turned Robby onto his stomach, stroked his upper shoulders with my hands, taking the time to be gentle and caring. I worked my way down to his bottom, massaging the soft, smooth skin with coconut lotion. His ass felt supple beneath my hands as I caressed it lightly with my lips. He raised his buttock slightly when I touched him.

"Do you want me to —"

"Yes," was his response to a question I hadn't fully asked. I put some lube in Robby's bottom.

"Here, get up on your knees." Robby moved up onto his hands and knees and I eased into him gently. I felt the heat of him as my cock was entirely inside.

"Are you okay?" I wanted to know if it was painful or if I was doing anything wrong.

"No," he sighed. "It's good, keep going."

In my head I had a flashback of the night Pete fucked me. I remembered his assertiveness and I started fucking Robby in the same manner. As Robby relaxed, I felt a growing confidence. My first time being inside a man was exhilarating. His ass was warm and enveloping. I pumped hard for a while, which he seemed to enjoy, then backed off and established a rhythm that was right for both him and for me. *With so much pleasure, I have to be careful not to go over the edge. Make this last as long as possible.* We changed positions a few times over the next hour. We tried him on his side. Then I put him on his back so that I could fuck him and kiss his mouth. He could also stroke himself as I touched his nipples and chest lightly with my fingertips as Pete had done with me. We stopped a few times to kiss again and then returned to anal sex, which I was eager to do. I told him how beautiful he was, how excited I was, how much I was enjoying being with him.

"Did you wanna cum together?" Robby asked breathlessly.

I pushed into him aggressively. "Yeah, I wanna see you cum with me inside you," I urged, borrowing some lingo from the gay porn magazines I'd read from the corner store. I was counting on my dirty talk paying off. "Ugh!" I grunted with each throbbing stroke.

"Oh, man, you're so far in me!"

"Okay, I'm real close!" I looked at Robby - this handsome young man flat on his back with his muscled legs wrapped around my waist as I stood at the side of the bed and made love for the first time... and then I began to cum. "Gawd," I gasped softly and shut my eyes. Robby growled and as I exploded into him, he sprayed semen to the base of his throat. I was motionless for a few seconds longer then kissed him and moved onto the bed beside him. I was once more dripping wet from exertion. Neither of us spoke. I drifted off then woke, though I don't know how long I was asleep for. Perhaps just a few minutes. Lying there, I wasn't sure what the next step was. For the first time, I had invited a man over to my apartment and did something I'd never done. Compared to having sex in a nightclub washroom it was very different. *Was I supposed to ask him to stay? Shouldn't he just grab a shower and leave? What's the protocol for an impromptu sexual encounter? I have to be up at 5 AM. It's gotta be late, really late.* I started worrying about the time as I lay beside him. *You fool, why can't you relax and go with the flow? Because it's probably after 1 AM, that's why. Get up, move around, send him a message so that you can get some sleep before practice.*

"I should go," Robby stated, getting up from the bed as though my telepathy had worked. "Your day starts early, doesn't it?" he asked.

"Yeah, 5 AM and it's gotta be pretty late now." *It's not like it's his fault.* "You're welcome to stay longer...if you want." *Please say no...*

"Thanks, no, I won't. But it'd be great to see you again. If you want to, that is. No expectations."

What about tomorrow night? What about every night? "I'd really like that, Robby. I'm at UBC guarding this summer, are you on campus, too?"

"No, I'm working a couple jobs until school starts up in the fall; stage assisting mostly."

"Okay. Let me give you my number." I scratched my phone number with a nubby pencil on a piece of paper from the bedside table and gave it to him. "I'm usually home from practice by eight o'clock at night. Maybe we could go for a run. Or go see a movie? I haven't seen Star Wars yet and my friend Lara isn't interested in seeing it."

"Star Wars? I doubt it's playing. It was out a couple years ago."

"Oh, right. I don't get out much."

"Everybody's talking about La Cage aux Folles. Next weekend? It's at the Royal Centre on Georgia."

Robby was pulling on his briefs and socks. His runners were at the door, his running shorts and his jade singlet were yet to be located. He left the room to look for them, my number in his hand.

"Sure," I called out, negating my concern about seeing a French film about a cage. "How's Saturday night?"

He came back to the bedroom, shoes on, shorts on, pulling a slightly damp shirt over his head, nodding. "Yeah, sounds good. I'll call you. Thanks for a great night or morning, or whatever it is. Did I tell you how handsome you look?"

"Yeah, I bet I'm lookin' real sharp right now," I said, disheveled, unshaven, hair askew and barely conscious.

"A lot of guys look like crap in the morning." Robby bent over the bed and planted a lingering kiss.

I want him to stay and I want him to go. I smiled and managed to say, "Thanks."

"G'bye."

Robby walked softly from the bedroom. I heard the apartment door close. I got up to lock the door and to find my watch, which I'd left in the washroom. I was surprised to learn the time was three forty-eight. I had just over an hour to sleep before heading out for practice. *I'm going to have a bad swim this morning.* Coach Lerner would be unsympathetic with my story of late-night lust with a young man who'd been cruising for sex in Stanley Park. Probably a poor explanation for a lousy swim. I quickly showered, ate two pieces of bread with peanut butter, brushed my teeth and plopped down on my brown leather chair and closed my eyes. I slept for fifteen minutes and woke, slightly panicked. It was just after 5 AM. Though I was completely exhuasticated, I was *not* going to miss practice. I gathered up my swim gear and headed out the door. *It's been quite a Sunday; Monday now.* I stumbled onto the deserted West End streets, barely awake and oddly found the Fastback right away.

26

TOUTE LA VÉRITÉ ET RIEN QUE LA VÉRITÉ ~ NOTHING BUT THE TRUTH

As I had anticipated, I'd been tired and unfocused at Monday morning's workout. Being lacklustre was unacceptable. Not only did I feel as though I was swimming through molasses, the effort I had put into running with Robby made for inefficient and sloppy kicking. The coaching staff wanted to know what was wrong; I feigned having the flu. I couldn't afford to do this again. Consistency was important in the water, especially now, when I was working towards the Edmonton time-trials. *Late nights without adequate sack time will have to go on hold…at least until next Saturday night,* I told myself, as I struggled to complete the workout under the unimpressed eyes of Coach Lerner. By the next day, I had rested and was back to form, however, I was not in a position to futz about with sluggish practices. I had to be at a certain performance level without exception. Just like Lara, there were people who'd made sacrifices in order for us to shine; it wasn't about just her or me.

The first Thursday in June, I had an afternoon off work and arranged to meet Lara by the Royal Vancouver Yacht Club in Coal Harbour. The afternoon was blue-grey, misty, damp, cool. The seawall was mostly deserted. I paced back and forth waiting for Lara when I saw her fast approach, red hair bobbing, no umbrella, blue Nike shorts, white runners and a bright blue tee-shirt with the slogan, *Stick with the Plan* in white letters written across her chest.

"Hi," I said, giving her a warm hug. "What's the *Plan*?"

"To go for a walk, of course."

"No, I meant the tee-shirt," I said, pointing at her chest.

"Huh? Oh! I don't know what the *Plan* is. Do you?"

"Haven't got a clue," I answered falsely. Truthfully, I had thought about one plan thousands of times. We started walking slowly past the Yacht Club, office towers across the harbour were our backdrop. After ten minutes, other towers came into a more prominent view, the tops obscured with mist and fog. I stopped when we could see the Marine Building. "Still the best in the city." I gestured with my hand across Coal Harbour to the iconic skyscraper.

"I know, Sunshine. Built in 1930, once the tallest building in the Commonwealth. There's depictions of geese, umm, pufferfish, biplanes, dirigibles and trains. It symbolizes a rock rising out of the ocean. And, one day, you'll have your own office there. How's that?" Lara looked pleased with herself.

"Wow, I'm impressed. You were listening to me," I said.

"You know I always listen to you," she said warmly.

"Good. Because I have something difficult that I'd like to talk with you about," I said in a quiet voice.

"Something serious, isn't it?"

"Yes. I'm probably going to struggle telling you, so please be patient with me."

"As Job," Lara promised.

I felt flushed, awkward and unready to talk.

"Gawd, I want this to be so polished and poetic, but…" I stalled.

"Please, you don't need poetry. Let's just walk," she said softly.

We started to stroll along Coal Harbour with skyscrapers as our foggy-grey backdrop and the totem poles at Brockton Point looming beside us. I began to fumble with my words. Lara was being patient as requested; each moment seemed like forever to me.

"Alright," I said, blowing out a deep breath. *Take your mark, ready…* "Lara, for a long time…from when I was a boy I've known that I was… you know, compared to the other boys, different…" *Different? I'm making it sound like I was born with an extra nipple.* Another deep breath. "I mean, not weird, but different in that, well…for me, I knew that I was… attracted to —" I paused, lost my breath completely, dreading the words I needed to speak. *Attracted to what? Edward Albee plays? Flower arranging? Walt Whitman poetry? Square dancing? C'mon…get it out, just say it.* "— men." The words flew out of my mouth like a bird in flight. Lara was silent and we kept walking, me going on carefully, beginning to weave my story, my throat constricted, dry, my eyes staring straight ahead. "I knew that I was gay, well not gay exactly, I mean I knew that I was attracted to males when I was a young boy, which of course makes me gay."

I recounted the story about riding the train with my mother and the Mountie in his scarlet uniform. Lara was quiet, listening carefully as we continued to walk.

"There was no doubt in my mind then or now. But I hid it or tried to. And growing up in my family…well, I got very good at hiding it. I figured if my father knew he might throw me out. And my mother, well, I hope she'd understand, but I'm not sure. Dad's influential. Maybe my father would convince her I was a worthless fag." I nearly choked on my words. "I've been an impersonator, ever since I was a child, all through school and university, with my family and with you, too. I couldn't ever be more than a friend to you even though I tried to be something else. I'm sorry if you were hurt or disappointed by me in any way. My friendship with you got me through and kept me going." I stopped and took a breath, looked at Lara and continued. "I regret that I had to be deceitful.…I just found it impossible to tell you, and the longer it's taken the harder it's been. I barely admitted it to myself all these years. And if you couldn't accept it and wouldn't want to be friends then…I don't know what I'd do." I stopped walking. Lara and I stood in the increasing rainfall. "You've always shared so much with me and I've held back. I feel like a shit-head." I felt heat rising off my chest and was likely crimson-faced. Lara remained wordless. "I never wanted to pretend, but I was afraid. Do you understand why…why it's been tough for me to talk with you about this?"

"Yes, of course I understand," Lara said eagerly. Her smile gave me an immediate sense that I was being unburdened of a great weight. "Sunshine, I'm so sorry. I've screwed up, too." Lara held my arms, "Vous étiez si tendre. Je l'ai pris pour la romance. Nos amitiés, c'est mieux que de romance. C'est l'amour, véritable amour."

"Lara, you know I didn't under —"

"You need to study your Français, Ensoleillement, for Montreal," Lara said, remonstrating me slightly. "I said that you were so very… tender. I took it for romance. I was confused, too. But our friendship, it's been better than romance. It's been a real love."

"Lara, I —"

"Let me finish. I had a crush on you in class. You tried hard, but God, you were abysmal at French. I felt sorry for you. I wanted to help and you were so appreciative —"

"I was grateful for the assistance - you made it possible for me to pass French - barely." I recalled the beginning of our friendship. There's a certain look when someone would like to be more than study partners.

"I mistook your attention for romance. I've made the same error with other men. I admit that I wanted more from you then. I thought that perhaps in time, well, somehow you'd come around. My ego was showing, wasn't it?"

"Ego? No, I'm flattered."

"Most every man I've met has tried to get every stitch of clothing off me in thirty minutes or less, but not you."

"Not me," I agreed quickly.

"But it wasn't just about sex. I sensed a big part of you was…locked up. I started thinking that you might be…*different*." She paused for a moment.

"Like I said?" I asked.

"Exactly like you said. I didn't know much about it - being gay - but I knew what I was feeling, and for more than a couple of years."

"Really?"

"Sunshine, how many straight men know the lyrics to 'Gypsy'?"

"I see your point."

"So, a while ago I went to Spartacus Bookstore and —"

"Hold on, you went where?"

"It's a —"

"Lara, I know what it is - it's a bookstore for anarchists."

"Oh, and much more. They were so knowledgeable. I even learned about handkerchiefs, you know, in your Levi's. Do you know what colour to wear?"

"What colour? You mean there's a colour?"

"There's a colour code for everything, Buttercup. And ask me about the Castro, where there's sex around the clock. That's in San Fran —"

"I know where it is, Lara."

"And there's Pier 48 and the Mineshaft in New York - have you heard what goes on there after hours?"

"Well, I haven't really —"

"A real eye opener. And you know about Tom of Finland?"

"Tom of Finland?"

"Oh, I think you'd adore him. I take it you know about cock rings?"

"Cock rings?"

"Yes, cock rings. Very popular with the leather men. Though I don't think you're one, right? I mean, I'm not sure. Artemus said it can be hard to tell."

"Artemus?" My head was whirling.

"Yes, from Spartacus. She explained that being gay is about more than sex, though that *is* such a fascinating part. She was so informative!"

"Sounds like it."

"And colourful. She had a silver ring in her nose and wore camouflage pants and a beret; she's the alternative type. Artemus sold me a couple of books and gave me a primer on life in the gay lane."

"You're on a first-name basis?"

"Yes, she was terribly nice! And I've been eager to learn. She asked me out for an espresso on Commercial Drive that same day."

"She wanted to take you for coffee?"

"Not just coffee, she also took me bowling at the Commodore Lanes and asked me to a vegetarian pot-luck at a Wymmin's party in Strathcona."

"And you didn't turn her down?"

"Why on earth would I do that? I had an amazing meal with wonderful women. Janice made these fantastic chickpea and onion fritters; there was a faux-meatloaf with a spicy red pepper sauce and salads to die for. Plus, Artemus made a killer baba ghanoush with roasted garlic. Reminds me…I gotta get that recipe."

"You don't cook."

"That's true. Oh, and I almost passed out from the triple-chocolate brownies - I suspect something other than cocoa was in 'em - that Trigger baked."

"*Trigger?* Okay, let me get this straight. You bewitched a lesbian anarchist, went on a bowling date and stuffed your face at an all-women's pot-luck? This is a lot for me to get my head around."

"Isn't it? Artemus and her friends made me feel so accepted. I'll be seeing them Thursday night for a baseball game at Nat Bailey's. I've met so many women who've created their own network of friends and girlfriends. A community without men," she sighed. "I can see the appeal. Is that what it's been like for you? I mean *with* men?"

"Not quite yet. It's a slow undertaking for me."

"How can I help?" Lara asked imploringly. "Please, how can —"

"You've been helping all along. Lara, I hafta ask - you've known for a couple of years?"

"At least. And when you finally told me that you'd had sex a while back I stopped myself from asking - who's the guy? I held my tongue until I'd done some reading and talked to a few people. I've made so many blunders I swore I'd keep my big trap shut until I was more informed and you were ready to come out. Good grief, do you know how torturous this has been for me?"

"I can only imagine."

"I should have told you that I knew and that it didn't matter - gay or straight. Maybe it would have been easier on you. It hurt me to know that you were alone with all this. Everybody had an opinion; I didn't know which was right. And I didn't..." Lara's eyes were suddenly shining. "I didn't want to embarrass my best friend and screw things up."

"You didn't screw anything up, Lara. You respected my privacy and waited for me to tell you. It was the perfect thing to do."

"It was? Then I'm quite proud of myself." Lara beamed, tears forming in her beautiful brown eyes.

"I guess I didn't have to be afraid of you dumping me after coming out, huh?"

Lara wrapped me up in her slender arms and looked straight into my eyes.

"What would I be without you, stupid? You know, I've managed to have a few relationships with men. How many have worked out?"

"Well..." I started to answer and Lara shook her head.

"It's rhetorical. Do you know you're the most solid relationship I've ever had with a man?"

"I dunno about that, Lara. Even without the mind-bending sex?"

"Idiot," she laughed. "Especially without. Oh, it's really starting to pour."

The clouds dropped tears upon us, washing away any lingering hurts or secrets. Viewing my mist-shrouded city, I finally knew what euphoria was. Lara's hand reached for mine as we strolled in the rainfall. Wordlessly, we walked past the boats in the Coal Harbour, past Deadman's Island as the eastern view to Burrard Inlet opened up. We were approaching the Nine O'clock Gun, and even though the cold rains doused us with each step, with Lara's hand in mine I felt warm.

"This is so nice. Last time we held hands was on the seawall, too. Such a long time ago, wasn't it?" she asked.

Four years earlier we'd danced at the Commodore, had an intimate dinner at the Blue Horizon, drove around the park and took a slow walk on Second Beach. It had been a dreamy late summer's evening that slowly turned to dawn. I was with the most beautiful creature I'd ever known. She'd told me all about her fantasies of being a singer as we'd walked. Clam shells crackled under her shoes, the tide ran over the sand and the sky turned violet with the approaching sunrise. I had aspirations that I shared as well, carefully metered out. As we'd walked, I'd taken her soft hand in mine - a gesture of wanting to be a different young man just for her. And perhaps for me, too. Things that I had hungered to do and longed to feel had happened to me, happened to Lara. There were more experiences to come for us, for everyone. *Life moves along for us all, we can't stop it; we can't even slow it down.*

"Sunshine, that night we'd gone out, I told you that one day I was going to live in a log house." Lara gasped, *"A log house?* With cracks in the wall filled with mud and braided rugs on a dirt floor...like Annie Oakley, maybe? What was I thinking?" Lara laughed softly and turned to me. "Remember?"

I sighed and nodded, deeply calm and pleasured with the shared memory. I held her hand a little tighter as we walked, no longer any need for me to be or act differently. The increasing rains were leaving us dripping wet but also renewed, once again alone together on the seawall. The same seawall we'd walked a thousand times, but everything seemed remarkably different.

"Yes, Lara," I said, sensing the enormity of this moment. My throat felt constricted as we walked past Hallelujah Point. My voice broke like an adolescent when I said, "I'm remembering it all."

27

HAPPY COINCIDENCES

In mid-June, I was relieved to have swum well enough at the Western Swim Meet in Edmonton to qualify for the Nationals in all three of my events. Lerner had me hold back significantly; he knew that I could swim faster, but he was cautious about me peaking too soon. I still had more preparation to do. Lara was also in preparation for her most important appearance to date: Festijazz. It was a striking coincidence that the Nationals and the Festival would be taking place in Montreal the same week. Lara thought it was providence, but I'm a skeptic about such things as destiny. I don't believe that there are divine cosmic forces driving how life unwinds for people. But I do enjoy happy coincidences and extraordinary opportunities. I'll admit that it was odd how some life events could come together, like meeting Robby at the lagoon. After all, I was just out for a run and couldn't imagine hooking up with someone, let alone a boy I'd fancied from high school. I was happy that Robby and I had been able to see each other over the last few weeks. Unquestionably handsome, he was also clever, which was a major attraction for me. Robby was showing me new things, like how to understand the directorial choices of Hitchcock, Orson Welles, Roman Polanski and Fritz Lang. It was exciting to talk about the arts with a man I was also sharing a bed with on a semi-regular basis. Pete had mostly faded into the back of my consciousness since Robby and I started seeing each other. I'd decided that while in training, only Saturday nights were possible for me to go out with Robby. Those nights we went to movies such as La Cage aux Folles and some graphic German films including Die Konsequenz and Das Ende des Regenbogens, which opened my eyes to fresh interpretations of gay culture. Robby took me to the Art's Club Theatre on Seymour Street where we saw a ribald Canadian play called Talking Dirty. He was also involved several creative projects such as a new stage on Granville Island. *Robby's a persevering type of guy. A real hard worker. Works as hard as my father but is also interested in other parts of living, too.* In the five weeks before Nationals, I also had a lot of work to do. I had to demonstrate that I was capable of doing times that had been out of my reach a few months ago. And I had to better them if I was to get to the podium. I eased off my guarding schedule for the next four weeks. Instead of working at the pool I increased all aspects of my training. I was under water for up to eight hours a day, swimming endless repeats of my events. In addition, there was distance and weight training, painful stretching with the physical therapist and treatments with ice-water baths. A slight increase in my musculature became evident. The improvements helped propel me through the water with more fire-power. It was these little extras that could potentially help me to blast past the competition, though it was taking many weeks to obtain slight gains. Swimming at a high level was consuming, but I was discovering that life was about much more - school, work, friends, family and possibly having a boyfriend.

With Pete's direction and support, Lara was also moving towards her objectives. For nearly a year, Pete had proved an extraordinary mentor. I can't say that Pete didn't occupy my thoughts since I had been seeing Robby. It was probable that Lara's assessment of Pete was correct; he might well have been a player. Or he was a sweet guy who wanted to connect with me because he liked me or liked having sex with me. What was wrong with that? I was learning slowly that things don't always make sense. *Still, that doesn't make me a nihilist. Stay curious. There's more to come. Watch what happens.*

28

POP-UP PETE

The last days of a balmy August were ticking down. Summer training had been tough. I was about to begin a taper - the decrease of intensive training strategically timed with the upcoming swim meet - and I was ready for it. I had done all of the work necessary and had to find the balance between staying fresh and staying competitive. It was a welcome relief for my tired and constantly aching body. However, the taper had to be perfectly timed so that there was no loss of speed in order to be competitive for Nationals.

Swim Canada was paying for my return flight to Montreal, but not for accommodation. For competitions, swimmers were usually billeted or stayed in low-cost motels. Though I hadn't finalized my lodgings, I told Coach Lerner that I preferred to stay by myself. I explained that I needed complete concentration. Lerner knew my style and consented to my wish. During the past four years I'd worked hard to secure his faith in me.

I was excited to be competing at the pool constructed for the 1976 Summer Olympics where American swimmers had swept the gold medals. Three years later, I'd be attempting to move through my heats and get into my own finals. The pool was pretty standard with eight lanes and fifty metres long. What wasn't standard was that the facility would be filled with five thousand spectators transforming it into a sports theatre. The meet was still ten days away, but I was already uptight. Merely thinking of heading to Montreal to swim with the top Canadian competitors was nerve-wracking. This was the time to settle my fears, to keep training smartly and ensure proper nutrition and rest. I had committed to a sequence of steps that I'd been taking since I was a youngster. Keeping mentally fit was as important as any series of swim sets I ever could do and nearly as taxing.

Lara was also experiencing the strain of having to sing at a new level of performance. Like an athlete, she had to warm-up, do countless scales and strenuously exercise her diaphragm daily. (I did them with her a few times and was challenged with the effort.) Her vocal teacher insisted she eat differently to maximize her singing prowess which meant a standard diet of mostly lean chicken, plenty of vegetables and fresh fruits. No Virginia Slims, of course. She was told to suck hard candies to coat her vocal folds with a constant supply of sugar, so she always had Jolly Ranchers and Life Savers. There were some hard and fast rules: four litres of water per day and limited alcohol consumption due to the drying effect on her vocal cords. This was okay; she could get by with less white wine. The clincher? No dairy. No thick spread of butter on crunchy French bread, no rich sauces on her pasta at Umberto's, no ice-cream on her favourite peach cobbler at the Aristocratic and no cheesecake. Lara willingly gave up all those things to be at her best, inadvertently losing another six pounds off her already slim frame in the process. Knowing how Lara enjoyed food, I respected her self-discipline. She had been spending a tremendous amount of time rehearsing with the trio, going over her arrangements, re-working some of the instrumental breaks, changing the song order, refining and perfecting any areas of perceived deficit. By the end of the summer, having sung at several dates in the Pacific

Northwest, she was as ready as me to make a real splash. We spoke most every day as we moved through the month, finding our conversations calming. I informed Lara that I was seeing someone. She was pleased for me but hadn't had the chance to meet him. I didn't quite know if I was ready for Lara to meet Robby. I wanted both people to really like each other. While Lara made it clear that romance was a distraction to her goal, I was liking the distractions in the form of Robby Berd. I'd been amazed at how another person could bring such satisfaction. There was potential for a deep attachment. (I was reading about Bowlby's attachment theory.) When I was near Robby I felt something inexplicable in my groin and chest. My infatuation was hard to explain in rational terms. It wasn't exactly a new feeling; I'd felt a rush with Pete, too. However, he was also quite different from Robby in that he was inconstant. That might have been a part of the excitement. When I did think about Pete, I rationalized that he could never have been more than an occasional secret lover.

On Thursday afternoon following practice, I was at a Chinese market on Davie collecting my feedbag of vegetables when I heard a voice from behind me.

"Excuse me, but do you know anything about this fruit?"

I turned around to see Pete holding an avocado his sun-tanned hand.

"Hey! I wouldn't know where to begin," I laughed, put my basket down and went to shake his hand.

"Why so formal?" Pete put his avocado back and gave me a long hug. He looked dashing in khaki shorts with a wide dark brown belt and a light-blue linen shirt, opened enough to see some dark chest hair. His smile was broad and sexy and his hair was considerably longer - hair that belonged in a Vidal Sassoon commercial. He had grown a short scruffy beard; very sexy. *And what was that eau de cologne?* Lemony, bright, distinguished. I was wearing Eau de Chlorine.

233

"You're looking great," I said. I'd never seen him look anything less than flawless. I worried I might have a caraway seed stuck between my teeth from the onion roll I'd had after practice. I discreetly pushed my tongue around seeking any potential kernel. "Getting some fruit, are you Pete?" Somehow I never imagined him doing something as mundane as shopping for apples and bananas. Shopping for a Porsche? That I could visualize.

"Nope. I saw an extremely fit young guy go into Chan's Produce. I had to follow him to tell him he was the sexiest man in Vancouver. It was no surprise that it was you."

Of course. I can never tell where Pete will pop up. He's got a knack for following people, catching them off-guard and charming the pants of them. Literally. I'm merely one of the many.

"Really? Well, that's quite a coincidence," I said coyly. *C'mon, you're going out with Robby, numb-nuts.*

"Truly." Pete then stated, "I hear you came out to Lara a couple months ago. Did you tell her about, ah, you and me?"

Hmm, is this why you followed me to the fruit and vegetable store?

I bent closer to his ear. "You mean did I tell her that you fucked me in a filthy washroom while your protégé was waiting upstairs? Wouldn't that've been in poor taste?"

"I'll take that as a no," Pete said, his white teeth gleaming. "It's just that I don't want anything to rock Lara's and my working relationship."

"I don't kiss and tell. Not my style."

"What is your style?" Pete asked, taking a look at my slovenly appearance.

"Well, as you can see, my style is a bit lacking right now. I've just come from swim practice which is why I have my sweats on and smell like chlorine instead of, well, like you."

"Oh, you manage to pull it off just fine. So, you like my cologne, do you? It's Eau de Savage."

"I might have noticed it," I sniffed. "Very nice."

"My dad told me to look good and smell better. It's great seeing you," Pete enthused, following behind me as I filled my red plastic basket with grapes, oranges, small potatoes, onions and cans of garbanzo beans. "Lara says that you're getting ready for a big swim meet in Montreal at the same time that she'll be there," Pete said, standing very close beside me as I surveyed the apples.

"Yes. It's the Nationals. Strangely, the time overlaps. I told her that I would go to her event if she would go to mine."

"Terrific. How're you getting there?"

"Flying, of course. CP Air."

"Maybe I could help you out with your flight," Pete offered.

"Ah, that's kind, but no thanks, Pete. Swim Canada's paying my way to the meet."

"And when you're there? I mean, you won't be sleeping at the pool. Where will all of you stay?" he inquired as I put some Macintosh apples in the rapidly filling basket.

"I found an affordable room, and pretty close to the pool. The other swimmers'll bunk at a motel, but not me 'cause I need the privacy. I told Lerner it wasn't for —"

"Cancel it," Pete stated abruptly.

"Excuse me?"

"Cancel your accommodation. I'm going to make a suggestion."

I stopped picking at the cantaloupes and looked at Pete. *Those dark lashes...gulp.* "Lara could really use a calming influence in Montreal. So I'd like to put you both up at the St. James Hotel in Old Montreal. I think it would be perfect; it's quiet and it's near the pool," he added for extra saleability.

Does he really want me to stay with Lara or was this a ruse? Is he wanting to bed me down? Do I want him to? Of course you do, but you won't, not with Robby, will you? No. Why is it so hard to resist Pete?

"And," he said, "I insist on paying the bill. It's all part of the expense for Lara's gig." He looked at me with intensity. "Personally, I'd like it if you were there, too."

"Oh. And you'll be staying there at the same hotel?"

"I will," he said plainly.

I thought a bit more. "And is the hotel expensive?" I asked.

"It's very affordable," Pete answered calmly.

"Tell you what, if it helps Lara, then I'll seriously consider it, but I can pay my own way."

Pete checked out if anyone was watching, then reached around my waist to the small of my back.

"Fine. Even when you're serious, you're sexy," Pete conceded. He slid his large hand to my bottom and squeezed my butt. "Whoa, that's a hard ass," Pete said with a wide grin on his face. "You need a hand taking that fruit home?"

"Who you calling a fruit?"

"If the banana fits," Pete said, grabbing the largest one from my basket and raising his eyebrows à la Groucho Marx. I hesitated. There wasn't any stated understanding about Robby and me being exclusive, but... *Stop rationalizing.*

"You know, Pete, I'm seeing someone right now," I said weakly.

"I heard. Lara told me. It doesn't mean that I can't walk you back to the Queen Charlotte though, does it?"

"No, of course not. I just meant that, well, you know."

"What? You're not afraid of the Big Bad Wolf, are you?"

I thought about being a boy and seeing that top-hat-wearing Wolf at my window, scaring me witless.

"Oh, no...I don't believe in Wolves anymore," I lied.

"C'mon, then. Buy your stuff and I'll walk you back." Pete moved along to the cashier with me a step behind. "It'll be nice to have a visit. You can pour me a big glass of Hawaiian Punch."

I scowled at Pete, remembering I still had it in my fridge. I put my items on the table and cashed out. The dull-looking bald Chinese lady in the brown-checked mismatched polyester outfit stood at the register and barked, "Seven dollah, twenty-tooo sens."

I rummaged for the cash in my pocket and counted it out in my hand. The cashier nearly snatched it from my paw. "Hey, careful, Miss Manners," I admonished. Pete and I left the market and walked down the hill with English Bay sparkling in the distance. I explained the tapering process to Pete. He seemed interested.

"So, what would it mean if you made the National Team?" Pete asked as we continued to walk.

"I'd have funding to train at a much higher level. As long as I'm competing, my tuition and some expenses would be looked after. I'd have a chance to go to some big swim meets like the Pan American Games. It'd be a great experience."

"All very exciting, eh?"

With pursed lips I let out a huge breath. "Exciting *and* anxious. It'll be the same in Montreal - right up to the moment I walk to my block. The anxiety'll go away when I hit the water. At least, that's the strategy."

"It's like an actor or a singer," Pete commented, "whose fears vanish when they step onstage."

"Yeah, I guess the pool is my stage. Didn't Shakespeare write about the actor that struts and frets his hour upon the stage?"

"Very good. Macbeth's famous soliloquy."

"Let's hope when this actor hits the footlights he doesn't barf his guts out in the water. It's not very dignified."

Pete laughed and tousled my hair as we walked. We turned up Nicola, away from the traffic and heat and onto the cooler, tree-lined street.

"Isn't body-shaving part of the preparation?"

"Huh?" I wondered where that question came from. "Uh-huh. It's a ritual. A lot of the guys do it the night before with each other. Not me; I'm a solo guy."

We were nearing my apartment. Pete smiled at me but I couldn't tell what he was thinking.

"And does it make a difference, or is it all in the head?" he asked.

"Hair creates resistance in the water. A swimmer'll do anything to take off a hundredth of a second, believe me." We had arrived at the front door. "Well," I said. *Okay, think about this. Do you really want him to come in? It's a bad idea. Something might happen. But only if I let it, and I don't have to let it, do I? No, it's wrong. It's stupid. I'd be tempting fate. Right, the fate you don't believe in. No, it's the worst idea ever. Say good-bye and get on with your afternoon.*

"So...how 'bout it? Aren't you asking me in?" Pete tilted his head and locked his dark eyes on mine.

No. No. No...

"Yes, come on up," I said, opening the door. We hiked to the third floor; me with my giant bag of produce, hair mussed, unshaven wearing my grungy UBC grey fleece sweatpants and a tattered and torn red sweatshirt. Pete, the contrasting player, looked refined, devilishly handsome; hair perfect, scented with cologne, clothes sporty and elegant. As we got to my floor, I noticed Mrs. McBride, vacuuming the carpet with her back to us. *Good, she won't see me. I don't want to explain yet another man coming into my apartment.* I fumbled for my key and in the process sent the bag of produce flying.

"Shit!" I hollered loud enough to defeat my stealthy avoidance of Mrs. McBride. She turned around immediately and said, "Oh, my dear!" as the apples and oranges rolled towards her like runaway boulders. Pete stood and watched, amused at the picture of me dashing after traveling fruit.

"Gawd, I'm sorry, Mrs. Mc - uh, Hannah," I said, collecting the items. Looking over at Pete, Mrs. McBride turned off the vacuum and tellingly said, "It seems as though you have far too much to handle, dear. And you've brought someone home with you, too. How nice. Perhaps he can help." She looked pleased.

"Uh, well...yes," I stammered.

"We've met before, haven't we?" She came towards Pete, leaving me to pick up my produce.

"Yes, Mrs. McBride. Some time ago." Pete smiled brightly.

"Of course, shortly after our Johnny Weissmuller moved in." She gestured at me. "I never forget when distinguished-looking gentlemen come by the Queen Charlotte." She smiled and appeared slightly coquettish.

Jeez, now even Mrs. McBride is making a pass at Pete. No one's immune.

"That's kind of you to say."

"Isn't it lovely that you have so many friends that come over to visit?" she asked, looking at me. Pete shot me a knowing grin. Under the circumstances, I thought it best not to respond and start a conversation about the frequency of my male visitors. So I merely nodded my head as I put the produce back into the bag.

"Here's the key." I threw a ring of keys at Pete. "It's the one with the purple doohickey on it." He looked at me with raised brows, as he located it. "Yeah, that one," I said, flustered and uncomfortable.

Mrs. McBride said, "Oh, I must tell you that I found what I've been searching for in the basement. You must come round and we'll have a look-see. Before you go away." She collected an orange that escaped my capture and put it in my bag.

"Um, sure, okay, I'll do that. I'm sort of busy right now, but —"

"Yes, dear. I can see that. No, I meant later this or next week. There's no rush, but surely before you go to Montreal."

"May I ask what you wanted me to see?" As flustered as I was, I was interested in what lay in store for me in the dark and ghostly basement.

"Oh, my, such a curious young man. It's meant to be a surprise. Every boy likes surprises, dear. Don't you?"

"Well, I guess..."

"Now, I must keep on with this hoovering. Besides, your companion is waiting for you, and he looks quite expectant." She glanced at the door that Pete was holding open for me.

"Talk with you later this week, okay?" I asked, anxious to finish up our conversation in the hallway. She smiled, nodded her silver head and went back to her vacuuming. I went through to the apartment with my bag, closed the door and blew out a lung full of air.

"She's wily like a coyote, isn't she?" he asked.

Hmm, my previous thought exactly. And you're more than a bit wily yourself - hunting me down in the West End, I thought, putting away my purchases in the fridge and cupboard.

"She's sharp," I said. "She wanted to know whether it was a girl or a boy I was going to be sharing the brass bed she gave me. Very direct, but never mean. Mrs. McBride's looked after me ever since I —"

"And you like being looked after?" Pete interrupted. "I wouldn't have thought so."

"I guess it depends," I said, putting vegetables in the fridge and regretting that I'd asked Pete into my apartment.

"Maybe I could look after something for you?" Pete asked with a searing gaze.

Oops, there's a tug at my penis. "Um, no, I dunno what you mean." I stopped putting items away and turned to face him.

"I think you know exactly what I mean," Pete said softly, taking measured steps towards me.

He either has a fever or he just radiates heat. I stepped back slightly and Pete immediately noticed.

"You're not comfortable."

"Pete, it's just that we haven't been alone like this. And I've been going out with someone...right; I told you that before."

"Listen, just relax and I'll give you Pete's Special." He paused. I didn't speak, I was frozen. "You're supposed to ask me what the special is," he said.

"I'm afraid to ask. Okay, what's Pete's Special?"

"A great massage. We were trained in theatre school. It's very therapeutic. Bet you could use one, too, especially on your shoulders and lower back."

"I dunno, my shoulders and back are tickety-boo," I lied. In point of fact, they were tired and sore.

"Uh-uh, I don't believe you," he said, putting his large hands at the base of my neck and squeezing firmly. "I've never seen that brass bed you've talked about. It's time you showed me."

"My bed? Oh, it's just a metal bed. No biggie, really —"

Pete stopped my babbling and put his mouth on mine. *Oh, Gawd. I shouldn't kiss him back.* His lips tasted sweet and felt soft as I yielded to his mouth. *This can't go well.*

"I wanna see you on the bed with your sweats off, buster. Now."

"Uh…" *This has gone too far. Why aren't you thinking about Robby?* I walked to the bedroom pulling off my top then my sweatpants and boxer shorts and lay down.

"Your chest is beautiful," Pete sighed. "I can see how hard you've been working." Pete moved his hand from my chest and traced the outline of my abdominal muscles with his long finger. It felt electric. "Now lie on your stomach…that's right, and I'll put some lotion on your back and do you."

Do you? What am I getting into? Okay, just a back rub. There goes the lotion - it's cold. But Pete's hands are so warm. He kneaded my shoulders like bread dough, releasing the muscles with a nimble touch.

"Ahhh, Pete, that's…really so…"

He compressed my shoulder and back muscles with his strong hands. Searching for knots along the way, he applied pressure on each vertebra all the way down to my lower back. *How much further is he going with those hands? Am I testing my boundaries with him? Idiot, you've already failed the test miserably.* He massaged my buttocks, then the inside of my groin, pulling, kneading, squeezing, releasing tight muscles until I was in another world of thought and mind. Pete continued to work the back of my thighs, then my calves and even my tired feet, which he flexed, rotated, palpated and soothed with expert hands. In thirty minutes I was a changed man.

"Wow, thank you," was all I could manage to say.

"I'm not finished," he said. "Roll over."

I did as I was told, turning over so that Pete could apply another layer of lotion and lightly massage my chest, my hips and my quads. He brought his fingertips to my temples and massaged them with a deft touch.

"Gawd, Pete. Imagine if you did this before my races? I'd fall off the starting block and drop to the bottom of the pool." I was completely immobilized. He stopped and I looked at him; he was sweating a bit at his forehead and there was a trace of perspiration on his linen shirt. "Hey," I said. "I never thought that you could sweat," I laughed. He climbed onto the bed.

"I'm full of surprises. You'll stay with Lara at the St. James?"

"Well, I —"

"Write down your dates and leave 'em in my pocket. I'll make the arrangements this evening."

"Okay. You win." *Why fight it? I just can't say no to this guy.*

"Good. Lara depends on you."

"Yes, she does. I depend on her, too. She depends on you. We're multi-dependable," I babbled.

"Right. You're not relaxed, you're incoherent. Get up. Let's grab a shower. I'm sweaty and you're slippery as the Shah of Iran."

Pete carefully removed his clothes, folding his shirt and shorts and placed them on the bed before going to the bathroom. We climbed into the tub and I turned on the shower full force, which was like a typhoon. There was a douche I'd attached to the shower. I started this cleansing routine since I was dating Robby. I could never tell when Robby or I needed to be ultra-clean. It made things a lot more sanitary. I hadn't turned the douche selection off; the water came out of the secondary nozzle at full force.

"Jesus!" Pete cried as he was blasted the harsh spray. "That's a lot-ta pressure," as the water hit his head. "Let's hope my toupee doesn't come off," he joked, as the stream pounded his long hair. I adjusted the lever and laughed as Pete washed my back. I'd never seen him fully naked before. His body was different from Robby's. Not athletic exactly, but lean, muscled lightly, with his pendulous cock swinging between his legs.

"Why don't I help you get ready for your swim meet?" he asked.

"How's that?"

"Well," Pete said, taking the Bic razor and the shave gel from the shower caddy.

"It's more than a week away, Pete."

"I'll give you a head start."

"*Pete,*" I mildly protested.

"C'mon. Better than you doing it yourself. You'll never reach where I can."

"You don't remember how flexible I am. Swimmers are quite bendy."

"I *do* recall," he said, re-directing the shower away from us and lathering up my chest. "Not much hair to get rid of, is there?"

Pete grabbed the Bic; put it to my skin and started stroking, re-moving the fine hair from my body.

"Oh, you're right. I prefer you do it. Much easier," I sighed.

Pete continued, finishing my chest in a few moments, then the faint trace of hair on my stomach then on to my legs, which were more of a challenge. I stood facing the shower as he swiped at any hair on my buttock and then he turned me round again. Pete soaped my cock, rinsed the Bic razor and started removing hair from my scrotum. The area was sensitive and I responded with an erection. He finished shaving my body until it was glassy smooth.

"Amazing," he whispered, admiring his work and putting the razor away. He ran his tongue from my chest to my mid-section, then began sucking my cock, touching my hairless balls and rolling them gently as my cock was lodged deep in his throat. *I shouldn't be doing this, but it's so hot.* Pete continued to suck me then told me to face the shower. He took the douche attachment, flicked the switch and placed it against my butt, filling me with and emptying the clear water down the drain. After replacing the douche nozzle in the stand he buried his face in my ass, tonguing it deeply, send-ing little shock waves through my body. He continued to rim me until I thought I was going to explode, so I turned round. Pete took my cock into his mouth and sucked me, overwhelming me with sensation.

"Oh, Pete, you'd better stop. I'm gettin' close."

"Turn the water off," he said and I reached back and shut off the faucets.

He stood up, grasped my hands and put them behind my lower back, then kissed me hard. Pete and I stepped out of the shower and walked back to the bedroom, soaking wet, water glistening on our bodies from the sunlight coming through the window. "Sit on the edge of the bed." Pete took my cock in his mouth and started to suck me, hard, gentle, using his saliva-moistened hand to glide over the veiny surface, the glans, the underside, brushing my ass with his fingers, probing into me. "Your ass is so hot." Pete went back to sucking me and I was once more getting close to orgasm.

"You gotta slow down. Oh, Gawd, Pete…you're gonna make me cum."

I grunted as he kept his mouth on my penis and I emptied into his warm, beautiful mouth. I drew a deep, satisfied breath and Pete looked at me, smiling. Without a word, he turned me over onto my stomach.

"Relaxed?" he asked, leaning over to get more lotion from the table.

"Mmm," I exhaled. I felt cool lotion on my buttock and then around my rectum. Pete's large cock pushed against me firmly.

"Whoa…" I said, gasping as his cock entered me. "Jeez," I said, not expecting there was going to be more to our encounter.

"You're warm inside." He pushed deeper into me then pulled all the way out. He reached for some more lotion and applied it to my now relaxed bottom. "You feel good. I wish you could know how hot this looks. Kneel more, that's right. Feels great, huh?"

"Gawd," was all I could manage to say.

"Like it? Like how this feels?" Pete was picking up the pace, quickening the strokes, reminding me of the excitement of Oil Can Harry's. He reached up to my head and grabbed two handfuls of my hair and gently tugged. My cock and balls were floppy, bouncing back against him as he pushed every inch into me and stroked with greater intensity.

"Yeah," I muttered, nearly hyperventilating. My butt was the centre of my universe now, not my penis. I felt deeply aroused, with each long stroke causing me to gasp. I'd thought that the pleasure would have stopped with me cumming earlier - I was wrong. After a half-hour of having sex - hard, fast, gentle, slow - I realized that it was a very complicated act and not merely relegated to my penis. Pete thrust into me, sweaty with the effort. He put me on my back as I had done with Robby - *Gawd, Robby* - so I could watch him fucking me. Pete's exertions were really showing. The muscles in his body were tensing. Sweat from his forehead and chest dripped onto me as he increased his pace.

"Ahhh!" He climaxed powerfully, then sighed contentedly. I leaned up and kissed his mouth then fell back, spent. Pete draped himself over me, drenched in sweat, exhausted. I sat up on the bed, towelling the dampness from my chest before collapsing back onto the bed. Pete shimmied beside me. He was still breathing hard. From his forehead, perspiration dropped from his brow like diamond projectiles. He kissed me briefly.

"It's times like this I wished I smoked," he quipped.

"I never got that. Smoking after the best thing ever? What a stinking thing to do. My Dad's a heavy smoker. It'll kill him before old age ever does."

"How old is he, your father?" Pete asked, pushing my damp hair from my eyes.

"Dad? Oh, he's gettin' up there. Must be fifty-one now."

"Oh, not that old."

I thought for a moment. Pete was a shrewd guy, career on track, owned a sports car, lived in an expensive building, money not seeming to be any issue. Young men didn't have what he did. I'd figured it was a good time to inquire about something.

"Pete, how old are you?" I asked abruptly.

"In dog years?" Pete smirked, the lines around his eyes crinkled.

"I'm serious. 'Fess up."

"Why? You never asked me before."

"Never thought of asking before. I was too dazzled by your smile," I said, which was an honest admission. Pete's smile was spellbinding to me.

"I'm forty-two…okay, I'm forty-four," he said.

I thought about this for a few moments. I was still twenty-one. Pete was seven years younger than my father. He was twenty-three years older than me. I'd just completed a sex act and was lying naked in bed with a man who was a whole generation older than myself; my father's generation. But it made sense. Pete was suave, accomplished, intelligent, a man of the world and old enough to be my father. *My father. Jesus H. Christ.*

"Really," I said, a bit dazed. "I'm surprised. I figured that you were in your thirties - and early thirties at that. I'd have never guessed you were so old. I mean, no disrespect. You look great."

Was it okay for a young guy to be with someone much older? Did this mean that I had Daddy issues? Stupid question. Of course I did. *He's an incredibly attractive man who turns sex into art. Pete's been kind to me and that's that. Full stop. Don't be a Gawd-damned ageist.*

"You okay with that?" Pete asked. "Scandalized, perhaps?"

I kissed him lightly, wondering if I really was. "Course not. I was curious, that's all."

"Wanna do it again? With an old-timer?" Pete's cock was almost fully hard.

I rolled over onto my stomach. "Go for it, Pa Kettle."

I gotta say, those fierce slaps on my ass hurt like hell, but he did make it feel much better later on.

29

HEARING AN OLD STORY ANEW

Pete stayed in bed for another hour then rose to shower. I wrote out the dates I'd be in Montreal as asked and slipped them in his shirt pocket. After coming back to dress, he sat on the bed and stroked my hair for a moment. "I'll see you in Montreal, okay?"

"D'accord."

Pete winked, slipped into his moccasins and left the apartment. I didn't see him out but stayed put. I viewed the room. Towels scattered, sheets knotted and twisted, the green comforter half-off the bed, some lotion stains affirming the afternoon's activities. I felt guilty. Was it cheating if Robby and I never discussed having sex with others? For the short time that I'd been going out with Robby, there'd been no declaration of fidelity, but was it implied? *Hmm, why should it be? I'm a free young guy.* So why did I feel like I'd betrayed Robby? Maybe men did think with their penises, but I had a conscience, too. I stopped putting myself on a guilt trip, got out of bed, put on my boxers, brushed my teeth, went to the kitchen and ate two litres of Heavenly Hash with a packet of ripple potato chips. I left the carton in the sink, crossed back to the bedroom, tidied up and fell onto the bed. I'd be seeing Robby Saturday night. I was looking forward to it, especially the witty conversations and laughter. *And the sex was very good, knucklehead.* I was fast asleep by eight.

The next morning, I had a couple bowls of Sunny Boy cereal with chopped apples and bananas, collected my bike and readied myself for swimming at Kitsilano Pool. Favoured by diehard distance swimmers, Kits was an outdoor saltwater pool. At 137 metres long, a lap was like swimming across a small lake. I cycled along Pacific and up onto the Burrard Bridge. It was a classic late-summer morning with big, white, cumulus clouds above the North Shore, a stiff sea breeze and visible whitecaps on English Bay. The heat rising off the asphalt of the bridge deck warmed me up nicely as I rode up and over the rise then coasted most of the way down. Traffic was light. *Probably lots of people away for the last week of summer.* I was more than half-way through my taper and feeling good. *My massage last night helped me feel so relaxed. It was good of Pete to do that for me.* I biked off the bridge and onto Cornwall. *He's a decent man, a decent, older man.* I cycled into the park, walked the bike to the complex's gate, locked it, paid my way into the facility and strode out onto the huge concrete deck. The spectacular pool took full advantage of the stunning views of the ocean, North Shore mountains and the West End in the distance. I took off my shoes and shorts, my Speedo already on. I checked out the other swimmers, stretched out my shoulders and hips, put on my goggles and jumped in. My shaved-down body felt fast. The cool water was lit by the sun, sparkling, glittering, splintered by the chop; an impressive underwater light show. I warmed my shoulders and lower back by doing some easy front crawl, then accelerated, passing other swimmers swiftly. After a kilometre of freestyle, I felt powerful but relaxed. I had time to think about my burgeoning relationship with Robby, exciting as anything Pete offered and with much more substance. Robby was super-bright, handsome and eager in bed. But long-term? He had career plans that might take him away. *So what? Focus on now.* Being with Pete was also exciting; his confidence and his experience succeeding in a complex world was extremely appealing to me. It was challenging - *okay, start flip turn now* - being involved with people and making choices. *Life is also about how I manage people who come into this life...my life.* It tested my boundaries, my principals, my mettle. *Pay attention to your arm position. Kick symmetrically.* I stroked the water, propelling forward through the rough. *Having sex has turned me into an idiot.* I smiled then laughed, blowing out a lung-full of air underwater. *You're an idiot, but you're learning to enjoy being stupid.* Then I pushed, pulled and kicked my way across 6 kilometres of shining waters.

Three days later I had my itinerary for the Nationals from Coach Lerner. He stated that after we arrived in Montreal on Monday, there would be mandatory dope testing and then an evening practice to try out the pool with one hundred other swimmers from across the country. After practice swims, heats started Tuesday. Assuming I progressed my finals - the 200 metre butterfly, the 400 metre free and the 400 metre IM - would go Thursday and Friday in the early evening. Things lined up well for Lara and me logistically; regardless of what might happen at Nationals, I'd be in the audience for her on Saturday night. *Now all we have to do is wait.*

On Saturday, two days before Montreal, I lay in bed until 6:30 AM, stretched, then ate a light breakfast with coffee. I never drank caffeinated coffee unless readying for a race. *A bit of extra sharpness would be helpful this week, but don't overdo it; you're already sufficiently anxious.* As hard as I'd been training, there were many competitors who were as well-trained and as eager to swim at Nationals. Swimmers like Matt Lowe, who had been scooped after his multiple wins at the UBC trials in '75 by the University of Calgary. Other high-performance athletes were considered to be contenders; swimmers I hadn't necessarily competed against. In the heats and finals I hoped to make, they would also be ready.

The Nationals weren't like any other kind of meet; swimmers had to qualify for time standards established by Swim Canada as I'd done in Edmonton earlier in the summer. Rankings through the year helped determine if a swimmer could compete. There was history in the Olympic pool I would be tossing myself into. Swimmers like Gary MacDonald, Stephen Pickerel and the amazing Graham Smith (who'd clocked 4:28:64 for the 400 IM) had competed there and made me suffer by comparison. I changed my train of thought and remembered that Mrs. McBride wanted to see me before I left. *I'll call on her later.* I looked around at my apartment. It was clean enough. There was nothing left for me to do. I'd eaten, stretched, tidied up. *Robby was working today and Lara's busy. What else can I do?* I sat with the Westender newspaper in my lap. After reading the local rag I started cutting out coupons that I'd never use while sitting in my comfy leather chair. *I've gotta call my parents. Jeez, I must really be bored.* I put down the scissors and dialled my mother. Of course, my father answered. I cradled the phone between my neck and chin, picked up the scissors again and continued snipping coupons.

"Dad? Hi, it's me." *Gawd, here we go.*

"Well," he exhaled, probably with a puff of cigarette smoke. "And how's my Number One Son today?" he asked with a bland voice.

"I'm fine, Dad...how're you? I'm surprised that you aren't at work."

"I'm going in later. Wait a second, I'll get your mother...Rose! Telephone! Long distance!"

I'm not going to lose it. I ground my teeth for a few moments.

My mother came to the phone, "So, you were speaking with your father?" she asked.

"Don't get too excited, Mum. He couldn't wait to pass me off to you."

"Oh, I'm sure that's not the —"

"Listen, Mum, I was calling to remind you that I'm going to be in Montreal for Nationals. Remember?"

"Yes, of course, the big swim meet. How exciting. When do you go?"

"I leave Monday, Mum. Finals are Thursday and Friday, if I make 'em."

"Of course you'll make them. You've been working so hard and I know what my son can do. Where will you stay?"

"We're staying at a hotel in Old Montreal." *Pete made the arrangements. You know, the hot man who was at the Sylvia Hotel? The man I've had kinky sex with a couple of times?*

"They're putting swimmers up in a hotel?" she asked, voicing her surprise.

"No, some swimmers'll be at a motel and Coach Lerner will be with them. I wanted to be closer to the complex and also wanted more privacy."

"Oh. But who is the *we* that you mentioned?"

Isn't it funny what we pay attention to?

"Mum, the *we* is Lara and me. Don't you remember? She's going to be in Montreal too, performing at the Jazz festival. We'll both be at the hotel."

"Together in the same room?" My mother sounded slightly alarmed.

Yes, Mum, now that I have gay sex all figured out I thought I'd take a crack at some crazy-hot straight sex during the most important meet of my life.

"No, Mum, not in the same room. The same hotel. It's actually a boutique hotel. It came recommended by Lara's agent."

"A boutique hotel? That must be expensive. How are you going to pay?"

"Well, I've —"

"What about your meals? I've been to Montreal. Do you know how much it costs to eat in those fancy French restaurants?"

"Mum, of course I —"

"You'll need some cash. I think I better get your father on the line."

Maybe if I plunged these scissors deep into my chest...

"No, don't do that, please. It's okay, I've got the expenses under control." I carefully lay the scissors on the table. "Swim Canada's helped, too. I don't need any money, but thanks for asking."

"Are you sure?"

"*Mum*...I'm sure."

"Alright, that's a relief. And where is Lara singing?"

"In a famous jazz club downtown. Very chi-chi, called The Rising Sun."

"Oh, sweetheart, do tell her to be careful. Those Montreal clubs are so dangerous."

"Dangerous? Why?"

"You know why."

"Mum, it's not Harlem at midnight. I'm sure it's safe. Listen, I just wanted to remind you that I was out of town so that you didn't worry. Wish me luck, Mum."

"Oh, of course. The best of luck, sweetheart."

"Mum?"

"Yes, dear?"

"Just before I go...umm, I was sort of curious about why you never went to my swim meets."

"Your swim meets?"

"Yeah. I'm not upset or anything. Just wondered about it."

"I'd have loved to have gone to more, dear. I enjoyed watching you swim, ever since you were a little boy."

"But, you didn't go to —"

"Well, of course I did. I stopped going, but you know why. You remember that old story, don't you?"

"Which old story?" I asked.

"Before we moved to Abbotsford. In Burnaby, I guess. You were on a team called the Bluefish or Catfish or some ludicrous fish name. There was a regional competition for the ten to twelve-year-olds. It was on a Saturday - that I remember. I worked Saturdays at the Bay, remember?"

"Uh-huh."

"Well, I took it off so that I could watch you compete. We bussed for an hour to the Canada Games Pool in New West. Your father couldn't come - he was working."

Of course you would have taken me. "I don't remember this, Mum."

"And when we got there you were so excited to get in the water. A bundle of energy. A real nerve-end."

"Yeah, that sounds like me."

"You finally got to swim after hours of waiting - I think it was the front crawl you were doing and something else. The backstroke, I think."

"Yeah, it would have been the 200 free and the 100 back."

"You swam your backstroke but never made the final. However, you got into your other race and you were so excited to climb up on those boxy things —"

"They're called starting blocks, Mum."

"Yes, well, after they fired the gun and you dove in - you and a bunch of other boys - I stood up and screamed bloody murder for you."

"You screamed? That's not like you."

"I'm more of a cheerer, but it's what the other parents were doing, so I followed suit."

"Jeez, Mum, I never knew you were such a conformist."

"Do you want me to tell this story or not?" Mum asked, once more vexed with my unsolicited commentary.

"I wanna hear the story." I swore to myself that I'd be quiet.

"You were swimming well, but in the final lap you just ran out of steam and fell back...incredibly far back. I think you came in second to last, poor thing. When you got to the end and saw where you finished...well, you looked right at me with the saddest face, got out of the pool and ran to the change room in tears. I felt horrible for you. You'd told me were going to win right in front of me, and I was going to be the proudest mother there. But I was proud of you regardless;

ALAN D. STAMP

it didn't matter to me. But to you? You pouted all the way home on that damn bus and said you never wanted me to go to another swim meet again. Never. You couldn't take the embarrassment. You said you were mortified that I'd taken time from work only to see you lose twice."

"Gawd, I actually said I was mortified?" I asked skeptically.

"Oh, you already had a flair for the dramatic. I tried talking to you on the ride home, but it was pointless. There was no reasoning with you. At your next swim meet you refused to let me go and watch. And the next three or four after that. So I did what you asked, I respected your wishes and thought you'd change your mind. Maybe I should have been more persistent. Even when you medalled you kept it to yourself as though it were a secret. You shut me out, sweetheart. And then you weren't a boy; you were a young man making your own decisions." Mum took a breath. "So, of course I'd have gone to watch you swim. You only had to ask. I loved seeing my beautiful boy fly through the water." Mum's emotion caught in her throat. I felt a heavy sadness smack in the middle of my chest.

"I think I remember this now, Mum." I was a stubborn, fearful boy. I never wanted people to see me lose or to be vulnerable, sad or dejected. If they could see that, what else could they see?

"Sometimes we forget the reasons why we keep others at a distance," she added. "And then it just gets to be the way we are, sweetie."

"Thanks for telling me the story, Mum. I'll call you when I get back."

30

CLOCKWORK CARRIE

Robby was going to be coming by after work. I hadn't any intention of telling him about my recent tryst with Pete. Instead, I decided to ask if he was interested in having a relationship with me. Perhaps my boldness was primarily motivated by guilt, but after my research on attachment theory, I was convinced there were advantages to being in a relationship. Before Robby came by, I needed to find Mrs. McBride. I'd given up calling her Hannah. She just seemed to be Mrs. McBride to me. She wasn't in her apartment. So I went downstairs with the intent of buying a book for Robby on a Scandinavian director I'd seen at a secondhand shop. From the lobby, I could see Mrs. McBride sweeping leaves from the front walk with a bamboo rake. There had been several wind storms that contributed to the trees dropping their foliage. The summer had started early this year, but perhaps it would be winding down early, too. I hoped not as I opened the door and stepped to the front landing.

"Mrs. McBride? Let me give you a hand," I called out, bounding down the steps.

"Oh, so kind of you dear. I don't like to admit this, but I'm not as strong as I once was," she sighed. Mrs. McBride stood still and straightened her posture, thrusting her shoulders back with a groan. Her silver hair was pushed off her lovely lined face with a beautiful pin of yellowed pearls, her eyes intensely blue in the afternoon light.

She was dressed in a pair of soft brown tweed pants and wore a black woollen turtleneck. Even raking up leaves, she cut a refined figure. I took the rake and started in on the leaves. They were plentiful, especially from the huge grouping of tulip poplars right out front which were starting to show autumn shades of deep orange. The tall maples beside the Queen Charlotte were shedding but not turning colour, not for at least another month. Bright blue skies were overhead and the air was slightly scented with the spice of the season yet to come. Once I stopped denying that summer was ending, I enjoyed the fall. Mrs. McBride took a break and sat on the gold toss-pillow she'd brought down from her apartment. She looked relieved to sit, cushioned atop the worn tiled steps of the building. She watched me piling up mounds of leaves to be put into large green plastic bags.

"My, you *are* a hard-working lad," Mrs. McBride declared, quite happy to have a break. While I was raking, I shared my excitement about going to Montreal. I told her in detail about my events and my competition, Matt Lowe. She listened attentively, eager to hear more about the meet. While I talked I filled three bags and took them to the garbage container at the rear of the building. Mrs. McBride thanked me and gave me a firm squeeze on my shoulders.

"Now dear, you've reminded me. I wanted to show you something in the cellar. Can you come now?" Mrs. McBride didn't wait for my answer but started to move towards the front door. She brought her cushion inside and left it on the lobby table. The birdcage elevator shuddered as it took us to the basement. Hopefully the ghost was occupied with haunting a different location. We stepped from the lift and into the dark, gloomy space.

"I finally came across it just last week. I wrapped it back up, then got distracted and forgot to take it upstairs. Over here." Mrs. McBride walked briskly to a painted wooden crate in a far corner, dimly illuminated as before with swinging lightbulbs. "I was worried that I'd never find it. There's been years of things to wade through," she said, tucking into the crate and pulling out something swathed in layers of old newsprint.

"What is it?" I asked.

Mrs. McBride unwrapped the paper to reveal an eight-inch copper figurine of a woman clad in a bathing suit with an outstretched arm posing gracefully atop a black onyx pedestal. It was dusty and dull, but I could see the aesthetic of it, clearly done in an Art Deco style.

"It's so beautiful; there must be —"

"Oh yes, there's a story to this."

She looked at the statuette and then carefully stood it up on the corner of the box.

"There was an open water race in English Bay in August... now, let's see, what does it say?" She reached for the statuette and squinted her eyes at the small engraving on the plaque. "August 17th, 1931," she read aloud. Mrs. McBride wiped the engraving with the sleeve of her turtleneck and put the statuette back. "Over forty-eight years ago. A young swimmer from Victoria was a late entrant, but she'd been secretly practicing for this very race for over a year."

"And you knew her?"

"Oh, intimately, dear," she chuckled. "She'd swum on a team in Victoria - won races, too - and was known for distance swimming. The Victoria press nick-named her Clockwork Carrie because her stroke was so efficient and precise. For this race, she was competing against accomplished swimmers like Percy Norman. I don't have to tell you who he was, dear."

I knew who Percy Norman was - a legendary marathon swimmer who became an elite swim coach. *A sixteen-year-old girl couldn't compete against Norman.*

"Forty-one swimmers had entered, but it was little Clockwork Carrie who captured the hearts of the city that summer. There were thousands who came out to watch all the swimmers battle the tides and swells but specially to see Carrie. Being a young woman, most thought she'd never finish." As she spoke, the gloom of the eerie cellar was gone; instead I was imagining the bright sunlight in the waters of English Bay. "The race was from Point Atkinson to Kitsilano Pool."

"Kits Pool was built by then?"

"Yes, dear. The swim was actually a publicity event for the opening of the pool earlier that summer."

"And Point Atkinson's where the lighthouse is, right? The blinking light seen from Stanley Park?"

"That's right. All the way over in West Vancouver. So, the swimmers were ferried over from the docks downtown. The Lion's Gate Bridge wasn't finished until 1938."

"No bridge? It's hard to imagine." I sat cross-legged at her feet and listened to Mrs. McBride's story.

"It was a very different Vancouver, dear. Now, let's see…the officials took the swimmers down to the rocks below the lighthouse. The competitors removed their city clothes —"

"I guess they weren't in wetsuits?"

"Wetsuits? Certainly not. Swimmers had their bathing costumes on underneath and waited for the race to begin. When the signal rang out they tumbled down into the sea. Soon enough, they were all swimming along the course. It took them a while to adjust to the cold water, to get their bearings with the swell. Though all the swimmers were vying for the first position, Percy Norman and Carrie had taken the early leads. But after an hour, it was Carrie who pulled out in front. *In front of Percy Norman, dear!* For the next two hours she was ahead, swimming like a machine, just as the press reported, living up to her name, her stroke powerful and exacting. Every once in a while she'd lift her arm up to acknowledge the cheers and to smile at the hundreds of people watching from boats, including those on the Harbour Board yacht Fispa. She carried officials and judges. There were cheers from the lifeguard rowboats and other pilot boats located across the bay. On the beaches, people made a real ruckus so the swimmers could hear them across the water. But even encouragement lasts so long. In time, several swimmers had to be plucked from the sea by the men in the lifeguard boats; exhausted and too cold to continue."

"What about Clockwork Carrie?"

"She was freezing and tired, but she swam on right out in front of all others, including Norman. Stroke after stroke. A revelation in the ocean and just sixteen years old! And then her course went wrong."

"What happened?"

"Her father - he was piloting the row boat near her - didn't make an important course correction with the changing tide. Percy Norman caught up, passed her and went out in front."

"Being passed is the worst feeling —"

"But the race wasn't over yet. Carrie pushed herself to exhaustion to regain her position, picking up the rate of stroke - so difficult after having been in the water for over three hours. She didn't give up, she kept on fighting. She regained her position, moving ahead of Norman for the next while. She thought she could maintain her lead. But Norman pushed hard and to his credit, passed her and put distance between himself and Carrie. He went on to win the race less than an hour later. Carrie fought to hold on to second place but she began to falter. She was seizing up but *refused* to give up. Others went past her as she swam to finish in sixth place. She was cheered when she came ashore near Kits Pool. Stumbling, frozen, shaking, exhausted with the effort of so many hours in the ocean. She was the only woman who finished, and her pluck was recognized by the city with this special statuette," Mrs. McBride said, taking a long, deliberate breath.

"Mrs. McBride?"

"Carrie was me, dear."

"Carrie was you?"

"I was Hannah Carrie, the sixteen-year-old who swam and lost, but swam damn hard." She picked up her statuette and held it in her weathered hands, her eyes glimmering with pride at her recollection. I'd expected to hear that it was her sister or perhaps a friend who was the young girl swimming ten kilometres in the open ocean. I assumed she told her tale in the third person to prolong a surprise ending and it worked; I was flummoxed, staring at a fellow swimmer with wide eyes.

"And I want you to have it."

"What? Oh, no...I couldn't. This belongs to you, for what you did..."

"I'm an old woman. I have no need for it, but you may, dear."

Mrs. McBride passed it her prize over to me. My mouth was open in stunned silence for several seconds.

"Why me, Mrs. McBride? I don't understand."

"My lovely boy," she said, patting her hand on my shoulder. "Perhaps I see something in you that makes me reflect upon my youth?"

"But Mrs. McBride?"

"Dear?"

"Why was it down here in the basement, forgotten and bundled up in newsprint? Wasn't this the proudest accomplishment of your life?"

"Well, people put away their old memories and create new ones. I was a young woman, and it was so long ago. But when you came to live at the Queen Charlotte and began telling me about your swimming... well, I started remembering that race and my statuette once more." She looked across the cellar, at the boxes and belongings of so many others who probably were gone. "Then I forgot where it was in all this mess. I've been looking for it ever since." She clucked at herself. "And my proudest accomplishment is another story, my boy."

After a moment I looked at what I was holding. I read the plaque again and asked, "Mrs. McBride? You were Clockwork Carrie? It's just...amazing. Why didn't you tell me about this before?" I asked. Mrs. McBride smiled widely.

"Modesty is underrated, dear." She laughed, took my arm and we walked to the lift. I pressed the button and waited in silence for the elevator. After it arrived Mrs. McBride flipped down the seat and sat down. I hit the third-floor button. We rose shakily from the dark, cold basement. In a calm, firm voice, Clockwork Carrie asked, "You'll take care of her?" She glanced at the treasure resting in my hands. Mrs. McBride saw my reluctance. Before I could say anything, she spoke. "Yes, I insist. Please, it would do my heart such good. If my story and this," she cast her eyes at the statuette carefully clasped in my hands, "inspires you, then I'll have done something useful for a lovely young swimmer. And it makes me feel a little younger, too," she said without melancholy.

"I don't know what to —"

"Dear, you don't need to say anything. Just take —"

"I'll take care of Clockwork Carrie," I promised, expressing my thanks as best I could. I was moved by her offering. The lift brought us up to the third floor. Mrs. McBride said her parting words before going down the hallway. She suddenly looked tired, as though sharing her story had exhausted her.

"And remember this one thing, dear." She fixed her stunning blue eyes on me.

"Yes, Mrs. McBride?"

"Think of how wondrously we can exceed our wildest dreams and be victorious. Even if we lose."

That evening I'd buffed my Clockwork Carrie statuette until it regained its lustre and placed it on the living room table. I stretched out on the couch, drowsily thinking about her narrative when the buzzer sounded. It was Robby, and though I was on a strict sleep schedule and couldn't have him stay overnight, a short visit was very welcome. He spotted the statuette as soon as he came through the door.

"Whoa, where'd you get this?" Robby asked, picking it up, examining the craftsmanship. He cautiously turned it round in his hands and looked closely at the plaque. "This Hannah Carrie...is she —"

"It's Mrs. McBride," I confirmed, though Robby had already figured it out. "There's an incredible story behind it," I said.

"I'd love to hear." Robby smiled, then kissed me and put the statuette gingerly down on the table. "Can you tell me in a horizontal position?"

"I can arrange that," I said, taking off for the bedroom, laughing. An hour after sex we lay in bed together, bodies completely entangled and I told him about Clockwork Carrie.

"Phenomenal," he spoke softly. "Who could have fathomed your landlady was a famous swimmer? What's the probability in that?" Robby reflected, pulling the green comforter over ourselves.

"Mmm, dunno," I said, enjoying the warmth of Robby's naked body. "This is nice," I said, stroking his chest with my hand. "You know, really, I don't need anything else."

"Were you looking for something else?"

"Huh?"

"I was thinking…would you like to go steady?" Robby asked unexpectedly.

I thought I was going to be asking him.

"That sounds pretty old-fashioned. Are you asking me if I'd like to date you? Just you?"

"Yes," Robby immediately answered. "I'm asking that exactly."

"Huh."

"That's the second time you've said that." Robby detangled and propped himself on his elbows. "I mean, if you would rather see other guys…well, I guess I'd like to be able to say that I was open to that."

"And would you be open to that?" I asked, curious to hear his response.

Robby paused and said, "Truthfully, I don't think so. I'd like to go out with you and see what happens. Whaddya think? It sort of bucks the trend, doesn't it? Instead of a different man every night? Wild orgies till dawn?"

"Yeah, it'll be a lot for me to give up. But I'd like to try," I said, seeing Robby's handsome face and looking deeply into his hazel eyes.

"Okay, let's give it a go." Robby looked happy. I kissed his forehead and felt his rough scar under my lips.

"You know Robby, no one's ever asked to date me before. I'm not experienced with any of this." I wanted him to know that I was not like a Pete or someone worldly-wise.

"Listen, I'm no expert, either," he stated, getting out of bed. Robby pulled on his jockey briefs and I noticed how beautifully he filled them out. "We can figure things out as we go along, okay? We're young, we're allowed to screw up," Robby laughed, pulling on his jeans. I thought of my recent encounter with Pete. Undoubtedly that would count as me screwing up. I cringed a bit as I thought of Pete and me in the bed I shared with Robby.

"So we'll just go slowly, right?" Robby pulled on his Venetian-styled black and white striped cotton-knit top. He stared at me lying under a tumble of blankets as he slipped into his jeans.

"What are you doing? You're not saying anything," Robby said.

"I'm watching."

"Watching me dress?"

"Yeah. It's very sexy. I've spent so much time sneakily watching men getting out of their pants I never thought it would be so hot watching somebody get back in 'em."

Robby fixed his smiling gaze on me. "You are a very queer boy."

"Well," I said, standing up from the bed and hooking my thumbs in the belt loops of his jeans and pulling him towards me, "we know who likes to wear the ruby slippers, don't we?"

Robby finished dressing then I walked him to the front door, saying goodnight with a lengthy embrace. After I watched him walk down the hallway, I went back to bed, smelling his scent in the sheets, recalling how it felt to have him beside me and fell quickly asleep.

I spent Sunday getting focused. I completed a set of stretches then went for a bike and swim at the Aquatic Centre. I practiced my flips and turns, did some speed work, kicked a bit and generally took it easy. I felt like I wanted to blast my way through the water; a good sign as my body was telling me that there was a lot being held back. I biked home - full of nervous energy - and decided to cycle around the sea-wall. By the time I got back I was still keyed-up and I wanted to speak to Lara before I left for Montreal. I rang her, but there was no answer. I couldn't shake feeling edgy. The waiting to go away was getting to me. I sat down in my brown leather chair with the sun streaming in across my face. I grabbed a book on Bowen System Theory and his complex scale of differentiation. Within twenty minutes I was losing the struggle to stay conscious. I was in the stage just before sleep and in a few moments I was in the water.

Am I in…? Yes, Boulevard Lake… huh…just a boy. Mum's watching me from the beach as I paddle out further, treading the water…dark, blue-black. The current's pulling me to the middle of the lake…so quickly. Mum's waving to me…now she's gone from sight. There's a man with brown hair and eyes… just bobbing in the water…heading toward me slowly, smiling, mouthing my name…someone I know? I can't figure out who he is. But the water moves him past me…and I'm alone…weightless on the water's surface. Untroubled. Happy. Drifting. Dreaming. Dérive, rêver.

31

MONTREAL

The next couple of days were a flurry of activity. I'd had a chance to speak with Lara, confirming our meeting late Wednesday morning at the St. James. There were meetings with Coach Lerner and the trainer before flying out to Montreal Monday morning. We flew Grouch Class, otherwise known as Economy - jammed into my seat alongside screaming babies, annoying adolescents, unhappy couples and the grumpy elderly with bladder-control problems. That just about covers all life-stages. For five hours, Lerner suffered along with the nine other swimmers from Vancouver. We all admitted having anticipatory anxiety, but we tried to keep each other relaxed. After we landed, Lerner gave me a stern warning to follow the practice schedule as we stood at the baggage carousel before we parted company. I took a shuttle bus to Old Montreal and found my way over to St. James-Jaques Street where the hotel was located. The building was a refurbished former 1870's bank with a spectacular antique-filled lobby. Flowers in gorgeous glass vases were everywhere. I registered, observing the elegance of the place. *This is going to cost me.* Entering my room, I noticed a good view of the city, artwork on the dark-grey walls, beautiful white linens, a comfortable bed and a snazzy grey marble bathroom. I didn't fully unpack my luggage, just took out some shorts and a couple of black tee-shirts and my toothbrush. The rest of my things - a paperback and chocolate cookies that Robby said he'd packed for me in a plastic bag - I left bundled up. The room was dead quiet. I lay down on the bed to rest and woke ninety minutes later.

My first practice was scheduled for Monday at 8 PM sharp. I was feeling a little off-centre; I wracked it up to the time-change. I had to give a urine sample at the pool before practice, so I drank a litre of water before I heading out. I changed from chinos to blue running shorts and a sleeveless cotton top. I put on my Nikes, collected my swim bag and headed to the lobby four floors below. The good-looking concierge with the dark hair and green eyes was very helpful in telling me in English (he'd been kind to ignore my attempts at conversing en Français) where to get the l'autobus to take me to Olympic Pool on Rue Pierre-de-Coubertin. I was pleased I could get there easily on one bus; a scant seven kilometre ride away. Montreal was exciting, different, frenetic, hot and close. I was overcome by the humidity and was quickly drenched by the time I arrived at the complex. I wondered if my constant sweating would affect my electrolytes. I kept drinking water and got myself registered, met with Coach Lerner, went to doping, changed into my Speedos and got into the pool for a practice swim with my contingent. I got the feel of the water. As I'd been told, it was a deep, fast pool. Instead of telling myself that I was getting butterflies, I swam my butterfly in 200 metre sets, but not at race pace. I practiced all the other strokes, did repeats of IM's, kicked for a couple of hundred metres, got out of the pool after forty-five minutes and returned to the hotel. That night I slept poorly and woke up Tuesday morning feeling agitated; nevertheless, I was ready for practice. It was important to shake off some of the nerves I was having. Nerves can translate into adrenaline in the water. Adrenaline helps to get off the starting block but it's short-lived. For me, a middle-distance swimmer, a build towards the finish was how I raced. I needed that jolt at the end. My first swim practice on Tuesday morning was just so-so; completely unacceptable for me. It was as though I didn't know what to do with my arms and legs. Finishing by about 11 AM, Lerner dressed me down for nearly half an hour and I listlessly headed back to the St. James. I didn't feel well. Though I'd had a cool shower, within a few minutes I was soaked with sweat. I chalked it up to pre-swim nerves and the high humidity. I also had an intermittently pounding headache. It's not something I would normally get and didn't want to take anything for it just in case I tested positive for substance. So I had a bite, relaxed, did an hour of stretches and then collected my gear for the second afternoon practice. I was going to be seeing Lara Wednesday, though after she arrived in Montreal she'd immediately start working with Pete and the trio on all the details for her performance. I was looking forward to seeing her, but I didn't want to lose any of my focus on Nationals. I wondered if my attention to the competition was giving me a stress headache.

The practice was meant to start at three o'clock, but it was put forward to four-thirty. I was glad for some extra time. I was waiting in the Ready Room until the other swimmers and I were called to the pool. I jumped in but wasn't eager to get in the water; completely uncharacteristic for me. Lerner had the practice-session charted out for me and I worked my way through it in two hours. I was not at my best; lacklustre in every way. At the end of practice my headache was increasing in severity. My swim goggles felt painfully tight though the strap tension was unchanged. My vision was altered, too. I was seeing haloes around lights. *Perhaps there's a different chlorine level?* I was fearful to ask anyone about it. I spoke with Lerner for a bit afterwards, complaining of a headache but neglecting all the details, fearing that I'd be dropped for medical reasons. He thought it was tension, told me to eat a full dinner and get as much rest as possible. I agreed and headed back to the St. James. As I moved through the streets it seemed that everyone in Montreal had a cigarette in their mouth. Being around smoke seemed to hurt my eyes and made my head throb even more. I got to my room at about eight o'clock. I was saturated with sweat and collapsed on my bed. Though the last time I'd eaten was at noon, the thought of getting some dinner left me nauseated. I wondered if I'd picked up something on the flight or perhaps before in Vancouver. I sat up and got some ice from the dispenser in the hall, dumped it into a large glass, topped it with the off-tasting tap-water and knocked it back. That did the trick. A few moments later I dashed to the toilet to vomit all that was in my stomach. My mouth was foul. I brushed my teeth and hung onto the bathroom counter. The toothpaste triggered intense nausea; again I made for the toilet, retching. I rinsed my mouth out, headed to the bedroom and stripped off my clothes. I sat on the bed, turned on the television, wanting any distraction to what was happening. The picture looked strange - just a fuzzy blue haze. I switched it off. Suddenly, in my peripheral vision, I saw glittering silver triangles stacked on top of each other. No matter where I looked the arc of shiny pyramids were there. My head felt as though it was going to explode. *Am I having a stroke?* I extinguished all lights; the bright blue haloes distressed me. I was hot and clammy though the air con-ditioning was on. I cranked the A/C to Arctic Blast and sat back down on the bed. My head spun, so I grabbed onto the mattress. I thought if I didn't I was going to fall off it. *Don't freak out.* It hurt in my head to breathe deeply. *This can't be happening, not now. This is the most important meet of my life. I can't be sick…it's stress, horrible stress. I need some sleep. I'll be fine by morning. My heats are tomorrow. Please God, whatever I need to do to swim tomorrow, I'm begging you, let me do it.* I'm a terrible hypocrite. In times like this I prayed to a God I otherwise never believed in. Stretching out, I closed my eyes. I didn't want to see those frightening triangles. I fell asleep briefly then woke, fever-ish, my head hurting with indescribable pain as I lay on the bed beside the air conditioner. The throbbing seared my eyes. Blinking sent an additional shock of pain to my brain. Any movement brought agony. At some point, I fell into an exhausted sleep. At 5 AM, true to form, I woke up. I was naked and felt as though I was encased in ice. Shaking with cold, I turned off the air conditioner and opened up the windows, allowing the humid, hot air back into the room. I still had a pounding headache. I grabbed my boxer shorts and a tee-shirt and put them on, shivering violently. I pulled the covers over myself and tried to fall back to sleep, hoping that the next time I woke up I would be healthy and ready to swim.

I was roused by the sound of knocking at a door. At first, I couldn't quite figure out if I was at the Queen Charlotte or if I was somewhere else - just for those moments between sleep and reality, it was unclear to me in which I resided. When I fully opened my eyes I determined that I was not at home. The knocking continued and I slowly rose, unsteady on my feet. My wristwatch said eleven o'clock. 11 AM? I'd slept for six additional hours since this morning. *Impossible. What day is it? Wednesday, right? What time is my heat this afternoon?* I shuddered. *Three-thirty. Lots of time.* I breathed out and opened the door.

"Sunshine!" Lara exclaimed excitedly, standing in front of me wearing a pair of black shorts, a green blouse and a pair of red suspenders. It was impossible for me to look at anything that bright without squinting. "What's the matter?" she asked, immediately seeing something was wrong with me.

"Lara, I dunno...I'm discombobulated. Don't get close to me. I might have the flu. I've had a vicious headache for the last twenty-four hours. I've been puking and sweating, then ice-cold...it's been...Christ, this light," I said as I staggered to close both the window and curtains I'd opened in the middle of the previous night. Lara quickly stepped beside me and touched her hand to my forehead. It was cool. I felt reassured that she was here with me.

"Sunshine, you're sensitive to light?" Lara asked with concern.

"It's like a bullet to my brain," I said, turning back into the dimmed room. I told Lara about the haloes and the shiny pyramids in my field of vision, which were thankfully gone.

Lara reassured me. "I think you've had a migraine, Sunshine," she said with confidence. "I don't think it's flu."

"I've never had a migraine. I barely get headaches." I seldom was unwell.

"Sweetie, I think it might be all this pressure - barometric and otherwise - and these sweltering temperatures. We don't have this heat or

ALAN D. STAMP

humidity in Vancouver. See what it does to my hair? I look like Chaka Khan." I noticed Lara's usually tame red hair was big and frizzy. "I've had migraines. They're nasty, but you should be okay in a few hours. Can you take anything?"

"No, I better not. Doping. I don't wanna come this far and get disqualified due to an aspirin."

"Have you eaten, Buttercup?"

"No, I couldn't even keep water down last night. No food since yesterday at lunch - I think. Frankly, the last day's been a blur," I said, shaking my head.

"How's your appetite now?"

"I think I could eat, but I don't want to throw up," I said, recalling the episode of vomiting the night before.

"No, but you'll need something in your stomach. Especially now," she said. I went to sit back on the bed; Lara seemed alarmed and took me by both arms and pulled me up. "No sitting in the dark. Stay upright. Walk around for a while," she insisted.

"Lara, I didn't overdose on heroin. I had a bad headache."

"Just do as I say, no arguments. Drink some water slowly, a couple of glasses to start, okay? You're probably dehydrated. Then grab a shower. And do something with that punk-rock hair; it's ghastly."

"My hair?" I touched my tender head. From sweating profusely the previous night my hair had formed five or six odd clumps; the rest was sticking out at every possible angle.

"Have you looked in the mirror? Your hair is giving *me* a migraine. After you're presentable we'll feed you something that you can handle. Pasta should be fine. Now, get into that shower or I'll start singing Schoenberg."

Lara singing dissonant music was all the motivation I needed. I grabbed some fresh clothes and swiftly padded off to the bathroom.

"There's incredible food on every corner in Montreal, and I'm just ravenous. After breakfast, I went by a patisserie a block from here and saw a beautiful treat filled with lemon curd and dusted with coarse sugar. I didn't have time to wait in line, but I can't stop thinking about

270

it!" she called out as I turned on the water. I looked at myself in the mirror. Lara was right, my hair and the rest of me looked ghastly.

"Ugh, not for me." I was nauseous at the thought of anything with curd.

"You're going to get some food into your system. Don't worry, I'll look after you. I'll make sure that you're ready to swim today." Lara's enthusiasm was welcome and I did as I was told. I drank some water very slowly and took a tepid shower. I washed my hair. The water from the shower hurt my still-sensitive scalp. A shave was next. I cleaned my teeth; my mouth was dry; my tongue was white. Perhaps being dehydrated was why my eyes looked puffy; otherwise I seemed to be myself. I dressed in a pair of dark-blue shorts and a white tee-shirt. I took my damp swimsuit from the towel rack and put it in my rucksack with all my gear. *Obviously, Lara is going to make me move my ass - thank Gawd. Having her here's making me feel better by the second.* I was so relieved that I became tearful. I took a couple deep breaths. I was really experiencing anxiety; I had to get control of it. I brushed my hair straight back, drank some more water from the tap - no vomit response - and emerged from the washroom.

"Better?" I asked Lara softly.

"Oh, you're a new man!" she said, assessing the change in my skin tone and a vast improvement in my hair-style. In a few moments, we were out the door. It was bright outside and she saw me narrow my eyes. From her oversized brown leather satchel, Lara fished out some dark sun-glasses and passed them to me. "Wear these whenever you're in the sunlight; don't remove them until you're at the pool. It's important; light could trigger another migraine."

I put them on. It made being outside much more agreeable.

"I think your Foster Grants help, Lara."

"Of course they do. Smart and stylish. If you haven't noticed, that's very important in Montreal," Lara advised.

It wasn't quite noon, but it was already a scorching 33 degrees. *I'm doing okay; no sign of a headache.* We were bound for a bakery along a busy, people-filled street where Lara had spotted her treat earlier. She bought her lemon delicacy - caillé de citron - popped it into her insatiable mouth and in a couple of chews, we were off to a bistro. After not eating for over twenty-four hours I was becoming hungry and in need of fuel. Eating was Lara's way of de-stressing, but for me, it was medicine for the swimming to come. At a Greek bistro, she ordered a lunch of calamari, orzo with tomatoes, caramelized onions, feta cheese and half a roasted chicken. I didn't glance for long at the heaping mound of food in front of her, fearing the return of nausea. I stuck to a diet of simple carbs; pasta with a whisper of tomato sauce and had a large green salad. Lots of water and some pita bread all worked to soothe and ready me. Eating very slowly, I quickly started feeling better. Lara's appetite was in full flight and she was tucking in vigourously.

"You think I had a migraine from all this heat and humidity?" I slowly chewed the last forkful of fettuccine and finished my third glass of water.

"Il est très probable. Au fait, have you been practicing your Français?" Lara had finished the chicken and was pushing her orzo around.

"My Français? Je suis morte."

"No, Slick, you're quite alive."

"Lara, I thought I was having a stroke. No, I haven't been practicing my French."

"Fine." Lara dabbed her mouth with a napkin and sighed contentedly.

"I have to swim well. I can't be sick and screw this up."

"Sunshine, we both have to pull a horseshoe out of our hats."

"Lara, I think you mean…never mind."

"Nous allons." She paid for our meal and we left the bistro. We walked down the uneven old street and I was careful that I didn't careen off the road. My balance was slightly off. After grabbing my arm, Lara explained that she still had to complete a technical rehearsal, several festival interviews, final sound checks and a few other details before the Saturday evening performance.

"I didn't tell you. There's a poster of me, at the club door. I'm on a God-damned poster. Jesus," Lara sighed.

"That's terrific. And I'm sure it's gorgeous. You're a true Jazz Debutante now," I said. "This is your coming out party." I stopped for a moment mid-street with people streaming around us. "I always figured I'd be the one coming out," I said, grinning.

"Hmm, something tells me you're feeling better," she said dryly.

Lara was correct, I did feel better, remarkably so. *Lara could find a way to turn me around. Funny, but Lara says that knowing me is lucky for her; that I'm her lucky horseshoe. What would I have done without her to put me back together again?* I hadn't much time, though. I was due at the pool in thirty minutes and had a big afternoon and evening ahead. After hugging, we parted company. I oriented myself to the swimming pool.

Wednesday afternoon and into the early evening I swam my heats, which given how I had been feeling, surprised me. I'd swum a decent 400 metre free and got into the final. But one of my heats was in question; the 200 butterfly. I didn't feel one hundred percent and it showed. I mistimed my turns and couldn't get my hips to coordinate the kick with my pull. They were uncommon and costly errors. At 2:08, I was a staggering 6 seconds off my best time. Lowe had a blistering heat at 2:01 and easily moved through, as did several other swimmers. Coach Lerner was shocked with my performance. I told him that I was holding something back for the final. I had to wait through the remaining heats to see if I qualified. I had a bad feeling about it. Twenty minutes later I found out that I'd failed to even make the semi-final. It was a huge disappointment and I was deeply humiliated. With one look, I could see the enormous unhappiness that Lerner had for my loss - our loss. I'd let him down tremendously and he made sure I felt the full weight of his dismay.

The 400 IM heat and semi-final proved a giant test. I felt like I was spinning my hands and not getting a proper hand catch in the butterfly and thus not generating speed. I had a wobbly backstroke, my kick was off completely in the breaststroke and I seemed generally out of synch.

Clearly, I wasn't ready for the task. I finished fifth overall with Lerner on the pool deck shaking his head in disbelief. Though I'd barely qualified for the final, I was a disappointment and had to swim better. I was having a hard time shaking off my illness from the day before.

I had the next day - Thursday - to work out in the pool, to loosen the kinks and to get myself mentally ready for the 400 metre freestyle final. The 400 IM that I'd barely squeaked into was set for Friday. For the IM, I'd routinely been doing 4:31 in practice; to win I'd need a better time or my competition would have to be off, which seemed unlikely. Matt Lowe was in great condition and ready to take the event. Matt was coming in consistently at 4:28:50 and I knew he could swim faster. Physically I was well-prepared, but mentally something needed to be overcome. Lerner gave me a sharp lecture, criticizing my poor performance in front of the other swimmers. But I needed something less confrontational and something more inspirational. I went back to the hotel feeling deflated. I was discouraged about whether I had the ability to transfer the years of hard work and effort into a few minutes of brilliance in the water when it really mattered. I felt a heaviness that was overwhelming me. *Maybe I should just pack it in and head back to Vancouver?*

Lara was with her trio, figuring out last minute details for Saturday night's performance at the Rising Sun, which meant that I had time to get myself together. I hauled out my luggage to retrieve a paperback Robby said he'd packed for me in a Super Valu bag. Something other than a small book and a tin of cookies was in the bag. I took it to the bed and removed the item, wrapped in layers of thick blue felt and held together with elastic bands. *Clockwork Carrie.* Robby had packed the statuette in my luggage. He knew how much I loved Mrs. McBride's story; knowing he thought of me made my heart lurch. I scrutinized the object and thought about sixteen-year-old Hannah Carrie leaping into the ocean for a six-mile swim. For a woman in 1931 to take on Percy Norman showed tremendous self-belief. Over several hours she didn't give in to the elements nor her fears. Even when she was passed she continued to swim, to struggle until she finished, exhausted and utterly spent. I held onto the statuette tightly, clutching it to my chest. What was it that Mrs. McBride told me? *Think of how wondrously we can exceed our wildest dreams and be victorious. Even if we lose.* I really thought about that. Since I was a child, I'd dreamed of a life that was congruent with who I really was. I had exceeded many of my dreams in the last three or four years. It proved to be a challenge, living my life under water. Who I was becoming was clearly the result of my losses, wins, struggles and experiences. Just working towards a dream was sufficient; first place finishes don't necessarily confer any greater personhood or success. I had to grapple with a lot of crap to become the swimmer and the man I wanted to be. And I hadn't finished - not by a long shot. If I wasn't gay, I wouldn't have had the life I'm living, with the people I care about and the confidence to say that I can get through whatever difficulty comes my way. If I wasn't gay, I wouldn't be in Montreal, having this extraordinary opportunity.

I looked at the statuette and felt my heart surge. "I understand what you meant, Mrs. McBride. I'll get my ass in the pool. I'll do my best. And for fuck's sake, I better swim fast."

32

MAKING A BIG SPLASH

I'd found and kept my focus as I left the hotel en route to the meet late Thursday afternoon. I was clear and positive in my head and felt ready, with a singular purpose. Changing into my Speedo, I jumped into the pool for a good warm-up. Afterwards I was calm as I walked into the Ready Room. In the remaining hour before the call I was focused and resolute. The officials announced that it was time for our race. As the other swimmers and I left the room to walk to our positions I was relaxed and alert. I stood at the back of my starting block, completed my rituals, stretched out my shoulders, waited for the noise and excitement to settle and anticipated the final announcements from the official. In the few moments before the race was to begin, I was primed and prepared. With the other swimmers, I took to the blocks for my 400 freestyle final. In my bright red and white Speedo, black goggles and a red and white swim cap, I practiced breathing right down to my toes, maintaining my composure. I was only vaguely aware of other swimmers around me. I tried to not allow the huge crowd to dissuade my purpose. Calgary's Matt Lowe, whom I had competed against for years, was beside me in lane 4. I was swimming in lane 5, a good lane. There was a large, boisterous crowd. I could barely hear them. Lights and television cameras were around me. I didn't acknowledge they were there. The coach was barking at me from the distance. I didn't hear anything he said. I was in my own world where my goal was clear. I only had a steady, determined focus on the job at hand. The starter began the countdown.

"Swimmers take your marks."

Marks taken.

"Ready."

Ready.

I crouched down, my hands grabbing my feet, tense, every muscle ready to spring. I waited for the sound of the gun, the sound that would propel me up and forward. My sister, in her childhood dislike of having a younger brother, had propelled me under a breaker in Lake Superior leaving me terrified. Now, in a split moment, I would explode off the block and propel myself purposefully into the water and...the starting gun fired!

I flew as all the pent-up energy was released from my body. I was weightless as I soared up and across the water before slicing into the unbroken surface. Deep into the water I went, forming a perfect arc. In seconds I was kicking back up to the surface, taking loping, muscular strokes. Chest forward. *Power. Stroke, stroke, stroke.* Breathing every other pull, I was aware of my strong shoulders, my movement, how the water boiled at my feet as I kicked with the assuredness of a young man who had spent fifteen years kicking thousands of kilometres. I felt confident, with a sense of the importance of each stroke, each kick. At the end of the length, I curled into a tight flip turn, hit the wall with a smack and pushed off with mastery and force. If there were other swimmers close by, including Lowe in the lane beside me, I was unaware of them. Near the 100 metre mark, I was conscious only of my breathing and of feeling no discomfort, no pain, no inhibitions. I flipped again, bouncing off the wall, firing my body like a torpedo under the water, my breath steady, assured. The metres raced by. I had the sensation of flying on the surface of the water, my hands and arms like wings lifting me above, skimming the water, perfectly centered over the black lane marker. Near the 250 metre mark I felt the exertion. My arms were no longer wings but oars stroking, pulling and pushing columns of water. I was not aloft as before but now powerfully using my body - my legs, my hips, my trunk and my arms to charge through the water, churning it behind me. Each stroke was becoming a taxing effort, my muscles were hurting, breathing was painful. *Close to the wall and flip!* I hit 300 metres. *One lap left.* My legs kicked hard, harder, raising me high as my arms swung out and stroked, grabbing, pulling, pushing the water backwards, gasping for air, starved for oxygen, coming up to the last turn and flip! *Kick, pull, push... not long now, goggles fogged, black line a blur, water foaming and seething all around me. Crowd's screaming. So loud. Gasping's hurting my diaphragm. 40 metres to go, hang on! 30 metres, body's failing, push, push, 20 metres, kick, stroke the water, please go, go, kick, don't think, just pull hard! Pull hard! Coming close, lungs screaming, burning, hurting, kick to the wall, can see it! Couple seconds more, go, reach, reach, touch!*

I took off my swim goggles as the water behind me moved forward and swirled around my chest. I looked at the clock in shock - 4:01:90. I was staggered with disbelief - the most surprised of anyone in the building. I watched as Matt came in two seconds later for second place, and felt his hand on my burning shoulder to congratulate me. The other exhausted swimmers came to the wall, all finishing what they'd started, too. Coach Lerner stood at the table, stoically nodding his head in recognition, a half-smile unfreezing his face, though he was still displeased with me. I'd given him a rotten scare the past couple of days with a final still to go Friday night. There was no cause to celebrate. After a hasty television interview a few minutes later, I sat in the hot tub after having my best 400 metres and thinking about what I had to do tomorrow - the incredibly difficult 400 IM. Matt Lowe would be gunning for the win - especially now. The IM was challenging mentally and I still wasn't as sharp as I needed to be. I showered, dressed, left the facility and headed back to the hotel room, walking for a couple of kilometres, trying to remove any built-up lactic acid. Picking up a large veggie pizza, I hopped on the bus to get the rest of the way back to the hotel. I ate it looking at but not watching television. I drank two litres of water, stretched for a half hour, completed a set of pushups, tried a bit of hypnosis to help me gear down for sleep, then undressed and got into bed. It was 9 PM. I wanted to get ten hours of rest whether I slept or not. When I last looked at the clock it was 9:10, then I was out cold.

The next morning, I woke at eight-thirty and was feeling good. I couldn't recall sleeping without waking up through the night before. *The after-effects of the migraine, perhaps?* I started to mentally and physically focus on my final as soon as I woke. I moved through the day drinking water, herbal teas, eating light foods like eggs, fruit and bagels until I was satisfied I had enough fuel in the tank to move through to my final. I rested - if not slept - for several more hours. Fortunately for me, the 400 IM was during the early part of the evening. I liked swimming tough finals earlier as I found it a challenge to keep myself psyched-up later at night. Lara was going to be at the pool for the IM. I was gratified to know that she was making the effort to see me compete. After all, she was getting ready for her Montreal debut. She came by the room after having lunch with Pete, who was also going to come to the swim final if he had time. There was much going on with Lara's coach, too.

"How far away will you be? Will I be able to see you? What's your lane assignment?" she asked in rapid succession.

Lara had many questions that I answered. I told her she shouldn't have difficulty seeing me unless I didn't surface after my start. A bit of gallows humour was something she could appreciate. I wanted to stay in the zone as much as possible and didn't want unnecessary distractions, so I limited my contact with Lara to a half-hour chat. I politely excused myself and started my final prep for the meet. I had a warm shower and a body-shave, rested for two hours, called Coach Lerner, then gathered up my gear and made my way outside. It was busy with people and traffic was everywhere. The late afternoon air was extremely humid. In minutes I was perspiring through my shirt; it clung to my back as I walked down the street and hailed a taxi to take me to the pool. *No grimy bus for me tonight.* I can honestly say that I was largely unaware of the ride there or even paying the fare. I can't recall going for urine tests or moving through the maze of people or getting my coaching session or being with other swimmers in the practice pool, but of course I had. What I remember was sitting and waiting to be called with all the other swimmers for the final. It was dripping wet in the facility. I told myself that my body had adjusted to the humidity; no migraine was allowed. My loose cotton shirt was wringing wet. Beads of sweat formed on my legs as I sat and waited.

There was a huge crowd watching the meet, but I couldn't sense them as we quietly waited. I briefly noticed that while some swimmers looked relaxed, others seemed tense and a couple appeared ready to bolt out of the building. I was trying to be composed and focused on my breathing. I kept one hand on my diaphragm and felt it moving outwards and inwards - just as Lara had taught me. It worked to keep me calm. I closed my eyes and visualized the race: me pushing off the block, slipping through the water, doing each part of the IM, my turns, breaths, kicks and pulls, closing on the wall and finishing. I did my best not to let the anxiety in the room affect or infect me. I stayed unruffled under the strain and refused to allow my attention to waver from the swim I was about to have. I had no headache, no physical pain, no anxiety. I was determined and ready.

Just after six o'clock, the swim officials called us to the deck. Seven other swimmers and I walked from the Ready Room and into the arena to the sound of thousands of people talking, clapping, shouting. I looked straight ahead, the stench of chlorine so potent my eyes watered. I went to the back area adjacent to the blocks, stripped off my soaked shirt and put it in the bag I'd carried out to the deck. There were live television cameras to my left. For a brief moment I wondered if my mother and father might be watching. Then I put it out of my mind; no distraction allowed. Lerner was back at the table the organizers had for the coaching staff and I sensed him watching me, but I didn't want to look him in the eye. I couldn't. Just like a child, I was afraid of what he might see. Officials assigned me to lane 2, a poor lane assignment because I didn't have a good heat time. *They always get you with something.* I spent a couple of minutes warming my shoulders, rotating them fully, shrugging them, stretching them with a two-hand-hold behind my shoulder blades. I did a few squats, twisted my torso side to side and pulled each foot backwards. Stretched, I began a set of rituals. I dipped my cap into the pool and poured the water over my head then pulled it over my long hair, tucking in any stray locks. The water felt bracing against my overheated skin. I put my goggles on, took them off, adjusted the tension, spat in them, rubbed the lenses and rested them on my forehead. I stood five metres to the rear of the blocks inhaling deeply, waiting, eyes forward, looking out across the fifty metres of still water. In a few minutes, all swimmers' names were announced, including a statement of where we were from. The PA was loud and distracting. I thought that I heard Lara cheer when my name was announced, but when I looked at the crowd I couldn't find her. I scanned to my right and saw her amidst the massive assembly. By herself, her hair had become an enormous crimson beacon. She was wearing a bright red tee-shirt and holding a white flag with something written on it. When Lara saw me looking at her she stood up and yelled. I beamed my best smile her way then I waved and mouthed, *thank you.* Lara blew several kisses at me, holding onto her flag as the swim official started the ready calls. I took one last long stretch and a last look at Lara, who gave me the thumbs up sign; the same sign I gave her at the Sylvia Hotel when she faltered before she wowed 'em. I nodded, then saw her cram her fingers in her mouth.

The official asked the crowd over the PA, "Can we have your attention? Quiet please." The crowd settled in a few moments. "We're ready to start the Men's 400-metre Individual Medley." The crowd got noisy once again. "Please, we're asking for quiet. Silence, s'il vous plaît. Thank you. Each swimmer will do one hundred metres of butterfly, backstroke, breaststroke and freestyle. Chacun recevra un…"

Okay, you heard him. There's no denying this. It's about to happen. You're not at your best, so get there fast. My focus changed; I let it slip. There was a restless excitement in the five thousand spectators in attendance. Everywhere I looked there were people and harsh white lights. I squinted. *Too bright for my eyes.* Television cameras; CBC, CTV. Glaring lights on metal towers shone down on the deck. I noticed a press box set up with reporters at the pool's communication station. The crowd became noisy again, the anticipation palpable. On-deck photographers flashed pictures of the remaining moments before we were to hit the water. A cacophony of sounds and sights. *Yesterday I was able to put it all completely out of my mind. Why can't I tonight? Anxiety's charging the air. There are so many people here.* I froze. *Too much pressure. Too many people.* I started to lose my focus a second time. I felt my confidence fading. I scrutinized the building. *How many others will be watching this? Watching me, the secretly gay swimmer. Can they tell I'm a pretender? Fuck, stop it. I have to get my focus back, right away…*

"Swimmers take your marks…"

I didn't feel prepared. *Not prepared? What's wrong with me?* My heart rate was rapidly increasing. The other swimmers moved to the line of starting blocks. Slowly I stepped from the rear of the pool deck and climbed onto my block, conscious of the extraordinary tension I was experiencing. I'd done so well controlling it all day and now I was feeling overwhelmed. I felt sick. Very sick. *Jeez, am I going to throw up?* My stomach churned. I swallowed and tasted blood. In my anxiety I had ground my teeth and bit my left inner cheek. The blood in my mouth was running down my throat. *Shit.* The metallic taste of blood made me feel even more like vomiting. *Don't puke, for Gawd's sake, not now.* The bile rose and tasted disgusting in my mouth. *Blood and vomit; terrific.* My heart rate shot even higher. *Get it together. Lower your heart rate. Get your concentration back. Focus on your breath. Breathe to your toes.* I turned my head and discreetly spat a modicum of blood and vomit onto the deck. I adjusted my goggles back to their correct position. Every part of me was bound-up with agitation that was ripping through my body. My head was pounding, throbbing with every heartbeat. For a moment I thought I was going to pass out and topple right off the block. I grabbed my feet in the starting position a few moments earlier than necessary thinking that it might help to get my head down. I could hear the restless murmur from the crowd and tried to tune it out. I fought to regain my focus. It was working. The nausea was going, then it was gone. I felt my focus coming back. *Focus, focus, focus...you know what to do. You can do this...*

"Ready..."

Focus, focus, focus...' fly, back, breast, free, ' fly, back, breast, free... better...getting it back...now take the biggest breath you've ever...

The electronic gun sounded with a sharp shot that nearly pierced my eardrums.

I used every bit of tension to launch myself on a skyward trajectory, tautness released like a slingshot. Moments later, my extended hands hit the water cleanly, my full lungs releasing trace amounts of air, the bubbles streaming behind me, dolphin kicking my way deeply from my hips and lower back with great effort. I could feel the tremendous water pressure against the soles of my feet - a good sign - as I soundlessly moved fifteen metres underwater before surfacing, taking my first butterfly stroke and first gasping breath. I powered my way through the water, keeping my chest forward, thinking, *pull, kick, kick, pull,* timing the arms with undulating hips, generating power and speed as I quickly hurtled down the centre of the lane for the first 50 metres. I could tell I was moving very fast. *Swimming downhill.* Breathing every other stroke, I'd muscled my way nearly to the end of the first length. I had my body in full stretch and touched the gutter with both hands. After taking a giant gulp of air at the end of the first 50, I launched myself off the wall explosively. It set me up for another strong underwater dolphin kick of 5 metres before coming up again. My shoulders were starting to hurt, nearly pulled out of their sockets by the strain of the blistering pull. I created a huge, rolling wave behind me. I was in the lead; there was no one that I could see at either side. I accelerated my stroke and dolphin kick as per plan. I was now breathing every stroke, taking a massive inhalation of air to aid my oxygen-starved lungs as I moved with break-neck speed to completing my lap of butterfly. I'd been fast in this first 100. At the wall I touched, turned, pushed off and started the backstroke. There was no one near me, though I was in a less desirable lane and vision was limited. I turboed my way through the backstroke; hearing the crowd hollering. I kept my eyes fixed on a ceiling sightline to keep myself centered in the lane, my head motionless, sweeping my arms back with my hips high and my kick strong. Increasing my turnover rate, I sped through the first 40 metres, saw the orange and blue flags above me and counted the six strokes remaining before I moved into my turn. I had a sharp back-flip that set me up for the remaining length. A brief glance from side to side informed me that I'd maintained a lead position. Out in front I felt the water churn at the sides where my hands exited at my thighs. My kick was strong, driving me faster as moved past the 85-metre portion of the backstroke. I was precisely where I should be, exactly what I'd planned. I was confident about my position as I rocketed closer to the wall at the end of the lap and.. *touch!* Now, the breaststroke. One underwater pull and kick and up to the surface for the start of my nemesis stroke. I could hear the spectators each time I surfaced, my head cresting the water at the end of the heart-shaped pull; the audience screaming, 'Pull! Pull!' The breast stroke pull was straining my shoulders, the kick was making my but and hips burn with lactic acid. After 30 metres any gains I had made in the butterfly and backstroke were being challenged by at least two other swimmers in lanes 4 and 5. I accelerated my pull and used my slightly-improved whip-kick. If I got too far behind in the breast i would be impossible to make up last 100 metres of freestyle. I pulled and kicked with as much technique and power I had, hoping that would keep me in front for as long as possible, but I was feeling desperate. I was hyperventilating, exerting so much effort to stay ahead compromised me physically. My breath was insufficient for the physical demands. My deficits were quickly showing up, wheezing with each pull. At the turn, I pushed off the wall and used all the strength I had to my advantage, but I was no longer in first place. Far as I could tell I was in second, or perhaps third. A couple lanes over, a white swim cap inched past - Matt Lowe, of course - but I hadn't anticipated he'd be so close after the first 50 of breast. *Shit!* Another 35 metres to go. *Christ! Pull, pull!* I swept my arms back with as much power as I had used in the butterfly, trying to compensate for my kick, the strain breaking me. My lower back throbbed with pain, my knees ached from the whip-kick I did shoddily. Each stroke left me further behind. I was getting closer to the wall - 15 metres, then 10 metres, but I was out of the pack. *Okay, closing on the wall, almost there. Hardest part is done, right? Looks like I'm third or fourth now.* I'd swum the breast badly. I touched the wall for the start of the 100 metres of free-style. I pushed off underwater...I had three seconds to make a decision. *Think fast.* I took a giant chance. Plan B. Instead of building to the finish of the freestyle, I decided to sprint the entire distance with a full-throttle kick. A very risky move for a depleted swimmer. A strong kick was a weapon for me and other competitors, used at the end of the race to give the best chance for a podium finish. But a big kick uses tremendous energy. Like a rocket, it fires and the fuel is quickly spent. It can sacrifice all aspects of a race finish. It was a chancy strategy. I was behind, maybe as far back as fourth. If I burned myself out with a bad sprint, I'd be lucky for sixth place. *Clockwork Carrie was sixth.* I surfaced to begin the 100-metre freestyle portion to complete the IM. In a heartbeat, I committed to the sprint and immediately began pulling with a high turnover rate, kicking deeply and fast, whipping my feet at the end for extra power, the water raging behind me. I told myself that my legs were fresh. But after only 20 metres my self-delusion wasn't working. I was already feeling the effect, but couldn't let up. I knew it was going to hurt so I persevered, my lungs bursting. My shoulders and forearms ached with each stroke as I pulled and pushed the water past my hips. My quadriceps and calves burned as I approached the 50-metre mark. Close to the wall,

I did a tight flip-turn; my hands pointed to the end of the pool with complete extension, my legs pushing off with so much force and speed that I felt an ear-splitting pressure as I sliced through the water. *Fuck! My turn was too deep!* I surfaced, legs piston-pumping, arms a blur of movement. I didn't know where any other swimmers were. I only knew pain as I gasped for breath. For a brief moment I had a flash of the IM's I'd swum over the years - from childhood to now - like a flare going off in the back of my brain, a picture in my mind. Reality brought me back. I felt the water churn around my body from shoulders to feet, a frothy white foam, my speed creating a deep trough to breathe from, snatching air with each stroke, expended and ready to collapse. I increased my rate of stroke and the power of the kick. *I can't do this...swimming uphill...don't think that...hold on.* My legs were giving out with the toil. *Where was I, where was the wall? Why isn't it in front? It should be... just..kick!...pull!* Each breath gave me the strength to go faster, harder, my body riding on top of the water, hands grabbing on and pushing the water backwards, propelling me faster and faster to the end. *I loved to see my beautiful boy fly through the water...Mum.* My brain flashed her image. *There! The blurry black cross, end of lane, close, 15 meters.* Knowing I was closing, I had a moment of renewed vigour. I swept my arms, pulled long, hard strokes faster and harder, chest, shoulders and trunk muscles straining. With each breath I grunted with pain, shooting a stream of exhaled air under water. *10 meters.* My feet and legs were beginning to cramp. *Come on!* I accelerated my kick, my hips ached. *Ignore the hurt...6, 5 meters!* I took one last gasping breath and put my head in the water, face to the bottom of the pool. *No more breathing...push the water behind you, pull yourself across the top of the water.* Suddenly I felt like I was flying, pain completely gone, no longer in the water but above it, gliding. *I see the end, I'm close! Just fractions of a second.* I pushed my hands past my hips for one more stroke, kicked and stretched my arms and hands out to the wall. *Touch!* I grabbed the gutter with both hands, holding on tightly. I couldn't get enough air; my chest burned. I stood in the pool, then my feet curled under with painful cramps, everything was blurry. I thought I was going to be physically sick; I covered my mouth. The Olympic complex spun in my head. I heard the crowd roaring, clapping, thunderous. In a few moments, other swimmers came in. I took my foggy goggles off; dazed. I looked upward to find Lara. I heard her voice above all others. She was yelling and waving her flag wildly, then stretching it out so that I could read it. She'd written my name - *Shepard* - on the banner. Though far away, I could see her glorious smile. The groundswell of cheering and applause hit me like a massive wave. I felt a quiet and profound satisfaction. All the years of practice had come together in a painful, first-place-winning time of 4:22:88. But I didn't need to look at the clock to know what I'd done, or watch Coach Lerner as he jumped up from the table and crazily screamed at his swimmer, or hear the announcer call my name. After fifteen years of training, I was confident I'd done everything that I could do.

33

WORDS AND MUSIC

I was relieved that my work was done in Montreal. I could relax and turned my attentions to Saturday night and Lara's Festijazz debut. Pete had been busy with sound checks, lighting, speaking with the producer; he was involved in everything pertaining to her and the trio's performance. He wanted her night to be a triumph. Lara had gotten some press coverage thanks to Pete and it was very favourable. There had been three newspapers clamouring to speak with her, including *La Presse*. In interviews, Lara proved witty, self-deprecating and enjoyed holding court. She told the press of her ungraceful entrance at the Sylvia Hotel and in a few minutes had reporters rolling with laughter. On the other hand, I was interviewed by CTV and CBC moments after my wins and the lights in my eyes, the microphones in my face and the attention being paid to me proved tough for an introvert. I muttered my way through for about 60 seconds, head down, made a prompt walk post-interview to the change room and had decidedly irked the reporters. My two wins might have been impressive; my interviews proved far less so. But it was enjoyable for me as I tagged along in Lara's camp and observed her outward confidence in the public eye that I was so uncomfortable in. I was aware that she had doubts, but she wasn't letting any press or public know what they were. Lara was garnering a lot of attention because she was different - a multi-lingual singer, well-studied in classical voice performing the American Songbook and an eclectic repertoire. Talented and different was good. Athletic and gay was not. How would the swimming community react if I had come out? Me waving the Rainbow flag at the podium would have resulted in an interesting response, but doubtfully a positive one.

Pete had asked if I could visit with Lara to settle any pre-show nerves. I went to Lara's room before she was meant to head off to the club. Her door was ajar; I stepped through to see several people there, though Pete wasn't one of them. Lara was quietly chatting with David, her handsome pianist from the trio. Lara was dressed in a stylish aubergine satin blouse and charcoal grey slacks. She spotted me immediately and excused herself politely.

"Oh, Sunshine!" She walked over, grabbed me with both arms and held me close. "Let's talk a bit, okay?" She led me to the washroom, locking the door behind her.

"Hey," I said softly. "How you holding up?"

"This waiting is the absolute shits."

"It's pretty nerve-wracking, isn't it?"

"No, I mean literally. Every few minutes my bowels have been exploding."

"Gawd, Lara."

"Sorry, that's vulgar, even for me. I know how you get squeamish."

"Um, no gay man wants to hear about exploding bowels. You're really looking flushed, though."

"Probably from all the deep-breathing I've been doing."

"Is it helping?"

"Well, I seem to be vacillating between passing out or seeing Jesus."

"You sure it was Jesus?" I asked, ever the agnostic.

"It could have been John Lennon."

"Imagine," I badly punned. "There's a lot of pressure on you," I commented.

Lara nodded, "I'm trying to be tranquil..." Lara hesitated.

"But?"

"It feels like I'm about to be shot out of a cannon in my undies." Lara drew a deep breath, twisted her hair around her finger. "Pete told me that music people are in full force for tonight's show."

"Really? Like —"

"Like recording producers and deal-makers and critics. Fuck," she whispered.

"Oh." I knew how unpleasant it was to be scrutinized.

"The only critics I've had are myself and my parents. Pete told me to relax and enjoy the experience and not to worry. It's just words and music, just like he's told me many times before." Lara began pacing in the small bathroom. "I know he's right."

"Yes, of course. Pete's giving you good advice. It makes sense that you're thinking all this through."

She nodded, striding in the tiny space, running her hand through her red hair, considerably mussing it. "Yes, thinking and thinking. Words and music…" Watching her, I thought about the past and all the struggles we'd both experienced.

"It's sensational that you're singing in Montreal."

"Isn't it?" Lara stopped pacing and shook her head, as if in disbelief.

"I'm proud of you, Lara. You've been told for so many years that you were foolish to pursue music," I said, but not by whom.

"Yes, and not just foolish. By singing, I was shaming my family."

"And look at you; poised on the brink."

"Hopefully not the brink of ruin."

"I don't think so."

"I honestly don't think so either. And yet my mother and father still think I'm some kind of street corner busker."

"Well, you know what you say about your parents."

"Fuck 'em?"

"Fuck 'em." Lara's eyes glistened. "I wish my parents could've understood. I've worked impossibly hard. I'm not a failure and I'm not a disappointment. I'm not someone they have to be ashamed of, am I?"

"Of course you aren't."

"Then why treat me like I've done something criminal? Why not just accept me for who I am?"

"Sweetie, it's a mystery. Maybe they can't admit being dead wrong. Pride's a powerful thing."

"Or maybe they've decided it's easier to hate me." Lara looked resigned.

"Lara, that's not possible."

"'No? It's how it feels. It's why I'm upset, yet again. It's so frustrating. Like an idiot, I've been waiting for my parents to call and wish me good luck tonight." Lara's voice was trembling. "It won't happen, will it?"

"No, I don't think so. I'm sorry, Lara," I said quietly.

"Stupid me. I told myself it shouldn't matter, but it does." Lara twisted her hair. "When I was a little girl, I used to sing Auprès de ma Blonde for my mother. I hated that song, but it made her happy. Now I wish I'd never sang it." Her beautiful brown eyes filled with tears and she wiped them away quickly. "It's just not fair."

"It's not…you're right," I offered quietly.

Lara grabbed the box of pink Kleenex from the bathroom counter, pulled out the last of the tissues, started mopping at her reddened eyes and sobbed for a few moments as I gave her a hug. Lara was thin and felt vulnerable in my arms. She cleared her voice.

"Damn it," she said huskily. "Crying is disastrous for my voice. I've gotta pull myself together or else I'm gonna sound like Janis Joplin tonight." Lara moved to the sink, cranked open the faucet, cupped her hands under the cold water to get a drink and spilled most of it all over her satin blouse before her hands got near her mouth.

"Remember the night that we went to the Starlight to see that Woody Allen flick?" I asked, passing her a hand towel.

"Annie Hall?" Lara looked up at me quizzically as she dried her hands and dabbed at her blouse.

"Yes. Afterwards, you were determined to pursue music."

"You didn't try to change my mind."

"Aren't you glad I didn't? When we were at UBC years ago you asked me, 'Where would singing take me?' Look where it's taken you.

In spite of what your family and a few stupid boyfriends have said, in a little while you'll be singing in front of a thousand people. You're stepping into your own future." I could sense an immediate change of mood. She sighed deeply.

"Since I was a girl, this is what I dreamt of doing. But I never gave it my full attention...and though I'm loathe to admit it...my parents' disapproval and rejection seems only to have pushed me harder."

"Kind of ironic, huh?"

"Isn't it?" Lara exhaled. "I have to figure this stuff out. It's exhausting to be angry and disappointed over things I don't have control over."

"Yeah, I know what you mean. It takes up so much time."

"Exactly. It's enough that I love to sing and make music." Lara looked relaxed and calm. "Sunshine, you always know how to centre me, just like magic. You're like my own taon chanceux."

"Translation?" I frowned.

"You know, a lucky horsefly," Lara said with utmost seriousness.

"Uh, I think you mean lucky horseshoe, Lara."

Even though her eyes were still red, she was looking much improved. She broke into a beaming smile.

"Yes, that's what I meant." She wiped the last tear from her cheek and took a couple deep breaths with her eyes closed.

"Better?" I asked, knowing the answer.

"Much. I'm ready to go," Lara said authoritatively.

"Good. Oh, just one more thing. I never did mention this to you."

"What's that, Sunshine?"

"Well...when you go onstage to start the show tonight..." I paused

"Yes?"

"This time don't trip on the mic cord and fall on your tits. Last time you wound up looking like shit."

Lara's smile vanished. "Except for that last comment, I was thinking what a good therapist you're going to make."

"I sure hope so. I can't stay under water forever," I said, only half-joking.

There was a knock at the door. "Lara? Hey, we gotta get you dressed; it's time. Everything okay in there? Lara?"

"Pete?" I asked Lara in a whisper.

Lara nodded her head and opened the bathroom door to reveal Pete's drawn and worried face. He looked at Lara's smeared mascara and messy hair, dropping his jaw in displeasure.

"Lara? What's happened to you?" Pete asked, seeing Lara's water-logged top, her red eyes and crumpled hair. "Christ, please tell me everything's okay."

"Of course it is, Pete," Lara said poker-faced. She looked at her agent and said crisply, "I've got a lucky horseshoe up my ass."

After I left Lara in excellent hands, I retreated to my hotel room. On the bed was a box wrapped in glossy black paper. Atop was a scarlet card; it read, *'For Aquaman - Yours, Pa Kettle'*. I laughed and opened the gift. Inside was a beautiful grey linen shirt that I had admired in a shop on Avenue Laurier when I was with Pete earlier in the day. I dressed and made my way to the Rising Sun by taxi. Montreal was alive with people and smells and noises and lights. I was craning my neck to capture all the visuals as the driver slowly inched through heavy traffic en route to the club. I stepped from the cab, paid my fare and moved through the throng. I took a moment to admire Lara's giant black and white poster outside the club's entrance. She was photographed in profile and looked like the pictures of Hollywood stars from the 1940's. I presented my ticket and stepped into the noisy nightclub and wandered for a bit before going into the main hall to locate Pete. Inside, hundreds of music lovers were packed into the vast hot and smoky venue. I wore a pair of black pants with the grey linen shirt that Pete had bought me. I set out looking for him near the front of the stage. I found him at the table, looking his best in a dark blue suit with a crisp white dress shirt and a bold crimson tie. He looked pleased to see me.

"Your shirt looks good on you," he said approvingly.

"Someone with great taste bought it for me. Thanks, Pete."

Sitting beside him I noticed he'd lost more weight. The effort he was putting into getting Lara launched was taking a toll. As we waited the excitement took me right back to the night we met at Oil Can Harry's. *Pete's the sexiest man I'd ever come across, regardless of age.* With his eyes glued onstage, I took the liberty of some lingering glances. I didn't really know much about Pete, even after all this time. I wondered if that made him more irresistible. Every couple of minutes Pete glanced at his watch, fidgeted with his hair then scanned the stage. His OJ was untouched. Like me, he was impatient for Lara to step onstage. *Pete's as tightly wound up as Lerner ever was.* Pete reported that the instrumental group had been off the stage for over a half-hour.

"I'm sorry that I couldn't see your race," Pete apologized, explaining that the timing was impossible. "I heard that Lara held up a big flag and waved it like a maniac," Pete commented.

"Yeah, did she tell you?" I laughed.

"You kidding? Three, four times. Couldn't stop talking about it," Pete said.

"Lara was incredible. At the end of the final I heard her scream out my name. Hope she didn't hurt her voice." I smiled at the recollection.

"That reminds me, you never did tell me how you got your name. Your father named you after someone, right?"

"Uh-huh. Dad was a huge fan of the US space program - from the beginning - when they were flying those X-15 things. He was on a business trip in Chicago one time and chatted up a group of pilots at a bar. Apparently, he was taken with a good-looking young man in particular."

"Hmm, exactly what type of bar was this?"

"No," I laughed. "Just a regular bar. Anyway, this guy was a test pilot who claimed he had bigger plans for himself. Like going up in space and becoming an astronaut. The other guys ribbed him as though he was just another pilot with an over-inflated ego. But Dad told me the pilot knew exactly where he was bound. When I was born just a few months later my father decided to name me after him. Guess he knew something."

"What was that?" Pete asked.

"A couple of years later a pilot was announced as one of the Mercury 7 team of astronauts. He was the first American to blast into space on top of a Redstone rocket in 1961 - Alan Shepard. My father said Shepard was the bravest man in the world. He still talks about that Mercury-Redstone flight. Riding on a ballistic missile at 5,100 miles per hour and thrown into space for fifteen minutes. He wanted me to have a special name. Said a name like Shepard would make me different. I guess he had no idea *how* different," I chuckled. "Honestly, I didn't like my name because I've always had to explain it to people. But perhaps there was a scheme behind it, after all."

"Some scheme. I'm sure your Dad's gotta be proud of how you swam last night," Pete stated, tousling my hair. He seemed to like the distraction I was providing.

"Hope so," I said, smoothing my hair back into place with my fingers.

"Lara should have come on. I wonder what's happening?" He looked at his Rolex. "Christ, it's almost nine thirty," he complained, shaking his head.

"Maybe she's having a bite," I quipped, which under other circumstances might have been humorous. Pete continued looking expectant, checking his watch frequently and chatted with me absently for the next few minutes until the house lights dimmed and the last performer was about to be announced. I heard him let go of a monstrous breath. A large, well-dressed man stepped up to the microphone.

"That's Doudou Boicel, the festival organizer," Pete whispered to me.

"Bienvenue, mesdames et messieurs, ladies and gentlemen. We're proud to present an exciting singer from Vancouver to perform at Festijazz tonight. Please welcome our chanteuse to Montreal…

Lara Jean!" Boicel left the stage and the house lights went to dark. Applause followed. Within a few seconds there was a small spotlight. Lara purposefully strode out into it. Her large brown eyes sparkled. She wore a mid-length emerald-green silk dress in a halter-top style, emphasizing her slender physique. There would be no bouncing boobs tonight. In her coif was an ivory-coloured gardenia. Her red hair was tamed; it flowed down to her shoulders. Something was different about Lara. Before she began to sing she looked confident, poised, relaxed, smiling, captivating. She moved several feet past the microphone. No trips, no falls, no errors. Lara stood alone in the spotlight and the club became hushed and expectant. After several long seconds, she started to snap her fingers and sang a cappella:

> *'Grab your coat and get your hat,*
> *Leave your worries on the doorstep,*
> *Just direct your feet,*
> *To the sunny side of the street....'*

With each subsequent line, the trio quietly came onstage, picking up the drumsticks, sitting down at the piano and standing next to the bass, then instrumentally joining in to accompany Lara's soaring vocals. The trio shifted to a different time signature. Lara, completely at ease, utterly in control, began singing a full-throated second verse. Voice booming with no need for amplification, she easily filled the hall with her gorgeous soprano. She didn't hold back as she reached the end and sang the last phrase by effortlessly moving up a full octave and a half:

> *'Life can be soooooo sweet,*
> *On the sunny side of the streeeeet!'*

Appreciative applause followed, but she didn't hesitate long to acknowledge it and instead stepped quickly to the microphone to begin her first set. Arlen, Porter and Gershwin were well-represented in a selection of standards. Then a Piaf medley; 'Milord', 'La Goualante du Pauvre Jean', 'Mon Dieu' and an exquisitely performed 'La Vie En Rose'. She covered Joni Mitchell's 'Both Sides Now' with a jazz-inflected twist. A few Gallic songs were beautifully rendered. There would be no break; instead she decided to move through the songs without pause, building excitement as she went along, her voice strong, clear and rangy. Lara's performance was sometimes wistful, other times vulnerable, then strong, defiant, funny, touching and quiet. In a song list that captured many moods she was never less than stunning. She included many songs from her appearance at the Sylvia Hotel, including 'Any Place I Hang My Hat', her stratospheric top note nearly blowing the roof off the club. She sang 'When Your Lover Has Gone' with just the piano as accompaniment. She did a stupendous rendering of 'Lost in the Stars', with Lara's plaintive voice moving me to tears. She belted out 'Some of These Days', with a nod to Sophie Tucker and offered 'Blues in The Night', which delighted the fans, her vocal pyrotechnics sounding like a train coming down the tracks. There was a scattering of Duke Ellington numbers that honoured his musical contributions. Her performances of 'Sophisticated Lady' and 'Come Sunday' dazzled. The trio supported her and were sympathetic to her spontaneous improvisation. Her rapport with the audience continued to build as each number was unfurled. She quickly rose to being what Pete had called her - exquisite. He was observing his client, gleefully noting the reception Lara was getting, a fresh talent giving a fascinating performance. I watched, listened, cheered like I was at a swim meet and nearly clapped my hands raw. She was incandescent, transformative, electric; super-charged by the audience. By 11 PM, both encores had been performed: Gershwin's 'Summertime', where she accompanied herself on the piano, surprising the audience with her virtuosity, her soaring bel canto voice in full display. The next encore was Noel Coward's 'Sail Away', sung with enough lung power to push back the curtains. The audience roared, stamped their feet and clapped in unison until she came back onstage.

"We have one last song," she said, slightly breathless as they slowly quieted. "Thank you for being here tonight, Nous avons une chanson plus pour vous pour écouter ce soir. J'espère revenir bientôt," she said soothingly and stepped away from the microphone. Lara ended the night the way that she had started, her trio quietly leaving as she stood on an empty stage with only a spotlight framing her shining face. The nightclub fell silent. Lara closed her eyes and purely sang.

> '*I'll be seeing you,*
> *In all the old familiar places,*
> *That this heart of mine embraces,*
> *All day through,*
> *In that small cafe,*
> *The park across the way...*'

Lara continued to sing unaccompanied; each moment alive with meaning.

> '*I'll find you in the morning sun,*
> *And when the night is new,*
> *I'll be looking at the moon,*
> *But I'll be seeing you.*'

She finished the phrase with a high note, soft as velvet, the overtone ringing in the rafters of the club as she waved a triumphant goodbye, blew a kiss and left the stage to her first standing ovation. In actuality, Pete and I stood first, but others soon followed on their own. Lara had made us laugh with one song and choke up with emotion with the next. It was a transcendent experience. The audience knew that something unique had occurred, and so did Pete. The strain of the past few days had vanished from his handsome face. His coaching paid off in Montreal winningly. I was caught up in the magic spell that Lara cast as we pushed past patrons on our way back to her tiny dressing room. It was bursting with bouquets and packed with people congratulating her. Lara was flushed with the thrill of the night, smiling, gracious, shaking hands, kissing cheeks and glowing contentedly. The crowd thinned out in a few minutes; soon after it was just the three of us. Pete wrapped his arms tightly around her.

"Tu l'avez fait; perfection," he said, holding her and then kissing her on both cheeks. Pete was nearly in tears. She thanked him then turned her attention my way. Lara's luminosity seemed to create her own light. I was transfixed.

"So, what did you think?" she asked earnestly.

"Well, I thought you were pretty decent," I said, winking.

"Shepard, if you knew anything about theatre, you'd know this isn't the time for understatement. You're supposed to gush," Lara asserted.

"So now you call him by his name?" Pete asked, smiling.

"Yes, of course. He had to do something spectacular and he fulfilled his promise last night." Lara hugged me warmly. "So you thought I was *decent?*"

"What can I tell you? You sang your tits off, which, by the way, looked spectacular. I especially liked how they stayed in your dress this time."

"Sunshine, is that all you have to say? Why were you looking at my boobs anyway?" Lara beamed as I looked at Pete, both of us quickly laughing.

"Speaking of my boobs, I've gotta get 'em outta this dress."

"Where are the boys in the band?" I asked.

"They locked up the arrangements and took off right after the show. David said they were going for a quick drink, but let's face it, Montreal on a hot summer night? Have you seen the women in this city? They're gonna get laid. They do have a reason to celebrate; the trio was fantastic."

"It was the best evening ever," I agreed.

"Wasn't it? But it's not over, Sunshine. The evening's just starting."

"Oh, not for me. I gotta head back to the hotel. Coach Lerner wants me rested." Secretly I was hoping that I could tag along for a little while.

"I don't care what Lerner wants. It'll mean so much if we're all together tonight. It's so special for all of us. Right, Pete?" Lara collected her bag and moved to the back of the dressing room.

"On such a night as this? How can I persuade you?" Pete's dark eyes zapped me a penetrating stare, then he smiled. I was done.

"Consider me persuaded," I promptly said.

"Good. Gauthier's is just up the street from here, if we wanna grab a bite," Pete suggested.

"A bite?" Lara asked, tossing off her dress as she changed behind an old black dressing screen. "I don't wanna grab a bite. I want to have tourtière and try some of this poutine I've heard about. And cheesecake. For months I've been patiently waiting for a big piece of Montreal-style cheesecake!"

Pete and I exchanged a look with raised eyebrows. He took his large hand and surreptitiously patted my stomach. Lara emerged from the screen, jeans on, wearing the loose, bright-red cotton shirt she'd worn at the swim final, accessorized with a blue and red silk scarf. She had switched her heels for flat brown leather sandals. Her dress was left on the hanger to be collected later as were her pumps. Much of her make-up had been smeared off with a wipe of face-cream; just the gardenia in her hair and red lipstick remained. The transformation from glamorous nightclub singer to the freckled girl-next-door happened in mere moments and was nothing short of miraculous.

"So, c'mon, boys, don't look so stunned. Ready to go?"

Pete, Lara and I left the Rising Sun and went onto Saint Catherine Street past Place des Arts. The night air was electric with people, perhaps all having enjoyed music or dance or theatre. In fact, there was a type of live theatre being performed - the sounds of thousands out for the night, laughing, dancing, chattering, jostling, shouting, singing, joyous. *I'm a part of this, too.* Though we were walking arm-in-arm through historic Montreal - a hot and sensual city charged by the fantasies of what-might-come-next - Lara reminded us of the most important task at hand.

"I know, I know, Lara," I said, priming myself. "Vous avez un gros appétit!" I just nailed that one. Pete and Lara looked at each other and broke into a laugh that echoed along the ancient cobbled streets. Somewhere in Montreal that night there was a restaurant that would prepare a meal large enough to satisfy the hungriest and happiest singer in the world.

34

MY LIFE UNDER WATER,
AN EPILOGUE

I returned to Vancouver two days after Lara's and my adventure in Montreal. Robby had come to collect me at the airport. Catching his smile in a crowd of greeters was an unforgettable and new pleasure. Lara and the trio were hired to perform in Quebec City, Ottawa and Toronto for the next several weeks. She was thrilled to be well on her way.

I hadn't heard anything from Pete since we'd all had dinner together in Montreal. When I went to check out of the St. James Hotel, I was told that my bill had been paid. Pete had taken care of it, un-asked. I wondered when I'd see him again. Pete had a way of coming into the picture at unexpected times.

I began graduate school after Labour Day. Having made the National Swim Team, I began a familiar routine of training and studies. I always thought that becoming a therapist was the right choice for me. After all, I was fascinated to hear the stories of others. But I was experiencing how gratifying it was to participate in the story as well.

Mrs. McBride welcomed my return to the Queen Charlotte with a hand-picked selection of late-summer flowers grown at the side of the apartment. She was delighted when I explained how her swimming tale had motivated and inspired me at exactly the right time. I was to discover that her largest triumph hadn't taken place in the waters of English Bay in August of 1931. Clockwork Carrie married one of the spectators who had cheered her on, namely Harold McBride, a handsome young Scot, who had courted her for two years until they wed. They lived in the Queen Charlotte for over thirty years until his death from cancer. She told me her love for him was as deep as the bay she had famously swum in.

I called my mother when I got back; she was thrilled with my success in Montreal. She told me that she'd caught the IM final on the CBC. Mum had a front row seat in the family room and wouldn't be denied watching me compete. Lynda had come over with her child. Even my father had watched. Mum thought I'd lost the race after the breaststroke because I had fallen so far behind - in fifth place. She said the family was screaming at the start of the freestyle. "It was pretty tense for that final lap," Mum explained. As I kicked my way to the finish everyone hollered themselves hoarse. Everyone but my father. Mum told me at the end of the race he covered his face with his hands and turned away. When I'd phoned, my mother insisted that I speak with my father. He was congenial and slightly more talkative than normal, saying, "Looks as though your work paid off. Now, here's your mother."

Weeks after Montreal I was comfortably settled in at the Queen Charlotte, surrounded by treasures from the ghostly basement and the marvelous things my mother so generously purchased for me. Looking around, I felt a calm satisfaction. The pieces were coming together. I slipped my bare feet into some shoes, tossed my rucksack on my back, locked the door and walked down to the beach. The heat of the summer was gone, the late afternoon giving way to an early October evening. Leaves had changed colour and many had fallen to the ground. I kicked at them with my loafers. *Summer lasts just a brief moment in time. There's no stopping it. Life moves along for everyone and everything. But I'll remember this summer.* As I walked towards Second Beach I noticed the seawall was quiet, barely a soul in sight. *When summer's over the West End becomes such a tranquil place.* I continued walking past Second Beach Pool, closed for the season. There had been many children and adults swimming there only a few weeks ago. The wind was tossing waves and fiery red maple leaves onto the sandy cove where Robby and I first sat and talked. *Is the world really so wide? No,* I thought, remembering how I had met Robby again nearly ten years after junior high school. *Life has a funny way of driving events and people together, doesn't it? But I don't believe in fate, right?*

The sky was darkening earlier, the earth was tilting away from the sun, hurtling through space. Overhead the gulls soared, screeching. Other birds were sounding their calls, looking for a place to perch for the night, some calling out to their mates. I walked onto the beach, smelling the salt, the undeniable spice of autumn carried on the breeze. The waves rumbled deeply across the shoreline as I moved closer to the water's edge. Almost high tide. The water was so beautiful, so affirming and held such solace. I unslung my rucksack and placed it on the sand. As I kicked off my brown loafers I thought of that summer night when I'd driven out to the beach after being with Pete at Oil Can Harry's. That night was a baptism of sorts, a rite of passage. I'm not sure I fully understood my attraction or relationship to the water. Perhaps it replenished me, soothed me, transformed me. I unbuttoned my Levi's and pushed them and my boxers down past my ankles and stepped out. My red fleece pullover was next. I pulled it over my head and placed it with all my clothing on my leather rucksack. The air rushed over my body, chilling it to gooseflesh. I stepped naked into the ocean, felt the sand squeeze between my toes, the water cooled by October's winds. I ventured further into the sea. *The water's not treacherous,* I told myself, recalling my sister's failed attempt at temporarily ridding her bothersome brother in frigid Lake

Superior. My sister might have wanted me gone the way a child hates to be displaced by a competitor, but there wasn't any sinister intent.

I stepped deeper, past my midsection to my chest. The water held me in its bracing grip, lifting me off the bottom. A wave moved over my head, shockingly icy, a trickle of brine sharp on my tongue. As the sea buoyed me upright I bobbed in the ocean, sculling the water with my hands, agape at the brightly lit West End apartment towers. Riding atop the swelling waters, I faced the shoreline as I drifted further into the blackness of English Bay. The birds quieted as the skies quickly deepened to black. Cradled in the ocean I watched in awe as the moon slowly vaulted above the city skyline, shining it's reflected light on the water's surface. Aware of the wonder all around me, I slipped beneath the sea and slowly swam. Under water, I felt the tide pulling me from the darkness and towards my home. And with each stroke, I vowed to live the life that I'd been given without fear and without apology.

Alan D. Stamp is a Registered Psychotherapist and has practiced for more than thirty years. Stamp is a lifelong swimmer who swam competitively through his college and university years until age 28.

After attending UBC, Stamp completed an internship in Family Therapy, going on to work as a Clinical Director, instructor, speaker and therapist in private practice.

As a young person, Stamp was an observer of life but, with the passage of time understood the need to engage in living life fully. Stamp likes what Mae West once said: "You only live once, but if you do it right, once is enough."

He has written articles on topics such as birth order, marital and family conflict, sexuality, depression, anxiety and hypnosis. This is his first full-length book.

Stamp is a longtime West End resident, having lived in Vancouver, Canada for more than twenty-five years.

Made in the USA
Columbia, SC
20 April 2017